REQUIEM IN STONES

A novel of grief & grace

RICHARD WILE

Requiem in Stones

© Copyright 2016, Richard Wile

ISBN: 978-1-63381-095-2

All rights reserved. No part of this book may be reproduced in any form or by any electronic or mechanical means, including information storage and retrieval systems, without permission in writing from the author, except by a reviewer, who may quote brief passages in review.

Illustration features samples from
"The Sea! The Sea!" painting by Francis Cadell

Cover design by Amy Files

Designed and Produced by
Maine Authors Publishing
12 High Street, Thomaston, Maine 04861
www.maineauthorspublishing.com

Printed in the United States of America

For Laurie

CREDITS

Excerpts from "East Coker," "Marina," and "The Love Song of J. Alfred Prufrock" from *Collected Poems 1909-1962* by T.S. Eliot. Copyright 1936 by Houghton Mifflin Harcourt Publishing Company. Copyright © renewed 1964 by Thomas Sterns Eliot. Preprinted by permission of Houghton Mifflin Harcourt Publishing Company. All rights reserved.

Excerpts from *Rabbit is Rich* by John Updike, copyright © 1981 by John Updike. Used by permission of Alfred A. Knopf, an imprint of the Knopf Doubleday Publishing Group, a division of Penguin Random House LLC. All rights reserved.

Excerpts from Albert Camus's *The Myth Of Sisyphus,* translated by Justin O'Brien. Used by permission of Penguin Random House LLC.

Excerpts from Terrance Rafferty's Review of "Black Rain," *The New Yorker*, 3/12/1990, copyright © Condé Nast. Used by permission.

Excerpt from *Point Counter Point,* by Aldous Huxley, © 1928, by Aldous Huxley. Used by Permission of Dalkey Archive Press.

"('Til) I Kissed You"
Words and Music by Don Everly
Copyright © 1959 Sony/ATV Music Publishing LLC
Copyright Renewed. All Rights Administered by Sony/ATV Music Publishing LLC, 424 Church Street, Suite 1200, Nashville, TN 37219. International Copyright Secured All Rights Reserved
Reprinted by Permission of Hal Leonard Corporation

"This is the Time"
Words and Music by Billy Joel
Copyright © 1986 Joelsongs
All Rights Administered by Almo Music Corp.
All Rights Reserved. Used by Permission
Reprinted by Permission of Hal Leonard Corporation

"Cat's In The Cradle"
Words and Music by Harry Chapin and Sandy Chapin
Copyright © 1974 (Renewed) Story Songs, Ltd.
All Rights Administered by WB Music Corp.
All Rights Reserved
Used by Permission of Alfred Music

"Theme From New York New York"
Music by John Kander
Words by Fred Ebb
© 1977 (Renewed) United Artists Corporation
All Rights Controlled and Administered by EMI Unart Catalog Inc.
(Publishing)
and Alfred Music (Print)
All Rights Reserved
Used by Permission of Alfred Music

> For more information about the author and *Requiem in Stones,* including study questions for group discussion, visit **www.richardwile.com**. Also check out his blog, **www.geriatricpilgrim.com**.

REQUIEM IN STONES

What seas what shores what grey rocks and what islands
What water lapping the bow
And scent of pine and the woodthrush singing through the fog
What images return
O my daughter.
—*"Marina," by T.S. Eliot*

Blessed are those that mourn,
for they shall be comforted.
—*Matthew 5:4*

Chapter One

1985

"How do you feel about God?"

Wrapped in a warm blanket of alcohol, Tom Jacobs thought the question made perfect sense. He watched the light from the lamp beside the couch in the dormitory lobby dance in Christine Shales's long black hair. Her high cheekbones and almond-shaped eyes reminded him of Audrey Hepburn.

At the same time, her question unsettled him. He set down his now-empty coffee cup of brandy. "I've only been attending church regularly for about five years," he confided. "I mean, I used to go all the time when I was a kid. My father moonlighted as sexton of our church."

"What denomination?" Christine touched his arm. "I've always been an Episcopalian."

"Congregationalist." Thinking: *Are her eyes brown?* "Both my parents were pretty active. I don't think they were terribly religious—the real religion in Ashton was high school basketball—but church is what everyone in town did on Sundays." *Maybe more dark gray.* "And as far as I know, they still do. Well, my father's dead, but my mother and her second husband go to church every week." *Sometimes they look purple.* "Anyway, I stopped going to church in college, and other than getting married in a church, didn't set foot in one until about five years ago, when my wife and I decided our daughter needed some religious training."

Tom pushed up his glasses and reached for his pipe, wondering if he'd ever seen a woman with eyelashes so long. He filled his pipe from his tobacco pouch and struck a match, trying to think of how to answer her original question. He failed to blow a smoke ring. "And, you know, I'm already on the Board of Deacons. All I can say is, the First Parish Church of Webber, Maine must be desperate for new blood. Our big issue is inclusive language—how to refer to God without masculine pronouns. Which I think is a good idea."

Tom gazed at a bulletin board and the ads for roommates with whom to share apartments for next semester. When was the last time he'd been in a college dormitory? He grinned. "So that must mean I don't think of God as some guy in a white beard anymore."

Christine smiled. "So how do you picture God these days?"

"I guess I imagine God as a…a…I don't know…." He held up two fingers to suggest quotation marks. "Creative Spirit. I know it sounds vague, but it's the best I can do." He shrugged. "I guess I'm confused, like most people."

Christine straightened and smoothed out her denim skirt. "Six weeks ago, right after Easter, Maggie, an eleven-year-old girl who goes…went…to our church, died of leukemia." She put both hands around her coffee cup and stared into it before drinking. "Since then, I've been quarreling with God." Her eyes grew wet and flashed black. "I sometimes think mothers care more for their children than God does."

She really believes God exists. Tom was impressed. And a little envious.

She finished her brandy. "I'm sorry. I get carried away sometimes. You want to get some air?"

1985

"Sure." He put his pipe in his sport coat pocket, stood up, and waited for the room to come into focus. How much had he had to drink? A Scotch on the rocks before dinner in Princeton. Wine with the meal. Then, when the six of them went to that bar with the band of pimply kids in ripped T-shirts, he must have had two or three more Scotches, and brandy just now. He felt sorry for any kid whose essay he was going to read tomorrow. Hopefully there wouldn't be many. The chief reader told them they only had at most a couple hours' worth of prompts to read.

They walked out the glass doors, down the walkway from the dorm to a wide mall, Tom's heart fluttering with the almost-forgotten jitters of a first date. At the same time, being with Christine felt completely familiar.

"Left?" he asked.

"Left it is."

Who was this woman? He'd met her earlier in the week and knew she was from Something-or-other Springs in Wyoming. That she had a husband and a son, eight or nine years old. That after years of adjunct work, she'd gone back to full-time teaching three years ago, and this was her first year reading Advanced Placement Essays for the College Board.

That she and God were on arguing terms and she had those mysterious eyes.

He inhaled. "I love the smell of a new-mown lawn. I mowed my lawn for the first time last week. I'm guessing New Jersey is a good month ahead of Maine." *For God's sake, Jacobs, can't you find something more exciting to talk about than mowing your lawn?*

He glanced over at Christine, who was looking up at the stars, only faintly visible over all the campus lights. "The weather in Wyoming varies a lot," she said. "We had snow last week. But on Mother's Day, it was over 80." She laughed. "I went rattlesnake hunting."

Tom stopped and faced her. "You what?"

Her hair seemed to shimmer. She giggled and hiccupped. "Well, all I did was hold the pillowcase. I have a friend, Wanda, and she and her husband sell venom to medical companies. They asked me if I'd like to come along."

"I'm still impressed," he said. "All the women in my life are scared to death of snakes."

They walked in silence. He felt her hand slip into his. She was about the same height as his wife, Martha, but with longer arms.

"Are you from Wyoming?" he asked. Her hands were larger, too, and thinner.

"No." Her voice seemed to come from far away. "I'm a New England girl. My parents live in Massachusetts."

"How did you end up in Wyoming?"

When she didn't answer, he thought she hadn't heard him, but just as he was about to repeat the question, she said, "The summer after my sophomore year in college—I was going to Vassar—I needed a break. Mostly from my parents. I love them, but when you're twenty-one and it's 1968, you don't want them quizzing you about where you're going and who you're going with. And they understood. My father contacted an old friend from med school who lived in Wyoming, so I went out there for the summer and lived with him and his family. Then I met this cowboy and, after I married him three months later, I transferred to the University of Wyoming."

"So your husband's a cowboy?"

"We have a ranch outside of town, but it doesn't pay the bills. If I weren't teaching, Zack would have to get a real job."

Does she sound bitter?

They walked under a large maple tree. The lights lining the mall dappled Christine's scoop-necked blouse. Tom imagined her riding a horse—maybe a palomino—cowboy boots, a wide Stetson hat, black hair flowing in a mountain breeze.

They came to a small pond. "Must be cool for your son, living on a ranch," he said.

"What eight-year-old doesn't love horses and cattle? But Nathan loves any animal. You should see his room. It's a menagerie."

Tom heard distant music and laughter coming from a cluster of brick buildings.

Christine giggled again. "Did I tell you already that I've had too much to drink?" She gnawed her lower lip. She had beautiful teeth. "What was I going to ask you? Oh, right. Does your daughter like animals? Didn't you say she was thirteen?"

"Fourteen," Tom said. "We've got a poodle she likes pretty well. But she loves the West. She's applied for a Girl Scout program in New Mexico this summer. I hope she gets it."

"It's different country than the East, that's for sure," said Christine.

He put his arm around her waist. The indentation between her lower back and the curve of her rear end made a lovely resting place. "I know. I spent two summers in Idaho when I was in college. Working for the forest service. The only time I've ever lived outside of Maine."

He felt her arm circling his back. "Maine's always sounded like a great place to live. I'd like to go there sometime."

"It is nice, except where I grew up there was always the smell of the paper mill. God, the sulfur in the air peeled the paint off the houses. It's better now, but I was happy to get out. Live closer to the coast."

"I miss the ocean. Every time I hear the wind blowing through the cottonwoods, I imagine the sound of waves breaking on the shore."

"I love the water. I don't think I could live anywhere far from it."

The next thing he knew, they were standing outside the dormitory, pelvises grinding, tongues in each other's mouths like teenagers. His head spun. *Why didn't I pay extra for a single room? Where's the closest motel?* But he was a married man. She was married. They both had kids.

He didn't know whether to be grateful or angry when she stepped back, stroked his face, and said, "I think we'd better go in…damn it."

At 4:00 a.m. he lay in his room, listening to his roommate snore, and staring up into the darkness. What an exciting and impassioned woman! What a contrast to his own life! She rode horses and hunted rattlesnakes in the Rocky Mountains; he drove a Ford Escort and walked a poodle around a housing development in a town of strip malls and abandoned shoe factories. She argued with God; he argued with the Board of Deacons.

His life flickered through his mind like an old black-and-white movie called *The Death of a Dream*. He saw Tommy Jacobs graduating from high school in the first year of John F. Kennedy's presidency, caught up in the young leader's vitality and vision. He saw himself running his hands over his flattop and nodding his head in agreement as he watched Kennedy on TV say, "Conformity is the jailer of freedom and the enemy of growth." He decided that the small Maine town in which he lived was filled with nothing but a bunch of dumb parents, dim-witted classmates, and old-fashioned fuddy-duddies. That all his mother did was gossip on the telephone all day, while his father spent evenings snoring on a couch surrounded by beer bottles. For the first time, he'd understood why his older brother, Ed, had left town. Tommy wanted adventure, romance. He read Hemingway's Nick Adams stories, Robert Ruark's stories of big game hunting in Africa, and most important, Jack Kerouac's *On the Road*.

And for his first two years at the University of Maine, he pursued his dreams, studying forestry, working summers in McCall, Idaho as a forest fire fighter. He read *The Dharma Bums,* agreeing with Kerouac that fraternity men and sorority women were weak-spined conformists on their way to lives built around the latest model cars, the newest TVs, and white houses with picket fences. He switched his major to English, and dreamed of becoming a writer who would change the world, dividing his time between Hemingway's Paris, the New York City of the Beats, and a cabin on the Salmon River.

Would it be too much, Tom wondered as light began to frame the curtain of his dormitory window in New Jersey, to say that his dreams died with Kennedy's assassination? That year was the unhappiest time of his life. He'd walk into the campus Bear's Den around 3:00 in the afternoon, when every table was full, and not know anyone well enough to sit with, self-conscious about his black Frisco jeans, khaki shirts, and Smoke Jumper boots amid all the pinstripes and chinos and penny loafers. At the same time, he couldn't go back to the dorm. There were times when the cinderblock walls of his room closed around him and he felt he couldn't breathe. So he went to the back of the Den with the foreign students and veterans, many of whom sat alone at a table for four, so he'd have to ask if he could join them. He'd sit across the table from someone whose name he didn't know, who usually never made eye contact let alone spoke, and watch the pulsating sea of laughter and companionship all around him, hoping a few drops of collegiality might splash his way. But then, if the guy he was sitting with tried to start a conversation, Tom would grunt and look away. After all, if the guy sat back here, he wasn't worth talking to.

And he always sat with guys. Two months after he'd entered college, his high school sweetheart, Linda, wrote him a brief letter saying she hoped he'd be happy with Bambi and his woodland friends, but she'd decided to marry Harv Giggy and his Impala convertible. After that it seemed as if every girl he met was laughing at him, so he avoided direct contact with the opposite sex, even as he undressed them from his seat in the back of the Den.

So maybe it wasn't Kennedy's assassination at all, Tom reflected, but the fact that his dreams of striding the road less traveled had withered away in a vast and barren desert of loneliness. So that when he'd met Martha at the beginning of their senior year, he was thirsty for love. Pleasingly plumpish, a home economics major, Martha was levelheaded and self-assured and, he realized now, looking for her MRS degree. After they'd first had sex, she began planning their wedding. Still, he'd admired her no-nonsense approach to life. "Honey, you think too much," she told him more than once. "Why must life be something to figure out? Why not just live it?" Besides satisfying his physical desires, she played bridge with him and did his laundry and ironed his jeans, all of which made him feel important, wanted. They married three days after graduation.

Intent on finding a secure harbor, free from the emotional gales of college, Tom had ignored the social upheavals of the 60s. After UMaine, he taught for two years at tiny Guntew High School in the western mountains of the state, teaching English, history, and public speaking, coaching JV basketball and girls' softball, and directing the school's entry in the state one-act play contest, before going back to the university for a master's degree in literature. A congenital lower back deformity kept him out of Vietnam, so he never needed to choose between serving in the military and running away to Canada. (*Either way*, he reflected as sunlight streaked the ceiling of the dorm, *my life would have been more interesting.*) Instead of smoking pot, protesting, or joining a commune (*like Christine?*), he became a pipe-smoking academic in tweed sport coats and vests, matching ties, and pocket handkerchiefs. His principal at Webber High called him "Mr. A.P.," because of the Advanced Placement English program he created. A lover of the Arthurian legends, Tom had come to see himself as Merlin, imparting knowledge to the brightest students in the school.

This morning, however, he saw his world as sterile, a watered-down imitation of what life should be. He and Martha spent their time together sniping at one another in passive-aggressive warfare, with an occasional furlough with their daughter when they went to a beach or a movie. He lived in the kind of housing development, complete with the white house and picket fence, he'd once ridiculed.

He had taken the road more traveled and he was still wandering in that goddamned desert.

After the morning reading and a largely silent lunch with Christine, followed by a quick kiss goodbye at the airport, Tom decided he'd stumbled into some kind of mid-life thing, succumbing to a combination of brandy, music, and forty-two-year-old angst. Seeing Martha and Annie waiting for him at Bangor

1985

International Airport, he was grateful that nothing had actually happened the night before, except some kissing.

He waved as he came down the escalator. There was no question he was meeting a mother and daughter. Same blue eyes, apple cheeks, turned-up noses. Same short, swept-back hair style. In their blazers and blouses and knee-length skirts, they both looked as if they'd just stepped from the pages of an L.L. Bean catalogue. For Martha, Bangor was the big city and she always dressed accordingly.

He set down his suitcase and kissed her familiar lips. "Good to see you." Hugged Annie. "How was your week, kiddo?"

"I had my interview yesterday for that Girl Scout Wider Opportunity in New Mexico," Annie said, as Tom picked up his suitcase and they headed for the terminal exit.

"How did that go?"

"They were really nice. I wasn't nervous at all."

"What did they want to know?"

"Oh, stuff about school, what my hobbies were, my family."

"You didn't tell them your father turns into a werewolf once a month?" he asked, as they left the building.

"Nah, I just said you snore when you fall asleep in front of the TV."

A small cloud darkened Tom's sunny spirits, as he thought of his father doing the same thing.

"They didn't ask if you were worried you were too young to travel?" He looked over at Martha. He knew Annie's age was one of her big fears, one that had almost made her tell their daughter she'd have to wait until the following year to apply.

"Subject never came up."

He nodded at his wife, as if to say, "See, I told you," but Martha just looked away.

Getting into the car, Tom asked her, "How was your week?"

"Fine," she said. "I got most of Annie's sweater done. Mom and Dad came over for supper one night. Mom and I went shopping Friday afternoon. I bought you a tie. I think it'll go well with your blue sport coat."

"Thank you." Tom started the car, waiting for his wife to ask him about his week. That she didn't was disappointing, but he remembered the previous year when he'd tried to tell her about the reading and New Jersey, and all she'd said was, "Glad you had a good time. Never mind that your daughter and I won't see you this week, either, because you'll be trying to catch up. I don't see why you people can't read those papers after the end of the school year."

As he drove off, he silently tried to relax into the security blanket she provided him. She bought his clothes, kept the house spotless, handled all the banking, even wrote his mother so he didn't have to. Tonight, he knew she'd have baked rhubarb pie for his homecoming.

But after they came home and had dinner and ate the pie, and Martha and Annie had opened the presents he'd brought them from New Jersey (a Princeton sweatshirt for Annie, a necklace for Martha), and Annie had gone to bed, and he and Martha had made love, his wife went back to her own bed and he went to sleep feeling Christine's fingers on his face, his hand on the small of her back. Two nights later, he dreamed of following Christine up a mountain trail to a promontory overlooking an expanse of tall pine trees, where they sat on a boulder and she read to him from the Bible.

He kept thinking of her asking how he felt about God. Until meeting Christine, when he'd thought about God at all, He/She/It was more of a problem to be solved. A puzzle, like one of the Rubik's Cubes his students played with. She had opened up a longing that he hadn't known he had. He wasn't even sure that this yearning really had anything to do with a traditional omniscient deity, but it was a desire to connect with something eternal and constant, something to give meaning to what he was now beginning to fear was a meaningless life, and since he couldn't think of another word for this longing, he might as well call it God.

The irony was, he thought the following Thursday night as he sat in one of those uncomfortable metal folding chairs in the library of Webber's First Parish Church, that for the last year or

1985

more he'd been spending almost all of his free time at church. The choir he could understand—he liked to sing—but why had he let his pastor talk him into becoming youth group advisor, when he spent all week teaching teenagers at school? And why the Board of Deacons, most of whom hadn't had a new idea since voting for a Democratic governor in 1955? He'd been at the church for three nights in a row.

As Bob Loring, Chair of the Board of Deacons, went over the budget, Tom gazed at a print on the wall of a very Italian-looking Jesus, enveloped by a circular rainbow, his arms held out as if he were dancing, sloughing off burial cloths that looked like they were made of crepe paper, while two women knelt at his feet. He thought of the previous Easter. While Christine had been arguing with God, he'd risen before dawn, driven to a hill in the middle of a cow pasture for the youth group's sunrise service, returned to church to fry sausages for the deacons' parish breakfast, helped sweep up, rehearsed the anthem with the choir, sung in church, driven twenty-five miles up the coast for dinner with his wife's parents, managed to work in an hour walking in the woods with his daughter, driven home, finished correcting a set of essays, and fallen exhausted into bed.

Where was God in all of that?

The air in the church library was dank. Dim florescent lights turned everyone's faces pale. The Board of Deacons resumed its discussion of inclusive language. At the last meeting, Tom had passed out an article by a woman whose father had sexually abused her and to whom worshipping a god called "Father" was abhorrent.

"As I said before, this is an article that's certainly influenced my thinking," he said.

"Do you always get your ideas from what you read?" asked Edith Trumbull. Tom might have known a more unpleasant woman than Edith, but if so, he couldn't remember one. She was a balloon-shaped woman with a hooked nose and false teeth that clicked when she talked. "Why can't you think for yourself?" she continued. "My guess is that the woman was at fault. They usually are in these so-called 'rape' cases. This whole language thing is a bunch of hooey as far as I'm concerned. Why do we have to keep changing things?"

Where is God tonight?

That week, Tom bought a small, spiral-bound notebook. At the top of the first page, he wrote "Thoughts on God." Each night he found a passage from his reading that seemed to relate to God, and he copied it down. The trouble was, the writings tended to rebuke instead of teach. After neatly printing the Twenty-third Psalm, he wrote,

> Where are my still waters & green pastures? I live in a housing development. The only still water I have is what pools in the corner of the cellar after a rainstorm. My green pasture is mostly crab grass.

Going to some of the novels he'd recently read, he quoted John Updike in *Rabbit is Rich*: "That's why we love disaster, Harry sees, it puts us back in touch with guilt and sends us crawling back to God." Then Tom wrote: "Is the reason I'm suddenly so interested in God b/c my life has become a disaster?"

He didn't really understand Chaim Potok's writing in *The Chosen* that God is a "spark" in every person. But when the author added that everything else is "evil, a shell," Tom wrote: "Is this image of academic 'excellence' I've spent the last twenty years creating just such a shell, a crime, if not against God, at least against myself?"

Aldous Huxley's words in *Point Counter Point*—"God's the total result, spiritual and physical, of any thought or action that makes for life, of any vital relation with the world"—gnawed at him:

> When was the last time I felt any kind of vital relationship? Probably 25 years ago, those 2 years I worked for the Forest Service fighting forest fires. Those years were the closest I've ever come to living the kind of life I used to dream of. Driving from

1985

Maine to Idaho w/, oh what were their names? Dave and Harry, I think, eating w/ long-haul drivers at truck stops, passing a whiskey bottle around the car. Yeah, I was vital then, independent, self-confident. There were fires to fight, which meant danger to confront, obstacles to clear away, a chance to measure myself, become strong, industrious, determined, courageous—all those things JFK called for America to be. & there was a spiritual component. I can see that now. The fire in Grand Teton National Park, when, after it was out, we stayed for another day checking for hot spots & making sure the fire didn't jump the fire line. I spent I don't know how many hours in the afternoon sitting on a rock mesmerized by Grand Teton's Upper Saddle, eventually watching the sun set behind the great mountain & the stars emerge, so close I knew I could grab any one I wanted any time I wanted. Yes, that day was holy.

But when he tried to tell his wife about those years, about the man he might have been, she replied, "So that's why you're so hot for Annie to go to New Mexico. You want to live your Smokey the Bear memories of the Wild West all over again."

He and Martha were sitting in the living room after Annie had gone to bed. They needed to make a decision. The day before, Annie had been accepted into the Girl Scout program outside Santa Fe for four weeks in August. The Wider Opportunity people needed to know by the end of the week whether or not she would attend. Annie didn't know it, but Martha was reconsidering allowing her to go.

"I just think fourteen is too young to be traveling across the country," Martha said.

"Well, I think New Mexico is a great educational and social opportunity," Tom said. He lit a pipe and tipped back in his red recliner. "And she's been the most excited I think I've ever seen her. I don't want her to go if she doesn't want to. She knows that. But I think she wants to go and I think she should be able to go."

"Shh! Keep your voice down. She's asleep." Martha sat on the blue couch. Jolie, their poodle, trotted in from the kitchen and jumped up beside her.

"I'm no louder than you are."

They glared at each other. She scratched the dog behind its ears and then lit a cigarette. "You must remember how homesick she was last year at church camp. That was only a hundred miles away."

Tom puffed on his pipe and tried to keep his voice even. "Of course I remember. She's going to be homesick. But she won't be the only kid out there missing her parents." Back in college, he and Martha had almost always been partners during their countless bridge games in the Bear's Den. Now, as usual, he felt as if he were competing against both her and the dog.

Okay, he'd play his ace. "Besides, when I picked her up at Pilgrim Lodge last summer, she told me she didn't want to come home."

"What about the flight out? It's two thousand miles each way. She'll be all alone."

"The Girl Scouts wouldn't be offering a program for girls Annie's age if they thought the kids weren't old enough to participate. There'll be someone there from the Scouts to meet her when she gets off the plane, and someone to put her back on it."

"What about on the plane? What if she gets homesick all of a sudden and falls apart? What if she gets airsick? What if she winds up sitting next to some weirdo?"

"You think someone is going to molest her on an airplane?" Tom pointed his pipe at his wife and threw down his trump card. "Maybe if you ever traveled anywhere except to Shop 'n' Save, you'd know that the airlines take good care of kids. You don't know because you've never flown. All you have to do is talk to the flight attendants and they'll look after her."

Martha slowly butted her cigarette in the ashtray. She scratched Jolie behind the ears one more time. She straightened the books on the coffee table, stood, and walked down the hall to the bathroom. When Tom heard water running into the tub, he picked up his book. That was the way most of their "discussions" ended. One of them forfeiting rather than admitting defeat.

Even after Martha agreed that Annie could go to New Mexico, however, Tom's discontent with his life grew worse. As the school year ended, he stood at his classroom window after his last exam, watching the sun light up the green playing fields behind the leaching pond, and sensing the collective disapproval of the sixty-four British authors (they'd come in a set) who peered down at him from the cinderblock walls of his room. Wordsworth wondered if Tom hadn't lain waste his powers. Keats had fears that Tom had ceased to be. Shakespeare shook his head sadly and said:

> "I behold in you that time of year
> when yellow leaves, or none, do hang upon
> those boughs which shake against the cold."

T.S. Eliot intoned:

> "I've seen the moment of your greatness flicker,
> I have seen the eternal footman hold your coat, and snicker."

Two weeks into summer vacation, Tom stopped by Webber High and found an official-looking envelope from Kidron Springs High School in Wyoming in his mailbox. His heart galloped. He'd thought of writing Christine, but held back. The last day of the reading, she'd been quiet, preoccupied. Tom decided she'd shifted her thoughts from him to her family. At the airport, she appeared as embarrassed by the previous night as he was. He was afraid that any kind of card or letter would remind her of something she'd rather forget.

As he took her letter to his classroom and closed the door, his hands shook as his eyes raced through two pages of professional chitchat about new classes for next year, a writing assignment that worked well, one student she enjoyed and one who gave her trouble. What he both wanted and feared came in her P.S.:

"I've had to move my desk; I stare too much out the window that faces east over the plains."

Raising his eyes from the letter, he felt dizzy, as if standing at the top of a two-story ladder, looking first down and then up to the heavens. Forgetting that he'd told Martha he'd be home for lunch, he picked up a pen and wrote his quasi-professional reply with his own P.S.: "My desk faces east but I'm still staring west."

From the walls above, Chaucer winked and Dickens gave him a thumbs-up.

By the middle of July, Tom and Christine were sending weekly letters from their respective schools, filled with observations, opinions, personal histories, and questions. Christine wrote about feeling overprotected as an only child, and admitted that dropping out of Vassar to marry a rodeo rider was a way to escape her parents. Tom replied that he, too, had been coddled by his parents and teachers for having potential to do more with his life than spend it in the paper mill, especially after his brother had gotten his girlfriend pregnant, dropped out of school, and then left both girlfriend and town.

They discovered they both loved T.S. Eliot. Christine sent lines from *Four Quartets*:"…moving/Into another intensity/For a further union, a deeper communion…" Tom responded from "The Love Song of J. Alfred Prufrock": "Do I dare disturb the universe?" He mailed her comments he'd written on the Sunday bulletins about his Congregational services. She sent him Xeroxed passages from C.S. Lewis, Madeleine L'Engle, and Thomas Merton.

They swapped concerns about their children. Christine worried that Nathan was too trusting. The kids in his class hit him up for money. He was often bullied by the bigger kids on the playground because he wouldn't stand up for himself. Tom was troubled about his daughter's introverted nature. He wrote that he and Martha had encouraged Annie to take music lessons, join children's theater, Brownies, the Girl Scouts. All of which she enjoyed, but despite a wide circle of acquaintances, she had few if any close friends, probably because she was a perfectionist and her hobbies—embroidery, wood burning, and ethnic cooking—were solitary.

They said little about their marriages, as if their respective spouses had somehow quietly and painlessly died. Instead, they wrote of their loneliness and how happy they were they'd met. To have become friends, they wrote for a while, and then, as their letters approached thirty pages a week, special friends.

At the end of July, Christine wrote that, while unloading groceries, she'd found the sterling candlestick holders her parents had given her for a wedding present, wrapped in a horse blanket in the back of their pickup. Her husband said they never used them and that they needed the money, so he was selling them to a buddy of his. Christine wrote to Tom, "We don't need the money, Zack wants the money. He's got his eye on a new hand-tooled saddle. God, he makes me mad!"

Her letter gave Tom permission to open the floodgate. He replied by talking about how Martha had persuaded him to move from a small bungalow in the coastal village of Haran to Webber and "our house made of ticky-tacky." About the day she told him while she might be physically able to keep dropping babies, she wasn't "emotionally equipped" to handle more than one child. About the separate beds after that. The lack of conversation at any meal at which Annie wasn't present. The nights he stood in the living room after Martha had gone to sleep, filled with inchoate but powerful longings for something more in his life.

He described the previous Sunday at church after he'd watched Annie from the choir loft as she stood in the front row of the Youth Choir, radiating joy as she sang:

> When it was time for the adult choir to join in, I lifted my voice to hold the tenor note (the hymn was "Rise Up, O Saints of God," do you know it?) and I heard the voices of the sopranos soaring over me. And for a moment, I became, for lack of a better word, transparent, as if all barriers, all separation between myself and

others had disappeared, and I was connected—really connected—to the choir, the congregation, even the town I usually disdain.

But after church, when he'd tried to tell Martha about the experience, she'd barely glanced up from peeling potatoes. "That's nice," she said. "I guess."

"I don't know if it's 'nice.' I don't understand it. I mean, it seemed…I don't know…sort of holy. Is this how some people experience God?"

As Martha silently prepared dinner, Tom remembered Christine's question to him. He asked his wife, "How do you feel about God?"

Martha stared at him as if he were one of the local Born Agains at the back door, trying to give her a leaflet. "Tom, I don't know how I feel about God. I don't even know that God exists. I'm more concerned about what's happening to my husband."

"Not for the first time," Tom wrote to Christine, "my wife said, 'I just don't understand you.' And not for the first time, I replied, 'You sure as hell don't.' You know, I'm beginning to wonder if all my church activities have been ways to avoid staying home with this woman."

Later that week, the Jacobses drove to Bangor International Airport. For the third time that morning, Martha warned their daughter about talking to strangers. Annie sat in the back seat of the car looking pale and staring out the window. Tom sang, "I'm leavin' on a jet plane. Don't know when I'll be back again."

"Come on, Annie," he said, "sing along!"

"Oh, Dad," she said. He glanced in the rearview mirror and saw her frightened eyes. His heart clutched. When it was time to board and he kissed her goodbye, she seemed to have shriveled up. Her hands were frigid. She moved away from him down the accordion jetway, alone, hunched, walking slowly, as if she might stumble, growing smaller and smaller until she disappeared around a corner and he was left staring down an empty tunnel.

He and Martha drove silently home through stop-and-go tourist traffic. Tom smelled the exhaust from the Winnebago in front of him, and felt the heat rising from the road into the car. Pressure built behind his forehead. He couldn't shake the image of that empty corridor.

Returning to the housing development, he saw the leaves of some of the swamp birches already turning color. The glare of the sun off the vinyl siding of the houses hurt his eyes. At the back door, he heard the sound of the damn dog—her grating bark, the sound of her toenails scarring the floor. When he and Martha walked into the kitchen, he went to the refrigerator for some water, turned around, and started to cry. The next thing he knew he was sobbing, doubled up over the sink, as if vomiting.

Martha stood there, her eyes blank. "What's wrong?" she asked. "I don't understand. Tell me! What's wrong? You've never done anything like this before."

Waves of tears broke, subsided, broke again.

Martha's voice rose. "I thought I'd be the one to cry, but I can't do anything for Annie now, and you can't either. It's too late, so you might as well stop it!"

Anger at his wife helped him push away from the sink. He splashed cold water on his face and, although it felt theatrical, took a deep breath. Walking to the back door, he said over his shoulder, "I'm going to mow the lawn."

That night, after Martha had gone to bed, he wrote Christine:

Was I crying for Annie? She looked so frail as she walked away from me. Two thousand miles away, there's no way I can help her, protect her if she's in danger. Or was I crying for myself? Am I afraid that when Annie returns she'll never again be my little girl? That without her my life is empty of love? Was I crying because I'm living a lie, suffocating inside my "Mr. A.P." persona? That despite what might appear to others as an active life of teaching and service to the church, I've become disconnected from the world and from God, afraid to let myself engage either one?

In Christine's next letter, she thanked him for such a moving story.

> But please don't feel that you aren't loved. Annie will always love you. I'm sure, despite everything, Martha loves you. And (deep breath) I love you. After reading your letter, I picked up the phone and invited myself to my parents' in Massachusetts next week. I've told Dad and Mom that I met some people at the AP reading and might want to spend some time in Maine, too. I'm hoping you and I can meet somewhere for lunch, or maybe dinner, or something.

Or something. Tom stood at the window of his classroom, looking out at the lush leaves of the trees around the leaching pond, excited, afraid. Did he dare disturb the universe? He turned and looked at his British authors. Shakespeare stroked his little moustache:

"Let…not to the marriage of true minds admit impediments. Go for it."

Stopping on his way home from school at a phone booth outside McDonald's, Tom reserved a room at the Sheraton in Portland and began thinking of a name for the conference he would tell Martha he needed to attend.

Chapter Two

1988

"Jesus Christ is risen today, Alleluia!
Our triumphant holy day, Alleluia!"

Sunlight streamed through Gothic stained-glass windows as the St. Jude's choir processed down the aisle, followed by Father Gary Coffin. As he passed Tom and his family, the priest winked.

Tom grinned and looked down the pew at Christine, Annie, and Nathan, happily reflecting on the past three years. He and Christine were passionately in love. They had blended their two families together. Nathan was adjusting and Annie was blossoming. He was beginning to believe in a personal God—one leading him and Christine by the hand through the changes in their lives.

"Hymns of praise then let us sing, Alleluia!
Unto Christ, our heavenly king, Alleluia!"

Tom felt himself rising. The stone walls and red carpeting of the Episcopal church faded until he was sitting on the faded green cushions in the choir loft of the Ashton First Congregationalist

Church, looking down at the congregation, shoulders squared, heads tilted back, mouths stretched open as they sang:

"Christ the Lord is risen today, Alleluia!
Earth and heaven in chorus say, Alleluia!"

Easter had always been his favorite holiday. At Christmas, everyone seemed tense, in a hurry, and he always felt he disappointed his parents by not acting grateful enough for the bicycle or the baseball glove or the basketball they'd given him. Easter, however, was relaxed and intimate. On Easter Sunday, he awoke to the smell of shoe polish in the kitchen, where his father had lined the family's good shoes on the counter and put the Kiwi to them. Rising from bed, he discovered his older brother, Eddie, already hunting for the bright yellow marshmallow Peeps his father and mother had scattered through the house the night before. After breakfast he and Eddie put on new pants and socks, his father wore the suit he saved for Easter and Christmas, and his mother donned her best dress and a pink broad-brimmed hat that looked like a pastel frying pan. As crocuses budded and sparrows sang, the Jacobses strolled past white houses, Ashton's brick high school, and Sonny's Variety Store to the First Congregational Church. The air smelled of fresh dirt. After walking together up the walkway and through the double doors, the family split up: his father stayed in the back to usher, his mother sat with her cousin Edith in the old family pew with the brass Jacobs nameplate on the arm, and Eddie and Tommy went up to the balcony to sing with the junior choir.

"…where the angels ever sing, Alleluia!"

The words they sang here at St. Jude's Episcopal Church were different from the ones Tom used to sing when he was a Congregationalist. The difference was symbolic, he thought, of his new relationship with God. More intimate. More joyful. He put his arm around his wife, feeling for the small of her back. And

1988

surely it was God's doing. He and Christine had been drawn together by a completely incomprehensible power potent enough to extricate them from their sterile lives, a mysterious power—"higher" somehow than he'd ever known—that he experienced now, rising like electricity through his body as his fingers slid to the top of Christine's lovely backside, sensing himself lifted into another dimension where the physical and the spiritual became one.

"Sing we to our God above, Alleluia!
Praise eternal as his love, Alleluia!"

Next he heard Annie's ten-year-old soprano singing the hymn in the Sunday school choir back in Webber. He looked over at his daughter, now seventeen, who was smiling at her stepbrother. She looked good. A little tired, maybe but good. He liked the new haircut. Short over the ears, with a sweep of hair that fell over one eye, and a bright red streak running along one side of her hair. A quarter-moon earring dangled from the ear below. A lime-green birthstone hung from a thin chain sparkling against a black sweater that reached almost to her knees over the jeans. She'd pushed the sleeves of her sweater back, accentuating her thin wrists and long fingers.

As if watching a movie dissolve, Tom saw those fingers shrink into a pudgy five-year-old's grappling with a piece of chalk to produce spine-tingling screeches on his classroom blackboard. He watched the fingers extend, play scales on the piano, thread a needle, wield a wood-burning pen, a balloon whisk. These days, he knew those long, thin fingers held paintbrushes, modeled clay.

He used to worry that as an only child and only grandchild, his daughter spent too much of her time with adults or alone in her room, reading or going with her father to school on weekends. Now she had a circle of friends, two of whom, Alan and Jessie, had come with her from Webber to Newell last New Year's Eve for Portland's First Night Festivities. She was active in Amnesty International, volunteered at the Webber Soup Kitchen, and she would live in Europe next year on an American Field Service

Scholarship before attending Tufts the following year.

Standing at the top of the dais, Father Coffin extended his arms. "Alleluia. Christ is risen!"

"The Lord is risen indeed. Alleluia," Tom responded with the rest of the congregation.

Most important, he thought, Annie acted happy. The last three plus years had not been without stress for her. He knew that. Just a month after she'd returned from New Mexico, he and Martha told her they were separating, and he still remembered how she trembled when he put his hands on her shoulders and told her how he was always going to be there for her. How she'd flung her arms around him, her hands like ice through his shirt. How, just as he was leaving the house, he'd heard her vomiting in the bathroom. At first, she hadn't wanted to hear about Christine, then she hadn't wanted to meet her. She hadn't wanted him to move a hundred and twenty miles south to live with Christine and Nathan, and she refused to visit them for almost a year. Sometimes she hung up the phone on him and other times she used the phone to swear at him.

"Let us pray together," said Father Coffin. "Almighty God, who through your only-begotten Son, Jesus Christ, overcame death and opened to us the gate of everlasting life: Grant that we, who celebrate with joy the day of the Lord's resurrection…"

Tom listened to hear if Annie was reading the words along with the rest of the congregation, and was rewarded by the faint sound of her voice. Her attitude toward Tom and Christine changed after her first visit to their duplex apartment in Newell. Nathan met her with a hug before dragging her into his room to see his two hamsters, four guinea pigs, rat, cat, spider, and the king snake he'd brought with him from Wyoming. He spent the weekend with his arms around her, Annie laughing and saying he was trying to squeeze her to death.

The congregation sat as a woman in a powder-blue tailored suit walked to the lectern and began to read in a New York or New Jersey accent from Isaiah:

1988

> *"On this mountain the LORD of hosts*
> *will make for all peoples*
> *a feast of rich food, a feast of*
> *well-aged wines,*
> *of rich food filled with marrow, of*
> *well-aged wines strained clear…"*

Tom remembered Annie's first Christmas visit: she and Christine laughing together in the kitchen as they tried out recipes for bleu cheese sandwiches and triple chocolate bombe. He recalled the February vacation when a nor'easter buried southern Maine, and Christine and Tom and Annie and Nathan sat on the floor and played Parcheesi, Clue, and Yahtzee—Annie telling him on a drive back to Webber, "I had a good time this week. I like having a brother, and Christine is great. I'm pretty lucky. My friend Kimberly hates her stepmother."

But his favorite memory—one he knew he would cherish for the rest of his life—was of the April when they'd all stood on the rocky shore of Newell Landing, and Father Coffin had read them the Marriage Ceremony from the *Book of Common Prayer*, the liturgical services for worship Episcopalians refer to more than they do the Bible. Three black-and-white ducks dove and floated on the water in front of two gently rocking lobster boats. The air smelled of salt and seaweed and rebirth. Except for a faint line of black clouds on the horizon over the ocean, the sky was like faded denim. A breeze rumpled their hair, and the sun warmed the backs of their necks. Empty summerhouses on the shore smiled benevolently as Annie and Nathan each read a prayer, their voices rising over the sound of green waves lapping the shore. Annie, her head haloed in sunlight, grinned and gave him her two-fingered peace sign. As if a blessing from God, a bald eagle sailed across the bay.

> *"Then the Lord GOD will wipe away*
> *the tears from all faces,*
> *and the disgrace of his people he*

*will take away from all
the earth…"*

Through the next readings, Tom sat, half listening, half in blissful reverie, basking in the glory of his resurrection. He and Christine had found a duplex apartment in an old New England house and good teaching jobs in neighboring towns. Nathan seemed happy in his middle school. Tom was enjoying life without Advanced Placement English: not being "Mr. A.P." in his coat and tie, but "The Last Romantic," as he liked to think of himself, who'd challenged middle-class convention, dared disturb the universe, and whose beard was now long enough so that he could amuse his ninth graders by hiding pencils in it.

He reached over and patted Christine's leg. She reached down, covered his hand with hers, and squeezed. Down the aisle, Nathan giggled. Annie smiled and put a finger to her mouth. Tom smiled, too, at the boy's unabashed spontaneity. Slender like his mother, he'd also inherited her black hair and mysterious eyes. When he was happy, like today, they sparkled as if full of stars. When he was sad, they turned gray and glistened under long eyelashes like mist over a lake. When angry, they darkened like thunderclouds.

The first time he'd met Nathan in Kidron Springs during his and Christine's long-distance courtship, Nathan ignored Tom's handshake and hugged him around the waist.

"You're tall!" he said. "I like you. Would you like to meet my hamster, Huey?"

Nathan showed Tom how to feed Huey. He took Tom for a walk to his favorite toy store, where he talked him into buying a plastic jet plane. He introduced Tom to his favorite card game, which he seemingly played for the sole purpose of being able to yell "War!" at the top of his lungs.

When Nathan left to go to his father's ranch the next day, he hugged Tom again. "I sure hope you'll come back."

Tom dropped to one knee and put his hands on the boy's

shoulders. "And maybe you and your mom could visit me. Would you like that?"

Nathan's eyes twinkled. "That would be so cool!"

It *was* cool. As they stood for the second hymn, Tom raised his eyes to the stained-glass window behind the altar, depicting the Last Supper in bright reds and blues and greens, and sang,

*"The strife is o'er, the battle done,
    the victory of life is won,
the song of triumph has begun,
    Alleluia!"*

After an Easter dinner of baked ham and sweet potatoes and broccoli and a salad that Annie fixed of greens Tom had never heard of, followed by ice cream with Christine's chocolate sauce, they adjourned to the living room for coffee.

He sat in the stuffed granite-gray chair that had been his father's, surveying a room full of blessings. Christine sat on the brick shelf in front of the fireplace, while Annie and Nathan sat on the futon that served as the living room couch, sharing Claudius, the corn snake, Nathan's latest pet. Outside, the early April sun lit up an apple tree, which had apparently been part of an orchard back when the duplex had been half of a sea captain's house.

Tom raised his coffee mug. "Happy Easter, everybody."

"Happy Easter."

"And thank you again for coming down to join us," said Christine to Annie.

"Well, Dad's the one who came and got me and is going to have to spend another six hours driving me to Webber and back," she said. She looked at her father and grinned. "Thank you."

"It's worth it," Tom said. "If for no other reason than to see you eating. I think you've gotten too thin."

"Oh, Dad. You sound like Mom, now."

Heaven forbid. "Okay, how about I really enjoyed hearing you sing again in church."

Annie's smile faded. "Yeah, it felt good. We don't go to church these days. Mom's still pretty angry."

Tom shifted uncomfortably in his chair as he remembered the afternoon he and Martha had told their daughter they were separating. Annie said she wanted to go to her room, but then turned and went into the bathroom. When Tom heard her retching, he started down the hall, but Martha grabbed his arm. "I'll take care of her. Just get the hell out of here!" The memory of his ex-wife's next words rang in his ears: "I hope you and that woman and your God are happy with what you've done."

As if to change the subject, Annie reached over and rumpled Nathan's hair, which he'd combed across his forehead in imitation of his stepsister. Tom noted the boy wore the T-shirt she tie-dyed for him, and wondered if tomorrow he'd want a red streak in his hair, too.

"Did I tell you guys that Alan, Jessie, and I are going to have our picture in the local paper this week?"

"Cool!" Nathan said, gazing up lovingly at his stepsister.

"How come?" asked Tom.

"We folded a thousand paper cranes," Annie said. "You know, like in origami. It took us a month, but we got pledges and we've put the cranes on a mobile, and we're sending the money and the mobile to the Children's Peace Museum in Hiroshima."

"I've heard of that," said Christine. "Isn't that in honor of a girl who died after we dropped the bomb?"

"Sadako Suzaki," said Annie. "She was stricken with leukemia from radiation. She was twelve years old and she started folding paper cranes after a friend told her that, if she folded a thousand, she'd be granted a wish by the gods." Annie's long fingers pulled at a woven-leather bracelet loosely hanging on her wrist. "She died before she could finish." Annie brushed a lock of hair away from her eye. "But her friends completed the thousand and buried them with her. There's a statue of her now, and people send

1988

their cranes to the museum as a way to demonstrate for peace."

"That's wonderful," said Christine.

"Yeah, it was a great experience. You're supposed to say a prayer for peace every time you make one. It became my way of going to church, I guess."

Tom looked at the clock on the fireplace mantel. "We should be hitting the road."

"The next time we'll see you will be at your high school graduation," said Christine. "I imagine you can't wait for the next ten weeks to go by."

"Is it next week you're having that cyst removed?" asked Tom.

Annie ran her hands through her hair, stopping at the back of her head. "Yeah, the damn thing is driving me foolish."

"I remember Dr. Peterman saying that it might get bigger but that there was nothing to worry about."

"Well, it's getting bigger. A lot bigger. It's waking me up at night. I'm taking part of next week off from school to get it taken care of."

"Good," Christine said. "And then it's graduation and off to Europe, right?"

Annie grinned. "I'm hoping for France. And I'm hoping you guys will come visit me next year."

"You can count on it," said Tom.

"Wow, France!" said Nathan. "That will be so neat."

"It *will* be neat," said Annie, "I'd love to get Mom over there, too, but I don't know if I can get her on an airplane or not."

Tom rose from his chair. "Come on, kiddo, let's hit the road."

"Okay, Captain Kirk, here I come." Annie hugged Nathan and then Christine. "Thank you for a great meal and a great weekend." She paused in front of Christine. "Everything really has turned out for the best," she said, "if you know what I mean."

Tom mussed Nathan's hair. "You'll be asleep by the time I get back. Sleep well and I'll see you tomorrow." He kissed Christine. "I hope you'll wait up for me," he whispered. "Wear something sexy."

She put her mouth to his ear. "How about nothing?"

Monday morning, four weeks later, Tom and Christine stood with their arms around each other, looking out the bedroom window over the apple tree in the back yard, at a full moon sinking in the west.

"Thank you for last night," she said. "For the whole weekend."

"You're welcome," he said. "The skirt looks good on you."

That weekend, even though they both disliked shopping, they'd gone to L.L. Bean on Saturday, where Tom had bought Christine a wool skirt and she'd bought him a Greek fisherman's cap. Sunday after church, Tom, Christine, and Nathan walked the beach at Reid State Park, and after Nathan had gone to bed, Tom and Christine had taken a bath together.

They kissed and finished getting dressed for the next school week.

After breakfast, Tom, Christine, and Nathan walked out the door together. Despite a vivid sunrise, the day had quickly become overcast, with a damp wind coming off the ocean, so Christine made Nathan go back in the house for a heavier jacket to go over one of Annie's tie-dyed T-shirts. Then Nathan walked to the bus stop, while Tom and Christine got in the car for their morning commute.

Twenty-five minutes later, Tom dropped Christine off at Aronson High. "See you this afternoon," she said. Kissing her goodby, he tried to open her mouth but she giggled and pulled away.

"Let's not go to school today," he said. "Let's drive into Portland and rent a room and make wild, passionate love."

Christine's eyes turned that sexy, smoky blue that he loved. "Hold the last part of that thought for tonight. Bye."

He drove across the river and down Jordan Mills' Main Street. When he passed the town's Episcopal Church, St. Mark's, he remembered he and Christine had a kerygma class at St. Jude's that night. They'd spent the week memorizing the books in the Bible and planned to recite them together. It hadn't taken long (although he still confused Joel and Jonah and Zephaniah with Zachariah);

1988

he'd memorized the names when he was in Sunday school back in Ashton. Even won a jackknife for it, which upset his mother no end.

Thinking of his mother, Tom once again counted his blessings. After his father's death from liver disease, she'd become a bitter woman. According to her, her husband had been "a nasty lush," Martha had been "a bitch," and Christine "a tramp." But after her marriage last year to Cal, a widower with a terrible toupee and a wonderful sense of humor, she was learning to enjoy life—taking up golf and going on cruises to the Caribbean, Alaska, and Canada. A few days ago, he and his mother had actually had a good phone conversation.

Tom was whistling as he pulled into the high school parking lot. Unlike the more recently constructed Aronson High, Jordan Mills High School was a traditional brick building, nestled under towering oak trees. He walked into school, up the stairs to his classroom, and began the day.

The kids in his homeroom seemed relaxed. Even though there were only five more weeks of school, the weather was still cool and today it was cloudy, so they weren't too antsy. As Allan Jessup, the principal, pointed out over the intercom in his morning announcements, both the boys' baseball team and the girls' softball teams had won.

After his first class of the day, in which Tom led his sophomores through the scene in *Ordinary People* in which Conrad has a breakdown and admits that he blames himself for the death of his brother, Buck, Tom and his juniors began *Macbeth*.

"So what's significant about Macbeth's first words in the play, 'So foul and fair a day I have not seen'?" Tom asked.

A voice crackled over the intercom: "Mr. Jacobs?"

"Yes?"

"Could you come to the office? You have a phone call."

Nothing would ever be the same again.

Standing in the main office, he listened on the phone to

Martha's broken voice: "...results...biopsy...malignant."

The walls spun. "I don't understand. She's had it on the back of her head for years. Peterman always said it was a harmless sebaceous cyst."

"Well, he was obviously wrong. Tom, what are we going to do?"

The desks, the counters, the secretaries, the walls all blurred, leaving only himself, growing dizzier, pulling into a shell, his blood draining—no, flying—away, his face hot, his arms cold, as if he were on the old, giant swing at the carnival. Colors ran together, became black. A cold knot formed in his stomach, rose into his throat, burning. A metallic, midway voice whined in his head:

> *"Things fall apart; the center cannot hold;*
> *Mere anarchy is loosed upon the world."*

He told himself to focus. Listen to Martha's voice. Tight. Tearful. As if she were biting her fist. "I don't know how I'm going to tell her."

His voice sounded far away, "I'll drive up, and we'll tell her together."

A yawning emptiness opened beneath him. Someone said, "I have to go. I'll see you tonight."

He willed the phone back to its black cradle. He left the main office and walked down the hall as if he were built of glass, afraid of stumbling and shattering on the linoleum tile. Students turned to shadows and the walls whirled. Under him, the void.

He refused to look down. Refused to acknowledge it. Refused to sink into it. If he fell into that chasm, he would disappear.

Instead, he would hold on. To what?

The carnival voice wailed: *"My God, my God, why have you forsaken me?"*

Chapter Three
1989

On the day after Annie died, Tom folded up the cot in the small upstairs bedroom where she used to sleep when she visited, pushed it into the corner, and covered it with a gray blanket. He went downstairs to the living room and brought up a small wooden cabinet in which his grandfather used to keep his corncob pipes. After rummaging through a cardboard box in the hall closet for a glass ashtray that once belonged to his father, he returned to the living room for two pillar candles on the fireplace mantel, carried them up, and carefully positioned them on the bookcase already in the bedroom.

On his next trip downstairs, Christine called from the kitchen, "Is there anything I can do to help?"

He didn't answer, didn't hear his wife come into the room. When she touched his shoulder, he flinched. "The best way to help me is the get out of the way," he said.

He pushed the coffee table against the futon. A card on the table fell to the floor. Tom glanced down at the words *Christ Is Risen!* printed in runny-egg-yellow. That's right, today was Easter Sunday. Anger radiated down his spine into his feet, one of which he watched, as if from some great distance, stomp on the card before kicking it out of the way.

He pulled his gray chair away from the wall, and put his arms around the back and his hands under the arms. He bent his knees and lifted. Crab-walking across the room, he banged the side of the chair against the wall, leaving a dent in the plaster. "Shit!" he growled. And when the chair struck the wall again, "Goddamn it all to hell!"

Christine said, "Let me help you!"

"Please," Tom said in a low voice. "Leave me alone."

He watched to make sure she was back in the kitchen before taking a deep breath and lifting again. At the staircase, he hoisted the chair three steps to the corner landing, where he set it down. Straightening, he felt a pop in his back. Pain shot down his spine into his right leg. He clenched his jaw and wrestled with the chair until the back of it faced the stairs. Tipped it upward, using his shoulder to bump it up the seven more steps to the second floor.

Once there, Tom slid the chair on its back to the doorway of the old bedroom. His lower back was on fire. Pulling the chair onto its side, he swiveled it into the den, gouging the door. Lifting the chair didn't hurt too much, but when he stood up, pain took a hammer to his lower back. He sat down heavily, looking at the enshrouded cot and pallid walls. Listened to a cold, March wind rattle the window. Convulsed in tears.

An hour later, he stood at the window, both hands kneading his back, staring out over the apple tree in the back yard. Low leaden clouds blew over the remnants of dead leaves and old snow. He heard footsteps on the stairs, Christine's voice: "Would you like some lunch?"

His eyes fixed on a jagged limb of the tree and the broken branch that lay beneath it. "No, I'll come down later. You go ahead and eat."

1989

He shut the door and opened the brown portfolio of Annie's artwork. Dropping to his hands and knees, he spread the unframed pictures on the carpeting. He ran his fingers lightly over the fibrous paper, smoothing out wrinkles. He arranged the pictures. Kept rearranging them until he had them grouped the way he wanted. Getting up was like trying to rise with a hot rod running diagonally across his lower back. With mounting tape left over from putting up posters in his classroom, he began to hang his daughter's work. He went slowly, focusing all his attention on measuring with a yardstick. He marked with a pencil how far down from the ceiling and away from the corners to begin, and how far from each other the pictures should be. On either side of the room's single window, he stuck two watercolors of flowers. One featured a spray of lavender-blue blossoms against an inky background spilling across the painting. The other was of large blood-red petals. Over his grandfather's smoking cabinet, he arranged several charcoal sketches in various sizes, including one of a healthy nude with expansive breasts and a roll of comfortable fat around her middle—drawings Annie had done two years earlier at a summer art program. On the opposite wall, he aligned her charcoal self-portraits from the same program: one of her face when she wore her hair short on the sides, accenting the peace symbol dangling from her right ear; the other a waist-up sketch that showed his daughter's face clouded in shadows, her collar bones fanning out like wings above a low-cut jersey.

Finally, he picked up the largest watercolor and carefully positioned it over the bookcase and the candles. Holding his back, Tom gazed at a turquoise hand, reaching up through a pile of umber-colored stones, pointed like mountains toward a diaphanous petal drifting down from a cluster of orange and red and yellow flower blossoms. As he beheld the outstretched fingers, each vein pronounced and taut—they had to be Annie's—the pain in his back speared into his heart.

Christine's footsteps. Her voice at the door. "Tom, it's your mother on the phone. It's the second time she's called, and I can't convince her you don't want to talk with her."

He banged his fist on the arm of the chair. "Shit!" As he rose from the chair, he gasped in pain.

When he opened the door, Christine said, "I told her that you didn't want to talk to anyone today, but she said she wasn't anyone, she was your mother."

He stomped downstairs and grabbed the phone on the kitchen wall. "Damn it, Ma, what do you want?"

Silence on the other end of the line. Sniffling. "I won't be long." She sounded as if she had a cold. He could see her sitting in the captain's chair by the phone dabbing at her nose with a Kleenex. His anger drained, leaving behind a dirty bathtub ring of shame.

"What can I do to help?" she said.

Outrage gurgled up again. "You can leave me alone. I drove home a hundred and twenty miles last night in snow and rain on three hours sleep. I'm exhausted."

He heard sobbing noises. Shivered. Pain drilled his spine as he tried to stretch his lower back. Out the window, a crow perched on the bare branch of a maple tree.

"All right," she said, finally. "I won't bother you any more. Just one question. Can Cal and I ride up with you and Christine to the funeral?"

Tom's face flushed. "Christine and I aren't going to the funeral."

"What? You're not going to your own—"

"Annie didn't want a church service." His right hand twisted the telephone cord. "She wanted her ashes scattered over the ocean. If my ex-wife needs a funeral and a burial service at the family gravesite, fine, but don't expect me to attend the festivities."

"But I don't know what to do! How do you expect me to say goodbye to Annie? What will I tell people?"

He kicked at the molding along the kitchen wall. "Ma, if you want to talk your husband into driving a hundred miles to a funeral, hop right to it."

More sobbing noises. He thought of hanging up, and wished

1989

he had when she said, "When will the obituary be in the paper?"

"I don't know." He looked at the dirty dishes in the sink. *Damn it, Christine, this place looks like a dump.* "I'm not going to run one down here. Nobody knew Annie in this part of the state."

Which was a lie. Through her Girl Scout activities and work for Amnesty International, Annie had made a number of friends in southern Maine. But all Tom could think of were old classmates looking up from their morning papers and saying, "Too bad about old Tommy losing his kid," before dunking their donuts into their coffees.

"Oh, Thomas, no!" his mother wailed.

Years of guilt whenever he sensed he'd let his mother down seized him and held him in a chokehold. He was the son she'd needed to succeed, rescue her from the shame of an alcoholic husband, and an older son who'd dropped out of high school after impregnating his girlfriend and—if that weren't bad enough—leaving both the girl and the town. Tom was the good son. The junior choir member. The athlete. The class salutatorian. The teacher. So that when he'd come home drunk in high school, she'd slapped his face and screamed, "I can't have you turn out like your brother! Are you trying to kill me?" So that when he'd told her he'd left Martha to marry Christine, she'd sobbed, "My idol has feet of clay!"

He softened his voice. "Look, I'm sorry about the obituary. I'm sorry about the funeral. Maybe you and Cal and your minister can do something."

"Reverend Stiles did ask if I wanted him to come to the house." She blew her nose. "The Hastings—you remember them—will come, I'm sure…and maybe Cal's son. If you and Christine want to come over, you could join us."

Tom pounded the wall over the telephone. "Ma, how many times do I have to say goodbye to my daughter?" He burst into tears. "I've been saying goodbye for two months!"

His mother's voice filled with phlegm. "I'm so sorry for you, my son."

Her voice sounded labored. He knew she had heart issues. "My son" sounded awkward. Stilted. Did she mean that just as he was part of her—my arm, my leg—so too was his pain? Or did she simply want to say that she loved him? Should he reply, "I'm sorry, too, dear mother?" Shame turned to guilt for not being a better son. For not planning to take her to Annie's funeral. For not planning to run an obituary.

But instead of changing his mind, he straightened and dried his eyes on his sweatshirt. The notion of himself as "son" reawakened old resentments: Feeling strangled by apron strings; being responsible for covering up his father's drinking and his brother's fucked-up life; living under the pressure of being the first on either side of his family to go to college. He couldn't deal with it. Not now. He had to get her off the phone.

"Ma, I'll drive over to see you before too long. I just need some time."

"It's got to be this week, remember? Cal and I are flying to Miami week after next for one of those Caribbean cruises. I told you."

"I'd forgotten." *I had other things on my mind. Like watching my daughter die.* "If I don't make it over, have a good trip."

He hung up, knowing he'd never go to see his mother and stepfather before they left. He felt unclean, like the dishes in the sink. He stood for another minute at the kitchen window and looked up at a sky the color of scalded milk. He turned toward the cupboard over the refrigerator.

Gin, vodka, it didn't make any difference.

―――――――――

He sat at the kitchen table that night, enclosed by a fog through which occasional shafts of pain shot like lightning, his face and back hot, hands and feet frozen. His sense of Christine faded in and out. When he did notice her, she was staring at her plate, her eyes red. He knew she'd spent the day in the kitchen roasting a leg of lamb, baking bread and brownies, but he couldn't taste anything until it rose again into his throat. He heard her ask how the phone call had gone with his mother. Heard himself respond that he was sorry for her but that, damn it, it was his daughter who'd just died, and he'd grieve any goddamned way he wanted.

After Christine had eaten about half of her ice cream—he had no idea what kind it was—she put down her spoon and checked her watch. "Speaking of phone calls, I told Nathan I'd call at seven." She looked at Tom. "Anything you want to say to him? He was pretty upset last night."

It took several moments before he could put her words together. "Hell, he's twelve years old. He should have known how bad Annie was the last time he saw her."

Christine bowed her head. "I still think we should have said something to him."

Why does everything have to be my fault? He pushed away from the table, the noise from the chair like chalk scraping a blackboard. "Well, it's too late now. Say hello. Tell him I'll see him next weekend. I'm going to finish upstairs."

As Christine dialed Nathan's father, Tom went to the bathroom and chewed three more aspirin. He returned to the kitchen cupboard. Grabbed Scotch this time. Three fingers in a glass. Back in the den, he closed the door and took a deep drink. Put a bathrobe over his clothes. Lit the candles on the bookcase, and then one of the small cigars he'd brought back from Bangor. Sitting in the granite-gray chair, he positioned a pillow behind him, pulled the hood of his bathrobe over his head, and gazed through the encircling smoke at Annie's watercolor over the bookcase.

The green shading on the stones in the painting reminded him of rocks jutting into Casco Bay off Newell Landing, and of his second marriage ceremony. The black clouds on the horizon. The unearthly aura around his daughter's head. He began to cry, then to sob angrily, pounding his fist on the arm of the chair. When his tears slowed, he wiped his eyes and dropped the cigar into the ashtray. Slowly and painfully, he walked to his and Christine's bedroom, where he found a pad of paper, an envelope, and a pen from the jelly jar that Annie had once painted blue, except for the word "Dad" in red.

Back in his new den, he started writing:

Father Coffin:

When I got home yesterday after driving from Bangor, what did I find in the mail but an appeal for money for St. Jude's capital campaign. Is that why I never heard from you for two months—because you've been too busy drumming up money for that goddamned addition instead of looking after the people who are going to sit there? Okay, I was 120 miles away, but you could have picked up the phone once or twice—Christine had my number at the Ronald McDonald House. And speaking of Christine, couldn't you have stopped by once or twice to see her and Nathan? Or were you too busy kissing the asses of those parishioners with the big bucks? Good luck raising the money for your new addition, but I can tell you one family that will never set foot in it.

Tom Jacobs

There, damn you. For a moment, the pressure pushing behind Tom's eyes eased. He finished his Scotch in three more swallows. Over the last two months, he'd fallen out of the habit of drinking, but now the burning tasted good in a perverse sort of way. He felt better than he had all day. Maybe the aspirin was finally kicking in.

But as he sealed the envelope, his hands trembled as he thought of Gary reading the letter. He'd never written anything like this—or s*aid* anything like this, for that matter—to anyone, let alone to a man of God. Tom's parents, especially his mother, had raised him—and his brother, Ed, for all the good that did—to respect the law, religion, and education. They'd taught their boys that gaining and giving respect was perhaps the most important thing a person could do. He'd learned to measure every action by "What will the neighbors say?" Well, what would the neighbors say now, about his swearing at a priest? More hot tears rolled down his face.

1989

His back spasmed. Damn it, he was tired of thinking about what the fucking neighbors or his fucking mother or that fucking hypocrite, Gary Coffin, would say. He took the letter downstairs, found a stamp, and, since he was there anyway, headed for the kitchen cupboard. Christine was still on the phone with Nathan. Another wave of anger rolled over him. How much was this call to Wyoming costing?

"Honey, I can't read anymore," Christine pleaded with Nathan. She smiled weakly at Tom and held up a copy of *The Hotel Cat*. "I've read the story to you twice already. I'll read to you again tomorrow night when I call, I promise. Meanwhile, I hope you're having a good time with your old friends and we'll see you soon." She offered Tom the phone. He shook his head, thinking, *Isn't twelve a little old to be read to?* He snatched the bottle of Scotch and stopped in the bathroom on his way upstairs for three more aspirin.

Tom smoked another cigar and drained two more inches of Scotch from the bottle, before his head fell back on the chair. When he awoke two hours later, the burning in his back had risen into the right side of his neck. Sawdust coated his mouth. He staggered to bed, where he fell into a restless sleep, punctuated by back pain.

At some point in the night, he dreamed that he and Annie were walking under a cobalt sky, along a sandy beach enclosed on three sides by rocky hills. A breeze blew and cold surf rushed in and out over their feet. Seagulls flew overhead. They met other people, but no one Tom recognized until he saw John F. Kennedy, tanned and healthy in a navy blue bathing suit, standing beside a tall black rock—a polished obelisk. Kennedy smiled and said hello. Tom stopped to talk. He wondered whether or not to ask JFK what he'd been doing since the assassination, but realized Annie had gone on without him. He saw her disappear into a cave in a wall of rocks up the shore, and ran after her, his feet sinking into the sand, slowing him down. Finally, out of breath and sweating, he reached the cave, ducked his head, and entered. Through the darkness, spots of light lay ahead of him. He heard water dripping and the sound of his own breathing. Annie walked from one spotlight to another, moving further and further away. Her footsteps echoed off damp stone walls. In the last spotlight, she turned and waved with two fingers, her face sad. When Tom tried to run after her, he couldn't move. His legs had turned to stone.

He awoke, feeling beaten up. His head throbbed. His back ached. One of his legs burned, even as the rest of him was cold. Trying to get comfortable, get warm, he rolled toward a gaunt, middle-aged woman in a flannel nightgown lying beside him. For a moment, he didn't know who the hell she was.

Chapter Four
1989

Most evenings, during the first month after his daughter's death, Tom left Christine and Nathan in the living room and went upstairs to his den. Shutting the door, he poured into a brandy snifter three fingers of Dewar's from the bottle he now kept with the cigars in his grandfather's smoking cabinet. He opened a window and turned on the small fan Christine insisted he use to keep smoke from the rest of the house. He lit the two pillar candles on the bookcase, snipped off the end of a double corona, and lighted it from the candle flame. Watched the smoke from his cigar rise like incense around Annie's watercolor of her hand reaching up through rocks toward the falling flower petal. Sat back in his chair and lifted his glass. *The cup of salvation.*

He'd first become aware of the lure of alcohol around the age of ten, when his father's friend, Don Daigle—who wore a fedora with the brim turned up in front like Ed Norton on *The Honeymooners*—used to come over to the house on Friday nights to drink Narragansett beer, eat Spanish peanuts, and smoke Camels in front of *The Life of Riley, Boston Blackie,* and *The Gillette Friday Night Fights.* Tommy sat on the couch, eating his bologna sandwich, transfixed by this male world of razor blades and cigarettes and violence and beer.

In high school, before he'd connected his father's unpredictable behavior and his brother's hell-raising to their drinking, guzzling Budweiser in the local sand pit was a way both to emulate his old man and to piss off his mother, which he was more and more inclined to do as part of his need to escape the confines of Ashton, Maine. During those summers in Idaho, he'd learned to drink Jack Daniels as part of being in communion with Kerouac, Neal Cassady, and the rest of the beats.

During his first marriage, his drinking became erratic (one more thing Martha said she didn't understand). By then, he'd recognized his father's alcoholism and there were months, in one instance, over a year, when Tom didn't drink at all—his way of making sure he didn't turn into the lout he saw on his occasional visits lying on the couch with a glass of *Old Crow* resting on his gut. But because alcohol also enabled him to see himself as sophisticated and intellectual (even less like his father) there were other times when he'd spend $100 to stock his liquor cabinet with Laphroaig, Courvoisier, and Bombay Sapphire, which he would sip in the evening while he smoked one of his meerschaum pipes.

From that night in the dormitory in New Jersey, drinking had been part of Tom and Christine's courtship, which included margaritas looking up at the Rocky Mountains and Manhattans looking out over the Maine coastline. They'd always had a pretty good supply of booze, even if the Scotch was Scoresby, the brandy was E&J, and the gin was Gordon's. More recently, they'd become fond of some of the beers from Maine's new micro-breweries, which they enjoyed by the pitcher on Friday nights with their pizza before going home and jumping into bed.

Now, however, most of Tom's drinking was solitary, a way both to dull his continuing backache, and to escape, even momentarily, the torments of the day—when opening a car door, putting away the dishes, or taking a leak, pain ripped through him, taking his breath away, and he'd erupt in tears, feeling as if he were drown-

1989

ing, even as part of him stood calm and detached off to one side, watching this damn fool bawl his head off.

Drinking was now more of a noun than a verb. A place rather than an action. An oasis in a sea of storms impossible to predict. Sitting with his Scotch and cigar in front of the candles, he could recapture, at least for a few moments, the comfort he'd experienced in the Eastern Maine Medical Chapel. During those weeks after Easter, when Tom had stopped going to church, his memories of that chapel became his place to worship, as he recreated it in his mind, inventing what he couldn't remember about the first time he'd found himself there.

Tom's story of the chapel began on a particularly ugly day at the hospital. Annie had developed a fever of 102 degrees. Christine's latest letter had whined about bouncing a check, Nathan's dropping garbage all over the front walk, and the cat's throwing up. He argued with Martha, who wanted him to complain to Dr. Godfrey, Annie's primary physician, about one of the nurses. To make matters worse, as he sat by his daughter's bedside while she was sleeping, a woman cried out from just outside the room in a shrill voice, "Where am I?" Plastic curtains rustled. There were footsteps. A bed rolled into the next room.

"Where the fuck am I?" the woman cried.

A deep, hoarse voice answered, "Damn it, woman, quiet down!"

"I want to go home!"

"Shut up and listen! You'll go home tomorrow. You'll see."

The woman's voice trailed off into a moan and Tom heard the man talking in the corridor with a third woman. His heart pounded at the intrusion. *If they wake up my daughter...* Peering into the hall, he saw a heavy-set man wearing a brown wool cap and a brown topcoat, buttoned only at the top button. The man needed a shave and the arm of his topcoat was ripped. The other woman appeared younger. Bleached blond hair. Black leather jacket and jeans.

Behind them, the new patient screamed, "Fuck off!"

He tried once more to read from one of Thomas Merton's books that Christine had left with him, but at the words, "All sorrow, hardship, difficulty, pain, unhappiness, and ultimately death itself can be traced to rebellion against God's love for us," he threw the book on the floor.

More moaning from the next room. The blond woman telling the man to phone someone in New York City.

Loud growling noises, followed by, "I can't find the fucking phone number!"

The woman yelled, "You asshole, just dial the operator!"

"I did. She told me to dial information. I don't know what the goddamn number is!"

Annie slept through it all, but by the time Martha came into the room later that afternoon, his head was splitting. His stomach churned. He left to go back to the Ronald McDonald House, walking to the elevator on gray and brown and white tiles of corridor, past rooms smelling of dirty diapers, past the metallic jingling sound of a curtain being pulled, past an ancient voice softly sighing, "Help me…help me."

Later, all he could figure was that somehow he'd gotten off the elevator on the wrong floor, and in his confusion and frustration about the day, hadn't even noticed until he found himself in front of a door with a metal sign that read "Chapel." He didn't even know EMMC had a chapel. He opened the door and entered a small room with white walls, four rows of metal and blue-cushioned chairs, and a walnut-colored altar, unadorned except for two pillar candles. No crosses. No hint of any religious denomination. No indication of any religion whatsoever. Behind the altar, filling an entire wall, a round window framed by shards of brown, gold, blue, and red glass faced out over the river. Along the riverbanks, birch trees bent in the wind. It was like viewing an animated stained-glass window.

Tom fished a book of matches from his shirt pocket and, after lighting the two candles, sat down in the front row of chairs and stared past the flames, out the round window at the rushing water. The room was so quiet. Even in Annie's single room at the end of the hall, he could hear a steady undercurrent of noise from machines or voices in the hall like those assholes this afternoon.

But as Tom thought of the man's words—"She told me to dial information. I don't know what the goddamn number is!"—he nodded his head. He wanted information, too. Like why did Annie have a fever? Why wasn't she eating? Why did she get this cancer in the first place? Why was she dying?

He stared into the circle encompassed by stained glass, the question *Why?* pounding in his head and heart. The window blurred. Wet flakes of snow lathered the glass, turned the circle white, scoured him to bone. The candles on either side of the altar glowed brightly, their light dancing. As Tom watched, the flames drew together, enfolded by the stained glass around the white window. He, too, was enfolded, and from somewhere he heard the words, "Don't ask why, just ask for help."

It wasn't really a "voice," and yet it wasn't a thought, either. The words made no sense. Ask who for help? What kind of help?

Tom heard the words again. "Don't ask why, just ask for help."

Okay, help, he thought, bitterly. *Help me make sense of this mess. Help me understand the reason for my daughter's pain and why she's going to die before she's ever really lived.*

"Don't ask why, just ask for help." The words were gentle. Insistent. As if they had always been there, but that only here, in the silence of the chapel, could he hear them.

He couldn't take his eyes from the dancing candles. From somewhere in the ceiling fresh air bathed his face. His body softened. His breathing slowed. The stained glass drew him into its embrace.

After that, he'd spent almost every afternoon in the chapel, unwinding from the day before going back to the Ronald McDonald House. He never heard any more words, and eventually, as Annie's condition worsened, he almost forgot about them. Now, however, in the smoky, boozy silence of his den, Tom thought of that voice he'd heard the first afternoon he sat in the chapel. Not so much what it said, but how it soothed him. Embraced him. Cared for him. He wanted to hear that voice again.

But the only voice he heard was that of the rage he kept muffled up all day, and which, no matter how much he drank, eventually screamed in his ears like that woman in the room next to Annie's. In the faculty room, for example, trite, myopic, incessant chatter swirled around him. Tom wanted to shout, "Hey! What difference does it make who won an Academy Award or what Mrs. Motormouth on the school board said last night? I've been to the mountain and seen the face of Death. Who cares? Fuck off!"

He silently cursed colleagues who said they understood what he was going through because a grandmother or an old uncle had recently died, wanting to ask them if they knew what it felt like to wipe mucus from their child's lips after she'd stopped breathing. He cursed his principal, who stopped him in the hall, put his arm on his shoulder, and told him to keep busy. That's the advice he'd given his daughter when she was waiting to hear whether or not the college of her choice had taken her off its waiting list. Tom had smiled, imagined putting his hands around Allan's neck and shouting, "My daughter's not going to college! My daughter is dead. Fuck off!"

Worst were the people who went out of their way to explain how sorry they were for him. Father Gary Coffin answered Tom's angry Easter letter by saying he "ached with sorrow," and suggested he talk to Father Curtis Mathews of St. Mark's Episcopal in Jordan Mills, the town in which Tom taught. Jack Peterman, who as Annie's physician told him for years that the growth on the back of his daughter's head was harmless, wrote a rambling lamentation about the pain he felt whenever a child dies. Tom ripped up both letters. The bastards had no idea what it meant to ache. No clue as to what real pain felt like.

Fuck off. All of you.

He had little to say either to his wife or to his stepson. Afternoons and weekends, when not in his den, he corrected papers, got a haircut, or ran errands, leaving Christine to chauffeur Nathan to his friend Bart's house or to karate lessons. It was she, not he, who

1989

helped tend her son's array of animals, played cards with him, or got down on the living room floor with him and his toys.

Tom's throat constricted whenever he was around his stepson. Walking into the living room, he'd see the boy sprawled on the floor, with those mechanical toys—Transformers, Tom thought they were called—scattered everywhere, while on TV, shrill voices, loud music, and garishly clothed people assaulted his senses. He wanted to yell, "For Chrissakes, pick up this mess!" but instead, took a breath and said, "Does it have to be so loud in here?"

Nathan picked up a truck, converted it into an airplane, and pretended to fly it. "Zzzoom!"

Picking his way around the toys, resisting the urge to step on them and grind them to tiny plastic pieces, Tom walked to the TV and turned it down. "Come on, chum, let's pick up some of these toys, okay?"

Nathan picked up another Transformer and began an air battle. "Die, you Autobot! Bizzh! Broom!! That's what you think, Megatron! Kaploosh! Blam! Blam! Blam!"

"Damn it, Nathan, didn't you hear me?"

Nathan slowly looked up at Tom, his eyes becoming black holes. "I'm not finished."

Tom felt the boy's anger at him for intruding into his world. And why not? Nathan had an intuitive streak that seemed to pick up people's faintest emotional vibrations and reflect them back. Tom was sure that at some level his stepson sensed how much he'd dreaded the boy's return from spending Easter vacation with his father. How much he now resented Nathan's intruding into his grief.

And if Christine was within hearing distance, as she usually was, and said, "He'll pick up when he's done, don't worry," he sensed her condemnation for his not wanting her to tell Nathan that Annie had been dying. Her condemnation of him as a father. He knew he should sit down with his wife and stepson and tell them that he'd never talked with Annie about her dying because he thought he should follow the example of Dr. Godfrey, who, while he never lied to any of them about the seriousness of Annie's illness, never used

51

the word "death." He should explain that Martha thought that Annie knew she was dying, but didn't want to talk about it. He could admit to them that, by the time he decided to say something to his daughter, she'd slipped into a coma and it was too late. But trying to explain his reasons for silence would mean reliving Annie's death, and he couldn't do that. Any more than he could talk to Nathan about picking up his toys. Everything felt like confrontation and he'd had all the confrontation he could stand.

He knew Christine and Nathan were grieving Annie's death. Besides being silent and sullen around his stepfather, Nathan's grades were going down. He could only fall asleep curled up on the living room floor with the television set on in front of him, a fire in the hearth beside him, and his mother sitting with her foot on his back. Sometimes, for no apparent reason, he kicked a pillow or pounded the wall or stormed upstairs and locked himself in his room with his animals. One morning, McCafferty, the cat, knocked over an Easter lily that Bart's parents had given them, breaking both the pot and the plant's stem. Although Nathan had never, to Tom's knowledge, cried over Annie's death, he broke down in angry sobs over the loss of this plant. The lily, he said, was "dead."

Christine was sad and distant. Preoccupied. It was a rare day when a pot or a pan or a plate didn't fall on the floor. Twice, she burned herself on the stove. Besides her anxiety over Nathan and Tom, she was worried about her ex-husband, who'd joined some kind of Pentecostal religious group and called three or four times a week to make sure Nathan was all right. "Zack never spent any time with Nathan before, and when he did, it was only to criticize him. Now, he wants to talk with 'my dear, dear son.' I'm afraid he wants to take Nathan away from me."

Tom tried to appear sympathetic. But the truth—the truth that he could only admit to himself in his den after a couple of glasses of gin before dinner and half a bottle of wine with his meal, and his evening Scotch—was that it would be fitting for his wife to lose her child, too. After all, they'd already caused Annie's death.

They'd been blind. They should have known everything

1989

had been too easy. He hadn't even had to tell Martha about Christine; she'd found one of her letters. When Martha had confronted him, he moved out of the house (which he'd hated anyway) into an apartment owned by a former student. The following week, Christine left the ranch for an apartment in Kidron Springs. Their courtship had seemed like a romantic novel—Wyoming one month, Maine the next. In October, they ate sardines by the shores of Sebago Lake and read to each other from Thoreau: "If one advances confidently in the direction of his dreams, and endeavors to live the life which he has imagined, he will meet with a success unexpected in common hours." *(Yeah, right!)* In November, they drove down to Colorado Springs to a convent that Christine's friend, Diane, had recommended, where Tom experienced the same Rocky Mountain spirituality he remembered from his fire-fighting days. On Christmas Day, Tom drove to Belmont to meet Nathan and Christine's parents. Barney and Celeste James were incredibly gracious, making no effort to pry into their plans, and more important, providing a comfortable space in which Tom, Christine, and Nathan could plan their lives together.

So easy! Finding the apartment. Blending the families. He remembered the previous Easter, when Annie sat in his living room inviting Tom and his family to visit her in France this year. He hadn't noticed that afternoon how her wrists stuck out of her sweater like pipe cleaners. He and Christine had been too lost in the muck and mire of their lust to see what had really been going on before Annie's death. Now, in his den, his back aching, watching the smoke from his cigar frame his daughter's watercolor of her hand reaching through the rocks toward the falling flower petal, he realized that Annie had painted that picture almost two years earlier. Before her diagnosis, when her future seemed bright and limitless. What nightmares had spawned this vision of herself, buried under stones, grasping for one small shred of beauty?

Whatever they were, he—with Christine's willing assistance—had caused them.

He should have demanded the cyst be biopsied when it first appeared five years earlier. Should have insisted on a second opinion when it started growing a year ago. Should have paid attention to how much weight his daughter had lost during the last year. But no, he was too busy fucking Christine every time he had a chance, and thinking it was God's will.

Visions and voices pervaded his cigar smoke: The afternoon Annie came home and walked into the living room in Webber, looking as if she'd returned from college instead of high school. As tall as her mother. Her figure filling out. He couldn't believe she'd just turned fifteen. Her cheeks still kept some of the tan she'd brought back from New Mexico a month earlier, when she'd strode off the plane erect and self-assured.

A few minutes later, she began to die.

He saw again the way her body stiffened when he and Martha told her they were separating. Felt once more her cold face as he kissed her goodbye. Heard again her vomiting in the bathroom.

All his fault.

He heard Annie's voice at Pizza Hut two months after he'd moved out of the house, when he showed her Christine's picture: "I don't know, Dad, this is awfully sudden." At Christmas: "I can't leave Mom alone over the holidays." The following Easter, when he'd given her a stuffed bunny before telling her he was moving away to live with Christine and Nathan.

"Dad!" she cried, "how many more changes to you think I can take?" He saw her sobbing. Witnessed her heart break. When he moved toward her, she threw the bunny at him. "I don't want a fucking rabbit, I want you!"

All his fault.

He replayed the phone calls: Martha telling him his daughter didn't want to talk with him. Annie hanging up on him. His daughter screaming, "You never loved me!" Or claiming, "You don't want me. You've got the boy you always wanted now." All the time dying a little more.

All his fault.

1989

Some nights, he sat in his chair with his cigar and his Scotch and his aching back, his ex-wife's words spinning in his head like Nathan's hamster on its wheel: "I hope you and that woman and your God are happy with what you've done."

Was God happy? Did God even exist? Obviously, it hadn't been God who called him to be with Christine. Only forty-two-year-old testosterone. Was thinking of God as the voice in the chapel, a source of comfort in times of turmoil, just another self-deception? Was his daughter's cancer merely an accident of fate, a one-in-a-million chance, like being struck by lightning? Or was God a benevolent but limited Casper The Friendly Deity, who hovers around us without affecting the world one way or another, so that Annie's cancer stemmed from acid rain and people cutting down rain forests? Was God some glorified engineer who created a preordained world like one of those giant IBM computers, where her disease was part of a master plan to keep the universe running in harmony? Or maybe Shakespeare was right when he wrote, "As flies to wanton boys, are we to th'gods. They kill us for their sport," and God was a super-sadist, getting kicks from inflicting pain on innocent eighteen-year-olds?

He didn't know. All he knew was that his Puritan ancestors had it right. There *is* a serpent in the garden, and he and Christine had struck a deal with it. Swapped the lives of their children for their own selfish passions.

At some point during the evening, he'd hear a knock on the door of his den. Christine's voice: "Nathan's come to say good night."

When the door opened and Nathan stood in the doorway, his hair a black question mark and his face lined from the living room carpet, guilt for not spending more time with the boy stabbed Tom like an ice pick.

"I wish you were my father," Nathan had told Tom when he went out to visit him and Christine during that long-distance courtship. These days Nathan was on the phone with Zack every other night, undoubtedly saying, "I wish you were still my father."

And why not? Tom's deal with the Devil had damaged his stepson, too. Once, the boy had been open and spontaneous and happy. Now, he was sullen, guarded, distant. He no longer asked Tom to help him feed his animals. No longer went with him on walks to show him butterfly cocoons under milkweed leaves. No longer tried to sweet-talk him into buying another of those Transformer things. And he no longer hugged him good night. Just a half-hearted wave before the door closed again.

But as Tom continued drinking, he decided that guilt wasn't so bad, actually. Sitting with guilt was easier than trying to figure out what to say to Nathan or Christine. Required no effort at all, in fact. Guilt filled the void caused by Annie's death in such a way that he didn't have to think about his daughter. Better to feel the weight of his guilt than to feel axed in the heart whenever he remembered his child.

Tom observed himself growing larger. Guilt became a glow. His backache abated. The walls melted. The next thing he knew, his glass had fallen on the floor, his cigar in the ashtray looked like a wet turd, and it was midnight. He staggered to the bedroom and fell into bed. Rolling away from Christine, he shivered with cold, and tried to wrap up in what covers she'd left him.

But he woke only three hours later, with a headache and a parched mouth, smelling his sour sweat. The night pressed upon his chest like a boulder. He lay in the dark, fretting about Nathan's low grades, worried about Christine's upcoming mammogram, afraid that the pain in his back was a tumor.

As it was in the beginning, is now, and ever shall be.
All my fault.

Chapter Five
1989

He walked through the school hunched over, back aching, staring at the floors. His students said they couldn't hear him. He lost a set of exams. But at least trying to keep twenty-five adolescents focused for fifty minutes took his mind off his loss, his guilt, although by the end of the day and five of these classes, he was exhausted.

He found himself more drawn to unpopular students, especially girls, going out of his way to commend them whenever he could, as a way to make it up to his daughter for not having spent enough time with her. Not giving her enough praise. At the same time, he was more irritated by late papers and back talk, but found he didn't have the energy to confront students, so he muttered to himself about such behavior being another sign of America's decay.

The country seemed to be falling apart. After Iran's Ayatollah declared Salman Rushdi's *The Satanic Verses* offensive and sentenced Rushdi to death, some American booksellers refused to carry the book for fear of reprisals. Alaska's coast was still covered in oil. Oliver North was found guilty of illegally selling arms to support Contra rebels in Nicaragua, while the president was sending 19,000 troops to Panama. One Sunday, he read a piece by a columnist in *The New York Times* who'd returned to the United States after ten years abroad to find his country "over-ripe." Yes, he thought over his Scotch, "over-ripe" is a good word to describe modern American music, modern morals, modern integrity. Soft, rotten in spots. Even the athletic teams in school can't fail, so coaches cheat and bend rules so athletes no longer have to go to classes. They take steroids so they can be bigger and stronger and win more games.

The root of his country's problems, as he saw it, was fear. He lived in a frightened society. One afraid of dancing on the icy brink of life—pussyfooting its way along, trying to sidestep any kind of pain, from insomnia to depression to plain old boredom. No wonder drug use at Jordan Mills High School was on the rise. Kids used to wait until after school to get high but now they, like their parents, were more and more afraid of pain, not only physical pain, but any kind of emotional distress, and they didn't want guilt, they didn't want sorrow, they wanted to be "okay," and they wanted to be okay *now*.

He tried to feel sympathetic, but so many of his druggie students just pissed him off. The worst was Michael Keith, who'd transferred to Jordan Mills after being kicked out of Aronson High while Tom was on leave. A suspected drug dealer whose blurred eyes, sallow complexion, and smoky reek suggested he might be his own best customer, Michael often stormed into class late, collapsing with a loud groan in his seat. He interrupted discussion—"That's dumb! What time's this period get over?"—or belched in the middle of a quiz. When Tom told him to quiet down, Michael snarled, "Whaddya mean? Wadido?" Nothing was his fault. The world was persecuting him. Daryl stole his book so he couldn't study for today's test. Blame Sherry for talking, not him. Tom started to dread Michael's class, and often as he lay in bed at 3 a.m. with a dry mouth and dull backache, he saw the boy's pasty face smirking at him out of the darkness.

One Friday afternoon, when the bell rang at 1:20 for the end of class, Michael jumped from his desk, knocking his chair over with a metallic clatter. "I'm outta here!" he yelled, and raced for the door.

"Hey!" Tom cried, but Michael never hesitated. His voice called down the hall, "I'm gonna get smashed!"

The room emptied and Tom walked back and picked up the chair. Pain vibrated up and down his spine. Michael had printed "this school suks" on his desk. Tom looked at the clock on the wall. One more period to go, he thought, before he could go home, have a drink, and forget about that shithead.

As the next class poured into his room, he turned to the window and watched Michael and his friends piling into a beat-up Grand Am. By rights he should report them for leaving early, but Molly came to see about making up a quiz she'd missed, and class was underway.

"Mr. Jacobs," asked Jonah, opening his worn copy of *The Great Gatsby*, "I don't understand what Nick means here."

Tom liked Jonah, in spite of the black trench coat he still wore in the middle of May. "Why don't you read us the passage?" he said.

Jonah cleared his throat. "'When I came back from the East last autumn I felt that I wanted the world to be in uniform and at a sort of moral attention forever; I wanted no more riotous ex... excursions with privileged glimpses into the human heart.'"

For the first time in weeks, Tom felt a glimmer of excitement. How many times had he read that sentence and never paid attention to it? "Well, let's look at the two parts of the sentence," he said. "See the semicolon in the middle? That divides the sentence. Okay, now in the first half, what words stick out?"

Unlike last period's class, with that asshole Michael Keith, this class was good.

"'In uniform,'" Richard said from the back row.

"'Moral attention,'" said Jonah.

"So what do you picture?" asked Tom. He looked at the overweight girl sitting beside the bulletin board. "Amy, what do the words make you see?"

"Soldiers?" Amy said. "Standing rigid?"

"Good," said Tom. Which, he realized was exactly what he wanted. Students in rows. No Michael Keiths. His family where he wanted them when he wanted them. No moody stepson. No broken heart.

"Why 'moral' attention?" he asked. "What does the word 'moral' suggest?"

"Follow some kind of ethical standard?" suggested Marcie.

"Or a religious one?" added her friend Stacy. "Like 'Thou shalt not kill?'"

Or Thou Shalt not Commit Adultery.

"Great," said Tom. "Now, let's do the same thing with the other half of the sentence. What words grab you?"

"'Riotous excursions,'" said Josh. "What are 'excursions'?"

"They're trips somewhere," said Molly. "Right, Mr. Jacobs? Mr. Jacobs?"

Tom was thinking of the weekend he'd flown to visit Christine in Cheyenne. Although only 4:00 in the afternoon, they'd gone directly from the airport to the closest motel. He thought of the sweat on the small of Christine's back, the feel of her haunches in his hands as he entered her from behind…

After class, Tom returned to the window. He should have felt good. The previous class was the best he'd had in weeks. But his shame over his and Christine's "riotous excursions"—two animals in heat was more like it—stuck to him like tar and feathers.

He thought again of Michael Keith—"this school suks" and "I'm gonna get smashed!" How was Michael any different from his teacher? Didn't Tom think school sucked, too? Wasn't he counting the minutes until he could go home and get smashed? How much of his waking up at 3:15 this morning had to do with knocking down two glasses of straight gin, half a bottle of wine, and two big brandies in about three hours the night before?

By the time he reached home that afternoon, Tom had started doubting Michael ever said "smashed." Maybe he said he wanted to "crash"—relax before going out tonight. *Maybe I'm the one who thought about drinking during school.* Maybe he hated Michael Keith because he hated himself.

Well, in that case, he wouldn't drink. Instead, he went for a walk and tried, despite the damp breeze and fog, to find beauty. He admired the yellow and white daffodils growing beside old and elegant houses, and smelled salt air from the bay. Sparrows sang out of newly green bushes. The fog washed his face. For a while he was ten years old, walking to church with his family, ignorant of death and grief.

Later, he and Christine and Nathan drove to their usual Friday night pizza place. Tom felt strong. He hadn't had a drink that afternoon, and he'd gained an insight into his behavior since Annie's death that gave him a sense of control he hadn't had in months. He gave Nathan a couple of dollars for video games, and he took Christine's hand and told her about Michael Keith and that afternoon's epiphany.

"I really need to change," he told her.

"I think you're being too hard on yourself," Christine said. But she gave him a smile he hadn't seen in weeks.

He squeezed her hand. "No, I can do more. I need to get more exercise. My back feels better after that walk than it has in weeks. I need to stop holing up in that den every night." He nodded his head toward Nathan, who was absorbed by some game that involved jet planes and machine guns. "And the three of us need to start going back to church. Let's try the one in Jordan Mills."

"Okay, sounds good." Her eyes were lovely. For the first time since Annie's death, he thought about sex.

"And I think I'll ask Myles Georgitis in the history department about team-teaching a humanities course in the fall." He squeezed her hand again. "I need to get some creative juices flowing."

Mickie, their favorite waitress, came to the table. "Can I get you guys something to drink?"

"Sure," Tom said. He winked at Christine. "Because I didn't have that drink this afternoon, I'm going to treat myself to a Rusty Nail. You want one?"

Christine's smile faded, then reappeared as if she understood. "No, you go ahead. I'll stick to beer."

And because he and Christine were playing Hangman on a

napkin ("Winner gets a back rub tonight"), he gave Nathan another dollar and drank another Nail before ordering a pitcher of beer with the pizza. That tasted so good he talked Christine into splitting another pizza and another pitcher of beer for dessert.

The next morning Tom woke to the sound of rain beating on the windows. His mouth was fuzzy and his head ached. Staring up at the ceiling, he remembered the drive home. Past Newell Video, Nathan had asked if they could rent a movie for the weekend. Tom made a quick U-turn, almost clipping a car coming the other way out of the fog. He ran over a curb and blew a tire. He recalled the frightened faces of his wife and stepson, flashing red and white in the lights from the AAA truck. After they got home, he went to his den to nurse his guilt with more Scotch.

His head throbbed to the sound of the shower down the hall, of galloping trumpets, explosions, and "bee-beeps!" from the TV cartoons downstairs. He began to shiver and wondered if he had a fever. He couldn't face the day. A house full of dirty dishes and ripped furniture. A stepson sprawled on the floor, whining about how glad he'd be to see his father this summer, while those damn Transformers cluttered every part of the house. A wife trying to please both husband and son, rebounding like some ping-pong ball back and forth between them. A stack of uncorrected papers from students who didn't respect him.

All his resolutions from the day before returned and stood over the bed, laughing at him. He heard his father's voice: "You think you're so much better than me. Well, look at you. Who's the dumb drunk now, Tommy Boy?" Tom saw himself pacing in the fog while the guy from AAA put on the spare. Saw Christine holding Nathan close. The fear—or was it disgust?—in her eyes as she looked at this idiot she'd been stupid enough to marry. He'd been lucky only to drive over the curb and not into a telephone pole or that other car.

He pulled the bedcovers over his head, sobbing into his pillow.

"Are you all right?" Christine had come into the bedroom.

1989

"No," Tom said. "I'm cold and hung over and ashamed of getting drunk and blowing a tire, and I still haven't written thank-you cards to everyone who gave money in Annie's name to the Tumor Clinic, and I haven't written to thank your parents for giving us money to get us through when my bereavement leave ran out. I haven't called my mother. I need to buy a goddamn tire. I can't do any of it. I can't even get out of bed!"

Christine sat beside him and said gently, "It's raining and it looks like March. Probably you wish you were sitting in the hospital by your daughter's side."

She stroked his arm. Tears glistened on her cheeks. Her face was gaunt and haggard. How much weight had she lost? He remembered the weight Annie had lost before her diagnosis. Would he kill his wife as well as his daughter? He doubled up, holding his stomach and sobbing. Colder than ever. Christine covered him with another blanket. "You don't need to do anything today if you don't want to. Stay in bed all weekend if that's what you need. Take Monday off. Tuesday as well."

Her compassion, her selflessness shamed him. She had left her husband and her home and moved two thousand miles to live with a man she barely knew. Her only real friend, Diane, lived in Wyoming. Tom thought of Nathan, trying to fit into a small Maine school system where almost every kid had known each other since kindergarten, and whose parents drove new Volvos instead of a rusting Ford. He knew he needed to do something to bring them all together as a family, but he was too cold. Too afraid. He fell asleep, Christine's fingers stroking his hair.

He awoke around noon, hot and sweaty, rose from bed, showered, ate lunch, and drove Nathan over to his friend Bart's house. He bought a tire and corrected a few papers while he waited for it to be mounted, and then returned home to phone St. Mark's Episcopal Church in Jordan Mills, where he left a message asking if he could stop by sometime to talk to the rector.

On Monday, Tom went to school as usual, but by the last period he was wiped out. His back throbbed. He came home, poured some gin, and went to the den, where he sat in his gray chair in front of Annie's hand, stretching up through the stones in that desperate attempt to touch the falling flower petal. He soon fell asleep. He dreamed of walking through streets filled with gray rubble and twisted pieces of metal. People lay dead from some dread disease. Tom thought he might be dying, too, and yet at the same time he knew he wasn't. He was searching for something but didn't know what. He saw a bombed-out church, its roof gone, the steeple still standing. He started to walk toward it, but a bottomless crater opened in front of him so he turned back.

The phone rang downstairs. His head snapped forward.

"For you," Christine called. As he came into the kitchen, she whispered, "It's the priest from St. Mark's."

The voice on the phone was deep and well-modulated, like a radio announcer's. "This is Curtis Mathews. You left a message over the weekend that you'd like to talk to me?"

Tom's eyelids were sticky. The gin had left a sour aftertaste on his tongue. "Yes. Yes. I would. Gary Coffin suggested I contact you."

After a pause, the voice said, "That's right. Gary told me about you." Another pause. "You've…just lost a child."

"Yes, a daughter."

"I'm terribly sorry. Would you like to stop by the church tomorrow afternoon?"

"That would be great. Thanks."

Tom returned upstairs, pondering how, of all the times to call, the rector had phoned at almost the exact moment he'd been dreaming of trying to get to a church. Perfect synchronicity. Was this what theologians meant by God's grace?

He stared at Annie's watercolor. But if God were intervening in his life now, why didn't God intervene a year ago after Annie's diagnosis? When the cancer metastasized? The night she vomited green bile? When she took those last tortured breaths? Tom finished his drink. No, he was not about to start believing in divine intervention.

1989

Father Mathews appeared to be around forty. Tall, thin, and pale. Tom wondered if he'd been sick. "Call me Curtis," he said. "Let's go into my office." He offered Tom a wooden chair in front of his desk. Tom noted a bookcase of encyclopedias and Bibles, an oil painting of waves crashing on rocks, another wooden chair, and two windows, one of which looked out on three stone pillars standing in the middle of a garden of azaleas and rhododendrons. He was nervous. Twice today he had thought of canceling the meeting. He guessed that Gary Coffin had told Father Mathews—Curtis—that he was angry and unbalanced, prone to verbally attacking clergy for failing to live up to unrealistic expectations. But when Tom remembered that the only words he'd heard from his former rector during those two months in Bangor had come from a goddamned answering machine, he grew angry all over again. If this guy turned out to be the same kind of hypocrite, he'd walk out on him, too. He eased himself into the chair until his back felt okay, folded his arms, and waited for the priest to make the first move.

But instead of sitting behind his desk, Curtis pulled the chair from the wall and sat beside Tom, who was so surprised that he said, "Well, you know, the reason I'm here is because of Gary..." He spewed out his anger at the other priest. When he finished and Curtis said quietly, "It's too bad he let you down," Tom felt like a sniveling child.

Curtis asked about Tom's family, and he outlined his story: divorced, remarried, a stepson living with them during the school year and with his father in Wyoming during vacations.

"And your daughter lived with her mother?"

"Yes, they lived Down East. So that when Annie needed a hospital, she went to Bangor, which explains why I spent so much time away from Christine and Nathan."

"What kind of cancer did she have?"

Tom took a deep breath. "Primitive neuroectodermal tumor. PNET. One of the doctors kept calling it 'Peanut.' It started out as a bump on the back of her head. For years we all knew it was there. 'Sebaceous cyst,' her pediatrician said. 'Get it removed sometime,' he said, 'but these things are almost always benign. No hurry,' he said." Tom looked out the window at the three stone pillars in the garden. "Bastard."

"Cancer is a terrible thing," Curtis said, leaning forward. "Three years ago, my wife was diagnosed with ovarian cancer. It's in remission, but we live in constant fear...and continual prayer."

No wonder the guy doesn't look healthy. "I'm sorry," Tom said, wondering if Curtis had inserted the part about continual prayer for him.

"Thank you." The priest leaned back and touched his fingertips together. "Tell me about last year."

Tom stared at the gray carpet, clasping his hands and rubbing his thumbs. He described how, when Annie had found out the cyst on the back of her head was malignant, she'd canceled her scholarship to spend a year abroad. That when the results of chemotherapy appeared hopeful, she applied to The Portland School of Art, planning to continue her treatments while taking one or two classes. How less than a week before school started in September, her leg collapsed while she was walking downstairs. How she began physical therapy. Made plans to reapply to Portland School of Art in January. Found a job painting murals and designing menus for a new restaurant in Webber. How, by February, she'd lost the use of her legs altogether. "Every time she was knocked down, she picked herself up and started over. I kept asking myself, 'How much more can this kid take?'"

Curtis offered him the box of Kleenex for the corner of his desk. The priest took one for himself. "She sounds like an amazing young lady."

Tom wiped his eyes. "Well, I'm biased, but I think so."

Curtis smiled. "But what about you? What did you do to air out, especially after you moved to Bangor? Did you go for walks, watch stupid TV, eat junk food? Did you get any break?"

"Well, Christine and Nathan came up on a lot of Saturdays

and Sundays"—Tom thought of the weekends he and his wife had danced around his black holes of confusion and fear, playing card games with Nathan and making desperate love after the boy had gone to sleep—"but I guess that was its own kind of stress." He smiled back at Father Mathews. "So I smoked three cigars a day. I ate peanut butter by the bucketful. I walked probably two miles a day going back and forth between the Ronald McDonald House and the hospital. I kept a sort of a journal."

"Did you have anyone there you could talk to?" Curtis asked. "Were you and your ex-wife able to commiserate with one another?"

Tom's smile turned to a smirk. "My ex is not the commiserating type. We made decisions together, but most of the time we kept separate schedules. She usually arrived at the hospital between 8 and 8:30 in the morning to see how the night had gone. I'd come in at 9 to spend the day with Annie. We'd talk, I'd read to her, play cards—I watched her sleep a lot—and Martha would return at 3:30. I'd drop back in at 7:30 to say good night."

"Any kind of counseling available?"

"Oh, I spoke a little with Pam, the manager of the Ronald McDonald House, and to Sandy, Eastern Maine Medical Center's oncology social worker." Tom made a fist. "But I didn't have time to go around searching for counseling." He pounded his knee. "That's what Gary didn't understand. I was there to help Annie." He paused. "The hospital chapel, though…that was a big help. I'd go there for a half hour or so in the afternoons on my way back to the Ronald McDonald House."

He described how he stumbled upon the chapel by accident. The altar with the candles. The round window edged in stained glass overlooking the river. The voice—"Don't ask why, just ask for help." Tom said he didn't know if the words came from God or not, but that the chapel had become a haven of peace in the midst of chaos.

"I think my experience in the chapel is the reason I'm sitting here," he said. "I've tried to set aside a place at home where I can go to be close to God, but it hasn't worked." He admitted he'd gained ten pounds in less than two months. That his back ached all the time. That he was constantly tired and yet couldn't sleep. That he was probably drinking excessively.

"Those are classic reactions to grief," Curtis said.

Tom nodded. He'd suspected as much. He went on, surprised by what he didn't know he knew. Since Annie's death he'd had trouble focusing. He'd been forgetful and confused, frustrated by missing car keys and lost student papers. He no longer knew what was real anymore, except the pain of his loss. He said he understood he needed help, but that he couldn't find the energy to break the chains of inertia.

Tom took another Kleenex and wiped away more tears. Curtis didn't move. They sat in silence. A phone rang in another room. Finally, the priest uncrossed his legs and asked, "Do you remember the Israelites in the desert?"

Re-erect defenses. *What is this, a theology test?* "I think so," Tom mumbled. He clasped his hands and began rubbing his thumbs together.

"When we read the story," Curtis said, slowly, "we realize that God was always with the Children of Israel, not merely in oases and on mountaintops. God was with them when they were hungry and thirsty. God provided for them, even as they cursed what they thought was God's absence."

He paused. Tom's hands twisted against each other, as if trying to escape his own grasp. Curtis spoke even more slowly: "I'm going to suggest that God wasn't just in the chapel. God was with you when you learned of Annie's cancer, with you in the Ronald McDonald House, with you on the worst days in the hospital, with you when your daughter died."

Tom's hands stopped moving. He felt disappointed. Cheated somehow. He wanted to hear Curtis confirm that the voice he'd heard in the chapel was the voice of God.

"I have to tell you," Curtis said, "how moved I am by the way you left your job and your family in order to be with Annie for the last months of her life. Not every father would have done that."

1989

Tom shrugged his shoulders. He'd never thought of not being with his daughter. That's what fathers do.

"I'm also going to suggest," Curtis continued, "that you need to ask God for the same kind of strength in putting your life back together that you showed in handling Annie's illness and death."

Tom's mind flashed back thirty years to the sign on the wall of the old Ashton gymnasium: "When the Going Gets Tough, the Tough Get Going." Part of him wanted to laugh, but at the same time, he straightened and threw his shoulders back.

"I'm going to give you the phone number for the Family Center for Grief and Loss in Portland," Curtis said, walking behind his desk and flipping through a Rolodex. "It's a new organization, but it sounds good."

Tom stood up and took the number the priest had written down on a note card. As they shook hands, Curtis said, "And if you want a homework assignment, you might memorize the words from the *Book of Common Prayer* we sometimes say before the Eucharist: 'Deliver us from the presumption of coming to this Table for solace only, and not for strength; for pardon only, and not for renewal.'"

Walking to the parking lot, Tom legs trembled, but he also felt as if he were standing taller. Some of the weight he'd been carrying had lifted. His back actually felt pretty good. It was nice to talk to someone who listened. Someone facing his own problems. Someone who seemed to understand.

As he drove home, Tom realized that Curtis's "suggestions" were really challenges. That what the priest was saying was, okay, maybe Tom's students were spoiled and lazy, maybe the U.S. had become "over-ripe," maybe Christine couldn't fully experience his pain, maybe Nathan was messy and self-absorbed. But God was still there in the classroom and downstairs in front of the TV, just as triviality and weakness and fear were with Tom in his den, along with Annie's artwork and his cigars and his booze. Tom needed to learn that, just as peace comes from God, so does strength. So does renewal. That while he might have searched for peace in the hospital chapel, he'd received that peace by refusing to hide from the chaos, by going to Annie out of love instead of trying to avoid her pain.

It was simple, he told himself that night after his third Scotch. He needed to be stronger. He needed to be tougher.

Chapter Six

1956–57

All through the fourth and fifth grade, Tommy Jacobs heard the rumors.

"My brother says Mr. Bailey is really tough."

"Mr. Bailey was a Marine. He killed Japs in the war."

"My sister says Mr. Bailey is mean. He even yells at girls."

"If the kids on his basketball team don't do what he says, Mr. Bailey beats them up."

Sometimes Tommy heard a voice like a clap of distant thunder over the din of the playground shared by the elementary and junior high schools, or saw a shock of orange-red hair moving along the side of the wooden junior high building. For a moment, before returning to dodgeball or marbles or tag, he was both fascinated and afraid.

He got a better look at Mr. Bailey when he moved into the junior high to begin the sixth grade. The teacher was no taller than Tommy's father, but heavier, built like an oil drum. Under the fiery hair, he had fleshy ears and a flat nose. He never smiled, but plowed through the halls like a bulldozer. Sometimes Tommy heard his voice booming below his second-floor classroom.

In the seventh grade, Tommy's math class met downstairs, right across the hall from Mr. Bailey's room, where his voice resounded daily:

"Turn around, Lafano!"

"Hey, look at me when I'm talking to you!"

"Girls, shut up and pay attention!"

Although Tommy giggled when, after one of those outbursts, his friend Roland, whispered, "Look at me when I'm talking to you," his stomach knotted every time he saw Mr. Bailey. Like all Maine school children in the 1950s, Tommy had grown up with the threat of physical punishment. His mother's weapon of choice was a hairbrush, which she applied liberally when he swam in the polluted waters of the Androscoggin or gave her any lip. In the second grade, Mrs. Grover leaned students over their desks and spanked them when they misbehaved. In the fourth grade, Mrs. Adams slapped their knuckles with a ruler. In the fifth grade, Mrs. Jones twisted ears. But Mr. Bailey was no old lady. Tommy had never had a man teacher before. And not only had all his teachers been women, the strong personalities in his family were his mother and his two grandmothers. His brother, father, and grandfathers were distant and/or diffident. Tommy's mother's father was an alcoholic, Tommy's father was an alcoholic, and his brother was on his way to becoming one. As a result, he'd grown up in an atmosphere of uncertainly and anxiety, especially around men.

So when Mr. Bailey held tryouts for the junior high basketball team, Tommy did not go. He really didn't like basketball that much anyway.

That winter, however, his brother, Ed, left town. To Tommy's knowledge, their father never mentioned him again. Instead, Ike Jacobs turned his attention to his younger son. He invited Tommy to watch the Celtics on TV with him, pointing out some of the intricacies of the game. It was the first time his father had ever really talked to Tommy, and the boy began looking forward to those weekend afternoons. He started to appreciate the dribbling skills of Bob Cousy, the shooting ability of Bill Sharman. He liked some of the players on other teams as well, like Dolph Shayes and Bob Petite and Max "The Touch" Zazlowski. He put up a round Quaker Oats box on his bedroom wall and rolled up a pair of wool socks to make a ball, until he got a bright yellow Voit basketball for his birthday. Tommy and his father began shooting baskets together into the spring and summer. They had never been as close before—nor would they ever be as close again—as they were that year. He remembered his father, squinting through the smoke from his cigarette, flicking the ball two-handed into the basket on the side of the garage. Or, setting down his can of Narragansett, putting his arms around Tommy to show him where to put his hands on the ball. "Okay, son, now aim for the back of the hoop."

By the time Tommy entered the eighth grade in the fall, while he might have gone to church on Sunday with his family and listened to his pastor and next-door neighbor, Scotty Hughes, tell them about a loving God, his real worship service was in his backyard. Shooting baskets gave him the sense of first extending and then leaving himself, as if the ball were part of him, so that releasing the ball toward the basket was like soaring into the air, leaving the secular world behind. His scriptures became the sports pages of the *Portland Press Herald* and the *Portland Evening Express*. His icons became the pictures he cut out from *Sport* magazine—Hot Rod Hundley, Jungle Jim Loscutoff, Bill Russell.

As with church, basketball fulfilled more than a spiritual need. The sport provided him with the opportunity to fit into a community, one not only of friends, but of adults—a community where he knew the rules. In Tommy's family, the rules were blurred. In his family, he never quite understood how love and approval worked. He never heard the word "love" used, in fact, except in sentences such as "I'd love another piece of pie." His parents never hugged each other, let alone their two children. But Tommy, especially after Eddie left, was also babied in ways that his friends weren't. His mother picked up after him, bought his favorite foods, fried hamburgers for him in the middle of the afternoon. His father went into debt to buy Tommy the most expensive hi-fi record player on the market. But although Tommy knew that if he got A's in school and behaved himself in public, his mother would be happy and that if he didn't she'd tell him he should be ashamed of himself, he never understood why his father told him he'd caused his mother to miscarry because he hadn't taken in the laundry, when it wasn't his job to take in the laundry. Or why his mother paddled him with the hairbrush for giggling in the junior choir when he wasn't the only one and the other mothers hadn't been that upset.

Basketball was clear and simple. If you put the ball in the basket, you scored, and people applauded.

Lots of people. In the 1950s, high school basketball was the king of Maine sports. Communities rallied around their teams and the twice-weekly games were the social events of the season. Fights broke out, tires were slashed, babies were conceived after—sometimes during—games. Not only did schools shut down for the February basketball tournaments in Lewiston, Bangor, and Portland, businesses closed. Some townspeople took their vacations in February, not to fly to Florida but to drive to Lewiston, eat at Stickino's Restaurant, and watch the Western Maine Basketball Tournament at the Armory.

Selectmen from Ashton crossed the street to say hello to the players, and church ministers prayed for the team. The most envied girls in school wore varsity basketball players' class rings on chains around their necks. Few females wanted to play basketball, but dozens tried out for the varsity and junior varsity cheerleading squads, competing for the honor of prompting the crowd in chants of praise for the boys of the team, much like priestesses directing paeans to the gods.

When Tommy entered his homeroom at the start of the eighth grade and saw the back of Mr. Bailey's sport coat tighten-

1956-57

ing as he wrote on the blackboard, his stomach clenched. Yet instead of sitting in the back seat, as he had in every other class he'd been in since the first grade, he sat down in the front seat of the middle row, right in front of the teacher's desk. He knew that if he were going to play basketball this year, if he were going to go on to star in high school and then in college (and who knew after that?), he would have to impress the man with the red hair, black eyes, and flat nose who turned around and glared at the class.

His voice boomed like a cannon over Tommy's head. "I'm going to call the role. Pay attention." He picked up a piece of paper from his desk. "Adams, Annette."

"Here."

"Arsenault, John."

Down the list of names he went.

"Jacobs, Thomas."

"Here." Tommy wanted his voice to sound strong and deep, but what came out sounded squeaky, like the alien on the Flying Saucer record everyone was listening to.

"Kinnelly, R—."

Just then the door opened and Freddy Gallant sauntered into the room. Freddy was one of those kids Tommy had grown up with who had failed fifth, sixth, and seventh grade, sometimes two or three times, while they waited for their sixteenth birthday, when they could quit school. At least six feet tall and probably weighing 180 pounds, he was a playground bully who had once twisted Tommy's friend Richie's arm behind him until he cried.

But he looked spindly in front of Mr. Bailey, who walked toward him. "Do you belong in this class?"

Freddy grinned. "Yeah, I suppose so."

"You're late!"

"So? What's the big deal?"

Mr. Bailey grabbed a fistful of Freddy's plaid shirt. "I'll tell you what the big deal is, young—Look at me when I talk to you!"

Freddy stared at Mr. Bailey. "I heard about you. You think you're a big deal. Well, you ain't so goddamn tough."

With one hand still on Freddy's shirt and the other on his belt buckle, Mr. Bailey shoved Freddy into a corner between a wooden bookcase and the wall. He removed a big ring with some kind of insignia on it from his right hand and dropped it in his pocket. "Swear at me, will you!" He slapped Freddy across the face. *Whap! Whap! Whap!* The sound reverberated through the room. "When I'm through with you, you won't be swearing at any teacher again."

The high white walls pulsated: *Whap! Whap! Whap!*

His face florid, Mr. Bailey lowered his arm. "Now, are you ready to apologize?" He slipped the ring back on his finger.

Freddy straightened and pushed himself away from the wall. Then the damn fool doubled up his fist.

Mr. Bailey's fist, complete with ring, smashed Freddy's nose, sending blood into the air. Tommy felt a cold kick in his stomach, and his morning Wheaties rose into his throat. Freddy slid down the wall. Mr. Bailey hit him again, and again, his fist rising and falling like Tommy's father's hammer as he shingled the new addition to their house.

Tommy never saw Freddy Gallant again, but for years afterward, usually when he awoke in the morning, he'd hear the crunch of bones breaking, see Freddy's nose collapsing against that ring and spurting blood, feel his stomach churn and his legs tremble.

In his driveway that fall, Tommy had imagined himself on the basketball court as the star of the team. Lying on his bed after school before the first basketball practice, listening to Bill Haley sing "See You Later, Alligator," he envisioned himself stealing the ball from his opponent, dribbling behind his back, driving through the lane, leaving his feet at the foul line, switching the ball behind his back in mid-air, and slamming the ball down into the basket, while Mr. Bailey stood on the sidelines cheering.

But at the first tryout, Tommy's stomach knotted the minute he saw his coach walk on the court, and he almost ran from the gym. He pictured Mr. Bailey yelling at him. He imagined him grabbing his shirt and slapping him across the face. He saw him double up his fist. Saw the ring. Felt his nose shatter.

"Get in rows!" Mr. Bailey shouted. He had swapped his sport coat for a sweatshirt, and his spit-shined shoes for sneakers. Tommy and the other boys began by doing calisthenics. Then they ran laps around the gym. They lined up for layups. All the while, Mr. Bailey's voice exploded over their heads, "Come on, move it! Move! Move!"

Despite Tommy's dreams of being as agile as Bob Cousy or as muscular as Wilt Chamberlain, he was, in fact, a slow and clumsy thirteen-year-old, a hundred and seventy pounds of baby fat. He began to sweat after a few jumping jacks. He was out of breath before he'd run twice around the perimeter of the basketball court. Still, he pushed himself to make it around again. If he wanted to keep Mr. Bailey from lacing him out, he needed to make sure his coach didn't see him as a wiseass. That he saw him as someone who would do anything he wanted, even if it meant running ten times around the goddamn basketball court.

The good news was that Tommy made the team. The bad news was, that meant more exercises and drills. Mr. Bailey increased the number of laps around the gymnasium to twenty. ("Do you see that sign—'When the Going Gets Tough, the Tough Get Going'? Well, get going! Move!") The team formed circles and passed around a ten-pound medicine ball. They ran three-man weaves, practiced pivoting, layups, rebounding, passing. Before they scrimmaged, they repeated set plays again and again, most of which involved Tommy setting picks—blocking out an opponent—so that Willie Dunbar, who was the real star of the team, could get a shot off.

But no matter how hard Tommy worked, Mr. Bailey yelled at him. "Move it, Jacobs! You run like a duck," he'd bellow, his face getting redder and redder. "Toughen up! Do you want to wind up like your brother? Look around you! Get your head up!"

One afternoon, when Tommy couldn't seem to go where Mr. Bailey wanted him to go, his teacher stuck his finger in his face.

"No, no! Go here, not there!" He pointed at a spot on the court about three feet away. Tommy saw that ring catch the light from a caged overhead bulb, felt it breaking his nose. Then Mr. Bailey put his hands around Tommy's waist, picked him up, and set him down on that spot. "Here, damn it, you stand here! Understand?"

Their first game was against Yarborough in the Lewiston Armory, with a gymnasium that seemed twice the size of Ashton's high school floor. By the time Tommy had run up and down the court twice, he was gasping for breath. The first time Dougie Wilson passed him the ball for one of their set plays, Tommy turned and threw it a good three feet over Willie Dunbar's head as he cut for the basket. At the same time, despite the size of the Lewiston floor, it was in some ways too small, for Tommy kept running into other players and he fouled out of the game.

But he kept working, ever driven by dreams of glory and of hearing Mr. Bailey say "Good job, Jacobs." After the coach told them how Mike Sampson, one of the stars on the high school team, used to work on his footwork by jumping rope, Tommy started jumping rope out in the garage after supper. In the morning, before breakfast, he did sit-ups and push-ups. And any time he had a few minutes, he'd go out into the yard and shoot baskets. During their season, he sometimes played fairly well. Sometimes he played badly. It usually depended upon how he started. If he made a good pass or made his first shot, he'd play well. If he threw the ball away or dribbled the ball off his foot, he'd become more and more nervous that Mr. Bailey would start yelling at him, and he would screw up even more.

As Tommy continued to play sports throughout high school, it was Mr. Bailey's voice and not that of his high school coach that he heard when he did his morning and evening exercises: "Come on, Jacobs, ten more push-ups! Move it, Jacobs, Move it!" Whenever he saw his former coach's shock of red hair at practice or at the games, he always felt a rush of adrenaline. He ran a little harder, dove for loose balls. While never a star, Tommy was a good team player and Ashton High won several basketball championships.

1956-57

Perhaps his proudest moment came when he was a senior and one of the freshmen on their team told him that Mr. Bailey was using Tommy as an example of how hard work can transform an awkward butterball into a varsity athlete.

Thirty years later, Tom Jacobs thanked Mr. Bailey, not so much for whatever athletic success he'd had, but for showing him how to overcome fear through determination and self-discipline, values Tom felt he had somehow misplaced over the years. As he lay in bed before going to school, staring up into the darkness, his guilt over his daughter's death weighing on soul and body, images of Michael Keith leering at him, he heard his old coach's voice urging him out of bed: "Come on, Jacobs, you're better than they are. Toughen up! Move it!"

Chapter Seven

1989

The second week of June, Tom sat with Christine and Nathan in their living room, trying to get his back comfortable, as they watched a local news feature on the Family Center for Grief and Loss. Nathan was one of the children interviewed, and Tom noted not only how clearly his stepson spoke, but also how sad his eyes looked, how much softer and more serious the boy's voice had become. Nathan's black hair, parted in the middle, curled down over each eyebrow. His eyes looked directly into the camera, as if he were speaking directly to Tom: "I had my sister die just before Easter." Not his stepsister but his sister, even though he always called Tom his stepfather.

"I came to school, and like nobody talked about it. I mean, the teachers had told the kids, but nobody said anything."

Tom winced. He thought of all the nights he'd abandoned the boy for his den. He still blamed himself for not talking with Annie about her impending death; now here was Nathan piling on another millstone of guilt. He thought of when he himself was thirteen and how happy he'd been when his father had shut off that damned television set, put down his beer bottle, and come out to shoot baskets with him. What couldn't he do that for Nathan? He'd mentioned basketball, but his stepson hadn't seemed interested and, anyway, Tom didn't think their landlord would allow a hoop in the driveway. The old couple who lived in the other half of the house had already complained about the times their cat, McCafferty, had escaped outside.

Maybe he could at least go back to helping Nathan with the animals.

The news program cut to a shot of his stepson walking past two pink rhododendrons into the former furniture store where they all met, children with children, teenagers with other teenagers, adults with adults. Nathan hunched his shoulders and thrust his hands into the back pockets of his jeans. Tom shifted uncomfortably in his chair as he listened to Nathan's voice-over: "I was nervous and tense. If I studied my head off, I'd get an F on the test."

Saul Cohen, a former corporate lawyer who'd spent all his savings creating the Family Center for Grief and Loss, appeared next, sitting in a blue chair beside a tall aspidistra, speaking in his soft tenor voice of how, after the death of his brother, he would drive his niece to and from school. Every day she asked him to play the same song on his radio cassette. "We never spoke," he said. "I was usually thinking about my brother and how bad I felt. But one day I listened to the words of the song my niece wanted to hear. They were all about 'how much I miss you and how lonely I am.' And I thought, 'My God, we've been sitting beside each other day after day, both of us hurting, neither of us talking to one another. There needs to be a place for families to talk about their grief.'"

Another reminder to Tom of his failure to renew his life, become stronger, meet challenges head-on instead of hiding from them. In that first meeting at the FCGL, he'd briefly outlined the story of Annie's death, but he couldn't talk about his sense that he and Christine had sold their souls, not with her sitting next to him. Better to bear the weight of his guilt pressing down on him than accuse her of contributing to his grief.

Saul continued, "The kids draw, paint, finger paint, make collages. They're never forced to have to talk about anything they don't want to talk about, but the subject of death just comes up naturally."

Back to Nathan: "Some of the pictures and stuff basically relate to what happened and how we feel." He held up a small clay figure resembling a Tyrannosaurus Rex. He tapped the top of its head several times with his finger. "He represents, like, the anger." He stared at it and, for a second, his eyes turned from gray to black.

As the program ended with interviews with some of the other kids, Tom's back was killing him and he had a headache. He regarded his stepson, sitting on the futon next to his mother. His face was expressionless. Eyes inscrutable. Tom remembered the lively and demonstrative nine-year-old who'd come to him three years earlier. He wanted to go over and give him a hug. Say, "I'm happy you came into my life." But that would mean Nathan might think he had to say, "I'm happy you came into my life, too," and how could Nathan be happy when Tom had caused the boy so much pain?

Tom clasped his hands and rubbed his thumbs together. "Nice job, chum," he murmured.

Later, lying on his back in bed beside Christine, he continued to rub his thumbs. His legs and arms felt as if they were twitching. He wanted to tell his wife that he really was going to be a better stepfather to Nathan from here on, but shame for having ignored the boy in the first place, remorse over not being a better husband, and guilt for his daughter's death smothered his words. He realized she'd said little about the news program. In fact, she'd said little all evening. He wondered if she, too, wasn't feeling guilty—for leaving her husband, tearing her son away from his home, not talking enough to him here. A chill ran down his arms. Did she regret leaving Kidron Springs and marrying him? What would he do if she left him?

She spoke to him out of the darkness. "Oh, I forgot to tell you, what with the news program and all, I got a letter from Diane today. She and Sam are getting married."

1989

"That's great," Tom said. While visiting Christine in Wyoming, he'd met Diane and he liked her. A chunky blond with a bubbly laugh, she and Christine had known each other since they were young mothers together, and both had been active at St. John's Episcopal Church in Kidron Springs. Divorced for many years, Diane had started dating Sam after Christine moved east.

"They're being married in a couple of weeks," Christine said. "I'd really like to go out for the wedding. She's the only real friend I have."

Tom's stomach constricted into an icy knot and tightened around his lungs. Yes, she was leaving him. Next, she'd say that she wanted to fly out with Nathan next week when he visited his father for the summer. That she might stay for a while. That she needed some time alone. Some space. She just said she had no friends here. He'd driven her away.

"Why don't we *all* go?" she said. "You and I could take Nathan to Wyoming." She rolled over and put her arms around him. "I think the two of us need to get away."

The knot loosened. His body relaxed. His eyes welled with gratitude. He rolled toward her. "I think you're right," he said. "Let's do it."

They stayed at a Holiday Inn in a room with a view of aspens nestled beneath snowcapped mountains, and swam in the pool and sat in the hot tub, the jets of hot water loosening Tom's muscles. They joined Nathan at his favorite McDonald's. Tom bought a straw cowboy hat and a wide leather belt with a horseshoe buckle. He and Christine drank Margaritas and ate tamales and refried beans. He read *Lonesome Dove* and rode the range with Call and Augustus. They made love for the first time since Annie's death.

One afternoon, while Christine attended a shower for Diane, Tom walked across the parking lot of their motel to a cattle auction and stood with his foot on a split-rail fence, chewing a piece of hay, as if he were Tommy Lee Jones. Walking back, gazing at umber foothills against the high western sky, the image of Annie's watercolor of her hand reaching through the stones hit him. As his eyes welled, he heard Red Bailey: "Come on, Jacobs, suck it up!" He kicked the memory back to wherever it had come from and walked downtown to Kitty's Boutique, where he bought some massage oil and candles.

Diane and Sam took their vows in the garden behind St. John's, in front of a tall Gothic window in the red-brick church, and under an arbor woven with wild flowers. The five children they had between them and a small audience of friends sat in lawn chairs. A portable calliope pulled by a pickup truck played the "Trumpet Voluntary" and later, "Love Divine, All Loves Excelling."

Tom and Christine had parts in the service. Christine, radiant in a new blue dress that matched her eyes, read from the Old Testament:

"But Ruth said, "Do not urge me to leave you or to return from following you. For where you go I will go, and where you lodge I will lodge. Your people shall be my people, and your God my God. Where you die I will die; and there I will be buried."

Tom's groin stirred. He saw once more the seductive and mysterious woman he'd fallen in love with in New Jersey, who handled snakes and argued with God. Like Ruth, Christine had left her home and her friends to be with him. He straightened his back. He would be worthy of her. If, as he feared, they were paying for their sins, the least he could do was see to it that they endured their punishment together.

When it was his turn, he read from *1st Corinthians*:

"Love bears all things, believes all things, hopes all things, endures all things. Love never ends...."

He looked directly at Christine, speaking the words to her.

1989

He had wavered in his love for her, but no more. They would bear the burden of their sins; they would endure.

"When I was a child, I spoke like a child, thought like a child, I reasoned like a child. When I became a man, I gave up childish ways."

Yes, it was time for him to grow up, stop whining like a child, and look after his family.

Sun shone down on the pages of Tom's reading, momentarily blinding him. He found his place and finished:

"For now we see in a mirror dimly, but then face to face. Now I know in part; then I shall know fully, even as I have become fully known. So now faith, hope, and love abide, these three; but the greatest of these is love."

After Diane and Sam had said their "I do's," everyone drove to a reception at their house, where there was homemade carrot cake, picture-taking, and dancing to the Grateful Dead. (Sam, whose silver ponytail reached his turquoise-studded belt, was an old Deadhead, and for a honeymoon, they were off to catch the Dead in Denver.) Later that night in their motel room, Tom and Christine found an Oldies radio station and continued dancing, slowly removing each other's clothes. They massaged each other, Christine's fingers sending caresses deep into his skin. She straddled him, and he traced the sweat between her breasts with his tongue. As her magical eyes darkened with abandon in the candlelight, his heart rejoiced.

When Tom walked into his den after returning to Newell, he couldn't believe how small the room looked, how cramped, how stuffy. He threw out the rest of his cigars, and together he and Christine brought the big gray chair downstairs. He took down Annie's half-finished sketches from the walls, rolled them up and packed them away in the hall closet. He and Christine drove to Sears and bought a stationary bicycle to put in the room. Opening wide the window and smelling the sea breeze, Tom felt as if he were airing out his mind as well as the room, and he wondered how much that closed, smoky space had contributed to what he decided was depression.

They spent the summer sleeping late (he couldn't believe how much he slept), taking care of Nathan's animals, and going to the beach in the afternoons, where they threw themselves into the waves and lay in the sand and baked. In the evenings, they walked around town, admiring green lawns and white colonial houses and discussing what property they should buy. They played strip Scrabble, and dressed in costumes for role-playing games—alternating as doctor and patient, teacher and student, boss and secretary—before making love. On Sundays, they drove to Jordan Mills and worshipped at St. Mark's, where Tom heard the scriptures and the hymns with new ears. He who'd never much liked the Psalms, found himself drawn to lines such as

Your hand will lay hold upon all your enemies;
your right hand will seize all those who hate you.

And...

He satisfies you with good things,
and your youth is renewed like an eagle's.

He recalled the eagle that had soared the afternoon he and Christine were married. That eagle was a hunter, a symbol of strength and courage, a totem for Tom as he seized his enemies—fear, apprehension, bitterness—and wrestled them to the ground. His back felt practically normal.

They spent a pleasant Saturday with Tom's mother and Cal and Cal's son and his wife and two children at Cal's son's camp on Sabbath Day Lake. There was a lobster bake with corn on the cob and steamed clams to go with the lobster, and Tom's mother made an apple and a blueberry pie—their aroma wafting Tom away from their recent bickering and back to those Saturday mornings when he was growing up in Ashton, waking to the smell of his mother's baking. Cal made up one terrible pun after another ("The oriental couple's apartment was so small, they had a wok-in closet…When they asked the guy about his dog running into things, he replied, 'That's my blind Spot.'"), while messaging the back of Tom's mother's neck. Both Tom and Christine tried waterskiing, and although neither of them could stay up, it was fun trying.

On a Sunday afternoon in late August, after church and a butterflied leg of lamb on the grill, they sat in the back yard reading their novels. Tom rested Tolkien's *The Silmarillion* on his lap and gazed at three seagulls sailing across a cloudless sky. He glanced over at Christine, wondering what color her eyes were today behind those sunglasses. But all he saw was his reflection. He pondered yet again this mystery that had entered his life, which had changed it in ways he still didn't understand, any more than he really understood her. But it was okay. They had the rest of their lives. One thing he did know was that she was eagerly anticipating Nathan's return later that week. Tom too was looking forward to September and a chance to try again to be a decent parent. Teaching should be fun this year. Myles Georgitis had agreed to Tom's idea to team-teach a humanities course, and, at the end of July, Jim Silas, chair of the English Department at Jordan Mills, called to say that Don Wolfe had resigned to teach overseas, and would Tom take the Senior Advanced Placement English classes next year? No more Michael Keiths.

He thought back to the previous spring—his sorrow, his isolation, his guilt, his anger—as if he were looking back years instead of months. As if he were watching Tommy Jacobs struggling to run around the gym while Mr. Bailey's voice exploded over his head—"Faster, Jacobs! My mother can run faster than you can!"—or Mr. A.P. in his ties and matching pocket handkerchiefs, withering under the disapprobation of sixty-four British authors. "Mr.

Wimp," that's what he'd been, hanging his head like some whipped dog, sniveling through each day, mired in self-pity. Well, no more.

"How are you doing?" he asked Christine.

She raised her head from her reading and smiled. "Good," she said, "A little apprehensive about Nathan coming back, but, overall, good." She removed her sunglasses and her eyes took on that smoky hue they sometimes had. "And you?"

"I'm good, too," he said. "I really think we've turned a corner." He thought of saying more, but decided not to risk clouding up a perfect day with specifics.

Christine looked at him with a steady gaze. "I hope so, Tom."

"No, we have. I know it."

He returned to his fantasy.

Chapter Eight

1989

They sat on gunmetal-colored chairs in the Newell Junior/Senior High School Gymnasium, waiting for Nathan's first band concert of the year. Green and white banners hung over the basketball hoops bookending the portable stage. Tom thought about how much of his youth he'd spent in gymnasiums. He remembered the smell of sweat and damp towels, and Red Bailey and the lessons he'd hammered into him: how to push himself beyond what he ever thought he could do, how to handle pressure, how to become part of a team.

His athletic training, Tom decided, had helped him rise to Father Curtis's challenge to seek strength instead of solace. He'd stopped smoking and cut down on his drinking. He rode the exercise bicycle or took a walk every day. His students were smart and, for the most part. motivated, and the pain in his back had subsided to an occasional twinge if he happened to move the wrong way. Every Sunday he and Christine and Nathan drove to St. Mark's, and every Wednesday they went to the Family Center for Grief and Loss. Nathan had joined the youth group at St. Mark's and made friends at the Center. And, after months of hearing others at the FCGL tell their stories, Tom concluded that he and Christine were coping pretty well, all things considered. He still didn't say much, but few men there did. The women did the talking; most of the guys stared at the floor. Still, he felt a sense of community there, even if it was a circle no one wanted to be in.

He took Christine's hand; she gave him a weak smile. Not that everything was perfect. Nathan had returned from his summer in Wyoming talking about moving back to Kidron Springs to go to high school. Christine's ex-husband, Zack, was all for it. He had left the Pentecostals, and was, in his words, "finally growing up." He admitted not having been a very good father before—not to mention not being a very good husband—but he wanted another chance, with Nathan at least. Although Christine believed Zack did sound more mature and ready to look after Nathan, her concerns went deeper. "I understand that adolescent boys want to be with their fathers," she told Tom one day, "but I can't help thinking we've failed him." At meals, watching TV, reading in bed, he would catch her staring into space, her eyes a washed-out shade of blue. She'd lost much of the weight she put on the previous summer.

A month earlier, Tom had been ready to do more with Nathan, be more like a real father, but now it was harder than ever to talk to him. The boy spent most his time in his room with his heavy metal music and his guinea pigs and hamsters and rats and spiders and snakes, and refused Tom's offers to help feed them or watch the Red Sox or go for a walk.

I had my chance and I blew it. Now it's too late.

The band marched onto the stage, the boys in their white shirts and green ties, the girls in their green skirts and white blouses. Fluorescent lights turned faces pale. Tom studied his stepson, who towered over the rest of the trombone section. Nathan's shirt was half untucked and his hair fell over his eyes. He wished he could teach the boy some of the self-discipline Red Bailey had beaten into him. As far as he knew, the kid got no exercise. When he wasn't in his room listening to Guns 'n Roses and Def Leopard, he was watching movies that Tom

1989

thought were unsuitable for a kid who was still only twelve. Lately, Nathan had become obsessed with the *Alien* films, in which Sigourney Weaver fights a collection of slimy reptiles. For some reason in those films, the aliens need humans in which to lay their eggs. When the eggs get ready to hatch, the infected person's chest pulsates more and more until it explodes, splattering blood and loosing another alien into the world.

Nathan's favorite was the second of the series, in which Weaver's character, Ripley, defends a small, blonde-headed girl time and again against one of these creatures. In one scene, Ripley holds the little girl in one arm and some kind of huge gun in the other while she snarls at the monster: "Get away from her, bitch!" The time Tom watched the movie with him, Nathan snarled the line along with Weaver, his eyes flashing black. Tom had never seen his stepson that angry and he wondered if Nathan wasn't seeing the little girl in the movie as Annie, the alien dripping mucus from its jaws as death, and Ripley as himself, heroically driving the creature away.

The buzzing in the audience died, and the kids began to play something Mr. Abrams, their director, called "Arocknophobia." Tom's eyes drifted from Nathan to a girl with hair the color of corn silk leaning forward at the piano, eyes intent on the sheet music. A knot formed in his chest, then rose into his throat. Since last spring, except for a few dream fragments, Annie's memory lay walled-off in the darkest corner of his mind, but as he beheld Nathan's classmate, remembrance slithered through the cracks. He recalled his daughter's practicing scales in the living room over and over until he thought he'd scream, his nervousness as he sat in the audience at her recitals, the way his heart kicked when she hit a wrong note.

The last recital he'd attended had been four years earlier, on a rainy July Saturday, when he sat on the bleachers in the Webber Junior High School gymnasium, at least five feet away from Martha, thinking of Christine's last letter and planning his reply. Slowly, he'd realized that Annie was playing the Mendelssohn piece beautifully. She looked gorgeous that day, with a new blue dress and matching shoes. She knew she was playing well and her eyes radiated joy. Afterwards, when she said, "How was that, Dad?" he wanted hug her, tell her she was magnificent, but he'd been too self-conscious, afraid of crying, too timid to show his love.

His stomach iced and his throat burned. A bolt of pain shot down his back. He clasped his hands, rubbed his thumbs together, as he remembered Annie not at the piano but in a hospital bed. No hair. Eyes deep and recessed like sunken marbles. Drugged voice: "Whazz up, Dad?" He could have at least hugged her then, told her how much he loved her, but no, he'd still been afraid to show his feelings, unable to tell her what she meant to him.

The cinder-block walls of the gymnasium constricted and the lights hurt his eyes. "I'll be right back," he whispered to Christine. He stood, back burning, forehead slick with sweat, stomach queasy. He slid past the couple next to them to the aisle and walked out the exit, underneath one of the basketball hoops to the parking lot. Tom leaned against the wall of the school building with his hands pressed against his temples. The Indian summer night air and the sharp smell of dead leaves enveloped him like a body bag, and he started sobbing.

When he finally stopped crying, his legs felt wobbly, as if he'd been hit with a right cross. He felt ashamed of himself. Red Bailey's voice thundered: "Come on, Jacobs, what are you, some goddamned baby?" Tom straightened and slapped the side of the building. *You're right, coach. No more Mr. Wimp.*

Returning to the gymnasium, he told Christine he shouldn't have had that second helping of lasagna. "But I'm okay now."

He and Christine and maybe Nathan had been planning to walk a beach the following Saturday morning but his back hurt too much, so Christine and Nathan went with Nathan's friend Bart and his mother. Tom plugged in the electric heating pad and sat down in the living room to read Albert Camus's extended essay *The Myth of Sisyphus*, which he planned to use with the French writer's novel, *The Stranger*, in his A.P. class. Alluding to the

1989

Greek tale of a man condemned by the gods to forever roll a rock to the top of a mountain, from where the stone falls back because of its own weight, Camus sees Sisyphus as representing the human condition—trying to impose meaning on a meaningless world. The result is a condition the author labels "absurd."

Tom fidgeted around in his gray chair as he tried to understand Camus's absurd cosmos: "...the confrontation of this irrational world and a world longing for clarity whose call echoes the human heart." Okay, he understood. Somewhere upstairs he had a bag of notebooks, note cards, and other scraps of paper he'd filled during Annie's illness, with musings about life, death, and God, trying to comprehend things that nobody really knew anything about. He thought of his conviction that he and Christine had sold their children to the Devil and that Annie's cancer was his punishment for adultery. Absurd attempts to explain death. Irrational death. His daughter's death.

But at the thought of Annie's death, memories he'd repressed for months flooded over him. His daughter's face turning to chalk when he and Martha told her she had cancer. The sun hitting her red bandanna as she stood on the porch that summer, waiting for him to pick her up and take her to Newell for the weekend. Her head nodding toward the mashed potatoes while he tried to feed her in the hospital. Her cracked lips as he dabbed water on them with a cotton swab. Her thin legs bent together, a towel between them to prevent sores. The vein along her neck beating wildly, like some animal burrowing just under the ground. Her congested breathing that sounded as if she were saying, "Ash…es. Ash…es."

He had a vision of Dr. Godfrey—sharp nose and sad, brown eyes, white coat, buttoned-down blue shirt, chinos—making notes on a clipboard, speaking in a voice too loud for the hospital room: "Annie, can you understand me?"

"Yes. What's up?"

"We have the results of the latest tests." Godfrey speaks slowly and looks directly down at her. "The reason your leg hurts is because you have a new tumor in the muscle near the pelvis. It shows up on the CT Scan. We think that's the reason for your fever of the last few days."

Annie's voice trembles. "That's not good, is it?"

The doctor's voice softens. "No, it's serious. It's a real set-back for us, and I'm very disappointed."

Annie's voice rises. "I'll never go home! Never!"

Tom hurries to the bed. Puts his arm around his daughter's shoulder. She leans her face into his chest and cries. Godfrey turns to the window and gazes out over the river.

Annie pulls away. "Dad, you're hurting my hip. I'm okay. Would you move?" She uses the Kleenex he's offered her. "So what happens next?"

Tom recalled snatches, something about "…new treatment…experimental chemotherapy…VP-16…Mesna…monitor carefully…" Watched his daughter's long, thin fingers pulling at the Kleenex, tearing it apart. Heard Dr. Godfrey's pedagogical voice: "We sometimes have problems with lower blood counts, and low blood counts mean that she'll be more open to other kinds of infection."

The doctor turns to the nurse. (*What was her name?*) "Tomorrow, we'll put in another IV—this one in her shoulder—so we can feed her intravenously and keep her strength up." The doctor's sad eyes consider Annie. "I'm sorry. I didn't mean to talk around you. Did you hear that?"

She nods her head slowly. "What happens if this new treatment doesn't work?"

Dr. Godfrey steps to the bed and takes her hand. "We'll just have to go one step at a time. You know we'll do everything we can."

The doctor and nurse leave, and Tom returns to his daughter. Props up her pillow. She asks, "Things will get better, won't they?"

Was this when he should have said, "No, honey, I don't think they will," and talked about dying? What had he said? He remembered taking her hand, hearing her say, "I'm tired of being a cripple. I don't want to hurt any more. I want to go home, but it hurts too much to cut back on the morphine, and I can't eat. What am I going to do, Dad?"

1989

They had both cried. He'd held his daughter as tightly as he could, rocking her in his arms, trying to wrap himself around her, but his arms keep running into tubes.

The Myth of Sisyphus fell on the floor. Lurching his way through his tears to the kitchen, Tom poured a glass of equal parts tomato juice and gin, and drank half of it in two gulps. He returned to the living room window and finished his drink, attempting to focus all his attention on a spider web woven through the branches of the apple tree in the back yard, trying to push back his memory of his daughter as she slowly swung her head back and forth, her wet, haunted eyes staring blindly past him. But her voice wouldn't leave him, breaking off in sobs, rising: "I don't want to die, but I don't want to live like this!"

After another convulsion of tears, Tom made a second drink. His back ached, his head ached—hell, he ached all over. Falling more than sitting in the chair, he thought again about the prayer Father Curtis had given him, about asking God for strength and not for solace only. Well, now he didn't have either one. He stared out the window—the spider web, the apple tree, autumn leaves—and then nodded off to sleep.

When he woke, he finished his drink, and forced himself to pick up the book. He had to go over the next paragraphs several times before he could focus enough to continue reading, but when he did, he saw that Camus believed one could confront death in a world with no meaning and triumph; that Sisyphus serves as the model for what the writer called the "absurd hero." Coming down from the mountain after the rock to begin his effort again marks " the hour of consciousness," when Sisyphus is superior to his destiny—"stronger than his rock"—fully present to his fate, staring it straight in the eye, and defying it. "There is no fate that cannot be surmounted by scorn."

Tom felt an adrenaline rush. "Crushing truths perish from being acknowledged…Living is keeping the absurd alive…The only truth is defiance."

He repeated the last sentence out loud, as if carving the words in stone: "The only truth is defiance." He thought with disdain of Mr. Wimp holing up in his den last spring, of sniveling against the outside of the gymnasium earlier that week. Hell, what about his tears a few minutes ago? He wanted to slap himself across the face.

"Thank you, Albert," he said to the spider web. "I needed that."

He plunged into his life: making lecture notes on his reading, drawing up lesson plans, perusing the latest pamphlets from the College Board on teaching Advanced Placement. He joined the YMCA and began lifting weights, using the StairMaster, and watching young women in their leotards, their young bodies gleaming under the florescent lights.

"The only truth is defiance." One way to defy death was sex. Tom bought his first *Playboy* in twenty years. Grateful that he didn't live in the same town in which he taught, he started hunting Village Video for movies with explicit sex scenes to watch with Christine after Nathan had gone to bed. At first, he picked "art" films or kinky "cult" movies, which he and Christine agreed were sort of fun. Then one night when Nathan was staying at Bart's house, Tom went to the back room of the video store and rented *Lust in the Woods XXX*. After drinks and dinner, a shower and a second shave that day, he put on his bathrobe and nothing else, lit a fire in the fireplace, poured Scotches, pushed "Play" and nestled next to Christine on the futon.

She watched quietly as a man and woman took off their clothes and frolicked in the water, but shifted uncomfortably when the camera closed in on their genitals as they fell on each other in the grass.

Tom had just slid his hand under the hem of her nightgown. "What's wrong?"

Her voice trembled and her eyes grew wet. She stood and turned her back to him. "All this damn sex does is make me sad."

It took him a moment to react. "I don't understand."

She turned, her eyes closed, making circles with her hands. "I've never told you this, but ever since Annie died, all I've wanted was to have another child. It's my way of confronting death, I guess. I want to create new life." She opened her eyes and stared intently at him, as if trying to see something. "Lately, I find that what you want is to watch other people have sex."

Tom clasped his hands and rubbed his thumbs together. The idea of having another child to care for scared the hell out of him. "I don't see the connection. I just want to escape for an hour or so, indulge in a little fantasy." He stood and reached out to take her hand. "I don't know. Maybe it's a guy thing."

She pointed at the TV and a cunnilingus close-up. "Do you mean this turns you on?" she asked. "I'm embarrassed and insulted. Why the fantasies? What's wrong with the real thing? Do you know what a travesty tonight is—fucking instead of family?"

"You didn't mind indulging my fantasies last summer."

"That was when I was trying to forget how hard the last year had been, forget that my son was two thousand miles away." Her eyes turned bruise-colored. "Tom, I'm tired of playing games. I don't know who you think I am," she said. "I may have gone to college in the '60s, but I never did drugs, and I never slept around. I've had sex with two men in my life, you and Zack, both of whom I intended to marry and raise children with." He wished she'd stop staring at him like that. "Do you know—do you care—how hard it is for me to imagine not having Nathan with me?" Her voice rose in a way he'd never heard before: "All tonight does is make me understand why my son wants to move away. You used to at least try to be a father to him. Now, you're some guy he lives with—someone who can't wait to get rid of him so he can watch porno movies!"

Tom stared at the floor. His face flamed. "Don't you blame me!" he said, lifting his head and his voice. "Every time I've wanted to be a father to him, you've stepped between us. I tell him to pick up his toys, and you say he can wait. You let him watch any goddamn movie he wants to." he shook his finger. "I'm sorry you're upset because your kid might move away, but in case you've forgotten, my kid can't move anywhere. She's dead!"

Christine gazed at him silently. She brushed her hand along the side of his face. "I'm sorry," she said, as she walked away. "For all of us."

On the TV screen, the man ejaculated on the woman's stomach. Tom felt empty and sick. He heard Christine going upstairs. He shut off the VCR, and went into the kitchen to get another Scotch. Reaching into the freezer, he dropped an ice cube on the floor. Ignoring the pain suddenly coursing down his back, he picked up the ice cube and threw it against the wall. Next he threw the glass.

It was like watching his first marriage come undone. Sitting in church before the service began, separated from his wife by more than the prayer book and hymnal. "Spraying rose bushes," he used to call it when, after an argument with Martha, he'd go outside and spray their rose hedge for spider mites. "We must have had the cleanest rose bushes in eastern Maine," he once wrote Christine. But now Tom had spent the last week correcting papers, going for extended walks, working out at the Y, and having an extra drink before he went to bed, while Christine was the one who went upstairs in the evenings, going into Nathan's room to play games or look after animals. At night, they slept as far away from each other as possible, each of them clutching an edge of the mattress like a life preserver. *What's next, separate beds?*

Tom looked down the pew at Christine, who picked up another hymnal from the back of the seat in front of her and started leafing through it, a clear signal that they weren't going to be sharing this morning. Damn, she annoyed him! Not only was she a prude, she left as much mess around as her son, only instead of toys, she dropped clothes, folders from school, magazines, notes to herself, all through the house. This morning, he'd pulled a good foot of her hair out of the shower drain.

A stained-glass Jesus, holding a chalice, his face like a skull, loomed over the cross on the altar. *What kind of religion celebrates the torture and death of its leader?* And if Tom were going to celebrate death, why was he doing it in *this* church? His eyes swept the congregation. He'd gone to St. Mark's for six months, and seldom talked to anybody here except Father Curtis. He'd never been comfortable with all the doctors and lawyers and business owners and college professors slapping each other on the backs of their blue blazers during coffee hour.

The Episcopal liturgy had become repetitious and remote and obscure. "God from God, Light from Light, true God from true God"—what the hell did that mean, except another absurd attempt to impose order on a meaningless world?

As a matter of fact, couldn't you say that believing in God—whether it's the Smiling Deity who loves us but is helpless against evil…or the Great Engineer who created cancer as part of some divine plan to keep the universe running…or the Super Sadist who gets His kicks from inflicting pain on children…or the Oasis in the Desert…or the Source of Strength and Solace—was equally absurd?

His eyes followed the panels of another stained-glass window up to the apex, where a white dove descended, head down with extended wings outlined in blue and backlit by a stained-glass sunburst of gold. He thought again of the eagle flying over Casco Bay, and the symbolism he'd given it. It was just a goddamn bird, for Chrissakes.

The next week, Tom, Christine, and Nathan left after school on Wednesday to drive down to Massachusetts for Thanksgiving vacation with Christine's parents. Tom hadn't wanted to go, but Christine said that she and Nathan were going with or without him. Turnpike traffic was heavy, six lines backed up a quarter of a mile to the tollbooth. By the time they crossed the green bridge between Maine and New Hampshire, the sky was dark, trees and buildings looming out of the darkness like giant trolls. They stopped at the New Hampshire Liquor Store for some Sapphire

Gin for Christine's parents and some Dewar's for Tom. The people standing in the checkout lines looked like tired zombies.

Entering Massachusetts, real darkness set in, the road visible only in the headlights, reminding Tom of driving one morning about 3:00 a.m. across Nebraska—he wanted to say it was on Route 2—on the way back from Idaho. Dave and Harry asleep. Highway stretched out straight and flat before him. Occasionally, he'd pass a truck, but otherwise, he had the road to himself. Whether it was the endless cups of coffee or the third pack of cigarettes that day, Tom was wired. His eyes felt like the headlights cutting the night. On a distant radio station, Joan Baez sang, "House of the Rising Sun," her voice soaring. His body tingled. Every twenty miles or so, the road made an S around a grain elevator on one side of the road and a weathered house on the other, and Tom would feel sorry for whoever lived there, tied to a job and obligations. He was free then, following Sal Paradise and Dean Moriarty on the road, filled with a combination of joy and longing—for what, he had no idea. Thirty years later, his wife and stepson asleep in the car, he recalled a dream from last week, of careening down a mountain on a narrow dirt road in a school bus, two wheels hanging over the edge of a steep precipice. The future—on one side Sisyphus's mountain, on the other the Void—scared the hell out of him these days.

Route 128. Car dealerships. Technology buildings. Gas stations. Restaurants. Christine, her eyes closed, her head bowed almost to her chest. She looked tired, vulnerable. He recalled some of the roads they'd traveled in their two thousand mile courtship. Stops at Waffle Houses. Rooms at Motel 6. Holding hands and singing along with Willie Nelson: "Just can't wait to get on the road again." As he stared at the three lanes of traffic in the headlights, he saw that, if he could do it all over again, he'd still have left Martha and Annie for Christine. When he thought of a life without her, his heart raced and his arms and legs shivered. No matter how frightened he was, he couldn't let the marriage fail.

He thought about their argument the previous week, over

1989

the sex video. As if reflected in his windshield, he saw in his mind a series of smudged, gray and black postcards of a naked man and woman engaged in a variety of sex acts, some of which involved animals. He'd been probably thirteen and the week before, his friend, Jerry, had told him he'd discovered where his dad kept his condoms. So the next night, when Tommy's parents were both out, he went searching. When he pulled open the drawer in the knotty pine headboard that his father had built into the wall behind his and his wife's bed, Tommy found not only the red-and-white foil packs he'd been looking for, but those grimy postcards that had set his heart racing. Had sex always been something dirty? Had he merely swapped postcards for videos? One more legacy from his old man?

When they pulled into Christine's parents' driveway on Belmont Hill, Dr. James strode out the front door of his brick house to greet them. Standing in the door behind Barney was his wife, Celeste, holding her martini, pinky finger extended. Tom took a deep breath. He was grateful for all Barney and his wife had done for them during the last two years' turbulence. After Annie had been diagnosed, Barney had arranged an appointment for Martha, Tom, and their daughter with a specialist at Dana-Farber Cancer Institute, who had recommended Dr. Godfrey in Bangor. His in-laws had taken Nathan for weekends. They had helped out financially when Tom's leave of absence ran out. They had given them a car. But Barney James' lofty solicitude—not to mention the black Mercedes 500, the Rolex, and the home stereo system that took up an entire room—intimidated Tom and made him defensive. He recalled the cold efficiency with which Barney had quoted statistics and the odds against Annie's getting better, and his feeling afterward that his father-in-law would have been disappointed if Annie had lived.

Tom put on the smile he used on Parents' Night at school and, as soon as he got in the house, opened his bottle of Scotch. As soon as he felt he could without being impolite, he excused himself to go upstairs to their bedroom and read *A Savage Place*, another Robert B. Parker mystery. Parker's detective, Spenser, is tough, wisecracking, able to face down all his challenges, whether they're mobsters or girlfriends. Spenser, too, Tom decided, treats the absurdities of the world with Camus-like disdain. Still, the twin beds that he and Christine slept in that night made him aware of how much he missed his wife's body next to his.

The next day, he started in on Parker's *The Widening Gyre* until it was time for Thanksgiving dinner. Celeste and Christine had spent the morning in the kitchen and Barney and Nathan had set the table with a lace linen tablecloth, the family silverware with the monogrammed *J*, and the Wedgwood china.

"Nathan, why don't you light the candles?" Barney said, as they sat down. As Tom watched his stepson strike a match and light two candles in silver candlesticks, he envied the easy tone in which his father-in-law spoke to the boy.

They passed around the Beringer wines—both red and white—that Barney bought by the case directly from the winery in California, and then held hands as he said grace:

"*Bless this food to our use and ourselves to thy service; make us mindful of the needs of others; through Jesus Christ our Lord. Amen.*"

Tom wondered what Annie would say if she were here tonight. One summer day when he, Christine, and Nathan had driven up to Webber to see his daughter—that must have been when Annie was still refusing to visit them—she'd been working in the local soup kitchen, serving lunch. They sat at a table with a guy in a ripped straw hat and sleeveless T-shirt that showed his flabby arms and faded tattoo—"Born to Raise Hell"—a woman with no teeth, and a man wearing a dress. Behind the counter, Annie was ladling soup, and wiping sweat from her eyes. "There's no excuse for this country's gluttony," she once told him, "not with so many people going hungry."

Barney carved the turkey in expert strokes, the candlelight glinting off the carving knife. He filled the plate in front of him

1989

with half dark and half light meat. "I know what my lovely bride likes," he said, adding potatoes, squash, beans, cranberry sauce, stuffing, and gravy. He passed the plate to Tom. "Send that down to Celeste, will you, my boy?"

Celeste passed the empty plate in front of her to her husband to fill for Christine. ("White meat, please, Dad.") Christine passed her empty plate for her father to fill for Tom. ("Dark meat, I guess.") Tom passed his plate to Barney to fill for Nathan. ("Both, please.") And Nathan passed his plate to his grandfather to fill for himself. ("I'll have a little of both. And then a little more and a little more.") Barney's Pendleton sport coat remained spotless. Portrait of a successful man.

Tom saw his father excavating their clogged septic tank one hot Fourth of July. Digging down three or four feet through the rocks and clay that lay under the grass in their back yard. Stepping on the shovel. Lifting the dirt. Pausing. Turning the head of the shovel to drop the dirt where he wanted. Reversing the arc downward. Wiping the sweat and the dirt from his face, he took off his sleeveless undershirt. Ran water on it and tied it around his head. Pulled a pint of Old Crow from the pocket of his overalls. The cigarette-cured voice: "Goddamn septic tank (step down)…You can bet those goddamned shyster lawyers and Jew doctors aren't digging up shit today (lift up)…I spend the war digging ditches, they spend it back here making money (turn)…Why the hell do other people have all the luck? (drop)…Either that or they're fuckin' crooks" (swing down).

At the other end of the table, Celeste sipped her glass of Chardonnay. She wore a tweed skirt, white blouse, and pearls, both in a necklace and as earrings. Tom calculated that what was on the table—the silverware, the china, the food, the wine—cost more than his father had made in a year. He remembered how hard his mother had worked one afternoon to make their table presentable for an afternoon tea party for some of the women of the church. He was probably around ten years old and proud of himself for helping her, by taking his father's beer bottles down cellar and setting the table with those green plates decorated in oriental birds, following her instructions to give her the cracked one. But when the ladies of the First Congregationalist Church arrived and were gabbing downstairs (he could hear them through the heating vent in the bathroom, gossiping about somebody who wasn't there), he'd apparently embarrassed his mother almost to death by peeing in the toilet. "Everyone could hear you!" she said later, her face red and teary. "You should have flushed the toilet first to cover the noise. I was so ashamed."

Surrounded now by wealth and good lucks and intelligence, he knew exactly how she felt.

Two nights later, still in Belmont, he dreamed he was taking one of his old creative writing classes for a walk around the leaching pond in back of Webber High School. He recognized Wendy and Phillip and Lori standing around the pond, motionless as tombstones under skinny trees with limbs that looked like bones. Yellow pollen settled on the algae that grew in vomit-like patches along the water's edge. Blackflies buzzed. Moving up a slight rise, Tom saw Annie—looking about eight years old, when her hair was still shoulder-length—crouched below him, peering intently into the mud and reeds. As she leaned forward, he beheld the largest frog he had ever seen, squatting, shiny and green-black in the shadows, throbbing like a slimy, warted heart. It grew larger and larger, until he felt as if it would devour him if it opened its mouth. He gazed at its indifferent eyes, its reptilian smirk, its undulating relentlessness, and somehow recognized the creature, feared it, and would bow before it.

Annie knelt, her fingers slowly tracing the frog's taut, glistening skin. Tom could feel the cold as surely as if her chubby finger were his. Carefully, she took a silver pen, one of those with two hearts on the clip, and softly prodded a protuberance the color of wet bark just above one of those glassy eyes. The eyes seemed to dilate and contract to the rhythm of the frog's breathing.

1989

Suddenly, the frog sprang into the pond, the pen shot into the reeds, and Annie toppled backward into the mud. Tom heard his daughter gasp, saw her wonder turn to fear, and felt his stomach freeze and then erupt in briny rage. He charged down the bank toward the muddy water. He knew the damn thing was gone but he attacked anyway, plunging his arm through the water and the mud until his hand closed on a rock, hard and heavy and misshapen, a Truth, suddenly palpable in the midst of the muck and murk. He straightened and heaved, and the dusty, unruffled scum on the surface of the pond shattered into thousands of polished pieces of glass. The sound of an explosion echoed through his head. He felt himself following the rock as it drove straight and true toward the bottom.

As he came up for air, he felt his insides percolate down through his feet, into the water in which he stood. He heard Phillip laugh. Wendy, Lori, and finally the whole class joined in, cackling like crows. He realized he was covered in mud. They were laughing at him. Pointing in derision. He knew he could never resurrect their respect. Tears of shame mixed with shit-colored slime slid down his face.

The next morning, instead of going to church with everyone else, he walked to the bookstore in Belmont Center to see if he could find any more Spenser mysteries. On his way back, a cold rain began to fall, so Tom followed a sidewalk to a small tunnel under the commuter railroad tracks. As he entered, he recalled Annie telling him in the hospital of the dream she'd had in which she stood in a stone tunnel that stretched away into nothingness at either end. She was frightened, and when she saw a man walking away from her, she yelled to him to wait.

"There's nothing I can do for you anymore," the man called back, and disappeared into darkness.

Tom's footsteps echoed off the damp stone walls, many of which were covered with graffiti—a florescent orange "Fuck you," obscene drawings, swastikas, and a crimson Devil with a pitchfork over the words, "Keep Up the Good Work."

Someone or something kicked him in the chest. After a second pain, he couldn't breathe. He was dizzy. His ears rang. Throat on fire. Was he having a heart attack? A belt of pain tightened around his temples. What the hell was going on? His legs buckled. The other side of the tunnel appeared miles away. He turned around, but the first entrance looked even further behind him.

He pushed himself—*Come on, damn it, move!*—willing his legs to advance, eventually staggering through the mouth of the tunnel into the November rain. Leaning against an embankment of withered grass, he tried to breathe deeply and evenly. His heart pounded, and he thought of the characters in Nathan's *Alien* movies, infested with the creature's eggs, and how their chests begin to pulsate prior to bursting open. He imagined himself exploding, blood splattering the grass and the trees and the rocks around him.

And what kind of creature, he wondered, would he loose upon the world?

Chapter Nine
1989–1990

Another gymnasium. This one at Jordan Mills Junior High School. John Denver sang "Sunshine on my shoulder makes me happy" through two sarcophagus-like loudspeakers on either side of a podium beneath a basketball hoop.

Camus was right: we live in an absurd world.

Tom walked up the center aisle of gunmetal gray folding chairs to the last row. He sat, slumping down so that the chair wasn't pressing against his lower back, and gazed up at the bleacher seats along the walls, wishing he had the nerve to sit in them, as far up as possible above this foolishness.

He watched teachers from the elementary school, the junior high, and the high school file in for this day-before-Christmas-vacation workshop, "Wellness: Concern for the Whole Child." Administrators sat in the front rows. The jocks plus Jim Silas, his department chair, headed for the back with Tom.

He'd tried to find an alternative activity, signed up for a workshop in another district on improving the teaching of writing, but it was canceled at the last minute and so here he sat. Tom had only heard guidance counselors use the word "wellness," which made him suspicious, and talk of the "whole child" reminded him of a professor he'd once had who said that if schools succeeded in creating "well-rounded students," the country would become a nation of billiard-balls. Tom didn't want to teach the whole child. He had all he could handle trying to educate the kid's mind.

He certainly wasn't having much luck with the minds of this year's Advanced Placement students. They seemed smart enough, but their immaturity and self-centered arrogance appalled him. Two students complained to Jim Silas when Tom assigned them homework over the Christmas break. He was starting to question the way he taught. Had the kids at Webber High been like this? Had he ignored their human failings because those A.P. classes had fed his own hubris?

He remembered one Fourth of July when he and Martha and Annie had walked down to Webber's town green for the annual parade and craft show. He'd been teaching in Webber for fourteen years, and while Annie and Martha surveyed the painters, photographers, potters, and leather smiths, he searched the crowd for students, present and former. He found them. Many said hello. Some who were still in college stopped and talked: Emily, attending Penn State; Dennis, going to the University of Maine; Cheryl, attending the University of Chicago; Stephanie, finishing up at Macalester. They said nice things about how well they were doing in English, how thoroughly Tom had prepared them for college expectations. Cheryl said he'd taught her not only how to write, but also how to think.

He'd wished them all the best, lit his pipe, and blew a self-satisfied smoke ring. Above the clamor, a voice cried, "Hey, Mr. Jacobs!" He looked around for another student. Behind him, the voice said: "Mr. Jacobs?" Turning, he saw Annie—she was eleven or twelve—her eyebrows raised, her forehead furrowed. "I've been saying 'Dad' for the last five minutes, but you never noticed me."

Reflecting back, he saw himself through Annie's eyes. Distant. Self-absorbed. More interested in having his ego messaged than in spending time with his daughter. Had she been right? His stomach kicked up a cold rock that began to burn in his throat.

Joe Ashley, Director of Guidance, stood up beneath the scoreboard clock and introduced the coordinator for today's workshop, a Dr. Piper whose red bow tie matched his suspenders. Piper bounced from his seat. "You're going to have fun today! You're going to feel good about yourselves, you're going to develop a positive attitude, and you're going to take that attitude back into your classrooms and teach it to your students!"

Whoopty-fuckin'-do.

Dr. Piper nodded at a stack of papers on one of the chairs and Joe divided them up among the other guidance staff to pass out. When he received his handout, Tom stared at the top:

☺ MAKING THE WORLD WELL ☺

Remember Camus. There is no fate that cannot be surmounted by scorn.

"How many of you have stopped smoking?" Dr. Piper asked. Tom started to raise his hand and stopped, irritated at himself for being conned into playing this clown's game. "I want you to turn to the person closest to you with their arm in the air. Now shake their hand. Do you know how much you've cut your risk of cancer?"

Tom smelled his morning cigar as he walked from the Ronald McDonald House to the hospital. Tasted the one he had before going to bed after a day by the side of his daughter dying of cancer. His daughter who'd never smoked. Those cigars had helped keep him sane for two months. He glanced over at Jim Silas, who also held his hand half in the air. When he saw Tom, he shrugged his shoulders. Jim's sheepish expression was embarrassing—a man of wit and compassion reduced to junior high expectations.

As Dr. Piper read to them definitions off the handout of "attitude," "diet," and "exercise," Tom looked at the black curtains of the gymnasium stage behind him, and saw Annie, shoulders back, head erect, receiving her high school diploma. He, Christine, and Nathan sat in the Webber High School gymnasium as Annie turned to the crowd and waved her two-fingered peace sign.

Nathan jumped up from his seat and waved back. She'd styled her hair to hide where the back of her head had been shaved for a second surgery. The following week she would begin chemotherapy. Tonight, however, she was a high school graduate with a bright red dress and a date for an all-night party. Proudly, Tom watched her join the other graduates of the Class of 1988 in singing:

"This is the time to remember
Cause it will not last forever.
These are the days
To hold on to
Cause we won't
Although we'll want to."

Eighteen months later, instead of Billy Joel, Frank Sinatra resounded from a different set of loudspeakers:

"Start spreading the news. I'm leavin' today!"

"Sing along!" cried Dr. Piper. "You'll feel better and you'll live longer!"

Tom's heart pulsated against his chest. He straightened his shoulders and then, before realizing what he was doing, stood up, turned and marched to the music out the back door of the gymnasium. In the lobby, surprise at what he'd done twisted to anger as he paced back and forth listening to Piper's metallic voice crying, "Sing!"

"I'll make a brand new start of it in old New York!"

Tom threw his smiley-faced handout against the wall of the lobby, and pushed open the glass door. He walked outside, around to the lobby by the cafeteria, and grabbed his hat and coat before going back into the gray winter's day. For the next two hours he roamed the icy streets of Jordan Mills, through housing developments of pale Christmas lights, faded lawn Santas, scraggly wreaths, his rage feeding on itself. He thought of Trudy Mathews, Curtis's wife, whose cancer again had become active after three years in remission. Of Curtis growing thinner and paler behind the pulpit as he talked about God's undying love. He thought of his father, dying of oat cell carcinoma, lying on the couch in his faded blue bathrobe. Eyes filled with fear. Staggering to the bathroom, leaving a thin trail of shit on the floor behind him. He thought of his mother in the hospital in Arizona the previous week, where she'd had fluid drained from around her heart after she'd been taken by ambulance to the emergency room when she couldn't breathe. Her wheezing voice on the phone when he asked her how she was—"I am fine. How are you?" His irrational guilt that somehow he was responsible for her congestive heart failure, too.

He heard his stepfather from the Phoenix time-share (*Did his voice really sound like Piper's?*) telling him to cheer up: "Hey, we're great! Nothing to worry about. She'll be back on the golf course in no time. You just need the right attitude, that's all, and your mom's got that in spades."

Oh yes, the right attitude. Sitting by his daughter's bedside in the hospital. The IV catheter. The Get Well cards. The disinfectant smells. Voices from the hall. She was asking him to read to her.

"Sure," he said. "What would you like?"

Instead of wanting to continue *Children of Dune*, she asked him to read from some kind of alternative health magazine she subscribed to. Tom leafed through glossy pages, reading to his daughter ads for Royal Jelly, Ayurvedic ginseng, macrobiotic hair care, and articles titled "Refreshing Summer Seaweeds," "Nontoxic Alternatives to Mercury Fillings," and "Curing Infertility Through Chinese Medicine."

He turned a page. Before thinking, he read to her, "Alternative Cures for Cancer."

"I want to hear that one," she said.

Tom hesitated before he began: "'I am bothered not by conditions imposed by nature, but by the illusions conjured up by technology.'" He stopped. "Are you certain you want me to read this?"

"Sure. What's wrong?" Her voice grew impatient.

He looked at his daughter. Her eyes began to close. *Maybe she's not really listening. Maybe she's already asleep.* So he read to her about the arrogance of a medical establishment that insists that it alone has the answers regarding how best to treat cancer, when in fact there is no real evidence to support the use of deadly chemicals and mind-altering drugs on millions of patients. About how this establishment has continually repressed evidence that indicates that a healthy, positive self-image is the best cure for disease.

"'Indeed,' he read, "case after case suggests that with the right mental attitude—one built on love and faith—miracles can and do occur every day. Eighty to ninety percent of all cancer is preventable.'"

He stopped. Annie's eyes remained closed. He waited. Just as he started to breathe naturally again, he heard a slow, thick voice: "I've tried to be positive…I guess I'm not strong enough…I wish I wasn't such a baby."

Just off Main Street in Jordan Mills, Tom pivoted and walked back to the high school, to the English office that had one of those new computers. His chest pulsated, his ears rang. He sat down, and typed a letter addressed to the superintendent of schools, the high school principal, and the director of guidance.

He wrote: "I am embarrassed and enraged. In other words, I am not 'well.'"

He wrote without notes, without stopping—an explosion of words: "This workshop is symptomatic of what has lowered the quality of education in this country today."

He wrote about smiley faces, John Denver, Frank Sinatra, being read to from a dictionary.

Three pages later he was still writing:

> Last Easter my eighteen-year old daughter died of cancer, convinced until the very end that, if she'd had a more positive attitude, she wouldn't have been sick. Being told that 'wellness' is under our control does nothing but add guilt to all the

other burdens victims of cancer, diabetes, MS, and other diseases face. Wellness is dangerous and wrong!

Signing the letter, he felt as if he'd lanced a boil.

On the Monday following Christmas vacation, Tom sat in his principal's office, staring through the venetian blinds at a leaden sky spitting snow, trying not to snicker at Allan's prattle about the need for a well-rounded education. In Tom's mailbox that morning were letters of reprimand from Allan and the superintendent of schools. The superintendent's letter was brief: Tom had violated the terms of his teaching contract, which required him to attend district workshops. His choosing to stay in school instead of going home meant he would not lose a day's pay, but he needed to know he could have. Allan, on the other hand, wrote a rambling rebuke, expressing surprise at Tom's "lengthy letter," which he said "ran the gamut from being opposed to a point of view to being sarcastic."

"Don't get me wrong," Allan said as he tightened the knot in his tie, "I'm proud of Jordan Mills's academic programs. We've always had a good track record of high A.P. scores and acceptances into top quality schools."

Here comes the "but."

"But times have changed. More and more kids are coming to us from broken homes…"

Thanks, I needed that.

"…and more and more children are being diagnosed with learning disabilities, and need alternative programs where they can succeed."

In other words, it's better to take a class where you can sit around talking about a movie based on a book, rather than one where you have to spend extra time learning to read the book. Who needs to read, anyway?

"Tom, I understand your concern, but that letter went too far. At first, it made me really angry. I thought you were attacking me personally." Allan glanced into a mirror tucked into some photographs on his desk and smoothed his comb-over. "But eventually I realized that you were merely acting out of grief."

Tom's forehead tightened. His eyes stung. He blinked back tears, put his hands on his thighs, and pushed himself straight against the back of his chair. The last thing he wanted was to let this bastard see his "mere" grief.

Allan looked across his desk at Tom and smiled. "Look, you understand that my letter and Sid's will have to remain in your permanent file, but I've talked to him and we're both willing to forget this incident, as long as such a thing never happens again."

Tom sat silently, inhaling Allan's legendary halitosis. His principal had missed the whole point. The letter was about the dangers of wellness, not about himself. Through the window, he watched a student with a black baseball cap on backwards dash toward the smoking area behind the school garage.

What's the use? Roll your rock, Jacobs.

He thanked Allan for his concern, shook his hand, and left.

To find he'd become a faculty hero. At least, that's what Jim Silas and Myles Georgitis told him that afternoon when they'd come into his room and invited him for coffee.

"No shit, man," said Jim, as they sat at Dunkin Donuts, "We all thought the day was a complete waste of time, but you're the only one who protested. I wish I had your guts."

Tom shrugged modestly, but felt his ego inflating. Like Sisyphus, he'd challenged the gods. Achieved some degree of respect in an absurd world. He told Jim and Myles about his meeting with Allan. "All in all, I was surprised he wasn't more upset. I figured he'd try to dock me a day's pay."

"Allan's not completely stupid," said Myles.

"Only around 97 percent," said Jim.

"No, he's better than that," said Myles. "I've been at this school for over twenty-five years and, believe me, Allan's not the dumbest principal I've ever had. He knows that workshop was a disaster, and he's afraid Tom will write a letter to the school board, telling them about how the school is spending taxpayer money."

Tom felt even stronger. Even more in control. Maybe while he was on a roll, he'd write that letter.

"More coffee?" asked Jim.

Tom smiled at his department head. Jim was one of those people who never seem to age. Tom had seen old yearbook pictures and Jim had the same unlined face and full head of dark hair he'd had fifteen years earlier. Christ, Annie's face had looked older than Jim's. He certainly had more hair. Tom's smile faded, and a bitter coffee taste rose in his throat. And why not? Annie had gone through more in those last months than Jim had in his entire life. Than any one of them there had.

Tom looked out the window, past the parking lot and mud and piles of dirty snow. He knew he would never write that letter to the school board. Allan had been right all along. He hadn't acted out of principle but out of pain. His anger, once clean and pure, now felt desecrated with shame.

"No thanks," he said to Jim. "I've had enough."

Two days later, Tom drummed his fingers on the arm of the couch. "I explained to Nathan that Annie had hated violence of any kind and that if he wanted to honor her memory, he should learn to control his temper." He shook his head. "I was the voice of absolute reason, complete sincerity." Tried to smile. "And I never once thought about how much his anger mirrored mine."

Tom and Christine were checking in at their weekly adult session at the Family Center for Grief and Loss. Nathan was in the next room. John and Sheila, whose teen-age son Bill died of a heart attack during football practice, had talked about their spaghetti supper at the legion hall the previous Saturday night to raise money for a scholarship in Bill's memory. "We made almost a thousand dollars," said Sheila.

"Sheila worked her butt off," John said. He took her hand.

"Getting Shop 'n Save to donate food, contacting the local businesses to sell tickets…"

"It gives me something to think about, besides how much I miss Bill," Sheila said. She removed her hand from her husband's and bit her fist.

Tara had described a three-month birthday party she and her husband held for her daughter, Nicole, who'd died of Sudden Death Syndrome shortly after her birth. "I think her brother and sister really enjoyed it."

"I know it's a little early," said her husband, Stan, digging at his ear, "but we don't want them to forget their sister. We want to keep Nicole's memory alive for them."

"And for us," said Tara, reaching for the box of Kleenex on the coffee table.

The group's facilitator, Carole, whose ten-year-old son had been killed by a drunk driver as the boy played on the sidewalk in front of their house, praised Stan and Tara. "It's important to create and honor anniversaries—births, deaths, graduations."

Ruby, whose sister committed suicide—a bottle of sleeping pills washed down with a pint of bourbon—had spoken of another fight with her boyfriend. "Last night, I told that son of a bitch that if he slapped me again I'd cut his balls off." She sighed. Crossed her legs under her miniskirt.

"And how did saying that make you feel?" asked Carole.

"Oh, he apologized all over the place. But I know it won't last." She flipped back her florescent red hair. "I wish I had better taste in men. But hell, look at Sis. She married a prince of a guy, and she offed herself." She, too, reached for the Kleenex.

After that, Christine had talked about how, on the first day back at school after the Christmas break, Nathan got into a fight and received a Saturday detention. Her hands made circles. "As nearly as we can figure out, a boy named Ben Simons, who I guess Nathan doesn't like very much anyway, said something—Nathan says he doesn't remember just what—about Annie, and Nathan hit him."

"Did you talk to your son?" asked Carole.

Tom hadn't planning on saying anything, but then he'd had a rare moment of insight. "I did," he said. "It's probably the first heart-to-heart we've had since Annie died, and I've just realized I lied like a rug."

He went on to describe the Wellness Workshop. His problems that year teaching kids his daughter's age. The alien that had taken over his body, erupting at the mouthy clerk at the grocery store, over-ripe America, and his wife and her son for not picking up after themselves. He'd never talked this much before. It felt good, like an exorcism. He admitted how hard Christmas had been this year: "I mean, Christ, the three of us argued about where to set up the tree and how to decorate it, and nobody liked the presents we gave each other. Nathan spent a good hour on the phone with his father…"

He sensed Christine's discomfort beside him. He was getting better about reading her unspoken signs. They were keeping a precarious peace these days, balanced with a lot of silent compromises, most of which were for the sake of Nathan. Christine would be sure to pick up after herself and Nathan before she went to bed, if Tom would stop complaining about toys in the living room in the afternoon. Tom would go to the Sunday service at St. Mark's one week if he could stay home the next.

He knew he should strategically retreat. "Most of it, I'm sure, was my fault," he said. "I just couldn't get the memories of my daughter out of my head. I'm sure I didn't act as if I liked my presents because I kept thinking of the presents Annie used to give me…us." He felt tears building. "You know, when she was ten years old, she painted eyes and mouths on some small stones, and set them in modeling clay on a wooden base and printed 'Rock Concert,' on it." It was his turn to reach for the Kleenex. "And each year, after Christine and I were married, she gave us an embroidered Christmas tree ornament. Until last year." His voice broke. "How the hell could she do any embroidery when she couldn't even get out of bed?"

"What are you complaining about?" Behind her granny

glasses, Tara's eyes were huge. She burst into loud sobs. Her mouth twisted around her words. "You had eighteen years with your daughter. I never even had eighteen days!"

Tom hunched his shoulders and stared at the mud-colored carpeting, ashamed of himself for having taken up the group's time.

"Oh, Tara!" said Carole. "Talk to us about the way you feel."

Shame turned to anger. "Listen," he saw himself yelling at Tara, "you've got two other kids! You can have more children! Don't tell me not to complain!" But he said nothing, and when Tara apologized to him at the end of the session—"You know me, I'm always bursting at the butt about something"—he smiled. Mumbled that it was okay, that these were hard times.

That night, as he lay in bed, he wondered if Tara hadn't said what all of them there thought at one time or another: *My pain is worse than yours.* He recalled all the times he'd been impatient with the others' stories and began to question the whole idea of this kind of counseling. What were they, in some contest to see who can tell the saddest story? Cry the loudest?

More evidence of an absurd world.

The following Wednesday, Tom wanted to stay home from the Center, but Christine thought Nathan needed the weekly discipline, even though, after his impressive TV appearance, his enthusiasm seemed to have cooled. ("How did your session go this week?" "Okay.")

Just entering the room at the Family Center for Grief and Loss brought back Tom's frustration of the previous week. Why, he wondered, as he slumped down with Christine on the end of the couch, did they always have to sit in the same places? John and Sheila on the coffee-colored love seat under a painting of Whitehead Rock on Monhegan Island. Ruby in a faded black-and-green-checked chair across from him. Carole in a rocking chair by the only window. Stan and Tara beside him and Christine on a couch the color of dried blood? Why was check-in always the same? The memorial scholarship for Bill. Keeping what's-her-name's memory alive for Stan and Tara's kids. Ruby's boyfriend troubles. Nathan's mood swings. Carole's "How does that make you feel?"

His mind wandered in and out of the session, which had something to do with what people had done the previous weekend. The kids next door were playing some kind of game that involved laughter and cheering. He reminded himself that he needed to check out the slide projector from the library tomorrow morning for his lecture on Shakespeare's Globe Theater, which prompted him to recall Annie at around nine years old, dressed up as a gypsy for a children's theater production, make-up and hooped earrings and shoulder-length blonde hair giving him a glimpse of what a beautiful woman she would be. Then his memory fast-forwarded eight years, to when she'd lost her hair to chemo, her face had grown puffy and broken-out—something to do with steroid medication.

"John and I have stopped going to mass," said Sheila. Tom blinked back tears and looked at the couple sitting under White Head Rock. "In fact, it's really hard to even believe in God anymore, after Bill's death."

"What was it Dostoevsky said?" Stan pulled his ear. "'The death of children is the greatest argument against the existence of God'—something like that. Anyway, it works for me. Religion is all superstition."

"I have a friend who's got one of those Ouija board thingies," said Ruby. "They're pretty weird, so maybe there's something out there."

"I couldn't believe in God before Nicole died," sniffed Tara, "and I sure as hell can't believe in Him now."

Carole raised her eyebrows at Christine and Tom. Across the hall, the kids cheered and applauded. Tom heard Nathan's "Yahoo!" He cast his eyes to where Ruby's legs disappeared under her skirt. When neither he nor Christine responded, Carole said, "My faith has grown stronger since Jason died." She ran both hands through her chestnut hair, exposing gray roots. "I have to believe God wanted him to die. He was such a beautiful boy, I think God needed him in heaven to be one of his angels."

Tom's face flushed and his forehead tightened. His chest exploded. "What kind of a sadist do you believe in?" He slapped the arm of the couch and pointed at Carole. "If that's the way God operates, send me to Hell."

In the abrupt silence that followed, he sensed Christine's body stiffen. Others stared at the floor. Carole scanned the room, scratched her double chin, and rocked back and forth in her chair. "Well, I guess we all have to decide for ourselves, don't we?" She rubbed her hands together and peered at her watch. "Maybe we'd better break a little early tonight. We can chat over coffee before the closing ceremonies."

Tom didn't want to chat. He wanted to drive his fist through the fucking wall. Without putting on a coat or waiting for Christine, he walked outside and paced the parking lot, kicking rocks and chunks of ice. He searched the sky for stars through the glare of the neon car-dealer lights and fast-food signs. He hadn't thought a lot about God lately, only about how much church—the people, the readings—irritated him. Camus had made more sense. Had, Tom thought, provided him with more strength and solace.

Still, if you're going to believe in God, how can you believe in that kind of God?

As he opened the door to the Center to join Christine and Nathan, Tom felt pain shoot from his back into his leg. Christine was waiting for him. She had a strange expression on her face: something between embarrassment and anger. "Our facilitator has been talking to me."

"Good. Did she apologize for being a stupid bitch?"

"She told me I shouldn't be coming to these sessions." Her voice trembled. "She said that, since I'm not Annie's real mother, I shouldn't be meeting with the rest of you. She liked your outburst, and she thinks you'd say more if I weren't here. She says I don't have the same kind of experience you all have."

"Oh, for God's sake!" He searched the room for Carole. Imagined walking up to her and telling her off in front of everyone. But he couldn't find her. "Okay, let's get Nathan. We're out of here. For good."

He put his arm around Christine and escorted her toward the door, motioning for Nathan to follow. As they drove home in silence, Tom replayed in his mind all the things he wanted to say to Carol. Once home, Nathan went immediately to his room. Christine followed him.

When Tom got out of the car, more pain went into his leg. Once in the house, he took three aspirin, and poured the last two inches of his Christmas Scotch into a glass. He stood in the living room and stared at the dead ashes in the fireplace. He cursed that bitch Carole, who became that bastard Dr. Piper, who turned into that asshole Allan. In a while, he heard Nathan's bedroom door open upstairs and Christine's voice: "Good night, honey. Sleep well." Fighting the urge to switch from Scotch to gin, he called, "Are you through down here?" He heard no answer, so he turned down the heat and switched off the lights. When he went upstairs, he found Christine still in her clothes, crying on their bed. Another slab of guilt fell across his shoulders. Not once since leaving the Center had he thought about how hard tonight had been on his wife. He lay down beside her. He took her in his arms where she sobbed violently, her body shaking against his. Soon, they were making frenzied love before retreating to their separate sides of the bed.

But even after they stopped attending the sessions at the Family Center for Grief and Loss, Tom couldn't stop thinking about Carol's God. At school, on his exercise bike, watching TV, at 3:00 in the morning, he saw her flabby face, heard her whiney voice: "God needed him in heaven."

He wanted to see both her and her God as more evidence of Camus's absurd world, but he was too angry to view either with enough detachment and scorn.

Chapter Ten

1990

On a Sunday morning at about 3:20, Tom lay in bed fretting about Carole and her God, trying to remember if he had to go to church that day. The phone rang downstairs. His first thought was that he was in Bangor, hearing the phone ring at the Ronald McDonald House in the middle of the night. He waited for the pause and a second series of rings, showing that Pam's private number had been called and that it was an emergency. When the phone kept ringing, he decided some drunk at a bar had dialed the wrong number. The phone rang twelve more times before it stopped—only to begin again a few minutes later. He went downstairs.

"Hello?"

The silence at the other end of the line seemed to confirm his suspicions about a drunk, and he was about to hang up, when a broken voice said, "Son, this is Cal…It's your mother…" More silence.

"What about her?"

He heard the sound of weeping. "I'm afraid, she's…she's passed on."

It took Tom a few moments to understand. "You mean she's dead?"

1990

"She passed about an hour ago...Earlier in the evening, we'd been watching TV when she had one of those spells..."

A cold fist hit Tom in the chest, sending pain down his back. Instead of Cal's voice, he heard Annie's the night he told her he was moving away: "How many more changes do you think I can take!"

"...And I want you to know that I called the ambulance even though your mom didn't think she needed one, and they came right away, so it wasn't a case of waiting too long..."

He recalled all the times his mother had comforted him when he was growing up. When he'd skinned his knee or put a tooth through his lip. When he was sick. A Sunday dinner—it might have been Christmas or Easter—when he had measles or chicken pox or one of those childhood things, and he lay on the couch wrapped in a blanket. His father reading the paper, his brother, Ed, wanting Tom to sit up so he could get on the couch, too. His mother in the kitchen preparing dinner. Grammy and Grampy Abbott, who'd been at the Baptist Church at the other end of town, coming into the house, bringing an apple and a chocolate cream pie. While the others went into the dining room, Tom's mother brought him in some homemade chicken soup and, before she gave it to him, she'd taken him into her arms and he'd buried his face between her comforting breasts.

How many Saturday mornings had she'd called him just after her homemade bread had come out of the oven, so he could tear off a hot hunk of it to slather with peanut butter? She'd worked weekends cleaning houses to help keep him in shoes that he seemed to outgrow every six months. She waited up for him in high school, no matter how late he was out. She rose the next morning to make sure he had a good breakfast. For years at Christmas, she made cookies, fudge, hand-knit scarves, hats, and mittens for him and his family (both of his families, actually). All this, as he now knew, while taking care of an alcoholic husband, cleaning up the vomit and diarrhea that she said came from his "nervous stomach," which she blamed on his years in the Army during World War II and stress at work.

She'd been a remarkable woman, and it was too late for him to tell her so.

But instead of sorrow and regret, all he felt was anger. "Yeah, I know, Cal, you did everything you could. Now what are we going to do about the goddamned funeral?"

The sanctuary in the Ashton First Congregational Church felt like a freezer. Worn pew cushions. Peeling paint on the walls. The pastor, Joe Stiles, with his buckteeth, permed hair, and cow eyes, appeared just out of seminary. Tom sat rubbing his hands together in the pew with the brass *Jacobs* name plate. Seated with him were Christine, looking pale and gaunt (Nathan was with his grandparents); his brother, Ed, bloated, tattooed, pierced, reeking of alcohol and pot; and Cal in his toupee, looking like a broken marionette beside his son, Phil.

When Tom had been Tommy, this church had been a familiar and comfortable place. He often helped his father clean or set up tables and chairs. Tommy knew the three staircases to the choir loft and the two staircases to the cellar. He knew the closet where the folding wooden chairs were stored, and the kitchen cabinet where the peanut butter and saltines hid out. The church's pastor at the time, Scotty Hughes, lived across the street and smoked and drank and told dirty jokes just like the other men in town.

At the same time, the boy remembered feeling a mysterious "otherness" in church, an interweaving of past and present, of things seen and unseen. In the cellar, on a stony ledge created by the uneven blocks of granite, a framed piece of parchment commemorated, in the most beautiful handwriting he'd ever seen, Deacon Noah Drinkwater's bequeathing a sledge hammer to the church in 1888. Sometimes in the echo chamber of the empty sanctuary, Tom sensed Noah and other old congregants applauding as he sang "Heartbreak Hotel" while picking up last week's bulletins from under the dark green cushions of the pews. Scotty Hughes, just another guy during the week, ascended the steep steps to the pulpit on Sundays in his black robe and became transformed, taller, more resonant, haloed by candelabra behind him. For Tommy, God was like Scotty—a nice guy who lives nearby, helps out when you need him, and every so often winks from behind golden clouds.

There were still a few people here he remembered: Mr. Johnson, his English teacher, who once walked from school to his house to show his mother a composition he'd written. Mrs. Thompson, his music teacher, who used to tell him he could be as good a trumpet player as Billy Frye, who once played with the Tommy Dorsey Orchestra. Red Bailey's widow. People who had protected and pampered and pushed him, feeding his dreams of success.

Maybe if he hadn't been such a dreamer, Tom thought, he'd be tougher now, more able to deal with the anger that threatened to overwhelm him. His objectivity, his reason, not to mention his concern for others—especially his mother—had been swallowed by a rage that slithered like a giant reptile out of the past into the present, threatening to devour the future. Self-absorbed in his anger at school policies, incompetent counselors, absurd church services, he'd never looked beyond his mother's "I am fine. How are you?" he heard every time he'd called Arizona. Why hadn't he flown to Phoenix to see her when she went back into the hospital? Why hadn't he at least asked Christine's father to find her a heart specialist?

As the congregation rose to sing his mother's favorite hymn, "O God, Our Help in Ages Past," Tom sensed himself singing in this same pew at the Easter service with his mother and her polka-dot dress and white gloves and that funny fry pan of a hat, his father in his gray suit, his brother, Eddie, in his navy-blue blazer. Today's funeral hymn faded, as Tom heard once more

> *Christ the Lord is risen today, Alleluia!*
> *Earth and heaven in chorus say, Alleluia!*
> *Raise your joys and triumphs high, Alleluia!*
> *Sing, ye heavens, and earth reply, Alleluia!*

But as the hymn ended and he sat down with the rest of the aging congregation, Tom realized he'd never thought in those days about the meaning of Easter—how or why "Christ the Lord is Risen Today." He'd simply accepted the Resurrection in the same way he accepted his mother's presence in the pew beside him, or the glow on Scotty Hughes's face. Now, the church seemed darker than he remembered, a different organ was in a different place, his mother, Scotty, and Connie were all dead, and Resurrection belonged to another era. A time of innocence. Before failed marriages, broken families, and diseased children.

Joe Stiles stood up and began to speak. His head above the pulpit made Tom think of the one-toothed dragon puppet—was it Kukla or Ollie?—he used to watch when he was a kid. The pastor talked about Rebecca Jacobs's lengthy service to the church, some of which, like her years as Moderator of the Church Council and delegate to the UCC's Maine Conference, Tom had forgotten and was grateful to be reminded of. But when Joe talked about her work with the Cub Scouts and the PTA, her raising two sons, Tom saw his mother standing in front of the refrigerator, her arms crossed over her chest. Heard her flat, Maine voice: "Thomas, I'm ashamed of you. If you'd mowed the lawn and taken out the trash, your father wouldn't be sick in bed. He's working two jobs to make ends meet. The least you could do is help him around the house. You know better."

As if from some security camera in the corner of the kitchen, Tom saw himself at eleven years old: pudgy with smooth round cheeks and blond highlights in his crew cut, a jersey with horizontal stripes, corduroy pants that whistled when he walked, black PF Flyers. As his mother talked, Tommy Jacobs stared out a tall window with light green curtains that looked down the street to the river. He spun the front wheels of a model racecar his father had given him the night before, trying not to think about his parents shouting at each other after he'd gone to bed—his father's slurred voice: "Goddamn it, woman, I'm working my ass off. If I need a drink or two to get me through, then who are you to bitch? I'm keeping you and the boys fed, aren't I?"

1990

Tommy pretended he didn't hear what his mother had said. He tried instead to think about playing baseball after lunch, but her words stung and his eyes burned. The plastic securing the axle between the two front wheels on the toy car snapped. He wanted to throw the damn thing at her and run away.

Was that when his fall from innocence started? When he had begun to shoulder some of his mother's sense of shame and guilt for being the daughter of one alcoholic and wife of another? When he'd started to feel it was his fault when one of his father's gifts broke or he couldn't ride that damn bicycle the old man had bought him? Why he'd come to feel he was somehow to blame when his parents fought, or when his first wife complained, or when his daughter died?

Now Joe was talking about "Rebecca's loving family," which sent Tom back to that morning's graveside service. Standing at Riverview Cemetery, shivering from the cold wind coming off the Androscoggin River, staring at an oval of Bean boots, dress shoes, and overshoes surrounding an inner circle of footprints in the snow, which in turn encircled a green mat of Astroturf, in the center of which stood an ash-colored urn containing the remains of his mother. The last of the family circle. Cal was moving closer to his son in Arizona. Ed—if he didn't pass out in the taxi to the airport—would catch this evening's flight to San Francisco. It had taken Tom days of calling his brother's old friends to find him and let him know of their mother's death, and all his brother had said to him in the cemetery had been, "You know, Tommy, the way Mom and Dad doted on you I really thought you'd amount to more than just a fucking high school teacher. I thought you'd become president of these goddamned United States."

Tom glared over at his brother in his leather jacket. Longhaired, bearded. But when he saw tears running down Ed's florid face, he felt ashamed of himself. After Ed had gotten in trouble in high school, his mother and father never mentioned their eldest son. It was as if he had never existed to them. That must have been hard, especially since, when Tom had been in grade school, it had been Ed who seemed to rate not only all his family's affection, but also the esteem of his teachers and coaches.

Not to mention his younger brother. When Tommy was little, he and Eddie used to watch cowboy movies on the family's new TV. Afterward, Eddie would throw his brother over his shoulder on to the bed in their room, the way Hopalong Cassidy did with the bad guy sneaking up behind him. Sometimes Eddie was Roy Rogers and Tommy was Gabby Hayes. Eddie taught him how to hold a baseball bat and spent time pitching to him. But once his older brother hit junior high and high school, Tommy became invisible, and Tom remembered doing just about anything just to get his older brother to notice him.

Shards of another image: two wide eyes…a tangled head of dark hair…bony arms flailing the air and the sound of shrieking obscenities. The vision came into focus. Scrapped knees below a ragged skirt and socks puddled around saddle shoes. A gangly, round-shouldered girl in a motorcycle jacket surrounded by anywhere from five to ten fifth-graders, hopping up and down like crows, and cackling, "Ester is a fart-smeller!"

Her name, Tom recalled, was Ester Morin, and she grew up in "Puddleville," a cluster of tarpaper shacks and rotting houses by the river belonging to woodsmen and dump-pickers, all of whom had intermarried so often that they were, in his father's words, "number than pounded thumbs." Today, Ester would get special services, but in those days, students who needed more help were simply held back, so that although close to Eddie's age, she was only a grade ahead of Tommy and his friends.

When Tommy saw Eddie and his buddies making fun of Ester on the street, he organized his friends into targeting her whenever they got the chance. In the halls, they tried to trip her or pellet her with spitballs. They waited for her after school, running around her in circles, baying like wolves.

Eddie never seemed to notice, but ridiculing Ester with names like "fart-smeller" and "cootie-lover" still made Tommy feel stronger—gave him what Joe Ashby and the other guidance counselors would today call "self-esteem." Deriding her helped him stop thinking of himself as fat, slow, and unpopular. Ester was a way to strike back at his confusion about his family, his fears, ridicule them with names like "fart-smeller" and "cootie-lover." Every time Ester screamed and waved her arms like some broken doll because of something Tommy had said, he felt more in control.

Because of Ester, he'd learned to divide the world into Us and Them. Red-blooded Americans and Dirty Reds. Good Guys and Bad Guys. Winners and Losers. Puddleville dummies like Ester Morin, and him and his gang. Now here he was, sitting in church, doing the same thing with his brother, just as his parents had. Ed and Tom. Loser and winner. High school dropout and college graduate. Druggie and respected teacher. And yet, as Ed had pointed out, Tom was no success. He drank too much. He was a lousy father and husband and son. Hell, he wasn't even a very good teacher anymore.

Standing behind the pulpit, Joe Stiles leaned into the microphone. "Remember, my friends, death is like the horizon: an end only because we can't see any further."

Tom stared up at the crack in one of the stained-glass windows. But it was all the suffering he could see—the physical pain, the aborted dreams, the isolation—that infuriated him. He thought again of Ester, and then of the afternoon Annie had come home in tears because some boys on the playground had made fun of her. Thought of Annie's sorrow when, after she'd started chemotherapy and lost her hair, younger kids would laugh at her. Even kids her own age whom she'd thought were her friends deserted her, as if cancer were somehow contagious.

Standing again for "When I Survey the Wondrous Cross"— *"Where the young Prince of Glory died..."*—he thought of the Crucifixion, and the ridicule that had preceded it. Annie, like Ester, had suffered ridicule. Worse, she had died in the morning hours of Good Friday, not upon a cross but upon a hospital bed, catheters piercing her body like nails. Tom had read that crucifixion was slow, torturous suffering that ultimately resulted in death by asphyxiation. How many times had he sat by Annie's bedside in those last days, listening to his daughter's breathing became louder and more labored as it rose and fell: "Ash...es. Ash...es"?

Resurrection might belong to the past, but crucifixion was very much a part of the present.

As he and Christine walked out of the church, the organist came down from the choir loft to the piano, where she played "Nola," one of his mother's favorite songs. The poor woman butchered the tune, stumbling over notes and losing the rhythm, reminding Tom of how he used to ride his stripped-down bicycle from Main Street to his house, and hear through the window his mother playing the piece on their piano. Coming in the door and seeing his mother, her back to him, her left hand bouncing up and down keeping rhythm, while her right hand glided gracefully, lightly, along the upper reaches of the keyboard. She'd been a natural musician, telling him she could pick out tunes on the piano as early as age three. When she was in high school, she performed at dances, minstrel, and variety shows. One year she saved up enough money to take the bus to Portland for a lesson with a famous music professor, but he told her she knew nothing about music and that she was wasting his time. After that, she always felt guilty about playing the piano, saying that she should be doing something more important.

In the cold March wind, Tom heard Annie at the keyboard as well, working on her piano lessons. He saw her sitting beside his mother at a piano in a cold empty room, the music echoing in and out of tune. He recalled a line from scripture: something about my father's house having many mansions.

Yes, and some of them are very cold and very dark.

Chapter Eleven
1990

Two weeks later, when Tom awoke at 3:13 a.m., Georgia O'Keeffe's vaginate flower on the bedroom wall mutated into the face of Ronald McDonald. He was back in Bangor, staring at the clown's malignant eyes and pallid face leering at him from the middle of a quilt hanging over a bureau. He saw himself getting out of bed, raising the window shade, and squinting at the sun flashing off the Penobscot River across the street. He felt the current pulling him over the waterfall, helpless, sucked by churning water to the cancer ward at the Eastern Maine Medical Center less than a mile downstream.

Next week would be the first anniversary of Annie's death, and the previous day he'd received a cryptic note from Martha: "In case you're interested, a commemorative plaque recognizing the contributions people made to the Tumor Clinic in Annie's name is now hanging in the Eastern Maine Medical Center."

The letter was the first he'd heard from his ex-wife since the week after Annie's funeral, when, at Martha's invitation, he'd driven to Webber to divide up photographs, go through their daughter's collection of music tapes, and take back the guitar he, Christine, and Nathan had given her for her eighteenth birthday. He thought it had been a pleasant meeting. They'd sat together on the couch, Jolie wagging her tail at their feet, poring over photo albums, reminiscing about their hike up Cadillac Mountain on Mount Desert Island, their trip to Campobello, Annie's first real Christmas (Tom: "She was more blown away by the wrapping than by the gifts themselves."), the time the power went out during a snowstorm when Annie was six months old (Martha: "I wrapped her in so many blankets, she could have passed for a parboiled beet.") Maybe if he'd stayed married to Martha, he thought now, they could have worked things out. He remembered her hearty laugh, her efforts to keep their house clean and tidy, the way she tended him when he was sick. Maybe if they'd stayed married, Annie never would have gotten sick in the first place.

Christine rolled up against him, and she began to purr. No matter how strained things were between him and his second wife, he still loved the sounds she made while she slept. Had things between him and Christine ever been as lousy as all those years of malignant bickering with Martha, his irritation at his ex-wife's curtness with clerks, the pressures she put on Annie's teachers, the way she'd bitched at him for having to correct papers at night and on weekends? What about the curtness of her last note? "You might be interested…" No greeting. No signature.

He remembered the afternoon in the hospital after Dr. Jacobs had told Annie that the cancer had spread. Tom had been holding his daughter, rocking her in his arms, both of them crying. Annie kept saying, "All I ever wanted to do was to make someone happy."

From the doorway, Martha's voice cracked like a bullwhip. "Okay, what's going on in here?" She spoke only to Annie. "Come on, babe, snap out of it. What's the matter? Tell Momma."

Annie pulled away from her father. "It's all right. I was just feeling sorry for myself."

As his arms emptied, Tom's face burned with anger and embarrassment. He retreated to the bathroom, stood over the sink, head down, biting into his fist as hot tears burned his cheeks.

1990

A year later, Tom's fists clenched all over again at Martha for driving him from his daughter. He felt the emptiness in his arms once more. His body went cold. He couldn't lose any more of Annie. He needed to hold on to whatever remained. He needed to keep his daughter's memory alive. He needed to go to Bangor.

That afternoon, after they'd all come home from school, Tom sat in the kitchen, flipping through the latest issue of *The New Yorker*, sipping gin, and watching Christine make bread to take to school the following day, something she often did for her classes. From upstairs in Nathan's room heavy metal music vibrated the floor.

"I think I'm going to drive to Bangor on Saturday to see Annie's memorial plaque in the hospital," he said.

Christine was silent for a while before she asked, "Could Nathan and I come with you?"

"No, this is how I need to observe the anniversary of my daughter's death. I guess I think of it as my Good Friday cross to bear."

His wife turned and inspected him in that way she did, her eyes somewhere between black and blue. "Good Friday isn't until April thirteenth this year." She returned to her kneading. "And why are you making such a big deal out of Good Friday when you're not sure you believe in God anymore, let alone Christianity?"

"I don't know. I don't know what I believe in anymore. All I know is that I want to go to Bangor...alone."

Silence shrouded the kitchen. Tom went back to his magazine, part of him ashamed of himself for not being a better husband and father and part of him convinced that, when it came to his daughter, he could do anything he damn well wanted to.

"Here's an interesting-looking movie," he said, trying to fill the emptiness. "It's called *Black Rain*, about the so-called 'survivors' of Hiroshima. Remember when Annie told us she and her friends folded all those cranes for the Children's Museum there?"

Christine didn't turn around. "Yes, that was a wonderful day. Maybe the last we all ever had."

Annie's voice drifted through the kitchen. "You're supposed to say a prayer for peace each time you fold one."

Peace. When was the last time he'd had any since that night? Tom downed his drink. Maybe if he knew who to pray to he'd ask for it. He looked at his watch. He'd promised himself these days that he'd wait at least fifteen minutes before getting another drink. He started reading the movie review. Part way down, he stopped and reread a paragraph.

"Listen to this," he said. "The reviewer's describing these 'survivors': They '…live in a perpetual state of suspension, a constant twilight. Their survival is too tenuous to give them much joy; it's more like a wary, static persistence. They're watching themselves, and each other, all the time—monitoring their bodies and spirits, looking for symptoms, signs, reasons to hope or despair…'"

He looked out the kitchen window at the gathering darkness. His sad face stared back at him.

"Go on," said Christine.

"'They're contaminated by uncertainty, and every gesture they make, every word they speak, is halting, self-conscious, tentative. They don't know what kind of story they're in…'"

He raised his eyes toward his wife. "Sound like anyone you know? God, I feel as if I'm reading one of my journal entries about my latest body aches and pains, and how I can't seem to plan for the future."

Christine turned toward him. Her eyes glistened. "Does it help to know that you're a survivor, too—that we all are—of a horrific catastrophe?" She went back to her bread. "The question is, where is our story going?"

Tom watched her fingers braiding three strands of dough on a flat pan. He glimpsed Annie's finger's sketching a picture. Folding a paper crane. "Look," he said, "I really need to go to Bangor by myself, but this summer, while Nathan's in Wyoming, we'll go somewhere. Just you and me, okay?"

Christine's shoulders trembled. "Okay."

Above the concrete monotony of Route 95, a stiff March

1990

wind drove a flotilla of clouds across the sky. Large, white, and puffy on the horizon, smaller overhead. Sometimes the clouds glowed in the spring sunshine. Other times they blotted the sun and turned the world dark. The grass along the interstate regressed from green to brown as he headed north. In a two-and-a-half-hour drive, he saw the remains of two skunks and a woodchuck splattered along the highway.

He listened to Annie's tape of Harry Chapin:

"And the cat's in the cradle and the silver spoon
Little boy blue and the man in the moon
When you comin' home, Dad
I don't know when, but we'll have a good time then
You know we'll have a good time then."

Somewhere he had a story Annie wrote for her eleventh-grade English class and then given him. "Playground Politics" was a fantasy, set on another planet, a world of innocence, where children play happily on a playground of terrashuttles and lunar jump games. One day, two girls from another planet show up. Although the girls are taller than the others and wear green plaid bows in their hair and yellow-and-purple striped shirts and red pants, the other children welcome the newcomers. They all play happily together, until one of the mothers shows up. She screams at her children. "Look at those freaks! I can't believe you've been playing with those two gooks!" Other arriving parents take up the shocked outcry. "I don't want to see you playing with those foreigners," one father says sternly.

Annie obviously meant to show how one generation instills prejudice in the next. Still, Tom took the story personally. He didn't like the tone of the father's voice. Was that how Annie heard him? He wanted to rewrite her story and make the father more understanding.

But he thought again of the way he'd treated Ester Morin, whom he couldn't seem to get out of his mind. Whether through conjecture or memory, he saw Ester in the hall of the elementary school. She was crying, her nose red and running, her eyes bloodshot, her shoulders stooped. Tom and his gang in their plaid shirts and Buster Brown shoes pointed their fingers at the gaunt and broken body. "Get away, fart-smeller. We don't want your cooties!" Maybe Annie was right and he was part of her circle of prejudice.

And it was too late to apologize to Annie or to Ester.

In Newport, the clouds gave way to gray shafts of light running almost perpendicular to the highway. Just before Bangor, a big black-blue-gray cloud first spit and then poured rain. He stopped first at the Ronald McDonald House. It was midmorning, and the downstairs was empty except for a volunteer receptionist, a fortyish woman with gray hair and a yin-yang medallion around her neck. She told him she'd spent time there when her son wasbeing treated for leukemia. "He's in remission now. The doctors are hopeful." Tom made out a fifty-dollar check to the Ronald McDonald House, and asked if he could walk around.

As he entered the kitchen, he saw the two refrigerators, the two stoves, the two coffee makers, the giant-sized jar of Jif on the counter. Morning after morning, he'd been in this kitchen, going to the larger refrigerator and a bag on which he'd printed his name to pick out a bagel and a slice of cheese. He wondered if that serrated knife was still in the drawer to the right of the sink, the knife he'd used to slice the bagel in half. Yes, same place. And the white coffee mug with the chipped handle that he'd thought of as his? He opened the cupboard over the drawer. Yup. Always drank out of this mug while he ate his bagel, spread with peanut butter and topped with a slice of cheese. He hadn't eaten that combination since.

He recalled the woman—What was her name? Husband getting treatment for prostate cancer—who used to fry sausages here every morning for about two weeks. Square and sixtyish, moving in slow motion in and out of the morning shadows cast by the light coming through the window over the sink. He saw himself saying good morning and hearing what came out sound squeaky, like Alvin and the Chipmunks on a Christmas record he and Martha had once given Annie.

He glanced into the dining area at the square tables and straight-backed chairs and thought of Jennie, her mother, and Jennie's stuffed penguin, Opus, sitting on the chair between them. At five, Jennie was the youngest person there at the time getting medical treatments. Radiation for a brain tumor, he'd heard. The table by the window was where he used to like to sit. One week Dave Shepherdson, a potato farmer from somewhere in Aroostook County, joined him every morning. Tom found his candor embarrassing, even obscene, as if he were unzipping his fly and exposing himself. Dave's nineteen-year-old daughter's transplanted kidney, the one he'd given her twelve years earlier, was failing and no one was sure what to do next. "I can't help her this time," he kept saying to Tom. "What the hell do I do?"

Tom's answer was always the same. "If you ever find out, let me know."

He wondered where Jennie and Dave were. How they were. Was Dave's daughter alive? Was Jennie?

He regarded another wall hanging of Ronald McDonald by the stairs leading up to the bedrooms. He suddenly wished he still lived here. Despite the isolation, the anger, the sorrow, the guilt of last year, there was a clarity and focus to his life here that he missed. He knew the minute he awoke what he should be trying to accomplish that day. The Great Truths, he guessed you'd call them—love, suffering, death—were always with him. These days, he seemed to be stumbling in circles through a forest of shadows.

As Tom walked out of the Ronald McDonald House, the slate-colored sky overhead opened like a zipper to reveal a golden sun against a deep blue sky. Two seagulls soared and swooped over the river across the road. Along the far banks, russet oak trees and white birches raised their boney branches to the sky.

He left his car in the parking lot and walked down the hill by the river. Past Cascade Park, up a hill past square houses with mansard roofs and pillared porches, to a low brick building next to a hotel. He opened a side door that led into the hospital and to what he always thought of as the bowels of EMMC. As he wended his way through the winding brick corridors, his stomach hiccupped and his legs felt weak. He passed rooms marked *Data Processing, Computers,* and *Housekeeping Maintenance.* Pipes and valves clunked overhead. Machines hummed. In the muggy air, he took off his coat and tucked it under his arm. Metal and wooden doors. *Records Retention Center Office, Respiratory Medicine Office, Hospital Staff Only, Procedure Room #1, Procedure Room #2.* He half-expected to run into himself coming the other way, after a day by Annie's side. He recalled Curtis Mathews's words, "Not every father would have done what you did," and experienced a faint, flickering pride for having made it through last year's adversity.

When Tom reached the laundry rooms, men and women in light-blue coats and plastic hairnets scurried around carts, baskets, and gurneys. Past a row of gray lockers, the brick walls turned to cinderblocks, and after walking past photographs of lighthouses and lobster boats, he came to the memorial plaques hanging like rows of wooden shields along the wall. It took him a few minutes to find his daughter's:

In Memory
Anne Sharon Jacobs
1970-1989

Tears. The cold knot in his stomach rising and burning his throat. Annie's name etched into the wooden tablet brought to mind his daughter standing in the cellar by his workbench, work goggles pulled tight around her head as she burned a coastal scene into a pine board. Black nail polish on her little fingers—some kind of peace thing. Tom wanted to make her hobby a foreshadowing, arrange all the pieces of her life together in such a way that her death made sense, but his emptiness obliterated all thoughts but one. *My daughter is dead.*

1990

Tom turned away, stood against a cement wall, and wept.

After washing his face in the men's room, he went to the second-floor cafeteria, bought the macaroni and cheese special, along with a donut, and carried his tray to a table beside a glass partition that separated the smoking from the nonsmoking sections of the room. Overhead, piped violins played "In Your Easter Bonnet." He smelled tobacco smoke and for a moment wanted one of his small cigars.

As Tom ate, he thought of Stan, his favorite orderly, entering Annie's room with a covered plate of food that would go to waste unless Tom decided to eat it. Stan did bird calls and sound effects—drum rolls, rocket explosions. Probably in his early twenties, he liked to flirt with Tom's daughter. They'd had a date to go out for drinks on Annie's twenty-first birthday.

Fighting more tears, Tom picked up the donut, his fingers coming away sticky with sugar glaze. The pastry smell brought back memories of his mother standing in the kitchen in her green-and-yellow apron on Saturday morning, baking, and he took a bite, savoring his sugary childhood. When he finished, he slowly licked his fingers, trying to prolong the taste. But when he saw Dr. Godfrey, his hair longer and grayer, walking out of the cafeteria, he grabbed his tray and hurried after him.

When he couldn't find him in the lobby, he walked by a table set up by "Home Care: Partners in Caring" and down the familiar corridor. He said good afternoon to a gentleman with closely trimmed silver hair, who pushed a wheelchair in which a woman in a white turban sat, her deep-set eyes staring straight ahead. He said hello to a nurse, who reminded him a little of Heather, Annie's day nurse. Thirty-five-ish, compact and "perky," as his grandmother might have said, she'd bound like a high school cheerleader into Annie's room to check the gauges on the morphine and saline solutions, and to examine the catheters on his daughter's body.

"Open those baby blues, honey. It's time to take your temperature."

Tom saw Annie's eyes open, wide with fright. "Where am I?"

"In the hospital with your favorite nurse. Now give me your mouth and I'll give you a thermometer."

Annie stared at her father. "Why aren't you in school with your students?"

When he told her he'd been there for almost a month, she started to cry. "I'm so confused. Damn it, I hate being like this!"

He went to the bed and took her hand, but she whined, "Get away—You're cold!"

"Okay, okay. Just trying to let you know I'm really here."

"I know. I'm sorry. I wish I were more stoic, then I wouldn't get so emotional." She sniffed and tried to wipe her nose, but she couldn't reach it because of the tube in the back of her hand. Tom got a Kleenex and did it for her.

Heather announced that Annie's temperature had fallen to 100. "I think we've got it under control, but we do need to get a bowel movement out of you. If the milk of magnesia doesn't work today, you'll have to have an enema."

"No!" Annie cried, both she and Tom remembering how a month earlier, some kind of medicine had given her terrible diarrhea for two days. Heather ignored her and spooned out the laxative, telling them a story about how she once saved a man's life with milk of magnesia.

Tom stopped at the plain wooden door with the small metal tag. As usual, the chapel was empty. He had sat in that room at least twenty times the year before, and only once did he have to share it with anyone. Instead of candles, Easter lilies on the altar filled the room with their sweet fragrance. He sat in the front row of seats, savoring the silence. Through the round window behind the altar, he watched the Penobscot River plunge over a waterfall in a cascade of rainbow-colored spray in front of an abandoned brick building on the far bank, the scene encircled by stained glass. He took several deep breaths and the knot in his stomach loosened.

His eyes, however, still smarted from his earlier tears. He felt like a hypocrite. Last summer, he'd embraced Camus's absurd world. That winter, he'd said he'd rather go to hell than believe in a loving God. Yet here he sat in the chapel, searching for some kind of peace. He was tired of rolling his rock. At least Sisyphus knew where he was going. Half the time, Tom didn't know whether he was pushing the rock up a mountain or following it back down.

The longer he sat looking through the window at the water churning over gray rocks, the more he began to wonder if he didn't belong here after all. He saw that all of his anger of the last year—at Christine and Nathan, at his parents and Ed, at Gary Coffin and Michael Keith, at overripe America and Dr. Piper, at Carole and the Family Center for Grief and Loss—was really anger at God. And if he was angry with God, didn't that mean that he did, in fact, believe in God?

Tom pulled at his beard. But the question arose: who or what was this God? He thought again of that voice or whatever he'd heard a year earlier when he sat here. "Don't ask why, just ask for help." Asking what kind of God he believed in was like asking why his daughter died: a pointless intellectual exercise. Maybe he needed to pay more attention to the second half of the injunction: "…just ask for help."

Help, however, from whom? From the Kindhearted God of Scotty Hughes, his former neighbor and minister? From Tom's old Creative Source of purple sunsets and primitive neuroectodermal tumors? From the vindictive God to whom he'd sold his child in return for a good fuck? From the insensate Patriarch of Emily Dickinson, whom he'd been trying to teach to his A.P. kids?

Of course—I prayed
And did God care?
He cared as much as on the air
A Bird—had stamped her foot—
And cried, "Give me"—

Wasn't he back to trying to define God?

But as the mist over the river thickened to fog, completely obscuring the water, Tom began to think that maybe it didn't make any difference who you asked when you asked for help. That the important thing was asking.

What did he have to lose?

And with that question, all the disparate fragments of the last year connected for him, as if he were peering into a kaleidoscope watching the pieces come together. Besides losing a child, he'd lost his passion for the most exciting woman he'd ever known. He'd lost his mother, a developing relationship with a stepson, enjoyment of a job that had given him satisfaction for twenty-five years, the solace of the Family Center for Grief and Loss, his past, his future, and every image of God he'd ever had.

"Help."

His voice sounded quivering, weak. He cleared his throat. His chest began to pulsate. The words exploded. "Goddamn you, help!"

Maybe it didn't make any difference how you asked, either. Tom sensed himself and the alien in his chest embraced. The stained glass around the circular window—random shapes of red, gold, brown, and blue fashioned together in one beautiful frame—cradled his anger and confusion. For a moment he felt reconciled, hopeful. Felt that behind all the gods he'd ever believed in, there might be a God of love after all.

But after the heady reassurance of the chapel, the Easter service at St. Mark's was like tepid tea. Tom sat beside Christine and Nathan in a crowded pew that hurt his back and listened to his stepson, supposedly over bronchitis, cough his way through the service. When the choir processed into the church singing "Jesus Christ is Risen Today," all Tom heard was a fourteenth-century vision of Jesus as some kind of Henry the Eighth:

1990

*"Hymns of praise then let us sing, Alleleuia!
unto Christ, our heavenly King, Alleleuia!"*

*"Now above the sky he's King, Alleleuia!
where the angels ever sing, Alleleuia!"*

Here he was, needing to continue the conversation he'd begun with God in the hospital chapel, and all the church could give him were images of a capricious monarchy and a two-thousand-year-old tale of Jesus coming out of his tomb like Punxsutawney Phil. When the service ended, congregants around him shook hands, laughing, wishing each other Happy Easter. Tom didn't know what to say. He ushered his family out of church as quickly as he could. Under a vast and sunless sky, they drove back to their duplex in silence.

Chapter Twelve

1990

Even at 9 p.m., aerosol clouds shimmered in sunlight. Tom and Christine sat at a wooden picnic table with Aaron and Peggy Green outside the Spade & Becket, a spacious pub with whitewashed stone walls and four tall chimneys, drinking Green King beer and watching tourists in shorts and sunglasses attempt to pole their punts along the gray-green waters of the River Cam.

Tom and Christine had met Aaron and Peggy at breakfast at Jesus College, and the Greens invited the Jacobses to spend the day with them and their rented car. In the morning, they'd attended Great St. Mary's Church in Cambridge. In the afternoon, they'd driven out to the ash-gray ruins of a twelfth-century castle at Saffron-Walden, and walked the nearby turf maze that, according to the guidebooks, measures exactly 1,500 meters. Still light-headed from the overnight flight from Boston to London thirty-six hours earlier, Tom thought he'd stumbled into a nursery rhyme.

Not once today, he realized, had he thought about Annie.

He felt ashamed of himself, as if he'd failed his daughter yet again, but he remembered what Christine had said as they boarded the plane: "We need to leave the past behind for a few weeks." She was right. Just as she'd been right to hold him to his promise that the two of them would get away this summer, before pointing out to him the advertisement for an Elizabethan Studies Program at Cambridge University. When he'd wondered if they could afford it, she had replied, "I'm not sure we can afford not to."

He wondered if she thought he was getting too obsessed with Annie's memory. After coming back from seeing Annie's memorial plaque, he'd put together a scrapbook, beginning with photographs of his daughter in her white christening gown and matching frilly hat, and ending with her in a red bandanna, standing with Nathan in front of the apple tree in back of the duplex. He added newspaper clippings and high school compositions. Then he spent fifty dollars to have her watercolor of the turquoise hand reaching through the rocks matted and framed before hanging it over the fireplace.

And he'd had plenty of time to obsess. In April, right after Easter, some kind of flu kept him home from school for three days and hung on for weeks. In May, he took another day off from school for tests, after the pain in his chest and throat got so bad he felt as if a bulldozer were excavating his rib cage. Results showed his esophagus scarred from severe gastritis. Dr. Solomon recommended a bland diet and told him to stop drinking. In June, he'd had to have a substitute administer his final exams, because he was in bed for a week after bending over to pick up some laundry and feeling a pop in his upper back. By that night he couldn't move.

He hadn't thought about his back today, either, come to think of it.

"Who'd like another pint?" asked Aaron.

Christine and Tom said sure. Peggy said that since she had to get up early tomorrow to drive to the airport, she'd pass. The Greens had been in England for ten days, and tomorrow she was flying back to their home in the college town of Franklin, Indiana, while Aaron stayed on for the same Elizabethan Studies Program that Tom and Christine were going to take.

Nice of Aaron and Peggy to take Christine and him with them, Tom thought, especially since this was the Greens' last day together for three weeks. They seemed like good people. She was tall, with curly white hair, while he was square-jawed, with a thick neck and laugh lines around his mouth. When Peggy had said something earlier in the day about their belonging to some fundamentalist church, Tom had worried, but both of them appeared healthy, friendly, and free of self-righteousness.

He couldn't remember the last time he and Christine spent time with another couple. Even before Annie's death, they'd isolated themselves. He wondered if both of them hadn't always at some level been ashamed to be in public after their adultery, their having broken up families. Christine occasionally walked with the mother of Nathan's friend Bart, but her only real friend remained Diane in Wyoming. He couldn't name even one friend, only colleagues like Jim Silas and Myles Georgitis, with whom he shared an occasional afterschool cup of coffee. A few members of St. Mark's made overtures of friendship, but whenever he and Christine went to a Christmas or cocktail party at a parishioner's house, they left early, Christine apparently as happy to go home as he was.

Aaron reached over and brushed a beech leaf from Peggy's hair. She smiled at him and winked. Sometime that day they said they'd been married thirty-five years, and Tom could see by their easy, loving relationship that it had been a good thirty-five years. He envied the way Peggy automatically passed Aaron the salt, how they finished each other's sentences. Sometimes Tom and Christine were able to resuscitate the good times—go out to dinner, take in a movie, make love successfully. Other times, they eyed each other warily from behind their respective barricades, as careful with their words as with sticks of dynamite, afraid some careless comment might light the fuse and blow their marriage to pieces.

Tom looked across the table at his wife. In the twilight, Christine's eyes looked the color of the river. How little he knew

1990

her! Once he'd idolized her as a free spirit from the '60s. Later, he'd made her his co-sinner against God. At times, he ignored her. At times he lusted after her. At times he wanted her to mother him. There were qualities about her he loved. When they disagreed, she never said he was wrong, only that she didn't agree with him. Unlike his first wife, she never complained, never raised her voice. She was a great cook. She liked a drink. As long as it didn't involve pornography, she liked sex. On the other hand, she hated to clean up. She left glasses, cups, homework, and magazines wherever she happened to drop them. She had no fashion sense or any interest in buying new clothes. (For example, tonight's faded-blue blouse, patchwork red-and-green skirt, safety-pinned, instead of buttoned.) She had no interest in buying much of anything, for that matter. She never stood up for herself. She never complained when her English Department head at Mount Aronson gave her the shittiest classes in the school. She did whatever Nathan wanted her to do, whenever he wanted her to do it.

What bothered him the most was that Christine no longer had that unconstrained passion for life that she'd had when he first met her. So often she seemed sad, distant, preoccupied, sometimes to the point of forgetting to eat. But he never asked her to tell him what was on her mind, afraid she'd reveal her sorrow for marrying him.

Who was she? He knew now that she'd never been a hippie. Never, despite living on a ranch, been a cowgirl. She was smarter than he was. She'd gone to Vassar, beat him regularly at Scrabble, and could explain theological concepts like the Trinity in a way that made sense: "Water comes in three forms—solid, gas, and liquid—why can't God?" She'd read everything Thomas Merton and Henri Nouwen had written. At the same time, she said she was struggling with God more than ever, and that she envied his experiences in the hospital chapel. As he became more and more disenchanted with the Episcopal Church, she grew more and more adamant about attending Sunday worship, as if she were clinging to the liturgy like a shipwreck victim hangs on to a life preserver.

Somehow, talk around the table turned to family. Peggy Green reached into her purse for her wallet. "Here's a picture of our daughter, Betty," she said, passing it to Christine. "She's the one we've been visiting in London. And behind her picture is one of her older sister, Kathy, with her husband, David. Betty's twenty-one, Kathy's twenty-three."

Tom's stomach knotted. His first drink in three months, so good a few minutes ago, now smelled like cat urine. He watched a punt filled with eight people in the middle of the river. "What beautiful girls!" he heard Christine say. Evidently, the punter's pole was stuck in the river bottom. The punt kept moving, bending the man backward as he continued to hold on to the pole. As the boat pulled away, the man tried to climb the pole, until both man and pole splashed into the river. Since the water rose only to the man's waist, he waded toward shore amid a chorus of laughter from the others on the punt.

"You must have some pictures," Peggy said cheerily to Christine. "Let's see them. How many children did you say you and Tom have?"

From across the table, Christine's eyes searched her husband's. He knew she was wondering whether or not to show Peggy photographs of Annie and Nathan.

He dropped his eyes.

"Come on, Christine. Let's see."

Christine opened her wallet. She showed Peggy a photo of Nathan at about three years old, dressed up as Spiderman, and his latest school picture.

Resentment at his wife for her healthy child spasmed into Tom's throat.

"I think he favors both of you," Peggy said.

No one had ever before suggested Nathan looked like Tom. The alien in his chest pulsated. He turned his attention to the man climbing out of the water on to the dock.

"Cheer up, mate," said a young bloke with a shaved head and a British flag sewed to the seat of his blue jeans. "'appens all the bloody time." He hopped into a punt and poled across the Cam toward the stranded punt, now on the other shore under some willow trees.

When Tom looked back at Peggy and Christine, Christine was gazing at him sadly. She folded up her wallet and put it away.

He thought of the line from *The Great Gatsby*: "*So we beat on, boats against the current, borne back ceaselessly into the past.*"

A week later, at around 10:30 at night, Tom leaned against a wrought-iron fence in front of a wall of Cotswold stone, around the corner from Trinity College, trying to ease the pain running from his back down into his hips. He was full of beer, and needed a bathroom. From time to time he peered through the panes of the red phone booth at Christine, switching the receiver from one ear to the other.

This was the third night in a row she'd called Wyoming, trying to talk to Nathan. According to his father, the boy was always out, having a great time with friends. Tom couldn't understand why this information should upset his wife. It was afternoon there. Why wouldn't Nathan be out? Tom walked into the narrow cobblestone street and started pacing. She'd seen the kid a month ago. Why couldn't they just go back to their room?

Finally, Christine pushed open the door of the phone booth and stepped out. Shadows fell across her skirt and blouse. "Nathan's at work. My old snake-hunting buddy Wanda got him a job at a wild animal farm. He didn't even tell me."

Tom started down the street. "You haven't talked to him for a week," he said, over his shoulder. "How could he tell you? Come on, I really need to get back to the room."

She caught up with him. "At least Zack could have told me Nathan had a job. I've talked with him every day this week."

Guilt supplanted Tom's irritation. It made sense (to him) that Zack was still angry at Christine for leaving (because of him), and that if she hadn't left (because of him), she'd be out in

Wyoming, taking Nathan to work, or picking him up, or both.

A corrosive mix of resentment at Christine any time she even mentioned Nathan, along with guilt at the thought that, if not for him, she'd be with her son, ate its way through the next week of lectures, plays, and pub crawls. One minute he felt as if he was clutching at his wife, the next minute doing his best to drive her away. The following weekend, on a guided tour of Bath, Salisbury, and Stonehenge, he did both, urging her to pose provocatively next to a fountain or a stone pillar, petulant when all she could produce was a thin smile. At Salisbury Cathedral, Tom became caught up in their tour guide's harried efforts to keep them on "shed-yule," snapping pictures as fast as he could take them. When he opened the camera to replace the film, he saw that he'd forgotten to rewind it.

"Damn it! I think I've lost the entire roll," he said, sinking onto a stiff wooden chair close to the main transept. "Shit, shit, shit!"

He realized Christine was no longer with him. *She's disgusted with me and I can't blame her.* He closed the back of the camera and rewound the film. Around him, tourists circled their tour guides. Cameras clicked and whirred. Tom hated tourists, had always hated tourists, and here he was, sitting here with a camera on his lap, one more goddamned tourist.

He sat, shifting uncomfortably as the straight back of the chair pressed into his spine. He saw Christine walking toward him. "Hold out your hand." She placed a small box in his palm. "I went into the gift shop and this said, 'Buy me and give me to your husband.'"

Tom gawked at her. A gift was the last thing he expected. Opening the box revealed a block of light gray stone.

"It's from the spire of the cathedral," she said. She sat down beside him. "They cut up and sell the stones they've had to replace."

The surface of the stone was surprisingly soft. Almost powdery. Limestone. Probably two inches wide and four inches long. Tom took the stone out of its box. Turning it over in his hand, he saw a folded piece of paper taped to the back that read "Certificate of Authority: Spire Stone Reg. No. 1460."

1990

Christine watched him with an embarrassed smile. "Do you mind that I overspent our budget? It's pretty useless."

Tom put the stone back in the box and placed it in the camera bag. He took her hand. "I love it. Thank you." He leaned over and kissed her. "I've been an idiot lately. I'm sorry."

Her smile expanded. Her eyes deepened to that lovely violet. "I'm going to wander," she said. "Do you want to come with me?"

Hand-in-hand they explored the cathedral. Seeing a docent pointing to a circle of marble pillars supporting the vast ceiling, they listened as the woman explained how the great weight of the spire—some 6400 tons—had caused the original pillars to bend. She directed their eyes upward, to where the pillars were reinforced. Tom looked up at the stone arches soaring overhead, lit by the sunlight coming through the stained, lancet windows. How could something so massive be built to allow so much space? Every direction he turned was like gazing down a tunnel, but unlike the dark and narrow tunnels in his dreams, these were lofty and bright. Ethereal.

Later that day, while Christine wandered around an open courtyard called a garth, Tom stood in the chapter house of the cathedral, an octagonal building that served as the meeting place of the cathedral clergy, who began their assemblies by reading a chapter from the Bible. Eight stone walls carved with Gothic arches surrounded him. Intricately carved figures stood in the spandrels over the arches.

Tom sat down on a stone seat built into the wall and savored the silence. He studied the statues. Once he identified Adam and Eve standing by the Tree of Knowledge of Good and Evil with the serpent wrapped around it, he was able to pick out other Old Testament heroes—Cain and Abel, Noah, Abraham, Isaac, Jacob, Joseph, Moses—figures from ancient stories depicted by stones even older, both story and statue created by a confluence of spirit, sweat, intellect, and prayer. He sensed himself taken up into these stories, imagined himself an Old Testament figure, Jephthah, perhaps, the Jewish general who sacrificed his daughter and only child because he swore to God that if granted victory over his enemies, he'd sacrifice the first to greet him after his return. But instead of becoming guilty and angry, Tom experienced the same strange peace he'd enjoyed in the hospital chapel the previous March.

After sitting in silence a while longer, he exited the chapter house through two Gothic arches, out to a covered walkway running around the garth. Sitting on a stone bench, he opened his camera bag, but instead of the camera, he pulled out his piece of Salisbury Cathedral. He turned the stone over and over in his hands, finding himself wanting to carve something into the smooth, clear surface. He pulled off the piece of paper taped to the back, unfolded it, and read the Certificate of Authenticity:

> Centuries of storm and frost, and, more recently, the deadly corrosion of acid rain, have eaten the medieval stonework away. This fragment is a genuine piece of the original masonry removed from the spire, to be replaced with fresh stone from the same quarry.

Tom stepped to the edge of the enclosed courtyard and shaded his eyes as he looked up to the spire of Salisbury Cathedral, rising into a cloudless blue sky. When their tour had arrived at the cathedral a few hours earlier, he'd been disappointed to see its famous spire encased in scaffolding. Now he wondered if the fact that this ancient stone monument to God and the human spirit needed to be—and could be—periodically repaired from damage might offer hope that he might rebuild his *own* life.

Across the garth, Christine stood in the sunshine next to the cathedral, enveloped in light and patting the stones.

Back in Cambridge, Ian, a member of their class on Shakespeare's world, invited some of them to a wine and cheese party in his room overlooking Trinity Quad. After an hour or so of a little cheese and a lot of wine, a woman named Sherrill started to go around the room, telling the others about themselves.

"You used to be a gymnast," she told the young woman who taught on an Indian reservation in Arizona. Michelle said yes, both in high school and college.

Under penciled eyebrows and a narrow nose, Sherrill smiled. "You've got that straight posture and bounce." She turned to Ian. "You write poetry. I can see it in your eyes."

The woman irritated Tom. "You can also see it in all those magazines he's left on the coffee table with his poetry in them," he whispered to Christine.

Sherrill came their way. "And you two met in a bar, right? You've each been married before, and I'm guessing you've been married to each other for a couple of years."

Tom's face flushed. "What makes you say that?" he said, trying to smile.

"Oh, you two still act like newlyweds. And where else do people our age meet? Hey, I met my second husband in a bar." Dramatic pause. "And that's where I left him, too, three years later, with some broad sitting on his lap, nibbling his ear." Her voice went up an octave: "'Oh,' she said, 'I didn't know Jimmy was married.'

"'Not for much longer, Sweetie!' I said."

Christine and Tom left the party shortly afterwards, just about the time Sherrill produced a camcorder and suggested they all tell it how they lost their virginity. They walked in silence across the Quad. Tom's back throbbed. As their feet crunched the crushed-stone walkway, he brooded over Sherrill's turning their marriage into a dirty joke.

Christine took his hand. A streak of evening sun lit up Trinity's clock tower, which Tom recognized from the movie *Chariots of Fire*. They wandered through Queens' Gate, under the statue of Queen Elizabeth I, and out to Trinity Lane. Although Tom wasn't sure where they were going, they turned left. Bicycles lined the narrow, winding sidewalk, so they walked in the cobblestone street.

"So where are you?" he asked Christine. "I'm still back at Ian's, wringing Sherrill's neck."

"I'm wondering what Nathan is doing." Christine walked in shadow and her voice seemed far away. "Sorry."

Behind him, Tom heard what was becoming a familiar ring. A bicyclist sped past them. "What are you sorry about?"

"Because I know it's hard for you whenever I talk about Nathan. But…" She hesitated before churning the words out: "…but I can't help it. I miss my son, and I'm tired of trying to keep quiet because I'm afraid of upsetting you. I know it's not the same loss you feel, but you need to understand that I miss my kid and it's tough."

Twilight through a narrow alley briefly lit up her face. Her eyes were moist. "I'm sorry, I can't always keep it bottled up the way you can." She reached into her pocketbook for a tissue.

"I'm sorry, too." His voice sounded weak, his words trite, probably because they weren't true. He wanted to commiserate with her. Sharing her sorrow would bring them closer together. But he couldn't. Not honestly. Not when the quagmire of his own grief sucked down any attempt to understand her suffering.

A tall man in a Greek fisherman's cap and tweed jacket walked toward them up the sidewalk. After he passed, Christine said, "I've never been good at confrontation, and I've never really known who I am." Her voice sounded far away. "I was my parents' only child. They protected me…and sheltered me." Her hands made circles as she searched for words. "I thought I was being independent when I married Zack, but I think I was actually using him to escape. After a while, I saw how he belittled everything I did. I couldn't do anything to please him. You…you made me feel loved and important. I could see myself through your eyes and what I saw excited me."

That Christine had never seen herself the way Tom had surprised him. One more indication of how little he knew her. Her voice grew stronger. "I haven't wanted to lose that love, that excitement, so I haven't told you how hard the last year has been—to watch you shut yourself off from me, from Nathan. I know what happened to you is the worst thing that can happen to someone, and I've thought one broken person in the family is enough."

She walked faster. "But Tom, it's not getting any better. The first months I could understand. But I can't keep going like this. Occasionally you come up for air and I know you love me, but then you dive back down into yourself again. It's what you used to say about your mother: I never know what you're really thinking."

Another ring. Another bicyclist. "Maybe the one good thing that's happened over the last two years is that I've had time to try to figure out who I am," she said. "And one of the things I am is a mother, and I'm not going to try to hide that anymore." She stopped and took his hand. "But I'm also your wife—and I want to stay being your wife."

The steel-blue flame in her eyes burned away Tom's fears that she regretted breaking up her marriage, his doubts about their future together. Just before the corner of Trinity Lane and Trinity Street, they stepped onto the sidewalk and embraced. Christine's body leaned into his, her hair soft upon his cheek. They kissed. He rested against a wall and felt the stones, still warm from the sun, on his back.

They walked on, turning right to Trinity Street, with its bookstores and clothing stores, and on to King's Parade running in front of King's College Chapel. Tom felt light on his feet, his back strong and straight.

"Tell me why you're so angry at Sherrill," Christine said. "I feel sorry for her. She struck me as a lonely, bitter woman."

Tom stopped under a crimson awning. Through the window, he inspected a green- and-white scarf that must have been six feet long. He didn't want to admit that Sherrill had shoved him back into the mire of old guilt, didn't want to set his pain up against his wife's. Christine took his arm. Finally, he said, "She made our life together sound cheap."

"Why, because she said we met in a bar?"

"Well, we did."

Christine moved directly in front of him. "No," she said. "We didn't meet in a bar. We met three days earlier, in the back of a shuttle van coming back from Macy's. You'd just bought a

Princeton sweatshirt for Annie, and you talked about how much you enjoyed reading A.P. essays because, for the first time in your teaching career, people treated you with respect. You were obviously crazy about your daughter and I'd never heard anyone so proud of being a teacher."

Tom shrugged his shoulders while his heart danced. "I keep forgetting that."

Christine pointed to herself. "Well, I haven't forgotten. You affirmed what I was doing—as a parent, as a teacher—and you made me believe I was important." She put both hands on his arms. "We didn't 'meet in a bar.' If you'll remember, we'd eaten dinner at the same table at Rider College and later we all went into Princeton together."

He realized that whenever he thought of meeting Christine, he always left out their ride together in the van. Before Annie's death, he liked the idea of two people meeting and falling in love the same night. After his daughter's death, thinking of that night in the bar enhanced his sense that he and Christine had sold, if not their souls, then their children's lives to the Devil.

Sherrill hadn't cheapened their story. He had.

Twilight turned to dusk. They walked down a cobblestone landing toward the river. After leaving the lights of King's Parade, he could see stars in the evening sky. Christine's voice said softly, "Sherrill did say we still acted like newlyweds. That's pretty good, considering what we've been through."

He'd forgotten that, too. Why did he only remember the shitty stuff? The stuff that fed his shame?

Out of the night, they heard singing. As they neared the River Cam, Tom could make out voices rising over the water:

"Gloria Patri et Filio, et Spiritui Sancto. Alleluia, alleluia."

They strolled out onto the stone bridge lined with people. Tiny lights twinkled against the trees on the other bank and reflected off the water. Tom and Christine were surrounded by light and song:

1990

"Magnalia Dei, alleluia"

Gazing over the heads of the people by the balustrade, he saw a boys' choir standing on punts, their candles flickering against their white robes, the entire scene reflected beneath them in the water.

"Repleti sunt omnes Spiritui Sancto"

As Christine and Tom stood with their arms around each other, he thought again of how Sherrill had talked about their marriage. Hers was a logical judgment. Perhaps he and Christine hadn't met in a bar, but they'd danced in a bar, they'd gotten drunk together in a bar, and they returned from a bar to kiss and fondle like tenth graders. The next time they met, they shacked up in a hotel. Christine moved two thousand miles to live with a man she barely knew. By rights, she should have moved back to Wyoming after a month. If not then, certainly after Annie died. Or now, with Nathan talking about moving back to live with his father. There was no plausible reason their marriage should last. But here they stood with their arms around each other, listening to a choir of kids praising God.

Could this be their real story?

"Gloria Patri et Filio, et Spiritui Sancto. Alleluia, alleluia"

The music ended, the choir blew out their candles, and like spirits, the boys drifted away. As Tom and Christine walked back to their room at Jesus College holding hands, Tom revised the past. It wasn't his divorce and remarriage that had brought about Annie's cancer. It was his sick first marriage that had produced a sick child. During her parents' "discussions," Annie had become expert at pleasing both Martha and him, agreeing with her mother while making him feel as if submission to her was something she and he had to do together. But at what cost? What did that kind of stress do to a kid? Clearly, his daughter's cancer must have been slowly advancing as his marriage became increasingly malignant. Didn't being pulled in two directions affect cells, cause them to mutate, turn into cancer? If he'd ended the marriage two years earlier, that cyst on the back of his daughter's head might not have formed.

Christine was blameless, but Annie's death was still his fault.

Every morning at breakfast before class, Tom watched Aaron Green pour a spicy British ketchup called Daddy's Sauce over his fried eggs and tomatoes. Every day, Aaron sat on one side of Tom as their class discussed Elizabethan music, art, and architecture. Several evenings a week, Aaron, Tom, and Christine wandered the pubs of Cambridge with the same group of summer students/winter teachers in search of the perfect pint. And every day reminded Tom of what he and Christine had not told their friend.

Two nights before their course ended, the three of them sat eating fish and chips on a wooden bench in Christ's Pieces, a green between Emmanuel Road and Jesus Lane.

"Aaron," Tom said, "you remember that night when Peggy was showing us pictures of your daughters?"

"When the guy fell into the water," Aaron said.

"Right. And Christine showed you folks pictures of Nathan, and Peggy said he looked like both of us?" Tom's leg started bouncing. "Well, we should have told you. We're a second marriage, and I'm not Nathan's father."

Aaron's eyes wandered to the other side of the green, to a group of men lawn bowling in the extended British twilight. "Oh. Okay."

"And the other picture we didn't show you was of my daughter, Annie. She died at eighteen, just over two years ago." He stammered out the story of Annie's diagnosis and death.

Aaron dropped his head and stared at the ground. "Oh, God, I'm sorry."

"We've felt bad ever since that night that we misled you," said

Christine. "But we're still learning how to talk about Annie, and your long and happy marriage…I don't know, intimidated us… That and your two lovely daughters."

Aaron's eyes returned to the green and the bowlers. He cleared his throat, started to say something, stopped, and cleared his throat again.

We've probably offended him.

"You knew we'd been in London visiting our daughter Betty before we met you, right?" Aaron said.

"Yes," Tom and Christine said, almost in unison.

"Well, the reason for our visit was because Betty and her husband are getting divorced after only six months of marriage. She says that she's still in love with her high school boyfriend. That two months ago, when she and her husband came back to the states to visit us, she met with him and realized she'd made a mistake. I'm going to London after our class ends to bring her back with me to Indiana."

"Oh, Aaron!" Christine put her hand on his shoulder.

"Our religion says divorce is a sin," Aaron said. He studied the grass under his feet, speaking more to himself than to them, Tom thought. "Peggy and I keep asking ourselves what we did wrong—whether we've damned our daughter." Aaron finished his fish and chips and wiped his hands on the greasy newspaper. "It's hard not to feel responsible, isn't it? But what you two have been through—it puts things in perspective. God, I'm sorry!"

We've all got our secrets, don't we? Our own losses, private griefs, struggles with God.

The three of them stood and awkwardly hugged each other. They went to their favorite pub, where they laughed loudly as they told stories about their time in Cambridge. Their sour-faced director and their clock-watching tour guide. The mother traveling with her daughter, obviously in search of a husband for her. Sherrill, whom Tom turned into a comic memory.

As they left the pub, they met a bearded, bald-headed elf of a man staggering toward the door. "What d'you call a deer with no eyes?" he asked them in a thick voice.

"I don't know. What?" Aaron said.

"No-eyed deer! No idea, get it?" the little man's laugh turned into a cough. "And what do you call a deer with no eyes and no legs?"

Aaron chuckled and rolled his eyes. "Okay, I'll bite. What?"

"Still no idea!" He slapped Aaron on the back and spit onto the sidewalk. He lit a cigarette and reeled into the pub, leaving Tom waving away at a cloud of smoke.

Later, as Christine, Aaron, and Tom wove their way past King's College Chapel, its four phallic spires rising in the night sky, Tom thought of Salisbury Cathedral, its tower encased in scaffolding, old stones replaced with newly carved ones, his new plans for carving out the rest of his life.

And realized he had no idea how to go about it.

Chapter Thirteen
1990–1991

Later that year, Tom still had no idea. He wanted to travel more—no, he wanted to settle down and buy a house. He wanted to return to school, get his PhD and teach at the University of Maine—no, he wanted to resign from teaching and write The Great American Novel. He wanted to take more of a role at St. Mark's—no, he wanted to leave St. Mark's and become a Quaker.

Or maybe a Buddhist. When Rashmi, Tom's exchange student from Sri Lanka, wrote a paper on her Buddhist beliefs, he was intrigued, especially the part about meditation. Which may have been why in December he decided to go to a program called "Meditation as Part of the Christian Tradition," held at St. Mark's on the first Sunday evening in Advent. He asked Christine if she'd like to come along. "Sure," she said. "Nathan has youth group at church and we can all travel together."

Their speaker was Jonathan Bennett, head of something called the Maine Chapter of Contemplative Outreach. Tom had pictured an authority on meditation as ascetic looking, perhaps dressed in monk's robes. Instead, Bennett (as he told them he liked to be called) and his ponytail arrived in faded jeans, gum rubber boots, a Red Sox cap, and an old checkered jacket that smelled of wood smoke. As he sat on the dais, his legs crossed, and leaned back against the rosewood altar, he looked like one of Jordan Mills's homeless, seeking warmth in the church sanctuary.

Although the other ten people in the pews with him and Christine looked familiar, Tom didn't know one name. Evidence, he thought, of his tangential, troubled relationship with the Episcopal Church. He still attended services at St. Mark's because of Christine and Nathan, but he remained disillusioned with the liturgy, and lately he'd been struggling with the church's various "seasons." Take Advent, for example. These four weeks before Christmas were supposed to be a time of hope as you waited for the birth of Christ—"the Prince of Peace," Father Curtis called him this morning—but it was also a time of penitence as you prepared for God's final judgment of your sins, for which you might be eternally damned. On one hand, Isaiah says the day is coming when swords will be beaten into plowshares. On the other hand, he warns this is the day when the Lord will make the earth a desolation, destroying the stars and the sun and the moon. Christine could fit it all together, but for Tom, Advent was a contradiction, another example of Camus's absurd world.

Thinking about contradictions, he realized that their speaker's voice—lilting and clear (*Is he Irish?*), just loud enough to make you need to pay attention—belied his appearance. Bennett began by describing meditation as one of several kinds of praying, along with repeating traditional prayers, singing hymns, and sitting with icons, and said that, until lately, Christians had largely ignored meditation as a way to become closer to God.

Tom took out his notebook. Because the intellect often gets in the way of prayer, Bennett said, the goal of meditation is to "let go of the head." He gazed at the ceiling fan and spoke of various techniques different religions use to help practitioners remove themselves from their thoughts. Eastern practices, he said, focus on the breath or the belly, while some Western practices concentrate upon a word or a phrase, a "mantra" which one repeats over and over to oneself. Bennett, however, believed that "centering prayer," which he called "receptive prayer as opposed to concentrative prayer like the others," is closest to the early Christian tradition.

"Instead of concentrating our efforts on our breath or a word," he said, briefly taking off his cap and running his fingers through graying-brown hair that needed to be washed, "we in centering prayer try to open ourselves up—become receptive—to God."

Tom wrote furiously, trying to copy his words down. Bennett scratched what looked like a three-days' growth of beard. "While centering prayer suggests you find a simple word, such as 'Abba,' 'God,' or 'Love' to signify your intention to surrender to God," he said, "you don't focus on the word, but merely use it as a pointer, away from all the thoughts which will rush into your head." He leaned back on his hands and crossed his ankles. "You simply sit, relax, and watch those thoughts pass by. It's as if you're sitting on the bank of a river, watching boats drift by. When you find yourself on board one of those boats—in other words, caught up in thought—use your sacred word to hop off the boat and get back on the bank."

Bennett sat up, slid off his rubber boots, and somehow folded his legs under the rest of him. "Okay, let's try it for twenty minutes."

Now wait a minute, chum! Tom had come to learn about meditation, not actually do it. He clasped his hands. Rubbed his thumbs together. Couldn't the guy at least limit it to five, maybe ten minutes?

He caught Christine's eye. She grinned, raised one eyebrow, settled back in her seat, and closed her eyes. Too embarrassed to leave, Tom closed his eyes and tried to figure out what to do with his hands, finally folding them in his lap. He felt like a fool for sitting in a dimly lit church—no lighted candles, the stained-glass windows inky—that must have been about the same temperature as a barn, trying to avoid what he'd spent over twenty-five years teaching kids to do: think. Searching his mind for a word to use, he thought of a movie he'd seen recently in which people sat around a candle, droning "Om." He stifled a snicker. His father's voice, slurred from Old Crow, muttered in his ear, "What kind of goddamned foolishness is this? I always knew you were an idiot." His old basketball teammates sneered at him for contemplating his navel with this guy, who looked as if he should be working the clam flats of Washington County. *This isn't me.*

But what about those Saturdays at the First Congregational Church when he was a kid helping his father, and the enjoyment of being alone in the empty sanctuary? What about all those solitary hours playing basketball in the back yard? What about the hours he sat on a rock in the middle of a burned-out forest, silently beholding the Grand Tetons? All the cathedrals in England he'd visited the previous summer—sitting with Christine on wooden pews surrounded by elaborately carved stones, never thinking about theology or God, most of the time just sitting, cradled by the silence? What about the chapel at the hospital? *Maybe I've been meditating all my life.*

As these thoughts kept surfacing, Tom found he was saying to himself his word from the chapel: "Help." Gradually, explosions of sparkling lights replaced the thoughts. The twenty minutes ended far more quickly than he'd expected, leaving him drained, but with a strange sense of satisfaction, almost like coming home after a good day's work.

Bennett unfolded his legs, slid into his rubber boots, and smiled. His eyes twinkled. "So if this is a practice—that's the word Buddhists use, and I think it's a good word—you'd like to continue, I'd suggest you form a group and set up a regular time to get together. Meditation seems like a solitary activity, but it works best when done together." He rose from the dais. "Twice a month works pretty well. I can recommend some books for you to read, so that you spend your time in both silence and discussion."

A woman, probably in her late seventies, with laugh lines incised around her mouth said, "I'll be happy to host a group at my house." She winked. "Just don't expect me to feed everybody."

Tom looked over at Christine, who shrugged her shoulders. "Okay," Tom said. He glanced again at Christine, who nodded. "You've got two takers."

1990–1991

The following March, Tom sat in the living room of a farmhouse on Goose Island, Maine with Bennett and fourteen strangers he wasn't sure he was going to like, drying off from walking from the ferry a quarter of a mile through the rain now hitting the windows, and nursing an especially bad back. They were gathered for an overnight retreat, one Bennett had titled "Resurrection into the Spirit."

"We're going to spend the next twenty-four hours meditating, talking about centering prayer and resurrection, and if the weather clears, walking around the island," Bennett said. He sat on the hearth in front of a blazing fire. Same rubber boots. Same Red Sox cap. Steam rose from his clothes, which must have been soaked from when he helped tie up the ferry they'd come over on a half-hour earlier. He reached over for another stick of wood. "It's also okay just to read or catch up on your sleep."

As Bennett talked about where the bathrooms were and the food available in the kitchen, Tom sat in a chair wedged between a china cabinet and a bookcase in the furthest corner of the room, and listened to the windows rattle. He guessed the other participants were, like him, between forty and fifty-five. They sat on chairs, a sofa, and the floor. Tom was one of five men, all bearded. Two women held hands. One woman knelt on the floor, resting her broad butt on a small wooden bench she'd brought. A man and a woman sat on round pillows. A thin woman in maroon sweat pants ran a chain of wooden beads between her thumb and index finger. Another woman with white hair sat knitting. Many people had ruddy complexions. On the ferry ride over, Tom heard one man telling another about a barn he was building. He shifted on his chair as the ache in his back—he seemed to have pulled something getting out of the car at the ferry terminal—reminded him that a good day's work on a farm would send him to the hospital, if not the funeral parlor.

He was self-conscious and apprehensive. He'd never been on a spiritual retreat before. But he was tired of trudging in circles through the desolate swamp of his anger, guilt, and sorrow. If he wanted to learn to work with his grief—shape it somehow, as he'd decided in England he should do—he needed to be able to confront his daughter's death without turning away or numbing himself with booze. Before coming here, he'd dug through the upstairs closet and found all the sympathy cards from two years earlier, as well as stuff he'd written during Annie's illness and death. He put everything, along with the scrapbook he'd made about his daughter the previous year, into a canvas tote bag and brought it with him.

"We'll begin with a twenty-minute meditation, "Bennett said. "After which, we'll break for a silent supper, followed by some socializing. Tomorrow morning, I'll do some talking about how meditation can resurrect the spirit."

Bennett picked up two circular metal discs connected by a leather string. "Let's begin." He struck them together in a piercing chime.

Tom watched the others shut their eyes, fold their hands, and straighten their backs. He tried to imitate them, but all the sacred words in the world couldn't slow down his mind. He thought of the ferry ride over, knowing his daughter would have loved to be on deck in the rain. The dark, spruce-covered island rising out of the fog, which reminded him of walks through spruce forests with Annie on Sunday afternoons. He wished that Christine and Nathan had somehow been able to walk with them during those years. His wife and stepson were driving the following day to Belmont to spend the weekend with her parents. Should he be with them? Was this whole meditation thing a direction he wanted to be going, or a colossal waste of time?

As far as he could tell, nothing had changed since he started meditating. His back still ached and he was still often sick. In fact, he'd spent much of last week on the couch with a bladder infection. He still often woke up at 3 a.m., worrying that he didn't have enough for his classes to do, or that he had lunch duty and needed to nab that kid who always left a mess on his table. While he didn't have the constant bitterness of the previous year, he sometimes lost his temper in angry spasms that frightened him.

His hands clenched. A few weeks earlier, one of Tom's colleagues had to leave school to take her child to the doctor's, and he'd ended up covering her study hall. Of all the goddamn luck, there was Michael Keith, his black-and-purple baseball cap pulled down over his eyes, talking nonstop, jabbing his pencil repeatedly into his desk, throwing spitballs, sliding out of his seat, and wandering around the room. When he asked for a pass to the bathroom, Tom gave it to him gladly, but twenty minutes later, when the little bastard hadn't returned, Tom was furious. When the kid finally sauntered into the room, Tom told him he'd written a note to his teacher about his behavior.

"Well, I had to take a shit!" The room brayed in laughter.

Tom followed him back to his seat. Michael sat down and smiled at Tom out of a face of uncooked bread dough, before turning to talk to a skinny kid with a fuzzy mustache.

"Listen, young man…," Tom said. Michael kept talking.

Before he knew what he was doing, Tom grabbed Michael's shirt with one hand and doubled up the other into a fist. For a moment, he was Red Bailey, about to break Freddy Gallant's nose. Thank God, the bell rang right then, and he stopped himself.

He saw again the fear on Michael's face and felt himself at thirteen, trembling as Red Bailey pummeled Freddy Gallant. Maybe Red wasn't such a great influence after all. His former coach had, he remembered now, died of a heart attack at sixty-one, five years after being fired for drinking on the job. Was that the guy Tom wanted to emulate? Come to think of it, what was he doing moving from English beer to Irish whiskey?

Tom unclenched his fists and cupped his hands in his lap. His heart was racing, and he tried to regulate his breathing—listen to the old house creaking in the wind, the rain, the crackle of the fire, the people shifting in their chairs. Dimly at first, he began to recognize that, even though outwardly his life appeared the same, there had been interior changes. He had never dreamed so often or so vividly. As usual since Annie's death, most of his dreams involved stones. Traveling through stones—sometimes sailing, sometimes walking, sometimes crawling. The previous week he'd had a series of dreams in which stones turned to dust. Once he watched a child pound a rock with a hammer, and once he dreamed of crawling along a walkway of slate, some pieces square, some only pieces in half-squares or triangles. In a few places, dusty squares indicated where the slate had been.

Listening to the farmhouse on Goose Island reminded him of the sounds in the duplex apartment during his morning meditation time with Christine. These days they rose at 5 a.m. to sit in a prayer corner they'd set up in their bedroom. No matter how preoccupied and apprehensive about school he was during that time of meditation, he relished the moment at the end when he and his wife stood and embraced. Even though they'd spent the night snuggled together, that instant their bodies met after twenty minutes apart helped him savor their love as once again new and unspotted and full of possibility, the uncarved block of Salisbury stone waiting to be shaped.

Meditation also seemed to have revived Tom's enjoyment of St. Mark's Sunday service. No longer did he spend his time trying to analyze how much in the *Book of Common Prayer* he actually believed. The liturgy—so repetitious, so irritating just months earlier—now allowed him to sink into himself, the words and the music and the candles and light through the stained-glass windows washing over him. Thanks to the meditation group that Tom and Christine had joined, they were finally getting to know some people in church. Marian, the woman who opened her lovely home for the group to meet in, was a long-time member of St. Mark's. A former elementary school teacher who seemed to be friends with everybody, she introduced Christine and Tom to a spectrum of people, many of whom belied Tom's stereotype of Episcopalians as supercilious doctors, lawyers, and retired CEOs. Last week, the meditation group ended their twenty minutes of silence with a party for their hostess's eightieth birthday.

1990-1991

Tom's thoughts continue to explode like fireworks: The shape of Christine's body under her night gown. Michael Keith's smirk. Freddy Gallant's nose exploding in blood. Annie at five years old, sitting in one of the desks in his classroom on Saturday morning. Annie at eighteen, IV tubes pinning her to a hospital bed. His mother's congested voice, "I am fine. How are you?" The senselessness of sitting here in a farmhouse with a gaggle of homespun yuppies near the anniversary of his daughter's death. Every so often, he'd go back to his sacred word—he'd settled on "ephphatha," meaning "be opened"—or listen to the rain on the roof, or the wind blowing through the spruce outside the window.

As if projected on his eyelids, Tom saw a pair of bright orange lips. Nothing else, just lips. Gigantic, cartoon like. The lips opened. They gaped wider and wider until he was staring down an orange throat. The mouth grew teeth, which turned into tentacles, reaching out as if to strangle him. He wanted to get up—at least open his eyes—but he sat petrified. Realizing his helplessness, he relaxed. At that moment, the tentacles lifted, extended over him, and grew into a bright red flower. As he watched in wonder, petals from the flower fell around him in a display of pink lights.

Bennett chimed the gongs. Tom wondered if he'd fallen asleep. The images—the lips, the teeth, the tentacles, the flower—were dream-like, but their clarity and his reaction to them—sweating, his stomach in knots—went beyond any dream he'd ever had.

At supper, they sat at two tables covered in red-and-white-checkered plastic, eating soup and bread in silence, while Bennett read to them from Meister Eckhart, a fourteenth-century mystic. Something about Christ's resurrection being symbolic of God's love flowing further into a new creation. Tom couldn't pay attention. He kept staring at his soup, which was the same orange color as those lips in his vision.

After supper, they went around the tables and introduced themselves. Everyone else had apparently moved to Maine from Massachusetts, New York, New Jersey, or Pennsylvania. At least two people there—the couple on the round pillows—worked as therapists of some kind, and a man with a thick beard that reached below his chest attended Bangor Theological Seminary. Tom heard stories of divorces, career changes, religious awakenings, and the death of the husband of a small woman with gray-and-brown hair and kind eyes, dressed in a beige blouse and slacks, a gold cross around her neck.

As the buxom woman who'd sat on the wooden prayer bench talked of her desire to leave her job as a lawyer and become a middle school teacher, Tom considered what he would say. Here was his chance to talk about Annie, about deciding to prepare for the second anniversary of her death by attending this retreat. But glancing at the woman in beige, all he could think was that anything he said would sound like "my story is sadder than your story." So when all the eyes in the room turned to him, he simply said that he guessed he was the only Maine native there.

Later that night, he closed the door to his attic bedroom on the fourth floor, turned on the overhead light, and studied the navy-blue tote bag on the bureau. He carried it to the narrow bed under the eves. He changed into his sweats and climbed into bed, painfully propping himself against the pine wall. He contemplated for a moment the small window and the darkness outside, and reached into the bag.

He read letters of condolence from old classmates and former students and colleagues. He read a note from Craig, his former principal at Webber High:

> I do want you to know that last year Annie and I chatted at an AIDS conference in Bangor. She spoke of you in such loving and proud terms. She was so happy that you were doing well. I was impressed with the empathetic, yet realistic chord she struck with me as we talked about the young man who had spoken (as an AIDS victim) earlier in the day.

Tom wondered how Craig was doing, and thought of the last time he'd driven by his old high school. October, two and a

1990-1991

half years earlier, part of the last trip he and Christine had made to Webber, when Annie still thought she could go to art school in January. He searched the bag for a cloth-covered journal with a Chinese symbol for creativity on the cover, a gift from a former student. He flipped the pages. *Okay, here it is.* He began reading:

A strange and exhausting evening…

Tom and Christine had picked Annie up at her mother's and taken her with them for two nights at a local motel. The weekend had gone well, with a drive to a beach and past the school and through the October foliage, but the next night, when they went to dinner at Annie's favorite restaurant, she had grown depressed. Tom wondered now if she hadn't been in pain. She hadn't eaten much of anything, and they'd left early.

As soon as we got back to the motel, Annie slept on the bed beside us for over an hour…

His daughter had complained earlier that day about not having slept for weeks, but when they returned from dinner, she conked out immediately, waking up briefly at one point to say, "I feel safe for the first time since they told me I had cancer. Don't ask me what I mean, it's just true." *What had she meant?* He'd like to think she was telling him she thought of him as some wizard protecting her from evil, but probably, after being housebound for weeks, she was simply happy to get out.

Annie had lain on the bed in the motel room, red socks to match her bandanna. Tom thought she'd gone back to sleep, so he turned on the World Series, just in time to watch Kirk Gibson of the Los Angeles Dodgers, who hadn't been expected to play because of a severely strained hamstring in one leg and a bad knee in the other, hit a dramatic pinch-hit home run to win the game in the ninth inning. As Gibson limped around the bases, and one talking head after another extolled his courage in the face of pain, he heard Annie say to Christine, "I know this cancer might—probably will—kill me, but hopefully not for years. I need to make the most of whatever time I've got left."

Those assholes on TV had no idea what courage is.

In the silence of his fourth-floor bedroom, tears stained his journal. He hadn't cried all year. The tears felt cleansing, like soft rain after dry weather. He put Craig's card in his journal to mark his place, turned out the light, and burrowed into bed.

He dreamed he was flying in an old biplane over some black rocks, trying to get from the plane to a similar plane directly overhead. Was there something wrong with his plane? Tom had no idea why he wanted to leave it, but when a ladder dropped from the plane above him, he started to climb it, apparently forgetting that he was afraid of heights. He clambered up to the second plane and, as he hoisted himself over the side, an old man dressed in a leather jacket and cap—your quintessential World War I flying ace—was waiting for him. "Welcome aboard," the man said.

The next morning, Tom wondered if the old man in his dream represented God. Was he climbing some sort of spiritual ladder? It felt more like being in a free fall. He looked around the tiny bedroom and out the small window at the foot of bed, where he could see nothing but white fog. He peered at his watch. In an hour, Christine and Nathan would drive down the turnpike to Massachusetts. He'd asked her to come on retreat with him, but ever since Nathan and his father had started making arrangements for the boy to attend Kidron Springs High School, Christine couldn't bear leaving her son, even for a weekend. Tom thought that she needed to loosen the apron strings. Besides, the boy wasn't leaving for another year. Tom had urged her to find a therapist to help her deal with Nathan's coming departure. Still, he felt guilty for not going with them this morning. Ever since he and Christine had started to resuscitate their marriage last summer, he'd been afraid of falling back into his old isolation. He imagined a tank truck filled with flammable gas, careening out of the fog and across the median strip. Crashing into her car. Screams. Both vehicles exploding in balls of flame. Blackened bodies smoldering in the wreckage. Smell of charred flesh and gasoline. A damp chill entwined his arms and legs.

He dressed and went down to the living room. No fire in the fireplace this morning, just the smell of dead ashes that made him shiver with fear more than with cold. The two women who'd held hands yesterday sat beside each other on the couch, sharing a wool blanket. The widow with the gold chain wore a red sweater over ski pants and bright blue socks. The man from Bangor Theological nodded to him. Tom took the same seat as he had the night before and tried to read the names of the colleges on people's sweatshirts.

Bennett walked into the room, wearing jeans and a hooded sweatshirt. He'd taken off his baseball cap and pulled his hair back tightly, holding it in place with some kind of turquoise medallion. He struck the metal discs to begin meditation, and Tom, still mulling over the cards and journals he'd read the night before, sank into a memory of Annie's eighteenth birthday. Her last. When he, Christine, and Nathan had taken her on a picnic by the shore and given her the guitar that now hung on the wall of Nathan's bedroom. He saw his daughter's wax-white face under a green bandanna. Sunken eyes. Slender fingers plucking the strings. Like two curtains, the memory drew apart to reveal a man's face, textured in blue and gold, like a painting by Matisse. A thin face with a turned-up nose and sad dark eyes that regarded Tom with compassion.

Is this the face of Christ? Well, if so, Jesus has swapped his white robes and sandals for a gray trench coat and fedora.

Feeling as if he'd stepped into an Ingmar Bergman movie, Tom joined everyone in the kitchen for a silent breakfast. When they returned to the living room, Bennett said they were going to do what he called "talking meditation." Everyone else closed their eyes while he spoke to them in his lilting voice about death and resurrection being the basis for Lenten observances, and that the story of Jesus's raising Lazarus from the dead was a model for spiritual resurrection.

"You remember how the story goes. Jesus hears his friend, Lazarus, is sick, and, by the time Jesus and his disciples get there, he—Lazarus—has been dead four days. Lazarus's sister says to Jesus: 'If you had been here, my brother would not have died.' Jesus replies, 'I am the resurrection and the life. He who believes in me will live, even though he dies; and whoever lives and believes in me will never die.' He commands that the stone in front of the tomb be rolled away. He calls in a loud voice, 'Lazarus, come out!' The dead man comes out, his hands and feet wrapped with strips of linen, and a cloth around his face. Jesus says to those who've been mourning, 'Take off the grave clothes and let him go.'"

Tom heard Bennett sip his coffee. As usual, these miracle stories of Jesus's healing, especially those involving raising people from the dead, made him angry. *Where the hell were you when Annie died?*

"Lazarus's 'death,'" Bennett said, "can be seen to symbolize our false selves, with all our weaknesses, ignorance, and pride, together with the damage lying in the unconscious, inflicted from earliest childhood to the present moment. All of which can make us 'dead'—unresponsive—to the love of God."

Tom shifted uncomfortably on his seat, but this made more sense than the literal interpretation. Still, he couldn't believe a God of love let his daughter suffer and die.

Lazarus, said Bennett, represents those who want to penetrate the mystery of God's love by being willing to die to their false selves and to wait in patience for God to call them to inner resurrection. "Think of the stone in front of Lazarus's tomb as emblematic of the false self," he said, "and the rolling away of the stone as the first stirring of hope." Again, the sound of sipping coffee. "But even when Lazarus comes forth out of the tomb—comes out of the shadow of compulsive behavior, addiction, bad habits—he's still wrapped in winding bands, still bound by the habits of the false self. He needs the help of others to become finally free."

Tom recalled his glimpses of God's love in the hospital chapel, at Salisbury Cathedral, his hope that he and Christine might resurrect their love. Was he, in fact, coming out of his tomb? Was the reason he was here because he was finally asking for help?

When the meditation ended, Bennett said they had the next four hours to themselves. He suggested they think about ways in which they might roll away the stones from their respective tombs. They could find fixings to make lunch in the kitchen. They could walk around the island, nap, or read. If they wanted, they could help him pile brush out back.

While everyone else either stayed downstairs or went outdoors, Tom climbed the three flights of stairs to his room and closed the door behind him. He'd felt less apprehensive after listening to Bennett this morning. But now the narrow walls, the low ceiling of his room, made him feel as if he were returning to his tomb, not leaving it. Did he really want to wallow again in all that anguish? Why didn't he go help Bennett pile brush? *With all my aches and pains?* He'd spent the last week pissing blood. Maybe he was supposed to be here a while longer.

Lying on the bed, Tom opened his cloth journal and pulled a blanket over himself. He was cold. He read again of his certainty that he and Christine had sold their children's lives to the Devil. He experienced anew the strain of his daily exchanges with Martha, his judgment of the nurses, missing Christine and Nathan. He waded through pages of quotations, most of which—"What will you drink, the water or the wave?"—now made no sense.

But when he switched to the spiral notebook he'd written in during the last month of his daughter's life, his tears washed away the musings, the questions, the self-flagellation, leaving only stony reality:

2-18: …Annie's failure to eat has worsened & she has contractions in her throat & pain in her esophagus…

2-25: Her morphine drip is at .12 & she complains of pains in her leg, ankle, and foot…

2-26: …She's gained 7 lbs. since the latest IV has been installed and she looks even more like my father…

2-28: It's after PT that Annie is the worst b/c she can see how much she's deteriorated…

3-2: "I only want it to be over!" she told me.

3-7: The nurses wheeled Annie to her bone scan. She looked small & pale in the wheelchair, hands crossed in her lap, eyes closed, but still defiant enough to wear her bright red scarf…

3-9: …Dr. Jacobs met with Martha, Nadine Bartlett, the head nurse, Sandy, the oncology social worker, & me to tell us what we already knew: there is no hope now for anything except to make Annie comfortable…

3-13: …Annie keeps asking, "What's next?" I don't know how to respond…

3-14: A melancholy, weepy day. Annie has pneumonia in her left lung…

3-16: Annie's more lucid. She said she's never had pain like she had this morning in her right hip. Her morphine drip has been increased & she's had 2 shots of Atavan.

3-17: More pain. Annie sleeps for ½ to ¾ of an hour, then contorts with pain. Martha & I both feel Dr. Jacobs is not being aggressive enough with relief…

3-18: …Annie has had an epidermal catheter put in so that the medication can be administered directly to the nerve endings. She is apparently receiving as much morphine as anyone has ever received at EMMC…

3-19: …There is indication that Annie may live longer than her mother & I expected. Her cancer continues to attack bone and muscle, but no vital organs.

3-20: Annie has less & less of an idea where she is or why she's in a hospital…

1990-1991

3-21: ...Annie's face is beginning to shine & I understand the comparisons with wax...

3-22: ...Annie has been more on her back, but her head remains turned to the left, thus her left eye has b/c swollen. Her left arm is useless & whenever the nurses move it, she starts crying & moaning...

3-23: Annie is groaning sometimes as she breathes & occasionally she seems to be gargling. Nadine has brought in some kind of oxygen suction device to clean out Annie's throat if it gets too full...

3-24: Anne Sharon Jacobs died this morning at 12:15 A.M.

In his mind, a phone rings. Stops. Rings again. Footsteps down the hall. Martha's voice on the telephone telling him he'd better come to the hospital now. This is it. He leaves the Ronald McDonald House and drives to the Eastern Maine Medical Center, swinging open the doors to the lobby, hurrying past a table where a skeletal woman in a red wig is selling Easter lilies that remind him of the lilies in the center of the table at Easter when he was growing up, so when he walks into Room 434 all he can think of is the sound of his mother's coffee pot percolating from Annie's bed, while Martha sits in the chair by the window, her forehead tight, her jaw clenched so hard it trembles.

"She started breathing like this about 5:00 this afternoon," Martha says. She turns her head away from him, and gives out a short sob like a pistol shot.

Annie lies on her back. Legs bent, pillow between her knees, four tubes running out of her body. He picks up one of her hands. Still warm. Stares at a small wreath of dried flowers hanging on the bulletin board over her bed. Listens to the air rattle as it tries to escape through the liquid filling her lungs.

At first her breathing is steady, but then it shifts to one deep breath followed by a shallow one. Soon, the shallow breaths become more frequent.

"Do you want to stand here by the bed?" he asks Martha.

She shakes her head, leaves her chair and goes out into the hall. Returns a few minutes later, eyes red, with Jen White, the head nurse that evening. They stand at the other side of the bed near the foot. He feels self-conscious holding his daughter's hand, as if he is posing, or acting a part. That's it: this is all a movie and when it's over the lights will come on and he and Martha and Annie will go home and make herbal tea and sit at the kitchen table and criticize the soppy ending.

"I've called for Sandy," Jen says. "Tom, would you like some coffee?"

He shakes his head. Jen leaves. Martha returns to her chair.

Annie's breathing shifts again. The deep breath becomes shallow and the other breaths fainter and fainter. Her hand cools. Her skin is like wax. A nurse named Tammy comes in and stands at the other side of the bed.

Mucus trickles from Annie's mouth. Not caring anymore what anyone thinks, Tom gets a handkerchief out of his pocket and wipes the mucus away. Soon, her breathing is nothing but a series of shallow breaths, growing fainter and farther apart. He holds his daughter's hand with his left hand and wipes her mouth with his right. His nose runs. Sandy enters the room. He's crying, tears and snot running down his face. Sandy rubs his back. "Let it go," she says, "Let it go."

No way there can be any more breaths. But there are. More mucus. Finally, mercifully, the mucus stops, along with her breathing. Although he can't feel the handkerchief in his hand, he wipes his daughter's mouth one last time and presses his lips against her forehead. When he straightens up, he looks to Martha, but she's turned her back and is pulling cards and pictures down from the walls.

On the third floor of the Goose Island farmhouse, Tom rolled over on his bed, pulled his legs up, and wrapped the blanket tightly around himself. Racking sobs tore his stomach. He slid, or fell, to the floor, dragging the blanket with him. Holding the wooden bedpost with one hand, he began to punch the bed with his other hand, driving his fist into the mattress. He grabbed the mattress with both hands, raised himself onto his knees and slammed his head into the bed. Leaned back and slammed his head into the mattress again. Again. All the while making yelping noises.

At one point, he thought, *this is stupid,* and at another point, *I wonder if I'm going crazy.* He didn't stop trying to drive his head through the bed, but he did start to ride his grief, the way he imagined one might ride the rapids of a river or wind currents over a canyon.

Eventually, he sank to the floor and listened to his heart pound in heavy-metal rhythm. He slept. He awoke on the floor, cold and uncomfortable. He climbed onto the bed and slept some more.

Tom had no idea what Bennett said to them before their final meditation or anything about his meditation until, just before its end, he saw a square package covered in shiny, wine-red wrapping. The wrapping—diaphanous, like a membrane—peeled away, leaving the package white.

Bennett ended the retreat with what he called a "group reflection." The man from Bangor Seminary gave thanks for this place. The tall woman with the beads thanked Bennett for his wisdom. One of the two women under the blanket gave thanks for new friends. The woman whose husband had died was grateful for Jesus's resurrection. The lawyer who wanted to become a teacher praised God for His love.

Tom rubbed his thumbs together. "I want to give thanks for this place, too," he said, staring at the worn, braided rug at his feet. "Two years ago, just before Easter, my daughter died—cancer—and this has been a good place to grieve. I don't know, it's felt safe, here, I guess, to do what I needed to do."

He didn't plan on saying anything else, but the sudden silence in the room scared him. "And I just hope that those of you who are wrestling with your own sorrows have received the comfort this retreat has given me. I'm certainly nowhere near being resurrected into the spirit, but maybe some day…"

He stopped, embarrassed. How could he say he'd been comforted when he'd spent God knows how long, a few hours ago, punching a bed? And what the hell did he mean by that last part? He had no idea what "resurrected into the spirit" meant. Still, the widow smiled at him and the man from Bangor Seminary nodded. Later, several people thanked him.

As he stood on the dock, waiting to board the ferry, Bennett sought him out. "I had no idea of what you're carrying around," he said above the low growl of the ferry's idling motor.

"Well, it's been quite a weekend," Tom said. He told Bennett of his strange visions during meditation. Lips turning to flower petals. Someone who may or may not have been Jesus. The dream of the biplane. Reliving Annie's death.

Bennett's eyes lit up. "That's really neat about the lips," he said. "What you saw reminds me of Tibetan death masks. In their Buddhist rituals, dancers put on masks and dance as if they were demons." A gust of damp wind blew off the water, and Bennett raised his voice. "They believe that, in what they call a shadow dance, they transform the dark forces within themselves into benevolent spirits. They feel that everything has its shadow side, and that the way to reverse its effects on our souls is to embrace it." Bennett put his hand on Tom's arm. "That's what you did."

Tom shivered in the wind. "Well, I didn't exactly throw my arms around it. I was just too afraid to move."

"But you didn't run from your fear. You acknowledged it and when you did, you transformed it. You turned your fear into a beautiful flower." Bennett tightened his grip on Tom's arm. "And the falling petals, in the Tibetan tradition, represent the ongoing circle of life. Unless the flower dies and petals fall, new flowers cannot grow and bloom. Jesus said the same thing: 'Unless a grain of wheat falls into the earth and dies, it remains just a single grain; but if it dies, it bears much fruit.' And there's this lovely haiku:

'Petals of poppies
how willingly
they drop.'"

Tom saw Annie's watercolor. The hand reaching toward the falling petal. His lips trembled and he began to cry.

Bennett's smile vanished. "Oh, damn it! I'm sorry, Tom. That was more information than you need." He gave Tom a hug. "Just know that God is helping you unload your subconscious—unwind those burial bands. Think of it as divine therapy." He pulled a card from his jacket pocket. "My phone number's on that. Call me any time you need to talk."

On the trip back, fog enveloped the boat. Tom stood on the deck, peering down at a gray-white ocean almost the same color as the fog. Too tired to think about the last twenty-four hours, he was aware only of a sense of moving through empty space. The past a bizarre dream, the future unfathomable, the only things real were the smell of gasoline and salt air, the clear clang-clang of a bell buoy somewhere in the distance, and the vibration of engines under his feet as the ferry eased over a ground swell—dipping into a trough and rising again, gliding through the fog.

Chapter Fourteen

1992

Nathan asked, "Can I stay home from school for the rest of the week?"

Tom looked across the dinner table at his stepson. Nathan was taller now and, since running cross-country and indoor track, thinner. His hair was shoulder-length, and some of it fell over his eyes. He wore black boots, black pants, and a black sweatshirt featuring four guys with white-and-black painted faces and very long tongues.

"Why?" Christine set down her knife and fork. "Don't you feel well?"

"No, I feel okay. It's just…" Nathan started tearing his napkin into pieces. "I mean, they're taking out all this asbestos from the school." Tom still hadn't gotten used to the deeper voice. "They were supposed to get it all out over Christmas vacation. But…well, some of the kids were talking about getting cancer."

At the word "cancer," chills inched up Tom's arms. He couldn't go through that again. Radiation, chemotherapy, doctors, nurses. He tried to keep his voice steady. "Did any of the teachers say anything?"

Nathan compressed his napkin into a ball. "Well, yeah, the principal had an assembly, and he said there was nothing to be scared of. The workers will be out of school by the end of the week. It's just..." He rolled the ball in his fingers. "Oh, I don't know, forget it." He threw the ball down on his plate. "I'll go to school!" He stomped up the stairs to his room and slammed the door.

Tom shrugged his shoulders. "I love adolescence."

"I'd better see what's going on." Christine left the table and went upstairs. Tom heard her knock on the door, her voice: "Can I come in?"

As he cleared the table, he found his hands shaking. *Relax. Focus on the breath.* When he was Nathan's age, the schools were full of asbestos. He swam in a river choked with sewage and paper-mill waste. He worked summers outdoors, hatless and shirtless, and never used sunscreen. *Concentrate on putting away the dishes. Don't get caught up in teenage angst.*

He'd just started the dishwasher when Christine came back downstairs, a frown furrowing her forehead.

"What's up?"

"I don't know. The only thing I could get out of him is that he wants to return to the Family Center for Grief and Loss. He says we should never have stopped going."

Tonight's meatloaf rose into Tom's throat. "But we left two years ago. Nathan didn't complain then." He pulled at his beard. "That would mean we'd have to go with him. They only take families. You know what happened last time."

"Why don't you go in the living room and sit down and I'll bring us some tea?" Christine picked up the teakettle and started to fill it. Above the sound of the water she said, "I'd like you to think about the two of you going together."

"What? How can you say that?"

She put the kettle on the stove and turned up the heat. "Tom, this is the first thing Nathan's asked of us since I can't remember when. If going back to the Family Center will help him, I think he should go."

"But why with just me?" he said. "Why can't we all go?"

Christine's eyes—gray-blue tonight—searched his face. "We

could, and if you insist on it, I'll go with you. But remember, I was told I didn't belong because I wasn't a real mother."

"You mean Annie's real mother."

Christine continued as if she hadn't heard him. "I'm already seeing a therapist to help me stop thinking God is punishing me for not being a good mother. I don't need to hear it from anyone else."

He rubbed his thumbs with his index fingers. "How did God become part of your guilt?"

"Do you remember the night in New Jersey when I told you I thought mothers cared more for their children than God does? What I meant was, 'I care more for my children than God does.' How arrogant could I have been?" Her voice cracked. "And in England, remember when I said who I am is a mother? What kind of mother drives her child away?"

"Christine, if anyone's to blame for Nathan's leaving, it's me."

She tore off a segment of paper towel and dried her eyes. "So maybe going back to the Family Center is something the two of you need to do together. Please, Tom, just go in the living room and think about it."

He scuffed his way to the fireplace, and stirred the coals of the fire he'd built before dinner. *Shit, shit, shit.* He and Christine had rebuilt their marriage. Established a prayer life. He was content with his classes at school. He was learning to live with his aching back. He and Christine and Nathan had spent probably their best Christmas together. Tom didn't want to slog back into that swamp hole of maudlin stories and twisted faces and soggy tissues.

But he thought of all the demands he'd made of Christine over the last three years, her struggle to cope with her son's leaving. He considered the times he'd ignored Nathan, the fact that, relatively soon, his stepson wouldn't be living with them any more, the previous summer when Christine's ex-husband thought Nathan had acted "clinically depressed." Since Zack was getting treated for depression himself, Tom thought the guy was just projecting his symptoms on to his son, but after returning from Wyoming, Nathan had acted so withdrawn that he and Christine met with a

1992

school counselor. They were relieved when Dr. Henderson said Nathan showed few of the classic symptoms of depression. Yes, he was moody, but what fourteen-year-old isn't? He had friends, he'd joined the cross-country team, he ate well, he slept well, and his grades yo-yoed no more than they ever had. The only thing teachers noticed was that he seemed sad. When Tom and Christine told the counselor that they had reluctantly given in to his request to attend high school in Wyoming the following year, Dr. Henderson nodded. "I wonder if he's grieving."

Tom prodded at the fire with the poker. Maybe Nathan's request wasn't so far out in left field as he'd thought. The wood flamed. And would it hurt him to talk with someone? When Christine had decided she needed to see a psychotherapist, she'd asked him if he felt he ought to see one, too. Was he really as well as he imagined? Despite feeling more settled—happier, he supposed, than he'd been since Annie's death—he still woke up around 3:00 every morning, and for the last year or so, he'd been experiencing strange attacks of anxiety that didn't always evaporate in the morning light.

They'd begun the previous summer, after he and Christine had taken Nathan to the airport, to the plane to Wyoming for the summer. From Boston, they'd driven up the coast and caught the ferry to Goose Island for another of Jonathan Bennett's retreats. This one was a completely different experience for Tom from the one he'd gone to on the anniversary of Annie's death. The weather was clear, and he and Christine walked rocky beaches and slept together in the farmhouse's largest bedroom. But he'd felt uncomfortable. Although he didn't want to admit it, he felt Christine intruding into his private space. At the same time, he was aware of something ominous hovering in that space, which he was just as happy to avoid. On the second morning there, he and Christine were meditating with about ten other people in the living room of the farmhouse, when he heard a noise he couldn't identify. Gradually the sound grew louder and louder, until it was battering his eardrums. He could barely breathe. His head spun. He left his chair and stumbled out the door to get some air. He'd thought the noise might have come from outside, but on the front steps he stood surrounded by silent spruce trees. Returning to the kitchen, he discovered his unbearable noise coming from a cast-iron teapot softly steaming on the woodstove.

He hadn't had a chance to talk to Bennett about the experience, and frankly didn't think it was anything particularly serious—probably just more unloading of the unconscious stuff. After the retreat, he and Christine drove home and spent the next four weeks taking a summer program entitled "Autobiography and the American Experience" for teacher recertification, which was both demanding and interesting. But in August, when they celebrated the sixth anniversary of their first illicit weekend by taking a trip through Canada, Tom, who had never had any trouble with heights, suddenly became terrified of them in Quebec City. Walking down the promenade from the Plains of Abraham to the Chateau Frontenac, he'd looked up at the pointed towers of the hotel, against the white clouds drifting across the blue sky, and his stomach started churning. Later, when he and Christine took the elevator to the top of the Frontenac and he tried to look out over the city, he thought he'd faint. He had to sit in a chair away from the window for while, before his legs felt strong enough so he could walk back to the elevator.

Worse, instead of a vacation filled with uninhibited sex as he'd imagined, he became impotent, his mind racing ahead of itself: *Tomorrow we need to be on a sightseeing boat at 9:00. When we get back, we need to try that restaurant. After that, we'll…*

Sometimes he still had trouble keeping it up. Christine told him not to be upset, that there were other ways of making love. But still, one more thing to worry about at 3:00 a.m.

Then, a week or so ago, Michael Keith and that other jerk he hung around with were lurking by the water fountain at school when Tom stopped to get a drink. Just as the bell rang to start the next class, he heard Michael's voice: "Did I ever tell you about my daughter, the one who died?" Tom froze in terror. He turned to see

1992

Michael walking into a classroom down the hall, and started after him. Then stopped. Had the son of a bitch really said what he'd heard? The more Tom thought about it, the more improbable it sounded. When he'd turned around, the kid had been too far away. Anyway, the remark had been too subtle for somebody like that.

Yet Tom heard his voice. What the hell was going on?

Christine walked into the living room, carrying two steaming mugs.

"Okay," he said, "I'll call the Family Center and see when Nathan and I can start coming."

Three months later, Tom watched his stepson saunter toward the Teen Room in the converted furniture store. It was hard to believe the boy was almost as tall as he was. Tonight, Nathan wore the tie-dyed T-shirt Annie had created for him, and besides being faded and full of holes, it barely reached his belt buckle. Tom remembered when it had reached almost to his knees. He noted that running had whittled away Nathan's baby fat until he was nothing but arms and legs. Watching him at last Saturday's track meet, appendages flapping like a marionette's, face grimacing as he headed toward the finish line, Tom had been proud of the boy. He wanted him to catch the runner in front of him, and he heard Red Bailey yelling, "Come on, move it! You run like a girl. Move!" But he was damned if he was going to yell at his stepson like that, so he merely applauded as the boy ran by. Now, he wished he'd yelled something like "Good job, son!" But Nathan wasn't his son, he was Zack's son, and next year they'd be together, which was probably the way it should be.

Probably.

He walked down the hall and into the room where the adults met. Fran, a young widow whose husband had been killed in an automobile accident, leaving her with three children under the age of ten, was telling Angela, their facilitator, about her youngest daughter's birthday party: "...She cried for her daddy when she went to bed, but overall, I think she had a good day."

Tom gave them a smile and sat in the black-and-green-checked chair that Ruby used to sit in two years earlier. So far, he liked this facilitator. Probably in her mid-thirties, with twin dimples and green eyes, Angela started them on time and kept them focused, sometimes even laughing. Still, he remained as uncomfortable as ever talking about his emotions and listening to others talk about theirs. What kept him coming was Nathan's improved disposition, and the fact that the Family Center gave the two of them something to talk about, even if it was only a sentence or two—"Nice-looking girl you were talking to." "Yeah, she's pretty cool." Last week Nathan admitted he was already sad because he was going to have to sell his animals when he moved back to Wyoming. He was especially sad about having to sell Cornelius II, the successor to his first corn snake.

Lannie, a tall woman whose willowy body appeared toned by daily workouts, followed Tom into the room and sat on the couch across from him. Last week had been her first time there. Her grandfather had died and she wanted to know how to explain his death to her children. Tom had trouble taking her grief seriously, but he forced a smile and asked how she'd been.

As she extolled the value of last week's session, Doug and Sally arrived. Tom's back began to ache. Although divorced before their nine-year-old daughter died of leukemia, they attended counseling sessions together "for the sake of our other two kids," in Doug's words. Standing probably six feet seven inches tall and weighing a good three hundred pounds, he tended to dominate the meetings. Sally, a tiny woman who always dressed in suits and high heels, had left him for a much younger man, a fact Doug often inserted into his tuba-toned monologues. Of all the people there, Tom found him the hardest to listen to. He didn't need to know any more about spending days in the hospital with a dying child and an ex-wife, thank you very much. The previous week, as Doug detailed for them the cocaine habit he'd acquired after Jennifer's death, Tom sat thinking okay, maybe

1992

drinking himself to sleep wasn't as glamorous as snorting coke. But he still wasn't impressed.

Finally Penny slipped in and sat in her usual place at the end of the blood-colored couch by the door, where he used to sit. A thin woman with a sallow complexion, she never smiled and seldom spoke. On his first night, and again the previous week for Lannie, she told them in a low monotone that her husband, from whom she'd just separated, had died of a heart attack.

As usual, the session began with everyone checking in about how the week had gone. Doug, who dealt in arts and antiques, talked about adding to his rare gun collection, Sally mentioned problems at work. Betsy and Lannie talked about difficulties raising children.

Tom wondered if he should tell people about hearing Michael Keith refer to Annie and her death. But he decided if he did, he'd have to talk about almost battering the little bastard's face a year ago, so he spoke vaguely about how hard he found these weeks leading up to Easter. How the longer days increased his memories of Annie's dying months.

He'd barely finished when Penny said, "It's been a really shitty week." At first, Tom could hardly hear her. "My daughter, Megan, was sick all last week with some kind of flu. She couldn't keep anything down. I was worried she'd get dehydrated. I needed to be home with her, but when I asked my boss for time off, he said no, he needed me. Christ, for the last month he hasn't given me any hours, and now he needs me." Head bowed, she spoke to the floor. "I wanted to quit right then and there, but I couldn't afford to." Her hair, which looked as if it needed to be combed, fell over one eye. "Working in that fucking Dollar Store is the only job I've been able to get."

She threw her head back and started sobbing. Words tumbled from her mouth. "It's all my fault. I never should have left Travis. It's just that I'd taken all I thought I could take. The drinking, the fighting, the physical abuse. I thought I was leaving him for the sake of the kids, but he never hit them. Only me." She bowed her head again. "I was selfish. And I killed him."

Angela gave her some tissues. "How do you mean?"

Penny wiped her eyes. "I knew he had heart trouble. He told me a week or so after I'd moved out he couldn't handle losing his wife and kids. I knew he was going to live on cheap whiskey and Big Macs. He asked me to come back and I refused." She reached for more tissues. She spoke slowly, her voice bitter. "I will always feel I murdered my husband, just as if I'd put a gun to his head and pulled the trigger."

While everyone else in the room tried to tell Penny how wrong she was, Tom sat in silence, his heart thudding. *Yes, and I will always think I murdered my daughter.*

He inspected his polluted pools of guilt, the guilt that had been there since Annie's diagnosis. When she died, he'd thought his divorce set off the cancer, but after that trip to England, he'd blamed himself for not leaving Martha soon enough. At the same time, however, he would also have said that his guilt was nothing more than one of Camus's absurd attempts to provide an answer to why his daughter had to die from a terrible disease. The other night, for example, at the meditation group when they were all talking about guilt, Tom had said how helpful meditation was at helping him unload his. That he'd committed adultery, not murder. That millions of people live and raise children while in unhappy marriages. In other words, he'd been talking the way the others were talking to Penny tonight.

But he knew he would never stop believing he'd killed his daughter, any more than Penny would never completely escape thinking she'd killed her husband.

Strange how much better he felt for having accepted it. His back felt better. Driving home with Nathan, he was relaxed, even drowsy. Instead of a drink when they returned, he made tea for Christine and himself, went to bed early, and fell asleep immediately. He did not wake, did not dream, until the alarm went off at 6 a.m.

1992

But the next night he *did* dream. In his dream, his group at the Family Center for Grief and Loss held its meeting on a school bus. He sat beside Angela in the front seat, behind a bus driver with a gray ponytail. (Jonathan Bennett?) Fran, wearing a bright red headscarf and Lannie in a floppy straw hat, sat behind them, across from Doug and Sally in matching blue-and-white Hawaiian shirts. Penny was by herself, behind Doug and Sally, wearing black shorts that accentuated her white legs. The weather was beautiful and warm, and as the bus left the parking lot in front of the former furniture store, Tom saw tall spruce trees lining the road. The bus turned and the next thing he knew they were driving up Cadillac Mountain on Mount Desert Island, a hundred and twenty miles from the Center.

He wanted to tell everyone about his discovery of the depth of his guilt. That whether or not it was true, he would always feel as if he murdered his daughter. He'd written his confession down in a journal—the one with the oriental cover—but now he couldn't, or wouldn't, read it, so he passed his journal to Angela to read to the group. The others listened politely but didn't act particularly interested, while Tom, embarrassed, gazed out the window at pink granite cliffs and tourists standing by square boulders in front of blue-gray water, stretching out under sunlight streaming through inky clouds.

The school bus stopped at the summit of creviced pink-and-green-gray ledges. In the distance, an eagle soared in a silver sky over humpbacked islands. Directly below, a cruise ship sailed into Bar Harbor. Everyone exited the bus except for Angela and him. She gave Tom his journal, and said, "I wasn't sure what to do with this other writing in your book."

"What writing?" He flipped through his journal and saw, spaced throughout—sometimes on top of his own writing—words written in green ink. Annie's tiny, circular handwriting. Tom turned the pages until, near the end, he found a page, blank except for the words

I love you.

The following weekend, Tom and Christine's wedding anniversary fell, as it had five years earlier, on the Saturday in April before Easter. They awoke early, sat for twenty minutes of meditation, shared an omelet for breakfast, and then moved into the living room with second cups of coffee.

Tom sat down beside Christine on their new couch. "How are you?"

"Good." She snuggled against him. "No, not good. Great."

He stroked his wife's thigh. Last night their lovemaking had been wonderful, their desire for each other flowing freely, unmuddied, he realized this morning, by guilt. "I'm feeling pretty great myself. Thanks again for last night."

They kissed.

"Do you remember," Tom asked, "that article Marian read to our group last week, about dealing with the thoughts that arise during meditation?"

"You mean about the 'the Three R's'?" Christine looked over at him. "Let's see, how did they go: 'resist no thought, react to no thought…' What was the other one?"

"'Retain no thought,' said Tom. "The author—I can't remember her name—even went so far as to say that it was important not only to recognize the emotions and thoughts that sail across your mind, but also to welcome them, no matter how painful."

"That's right. She said that welcoming the emotion takes away its power. Then you're supposed to let that emotion go, give it to God."

"I couldn't imagine ever doing that," Tom said, "but thinking about my dream the other night, I wonder if what I've done is to stop resisting the thought that I killed Annie, and that admitting my guilt—even, I suppose, welcoming it—is the reason for this strange peace that seems to have settled over me, even on the anniversary of her death. At least for now, I seem to have lost that fear, anxiety, whatever it was."

1992

He sipped his coffee and looked out the back window at the trees, their buds red in the morning sun. "Of course, I still can't let the guilt go, give it to God, the way Bennett told us to." The last of the snow had melted under the storage shed. "Part of the problem is that I don't trust God. I mean, how can I trust something or someone that I'm still angry at for Annie's death?" He finished his coffee. "Now that I've stopped blaming the two of us, and then Martha and me, that only leaves God, doesn't it?" Tom leaned forward. "I guess I'm more confused than ever about where God and I stand these days."

Christine rubbed his back. "Maybe what you need to do is fake it 'til you make it," she said.

"Meaning?"

With her other hand, Christine drank her coffee. He recalled the way she'd sipped her brandy on the night that changed their lives. "Even if I don't understand God," she said, "or if I'm angry with God, or if I can't trust God, I can still go to church, sing the hymns, read and listen to scripture, share in the Eucharist. Who was it who said eighty percent of life is just showing up?"

"Well, that's how I feel about meditation—that I'm just showing up. Waiting for God to say something."

"Exactly. But remember, even Bennett says meditation is just one way to pray. Sometimes I need the words of saints and prophets and poets to help me consent to God, even if I don't feel like doing it." She smiled. "Speaking of reading scripture, I know we're going out to dinner before The Great Vigil at church tonight, but you know what I'd like to do today?"

Tom looked into those mysterious eyes. "What?"

"It's a beautiful day. Let's go down to Newell Landing and renew our wedding vows."

Tom grinned. "Great idea. You want to do it now?"

Christine took his hand. "I'd like to wait until Nathan gets up, so he can go with us. He was there before, remember?"

Yes, and so was Annie. He forced a smile. "Okay."

Although Nathan complained at first, once he, Tom, and

Christine had driven to Newell Landing, he became the Nathan who first moved to Maine—lying facedown beside his mother on the rocks and gazing into tide pools, lifting sprays of seaweed and inspecting the mussels beneath. Meanwhile, Tom walked out onto a stone pier by some old wooden pilings. The tide was coming in, lapping worn, gray-and-tan-and-red rocks, which lay like the backs of sunbathing sea creatures. A thin mist hung over the horizon under a train of pink-and-blue clouds.

The first weekend Annie had come to visit since she'd started chemo and her hair had fallen out, she and Tom rented sea kayaks and paddled out into Casco Bay, not too far from where they now were. Annie had still been self-conscious, but at the same time determined "to beat this thing."

Despite some apprehension about going a mile down a tidal river and into an ocean bay—especially since Tom had only been in a kayak once before, at an end-of- the-year faculty party—he'd decided if his daughter wanted to kayak then goddamn it, they would kayak. They walked along the docks of the Newell Boatyard to a slip at the far end, where a wiry woman who might have been the mother of one of Nathan's classmates took Tom's money, untied two sea kayaks, and gave them paddles. As they paddled down the tidal river, Tom watched his daughter ahead of him, her thin neck, her narrow shoulders under a red, white, and blue Grateful Dead T-shirt. The sun lit up the tails of the blue scarf that fell halfway down her back. The tide had just turned and the channel of the river was lined with mud banks. As they rounded a bend, Annie pointed to a blue heron standing on one leg fishing. "This is so cool!" she yelled over her shoulder.

They rounded another bend and headed out into Casco Bay. They didn't go far—Tom was uncomfortable in the open water and Annie had gotten tired. Still, it felt good to be with his daughter as they paddled around the rocks and through shoals, avoiding seaweed and occasional dead fish and the shadow that hung over them.

Watching at least two dozen brown-and-white ducks float motionless, except for bobbing up and down on the rippling water

1992

offshore from Newell Landing, Tom heard Dr. Godfrey's voice drift across the water: "She was the bravest patient I've ever had."

Tom's tears felt cool in the April breeze. He was surprised to realize he wasn't angry, just terribly, terribly sad.

"Tom, do you want to come up here with Nathan and me?" Christine called from atop the rock they'd all stood on five years earlier.

He climbed up with them, and once again they read from the marriage service in the *Book of Common Prayer*, Tom and Nathan standing on either side of Christine as she held the book in her left hand. Tom took her right hand, shaded his eyes against the light glistening off the water with his other hand, and read:

"In the name of God, I, Tom, take you, Christine, to be my wife, to have and to hold from this day forward, for better for worse, for richer for poorer, in sickness and in health, to love and to cherish, until we are parted by death. This is my solemn vow."

Then Christine said her vows. Nathan read his prayer and Annie's in a newly discovered baritone. Still, it was Annie's voice Tom heard:

"Make their life together be a sign of Christ's love to this sinful and broken world, that unity may overcome estrangement, forgiveness heal guilt, and joy conquer despair. Amen."

And it was Annie's tiny, circular handwriting that he saw running over the words on the page. He blinked, but the words were still there, in the green ink she often used to write her cards to him:

I love you.

A trick of the light? Wishful thinking? He didn't care. He sensed himself gathered into a warm embrace, as if God or

Annie or the ocean or the sun or the rocks were saying, "Whether or not you're guilty of anything isn't important. What's important is that I love you."

Christine's voice seemed to come from far away. "Tom, are you all right?"

Tom placed his hand over hers and squeezed. He looked into her blue eyes. "I'm fine, love, just fine."

"Then 'the peace of the Lord be always with you,'" she said.

"'And also with you.'"

Chapter Fifteen

1994

Tom and Christine pulled into the driveway at 24 Emanuel Road in Jordan Mills, and parked behind three other cars.

"We're the last to get here," said Christine. "Sorry I made us late."

Tom checked his watch. "No, we're fine. Maybe a minute or so late, that's all." But it wasn't fine. Tom never liked to be late. Still, he didn't want Christine to see his irritation because he knew the phone conversation with Nathan (which is why they were late) had upset her.

Nathan had told his mother he wasn't coming to Maine for the summer. One of the veterinarians at the animal farm where he'd been working for the last four years had offered him a job as an assistant. This on top of the fact that he hadn't come to Maine for his spring break, either, saying that, because the vacations in Wyoming schools were different from those in Maine, neither Tom nor Christine would be home and he wanted to be with his friends.

"I think he doesn't want to come back because our apartment has too many bad memories," Christine said on the drive over. "It's too full of reminders of Annie."

"I don't think that's it," Tom said. "I think he's got a good job opportunity and he's made friends, both of which at his age are more important than parents. And besides, didn't Zack tell you Nathan's room was still full of Annie's artwork?" But even as he said, "His memories can't be all bad," Tom couldn't help wondering if *he* was the reason Nathan didn't want to come back. Which was probably, he realized now, the real reason his irritation had been building on the drive. Over the past two years, his guilt for causing Annie's death had ebbed, but he still had plenty of it when it came to his stepson.

They walked up the back steps into the house through the glassed-in porch. A wooden glider occupied one end, and two Adirondack chairs bookended the view into the back yard. Sometimes in the summer, when the screens were on, the meditation group sat out here. Opening another door, Tom and Christine went from the porch into a narrow hall that led to the kitchen. The smells of the house—fresh cookies (Marian had said, when she offered her house as a place for the group to meet, she wasn't going to feed them, yet her cookies had become a bimonthly staple) and a little mustiness from the cellar—wafted Tom back into his childhood visits to Grammy and Grampy Abbott, his grandmother's fresh apple pies or warm bread with a block of freshly pressed butter with salt sparkling through it.

He looked back at his grandparents' home as a harbor, safe from the unpredictable gales that blew through his own house. Tom wasn't sure why, because Grammy Abbott, encased in old-lady perfume and what felt like a shell underneath the soft fabric of her plaid dresses, never smiled, and Grampy Abbott, a short, bald man with a hearing aid that looked like some kind of mushroom growing out of his ear, was so fussy he wanted even his overalls ironed, and so critical of people who drank that Tom's father kept his booze in the cellar. Certainly, when Tom was growing up, he never felt particularly warm toward either the house or his grandparents. At sixteen, Tommy Jacobs had wanted Grampy Abbott to be like the men in the *True* magazines he

1994

read in the barber shop, or like his mother's father, Pop Kane, who was tall and wore faded flannel shirts and dark-green chinos with a flask of whisky peeping out the back pocket. Pop Kane spent his weekends hunting and fishing with his buddies; Grampy Abbott used his days off to drive his grandmother and her blue-haired friends to gatherings of women's groups called the Eastern Star and the Pythian Sisters.

But although Pop Kane kept saying he'd take his grandson hunting with him sometime, he always seemed to forget, while Grampy Abbott invited Tommy out to his shop in the garage and showed him how to use his woodworking tools. Tom knew now Pop Kane had been an alcoholic who couldn't hold a job, slapped his wife around, and once walked into the living room naked and drunk, before pissing on the wall in front of his ten-year-old daughter and a school friend. Grampy Abbott, who was really Tom's step-grandfather, had raised Tom's father from the time he was twelve years old, and while his dad might not have liked hiding his liquor, Tom never heard him say anything negative about his stepfather.

More guilt. How often had Tom ever invited Nathan to do anything with him? How much more time had he spent with his Scotch than with his stepson? Worse, although he would never admit it, part of him was relieved that Nathan wouldn't be coming to Maine this summer. Christine said her son was dating. And Tom didn't know how to talk about that stuff. His father never talked to him. He had just had the dirty post cards. Meanwhile, his mother gave him Pat Boone's *Twixt Twelve and Twenty*. Tom didn't know which was worse.

They walked into the kitchen, slipped off their shoes and coats, and headed for the living room.

"Sorry we're late," Christine said.

"Don't worry," Marian said, "we're just gabbing about the Easter Service."

Christine took her usual seat in the rocking chair by the doorway. (After four years, they all had their favorite places.) Their hostess sat in her wing-back chair by the window. Hard to believe she was eighty-three. Straight as a yardstick, her legs firm and free from varicose veins. Her hair was white, her jaw was strong, and her eyes were clear and piercing behind rimless glasses.

"Lovely to see you both," Lori Metcalf said from the swivel rocker across from Christine.

"You, too," Tom said. Lori always made him feel better. He noted that sometime in the previous two weeks, she'd had a haircut, possibly with a dull axe. A stocky woman, she dressed in brightly colored, shapeless dresses and several necklaces and enormous hooped earrings. An artist—a painter—her hands were perpetually smeared in oil paint. She'd never married, but over the two years she'd been part of the group, often referred to lovers, both male and female.

Tom took his customary seat in the wooden captain's chair opposite Marian, and beside Roger Bradshaw, who along with Marian, Tom, and Christine, was part of the original meditation group that had formed after Jonathan Bennett's visit to St. Mark's four years earlier. An architect whose wife died of breast cancer before he moved to Jordan Mills to be closer to his children, Roger sat in the straight backed chair he always moved in from the dining room. As usual, he wore a necktie, this one dotted with Bowdoin College polar bears, and instead of being in his socks or barefooted like the rest of them, he wore slippers he'd brought with him. When Tom looked over, Roger was checking his watch. He liked the group to start and end on time. Even after four years, Tom still didn't feel he knew the man. Still, he admired Roger: his precision reminded him of Grampy Abbott.

"No, I thought the music was great," said Bea Blanchard, a retired English and drama teacher whose accent clearly marked her as being from New York City. She flipped her dyed blonde hair off her shoulders and pulled at her paisley scarf.

"And Paul gave a great sermon," said her husband, Bud, who sat beside his wife on Marian's couch. He was a retired banker and avid sailor. Close cropped iron gray hair, striped shirt, chinos, and socks with sailboats. "I think he's going to work out very well as St. Mark's new rector."

Bea and Bud had moved to Jordan Mills and become part of the group a little more than a year ago. There were times when Bud's self-assurance—bordering on arrogance—reminded Tom of his father-in-law, and he'd had to overcome his prejudices against retirees with money. But there certainly were things Tom liked about the couple: Bea was a breast cancer survivor, and Bud was already on the St. Mark's Vestry, pushing for a small chapel to be used for meditation and reflection.

"And how was Easter for the both of you?" asked Marian. "I know this is a hard time of year."

Tom hadn't thought of this before, but although meditation was an integral part of his life, what made the meditation group important was that somehow—probably because of Marian—they had established an atmosphere of trust. They all knew each other's stories and were comfortable sharing them.

Tom held his hand out to Christine. "Go ahead, you go first."

She straightened up in her chair. "Easter was okay," she said. "I miss Nathan, but I did talk to him on the phone, and he was pleasant, even though he said he wasn't coming to Maine this summer..." Tom wondered if the others noticed her lower lip tremble. "But I still like my seminary class, and if Nathan doesn't come here, I'll take a summer course."

"Good for you," said Bea. "I've been thinking of taking a course at Bangor Seminary, too."

"Well, I'm not sure why I decided to take a seminary class, but somehow I think it's what God wants me to do. And I'm not going to argue with God anymore."

And she needs to fill her emptiness now that Nathan's gone. It had taken Tom a while not to feel as if he'd let his wife down. Why couldn't he fill that void? But taking a seminary course, he'd come to realize, was a lot healthier than some of the things *he'd* done to fill the emptiness left by a lost child.

"How about you, Tom?" Perhaps because she'd had a miscarriage and as she'd put it, "knew a little something about grief," Marian often tried to get him to talk about his feelings.

"I doubt if Easter will ever be my favorite time of year," Tom said. He drummed his fingers on the wooden arms of his chair. "But the grief, especially the anger, doesn't overshadow everything in my life the way it used to." Still, as he spoke, he realized that it wasn't just tonight; he'd been irritated by something ever since Sunday.

He leaned forward and rubbed his thumbs with his forefingers. *Do I want to mention this? Oh what the hell.* "I had this dream the other night. I was in the middle of a forest fire. Maybe out west, because flames ran across the tops of the ponderosa pines they have out there. Sounded like a locomotive. I hunkered down in a cave under some rocks, and when the fire passed by, stumbled out, feeling like a grilled steak. Ahead of me was a river, where boats floated like swans—white and serene. Behind me was nothing but cold ashes, and I remember feeling terribly sad. Ahead of me, red coals smoked along a path marked by gray-and-black rocks. I didn't have any shoes—maybe they'd burned up or something—and I woke up, knowing I was going to have to walk barefoot over the coals before I could reach the shore, which I think was lined by apple trees with white blossoms." Tom looked around the room and shrugged his shoulders. "So the big fire's gone out, but there are still lots of little ones."

"You have the most amazing dreams," said Roger. "I can't remember any of mine." He rose from his chair. "Anyway, let's do our thing." He reached into a carpet bag that he'd brought back with him after visiting Turkey and produced seven small square pieces of paper, which he'd cut from his apparently endless supply of handmade stationery. He passed them out.

"I forgot my pen again," whispered Christine.

Tom smiled—*has she ever brought one?*—and quickly writing down his prayers for Annie, Christine, and Nathan, passed her his pen. But while she was writing, he had a sense that he should have added another name. *My mother? My brother?* Sometimes he prayed for them, but neither had been on his mind lately. *My students? The meditation group? Damned if I know.* He stood, folded his paper, walked to the coffee table, and placed his prayer in a glass vase. He lighted a floating candle and placed it in the bowl of water beside the vase. When the others had deposited their prayers and lighted their candles, Lori struck her Buddhist gongs.

Tom took off his glasses, placed them on the bookcase under the window behind his chair, closed his eyes, brought up his sacred word, "ephphatha"—"be opened"—and sank into his breathing. He listened to Marian's clock on her mantle, and Bud or Bea shifting on the couch, and felt a familiar sense of floating, until an image of Harriet Dwyer, one of the young people at church, took shape before him. She'd read one of the lessons during the Easter service at church...*something from Isaiah wasn't it? "Sorrow and sighing shall flee away"?* He didn't know what it was about her that reminded him of Annie—*maybe the way she leans her head forward when she reads*—but it was ironic how her reading that passage made his sorrow return instead of flee...

Ephphatha.

Tom shifted in his chair and tried to sit up straighter. Usually his back felt better after Easter, like some weight had lifted, but not this year, not yet, anyway...

Ephphatha.

His mouth felt fuzzy and his head was slightly achy. He shouldn't have had that second drink before supper. Or not finished the bottle of wine. He figured it was okay to drink a little too much as part of celebrating Easter, but he was still drinking as if it were the weekend...

Ephphatha.

He breathed more deeply, down into his abdomen. A swatch of purple flashed before him, then evanesced into a vision of Jack Bridges, an engineer from Bath Iron Works, with whom Tom had talked at coffee hour a few times. Jack had helped his father—Howard, Tom thought his name was—to the railing for Easter communion. Tom had heard Howard was dying of cancer. *Why do the eyes of cancer victims look bigger? His looked like sunken marbles. Are the whites of the eyes accentuated by the dark circles around them? Or do those eyes see what the rest of us refuse to look at?*

And then seamlessly, as if Howard Bridges had never existed, Tom was looking at his father's face the last time he'd visited him—eyes sunken, wide, glazed—seeing in those eyes what he'd never seen before. Fear. Tom's back spasmed and his stomach churned. Bitterness toward his father—the old man's irrational behavior, his self-absorbed alcoholism—rose into his mouth…

Ephphatha.

He thought of those goddamn model airplanes that broke the first time Tommy flew them. Expensive presents like the Hopalong Cassidy cap pistol in a genuine leather holster that his mother would have a fit about because they weren't in the budget. Either way—if the wing came off the plane or his parents couldn't pay their phone bill—he felt he was to blame. And no matter what the gift, he could never seem to act happy enough. "Shit. He must not like it," the old man would say to Tommy's mother, as if he weren't standing between them. "I don't know why I bother."…

Ephphatha.

His mind continued to drift, through more interior lights— red, green, yellow—which became the lights on the family Christmas tree, reflecting off the red-and-silver bicycles his father gave Eddie and him the Christmas Tommy was seven years old. Tom remembered gazing stupefied at the cross-brace handlebars, the built in dashboard, the speedometer, the mud-flaps, the headlight, and the chrome carrier over the back wheel, hearing his mother's voice behind him as she tried to keep her exasperation to a whisper: "How could you have spent all that money? Thomas won't be big enough to ride that bike for years!"

Ike made no effort to keep his voice down. "It's my goddamned money and I'll do what I want with it!"

The first year Tommy couldn't reach the pedals. The second year he couldn't control the handlebars, and he and the bike wobbled for a few seconds before crashing to the ground in a heap. His father put on training wheels, but his friends in their stripped-down, smaller bikes rode circles around him.

The following year, he still couldn't stay on the damn thing. Eddie taunted him continually—"Tommy is a baby! Tommy is a baby!" One day, after falling yet again, Tommy burst into tears. He tore off the carrier, the fenders, the headlight, the speedometer, and the clock. He jumped on the bike, gritted his teeth, and pedaled like hell. Without the weight of all that extra chrome, he flew down the street. Soon, he was riding all over town.

"Jesus H. Christ from Baltimore," his father snorted when he saw how Tommy had modified the bicycle. "I don't know why I ever bothered to buy you something nice. You don't care about me."...

Ephphatha.

Marian's clock chimed its four-note indication of the quarter hour. *When did we start? Probably not even half way through the twenty minutes...*

Ephphatha.

Tom's mind drifted to another Christmas, this one when he was home from college. Having switched his major from forestry to English, he'd wanted to watch a public television production of Dylan Thomas's poem, "A Child's Christmas in Wales." His father lay on the couch, half-asleep, which Tom knew by then meant half-drunk, until the poet's melodic voice finished describing a fire in Mrs. Prothero's kitchen—the woman looking at the three firemen standing among the smoke and cinders and snowballs and saying, "Would you like anything to read?" His father lit a cigarette and muttered, "Good God. What kind of dumb question is that?"

Ike Jacobs groaned as he pulled himself off the couch. Ice cubes rattled in the kitchen. He thumped back into the living room and groaned again as he flopped down.

"What a faggot."

Tom looked at this lout lying there like a dying dogfish, pounded his fist on the arm of the chair, and stormed upstairs. As he slammed the door to his bedroom, his father called after him, "What the hell's wrong with you?"...

Ephphatha.

As if watching a merry-go-round, images of the last twenty years of his father's life circled through Tom's mind: Ike checking his watch shortly after one of his parents' annual visits to Webber—anxious to leave from the moment he arrived—heaving prolonged sighs, leaving in the middle of a conversation to go to the bathroom and swig from Pop Kane's flask, the one thing he'd taken from his father-in-law's house after he died, returning to say that whoever hung the bathroom door had done a piss-poor job. Ike losing his lure on the first cast and spending the rest of the evening with his shirt pulled over his head, waving his arms to ward off the black flies, and Tom vowing never to take the old man fishing with him again. Ike falling asleep on the couch while Tom was talking to him, then waking Tom and his family at 4:00 the next morning with his coughing. The weekend he stayed in bed with some kind of flu, lying there with a bell, which he'd ring every time he wanted his wife's attention—usually every thirty minutes or so, as Tom thought, *How does she stand that man?...*

So he decided not to be like him. His father kept his hair cropped short, Tom let his hair grow. His father shaved every day, Tom trimmed his beard once a month. His father got fatter, Tom subscribed to health food magazines. Most of all, he ignored the old man as much as he could.

Even when he was dying...

Ephpha—

After his mother called to say his father had been diagnosed with cancer and asked if Tom would come to see him, Tom had driven to Ashton, but spent the afternoon watching football while his father lay on the couch in his ratty bathrobe. He couldn't believe the old man was really sick. Ever since Tom could remember, Ike had suffered from cramps and diarrhea, moaning in his bed and running upstairs to the bathroom. But after the day—*what was I, twelve?*—when Tommy connected those lamentations with the garbage pail full of clamshells and beer bottles, he stopped paying attention to his father's bitching. Yes, doctors had given Ike

1994

two weeks to two months to live, but why did Tom have to be there that weekend?

After the game had ended, Tom waited a few minutes, then rose and called to his mother, who was down the hall paying bills. "I've got to hit the road," he said, "Correct a few papers before tomorrow." His father didn't speak. Reluctantly, Tom nudged his shoulder. "See you soon, Dad."

In his mind's eye, Tom saw his father's eyelids flutter open, those eyes that had been haunting him, he realized, since he'd seen Jack Bridges's father on Easter Sunday. Sitting in Marian's living room, he felt the same chill he'd experienced standing over his father fourteen years earlier. He'd searched for something to say then, but no words had come; instead he touched his father's shoulder. Before Tom could pull away, Ike squeezed his wrist.

He died the next day.

Lorie rang the gongs. Tom realized his cheeks were wet. He wiped them with his sleeve, stood, and led the meditation group on a slow walk around the living room, trying to "breathe through his feet," as one of the books they'd been reading suggested: inhaling as he raised his right foot, exhaling as it hit the ground, inhaling as he raised his left foot, exhaling on the way down. But with each step, pain ran from his legs into his back.

What's going on? Okay, take it easy… "Resist no thought. React to no thought. Retain no thought." *Resist no thought… Maybe I'm supposed to be thinking about Dad. Do you supposed I'm finally grieving?*

Marian's clock chimed, *da dee-dee da, da dee-dee da.*

He led them back to their seats. They sat down and Lori again rang the gongs. *Try to get comfortable. Inhale: Eph…Exhale: Phatha…Again: Eph…phatha.*

Out of the comforting darkness rose a mountain, a snow-capped mountain, beautiful. *Be fun to climb that.* Until Tom realized that what he thought was a pale-blue sky behind the mountain was another mountain at least three times as high, its summit disappearing into high, misty clouds. He felt small and weak, vulnerable.

Eph…phatha.

And then he was five or six years old, looking up at his father shoveling the walk of the church during the winters he served as sexton—top coat and fedora, methodically dipping his coal shovel into a bucket of ashes from the furnace at church and spreading the cinders across the icy walkway so no would fall, while he sang "Onward Christian soldiers, marching as to war." Meanwhile, Tommy, in the red-and-yellow hat and mittens his mother had knit for him, his gum rubber boots, tried to lift his own shovelful of snow, proud to be helping…

His mind kept drifting. Suddenly he was thirteen, standing back to his father in work boots and overalls, smelling the smoke from the cigarette he knew was in the corner of his old man's mouth. Feeling his arms around him as his father gave him the basketball. "Hold your arms like this. Shoot with your fingertips. Aim for the back of the rim."…

Then he was sixteen. His birthday. Somehow, he got his father to take him and his best friend, Jerry, bowling. Jerry asked Ike if he was going to bowl with them. "What the hell," his father muttered. He butted his cigarette, shuffled to the lane, picked up a ball, took three smooth strides, and bowled a strike. "Not much to this game, is there?"…

Eph…phatha.

He was a better athlete than I ever was. Somewhere at home were newspaper clippings. One referred to Ike as "Bullet" Jacobs, after he anchored Ashton High's winning swim team and set a conference record in the backstroke. Another article told of how, even though he gave up eight hits, he pitched the Rams to a 2-1 victory over Mechanic Falls, "bearing down in the pinches…"

I never heard him brag. Never saw him exercise. "I get my Christly workout walking up and down the stairs of that goddamned mill," he'd say. Still, even at the end, some seventy-five to a hundred pounds overweight, he had an easy, even careless athleticism Tom envied…

1994

The newspaper clippings were in a faded-red album, along with a photograph of his father in his baseball uniform and several of him from when he served in the Army during World War II. In one of the Army pictures, he smoked a pipe and wore his sergeant's stripes; in another he leaned against Tom's mother by the side of a car, one arm around her shoulder, the other on his hip, his elbow thrust out confidently...

In photographs taken after the war, he usually stood with his wife and two children in the yard, or sat at a family dinner table—his hair cut ever shorter, a sneer on his face, his stomach ever bigger, as his appetites began to bloat his body. Tom recalled his embarrassment on birthdays, when the family would go out to eat and his father would order the largest meal on the menu, if possible the two-lobster special, which he'd consume with single-minded determination, demolishing the lobsters, leaving nothing behind but a few shells...

Eph...phatha.

In a photograph of his father taken after he retired, his father was dressed in khaki—everything from his long-billed cap to the rubber-soled canvas shoes that he bought at Kmart for ten dollars a pair. This was about the time he was topping off his breakfast with a glass of Gallo's Hearty Burgundy, before moving through the day to Pabst Blue Ribbon beer, finishing with Old Crow whisky and falling asleep on the couch at 7:00 p.m....

In the last picture Tom had of his father, taken about two months before he died, he wore horn-rimmed glasses and although he and Tom's mother stood in shadows, he squinted as if the sun were in his eyes. Pasty flesh hung from his jowls and his neck. He looked eight months pregnant...

What happened? Had his father drunk up all his self-confidence? Or had he never been as sure of himself as he seemed? Listening to Marian's clock—*tick, tock, tick, tock*—Tom recalled one of his mother's old friends—*Carla, Carline, Caroline, something like that*—visiting one day and hearing her say to his mother, "I can still see Ike swaggering into class after he moved here.

The guys were all afraid of him, and we girls thought him the best-looking kid we'd ever seen." He remembered his mother replying, "That's funny. He told me that his first day of school here he was scared to death."...

Tick. Tock. What did he know about his father's background? From his mother, Tom knew that Ike's father, Abner, immigrated to the United States from Nova Scotia to work in a Marlboro, Massachusetts shoe factory. Tom didn't know how Abner and the woman he knew as Grammy Abbott met; only that she divorced her husband because he was abusive to their son. "I told him I could live with his womanizing, but if he ever took a belt to Ike again, I'd leave him," she once told Tom's mother. "He did and I did." For the next eight years, Ike lived in what was called "A Home for Wayward Boys," while his mother worked at a W.T. Grant's department store, visiting him on weekends. When she married Larry Abbott, a thirty-eight-year-old Hard Shell Baptist, she and Tom's father moved to Ashton, Maine, where, because he had little education, he was placed in classes two years below other students his age...

Some childhood. He heard his mother's voice over Marian's clock: "I remember one of the first dates Dad and I had." *Tick. Tock.* "We went to a high school dance. He walked me home afterwards and I said, 'I had fun. I like you very much.' He was quiet, and I said, 'What's wrong?' He said, 'No one's ever told me that before'"...

Tick. Tock.
Eph...phatha.
Tick. Tock.

For the first time, Tom saw what he'd never quite seen but always, at some level, known was there. His father's anger. Anger at Ashton High School for not preparing him to do anything except work in the mill. Anger at World War II for taking five years from his life. Anger at the men in town who'd stayed home during the war and made money. Anger at his mother, and—probably—anger at his biological father for abusing him. Now, however, Tom saw that his father's anger was his way of covering up his shame for being older than his classmates, for needing to work two jobs, for having a son who brought disgrace upon him. Shame was what Ike shared with Rebecca Jacobs—*Maybe what brought them together*—but while she covered her shame of being a child of an alcoholic with a façade of competence and a quest for social status, he drank...

Marian's clock sounded more distinctly in his ears: *da dee-dee da, da, dee-dee, da, da de-de, da.*

Tom could feel his own anger and shame—the letter to Gary Coffin, the Wellness Workshop, yelling at what's-her-name at the Family Center for Grief and Loss—realizing how often he'd felt as his father had: that he lived in a world of injustice, where God, Fate, Whatever, handed out unearned advantages to some and unwarranted disasters—like the death of a child—to others. And like his father, it made him angry but at the same time ashamed because he didn't have what he perceived others as having. *And yes, I've had more to drink today that I should have.*

Tom's body relaxed. His father's anger, his drinking, his inconsistent behavior, now made a little more sense. (Christine's voice on the cobblestone street in Cambridge: *"Occasionally you come up for air and I know you love me, but then you dive back down into yourself again."*) Ike Jacobs was no saint, but he'd been a hard worker who'd held two jobs and risen to the position of foreman at the mill. A faithful husband, he'd never physically abused his children. He did a better job as a husband, as a father, than his father had.

Can I say the same?

When Lori rang the chimes again, Tom was picturing the cemetery at Ashton, his father's stone:

ISAAC ROY JACOBS—FIRST SERGEANT WWII
AUGUST 31, 1919–APRIL 8, 1980

He and Christine needed to make a trip up there. For the first time he understood Martha's inability to let their daughter's ashes be scattered, her need for something specific and tangible and hard to leave behind in this transitory world.

He opened his eyes and gazed around the room at the others in the group, the paneled wall behind the couch, the old pictures on the bookcase, the valances over the windows that Marian said her late husband had made. If the goal of meditation was silence and emptiness, the last hour had been a disaster. Still, Tom felt relaxed. *What's that verse? Something about the peace I give to you being peace that the world cannot give?* He looked over at Christine and smiled. On the drive home, he would talk to her about ordering a memorial stone for Annie, to place next to his father's and mother's graves. One of those small rosebushes would look nice next to it.

Chapter Sixteen

1997

Outside tall, curtained windows, February sunshine gilded a metal cross standing in a snow-covered courtyard surrounded by stone walls. Inside, in one of the meeting rooms of the Society of St. John the Evangelist, an Episcopal monastery in Cambridge, Massachusetts, sofas and easy chairs arranged around a fireplace made the room cozy and inviting. Tom wanted to like it here, for since Jonathan Bennett had moved to Alaska two years earlier, Tom had searched for another spiritual community to complement his worship at St. Mark's and the meditation group that he and Christine now hosted. Christine had read of SSJE while researching a paper on Episcopal monasticism for one of her seminary classes.

Tom squeezed his wife's hand. They sat on a camel-colored loveseat. Seminary was going well. Christine loved her courses and had made friends. Although she was busy all the time, she laughed more, found the time to walk more beaches with him, and experiment more in the bedroom than at any time since Nathan moved away. Yes, there were still times, especially after talking on the phone with her son, when her eyes grew troubled,

213

and times when she seemed to withdraw into herself, but for the most part, these last three years had been the happiest they'd had since before Annie's death.

As a way to start their observance of Lent, Tom and Christine had come to the monastery for a guided retreat on the Parable of the Prodigal Son. Because the forty days before Easter so closely paralleled Annie's final weeks, Lent was the one "season" in the church year that Tom thought he understood. Lent was a time to fast from drinking, read daily scripture, and attend more worship services. In other words, go into training, get in shape for the big event which, in his case, was Easter and its memories of Annie's death.

As the retreat began, the fifteen participants sitting around the meeting room introduced themselves. They came from not only all of New England, but also North Carolina, Florida, and California. For the most part, they were the usual assortment of teachers and counselors Tom had grown to expect at spiritual gatherings, although one person here was an Episcopal priest on sabbatical. Christine introduced herself as a high school English teacher and seminary student. Tom said he was also a high school English teacher, who happened to be married to a seminary student. He smiled at Brother Bernard, the retreat director, a thin, sixtyish man in black robes and thick, rimless glasses, and squeezed Christine's hand again. After arriving at the monastery the previous night, he'd slept well. This morning, after a leisurely breakfast of hot cereal and wheat toast with the Brothers and those here for the retreat, he was rested and ready to learn.

Brother Bernard passed out the schedule and provided the usual information about breaks and bathrooms. "We'll spend the day reflecting on each of the three characters in the story," he said in a soft Southern accent. "This morning we'll talk first about the younger son and, after a break for coffee and bathrooms, the older son. We'll have lunch and a couple of hours for ourselves before returning to a discussion of the father in the afternoon. Tonight we'll have a silent service, focusing on Rembrandt's famous painting of the Prodigal Son."

Tom felt a mix of anticipation and anxiety. Besides wanting a weekend of "silence and slow time," as Bennett used to say, he also felt he needed some time to reflect about a father and two sons. He'd made a sort of peace with his father. He didn't understand the old man's solipsistic negativity that seemed to increase just when he'd had the time and the means to enjoy life, but now that Tom was less than ten years younger than his father had been when he died and more aware than ever of his own inconsistencies, his own addictions, his own difficulty in trying to talk with his children, he found himself more tolerant of Ike Jacobs's imperfections. But he still had a lot of work to do regarding his brother.

After a prayer for guidance, Brother Bernard began reading to them the Parable from Luke's Gospel:

"Then Jesus said, 'There was a man who had two sons. The younger of them said to his father, "Father give me the share of the property that will belong to me."...'"

Tom gazed around the room, at pictures of lofty cathedrals and bright landscapes. His father didn't have much property or money, but what he had, he gave to his children before they could ask. Whether they wanted it or not. All those gifts were the only way he knew how to express his love.

"'...the younger son gathered all he had and traveled to a distant country and there he squandered his property in dissolute living.'"

In Tom's family, it was the elder son who was the Prodigal. Voices crackled in his ears. Red Bailey: "Move it, Jacobs! You want to end up like your brother?" Coach Giddings telling Tom after the high school basketball awards banquet: "If your brother had had your determination and self-discipline, he'd have been the best basketball player in the state, but he threw his talent away."

His father, as blue lights flashed in the driveway: "I don't know where he is and I don't care!" His mother telling him before bursting into tears: "He's gone and I don't think you should ever mention Eddie's name to your father again."

"'...But while he was still far off, his father saw him and was filled with compassion; he ran and put his arms around him and kissed him. Then the son said to him, "Father, I have sinned against heaven and before you; I am no longer worthy to be called your son." But the father said to his slaves, "Quickly, bring out a robe—the best one—and put it on him; put a ring on his finger and sandals on his feet. And get the fatted calf and kill it, and let us eat and celebrate...."'"

Tom's father did not forgive. His family never said, "I'm sorry." Admitting you were wrong was a sign of weakness. Maybe that was why his dream of Annie's "I love you" in the face of his guilt for causing her death was—and remained—so powerful.

Tom realized he was rubbing his forefinger over his thumbs. That's the way Annie's presence was these days: when he wanted to remember her, she seemed far off, hazy, but when he least expected her, she—or rather her absence—would suddenly appear and kick him in the stomach.

"'...Now the older son was in the field; and when he came and approached the house, he heard music and dancing...Then he became angry and refused to go in.'"

Ed, too, had inherited their father's anger. As a kid he'd said things like: "How come Tommy doesn't have to eat his carrots and I do?" "Why do I have to take out the garbage and Tommy doesn't?" "Tommy always gets more Christmas presents than I do, It's not fair!" At their mother's funeral: "The way Mom and Dad doted on you, I really thought you'd amount to more than just a fucking high school teacher." The difference between Ed's anger and his father's and Tom's was that Ed never seemed to try to repress it.

"Alright," said Brother Bernard. "What is there about the younger son that resonates for you in the parable?"

A woman with turquoise eyeglasses said, "Well, the way the son felt that he had sinned against his father reminded me of the way I felt after my divorce. My mother never approved of the marriage in the first place, and I felt as if I'd committed some kind of crime. But she never said, 'I told you so'…she just took me and the kids in with her until I got back on my feet."

"The younger son makes me think of my younger brother," said a man with a salt-and-pepper goatee. "He's in jail for robbing a drug store—Oxycontin and other stuff—and the other day he sent the family a letter, saying he was sorry, that he knew he'd screwed up, but that he hoped we could forgive him and give him another chance. The reason I'm at this retreat is to help me do just that."

Christine spoke.

"I'm just so afraid my son is lost to me," she said. "He hasn't visited us since he left four years ago."

As she told the story of Nathan's leaving to live with his father, Tom recognized that his wife hadn't been as happy these last four years as he'd thought. *Damn.*

"Well, we do see him whenever we can afford to fly out there," he said. "And he's always pleasant enough…" *Come on, admit it. Stop being so defensive.* "But at the same time, he does seem distant…and, I don't know, mad at something, I guess."

"It's like there's this smog bank of anger hanging over him." Christine said.

"And he's got all these body piercings," said Tom. "Ears, nose, God knows where else. The last time we were out there, he'd shaved his head and gotten this tattoo on his arm of a skull with two snakes as crossbones."

"He's at Colorado State University, studying zoology," Christine said. "Last fall he was arrested. He was in a protest march against using animals for medical testing, and it turned violent." Her voice trembled. "I worry about him."

There was silence for a moment, before the Episcopal priest on sabbatical said, "The son in the parable reminds me of my own problems with alcohol." He sounded impatient. Tom stopped listening, thoughts of his stepson buzzing around him like wasps in a phone booth. Nathan's string of girlfriends troubled him. The two he'd met—out of how many, he'd lost count—looked just like Annie, and Tom worried the boy was still searching for his lost sister. Tom was also bothered by Nathan's hostility toward Christianity and his mother's taking seminary classes. "How can you participate," he'd said to Christine, "in a religion that's responsible for just about every war that's been fought in the Western Hemisphere?"

A woman's voice pulled Tom back to the present. "…never forget that, when I heard my daughter was in the hospital after flipping her car on an icy road…" Her voice grated, and he noticed a mole on her chin. "…I thought I'd lost her—that I'd never see Meg alive again," she announced. "But God returned her to me, and she's completely recovered. I'm so grateful! I know how the father in the parable feels."

Tom's forehead tightened. *Bully for you, bitch.* They were supposed to be talking about children, not parents.

He took a deep breath. *Where did that come from?* She had every right to be grateful. He directed his gaze out the window at the barren courtyard and the granite walls of the monastery chapel behind it. He tried to detach from his emotions. Watch them the way Bennett had taught him to watch his thoughts while meditating. Name them. *Resentment. Guilt. Anger.* Inspect them. Put them away. He focused on regulating his breathing and on listening to his heartbeat until it slowed.

After a break, during which Tom found himself alone since Christine looked to be in deep conversation with the man with the goatee, discussion turned to the older brother in the parable, especially his refusal to attend his father's party for the younger son, and the elder brother's self-righteous anger. Tom squirmed in his chair and rubbed his hands. Voices merged, faded, as he realized that in his mixed-up family, it was the younger son who was self-righteous. He'd been the one who had peered down his nose at Ed at their mother's funeral, like he was some kind of toad. He could have offered his house—Annie's room—as a place for his brother to stay. At least asked him to go for coffee. How would he know the reason for Ed's anger? Had he ever asked? Had Tom ever reached out to him? When was the last time he'd called his brother? At their mother's funeral, Ed had given Tom his address. Did he still have it? Had he ever reached out to anyone in need? Had he been as judgmental about Annie as he was of Ed? Of Nathan? *Look at how I talked about my stepson this morning.*

After lunch, Tom was grateful that, when they went on retreat, he and Christine stayed in separate rooms to give each other space and privacy (besides which, it made their return home to their double bed that much more fun). So after he ate he was able to go back to his room and dive uninterrupted into P.D. James' *Original Sin*. He needed a break from all this angst.

When they gathered later that afternoon to focus on the father in the parable, Tom smiled as he sat down beside Christine, but he was gripping his hands and rubbing his thumbs even before Brother Bernard asked the group to think of the father not as a personification of God but as a real parent.

"I want y'all to think of the father in the parable as also being prodigal," Brother Bernard said. He picked up a dictionary from the floor beside his chair. "If you look the word up, besides meaning wasteful, 'prodigal' also means 'to give in abundance, be lavish or profuse.'" His eyes slowly scanned his audience. "So the father, you see, was prodigal with his love for his son. He gave him not only his share of his inheritance, but also the freedom to take chances, risk failure, and push limits." He set the dictionary down. "And he welcomed his son back with open arms, not to mention the best clothing, fine jewelry, and all that good food." The monk appeared to be writing in the air with his right hand. "Even while the boy was away, you can see this prodigal love, because—and for me, this is key—since the father saw his son 'while he was still far off,' he must have been searching continually for his child's return."

"That's hard for me," the priest on sabbatical said. "My father was just the opposite of the father in the parable. I couldn't do anything to please him."

"My father has never been there when I've needed him," said a young woman, probably the youngest of them there. "And I've needed him a lot." She began to weep.

Tom looked out another window at another stone wall, this one around the monastery garden. Against the stones, dead leaves and broken branches poked through the snow. He thought of his father. Lavish with his presents, profuse with his criticism. Disavowing his older son. "I don't know where he is and I don't care!" Besides all those aggravating material gifts, Ike had bequeathed to Tom his anger, his shame, and his solipsism. Look at the way he always downplayed Christine's sorrow about Nathan. Like his father, he had difficulty relating with other people. The joy he felt in physically connecting with Christine, whether it was making love or simply holding hands, just further accentuated his inability to touch, hug, or even get close to others like Nathan or Annie. The first time he'd ever seen his daughter, twenty-seven years earlier, he'd stood trembling and dumb with wonder, separated from her by a plate glass window in the maternity ward. That invisible barrier had remained between them for the rest of her life. He had seldom fed her as a baby, rarely changed her diapers, hardly ever went to her when she woke up in the night. Maybe if he'd done some of the dirty stuff, he'd have been more apt to take her up into his lap, hold her in his arms. Embrace her. Kiss her. Tell her before she died how much he loved her.

Tom counted his breaths, but the air seemed stuffy. "I was happy to welcome my daughter back," said another voice, "but that was two years ago. It's time for her to leave." More talk of children. His stomach knotted and, for the first time in years, his chest began to burn. When he rose from his chair, pain kicked him in the back.

1997

After a silent supper, he returned to his room and *Original Sin*. He skipped the special evening worship service, preferring the logical mind of Adam Dalgliesh to sitting with the others. Still, he found himself staring through the mullioned window, through the shadows of trees, at the lights of the cars driving on either side of the Charles River. Things had been going so well. After years of chiropractors and osteopaths, he'd found a great physical therapist and, until that afternoon, his back had been practically pain free. Tired of commuting to school and to church from Newell, he and Christine had bought Marian Magnussen's house in Jordan Mills. (Marian to the meditation group: "I want to sell my house. I'm eighty-three years old and I want to take some of the money and see the Holy Land before I die. Know anyone who might want my house?" Tom: "Well, yes, as a matter of fact, I do.") They'd made a few friends in Jordan Mills. He was enjoying his classes at school, and last year Jim Silas noted in his annual evaluation that, besides being demanding, Tom was evolving into a compassionate teacher. He'd joined a new transition group at the Family Center for Grief and Loss, along with Doug, the art dealer he'd once disliked, but now found to be generous and kindhearted, a man with limitless energy who was always ready to try something new, and who inspired Tom to think about starting a bereavement group at church and getting more involved at St. Mark's in social action and pastoral care. Tom had even been considering taking a course or two with Christine at the seminary.

But as the wind outside picked up and cold air blew in around the window of his room, all his goals became either impossible to achieve or not worth doing. Join the Social Action Committee or the Lay Pastoral Visitors? He didn't know anybody in that crowd. Start a bereavement group? He didn't want to listen to people talk about their grief, anymore than he'd wanted to hear people that day talk about their children. Seminary? Who was he kidding? Christine was the theologian in the family.

Heating pipes clanged. Tom shivered from the cold. Not the frigid cold from being outside, but a more subtle cold that seemed to penetrate his heart. An icon of the Madonna and Child hung on the rough, stucco wall over a wooden kneeler. Something about the mournful expression on the face of Mary as she held her son reminded him of trying to hold his daughter in the hospital amidst all those tubes as she cried, "I want to go home, but it hurts too much to cut back on the morphine and I can't eat. What am I going to do, Dad?" His helplessness. His feeling ashamed of himself for not being able to answer her question, talk to her about death.

He wandered downstairs and made another cup of tea, wishing it were Scotch. He read and stared at the wall until after midnight.

The next morning, as they gathered for what Brother Bernard called "a sharing of the graces," Tom slumped in a wooden chair by the window. His back was on fire. A mix of snow and sleet pelted the courtyard while people spoke about their identification with one of the characters in the parable. Most saw themselves as the younger son—"wandering in wilderness, searching for a way home," as a man with a crucifix earring put it. A few people admitted seeing themselves as the older son: "I get so angry seeing the Church constantly changing, losing its traditions, trying to get people back on Sundays," said the woman with the mole on her chin. "All churches are doing is driving more and more of us old-timers away."

"But there's always a chance someone will return to God," said a seventy-something African-American woman. "Always a chance."

No, not always a chance. As the black woman repeated what she'd said the day before, about how the rector of her church had welcomed her back after a twenty-five- year hiatus, he saw that all of the previous night's doubts about his future were attempts to avoid what was really pulling him down into the old quagmire: the knowledge that he would never have a chance, like the father in the parable, to welcome his child home from her wanderings.

"I wrote a sort of a poem last night," Christine said. She was sitting alone on the love seat. "May I read it?" She glanced at Tom, next at Brother Bernard, who nodded. "The title's a little lengthy. It's 'Mary Reflects on the Prodigal Son as She Holds the Body of Her Crucified Child.'"

Tom's shoulders sagged with shame. *Shit. I read a mystery. Christine wrote poetry.*

> "You wandered far into a world unknown:
> Messiah, Lord, Redeemer—and now dead.
> And so I hold you here in my arms."

His face flushed, as shame shifted to anger.

> "You told a story of a son who left,
> Whose father grieved—surely his mother, too—
> As he wandered far into a world unknown."

Oh, for crying out loud, Christine. Nathan might be out there roaming the Rockies, but he wasn't dead. She could see him anytime she wanted to hop on an airplane.

She finished:

> "The son in your story came back, but you went on,
> Along a path that led to this stark tomb;
> You wandered far into a world unknown
> And now I hold you here in my arms."

The room at SSJE filled with audible sighs.
"Oh, that was wonderful!"
"So moving…"
"I'm glad you included a mother's feelings. I've always wondered where she was in the parable."

Tom seethed. *You have no right to my story!*

After everyone else had spoken, Brother Bernard turned to Tom. Through thick glasses, the monk's eyes bored into him. Tom said nothing. His stomach knotted and his back hurt.

Wringing his hands and rubbing his thumbs, he stared down at the beige carpet, envious of the father in the parable, angry at his wife, and disgusted with himself for having spent the weekend in hiding.

For the next month, the pain of Annie's loss was the worst it had been for years. Meditation, which had always helped Tom detach from his emotions, was like teetering on the edge of an abyss. Sometimes a belt tightened around his temples. Other times he trembled as if from cold. Sometimes he experienced desolation, fragmentation, frustration. Other times, fear.

He wrote in his journal:

> I realize that for the last few years, I have, without really thinking about it, equated the comforting silence that sometimes used to embrace me during meditation as God. Now I seem to be wrestling with an icy darkness that's trying to choke the life out of me.

Because he knew how hard it was to talk about God at the Family Center for Grief and Loss, he stopped going. His relationship with Christine began backsliding toward those early years after Annie's death—he, silent and self-absorbed, she, silent and sad. He went for solitary walks and drank more in the evenings. She spent more time at the seminary library.

One Sunday night, after a meeting of the meditation group, Tom told Christine that he was thinking about dropping out. "If I hear Marion tell me one more time to 'just stay with it. There's God's time and there's our time,' I'm going to puke. Let them find somewhere else to meet."

They sat in the study of their house, where Annie's watercolor now hung over a bookcase. For the past few years, he'd been able to see the falling flower petals the way Bennett had once explained them—as progenitors of new life. Now, however, he saw only Annie's cold, blue hand slipping away from him into the rocks. He wished Bennett were still around.

"I wonder if you don't need someone to talk with," Christine said, as if reading his mind. "Maybe there's someone at the monastery. I think the Brothers do spiritual direction."

"I'm not sure I know what spiritual direction is. Isn't that just for clergy or for people wanting to be clergy?"

"I don't know." Christine got up from her chair, came over to Tom and kissed him on the forehead. "Why don't we find out?"

She made the phone call to the guest Brother in charge of setting up spiritual direction sessions. In March, they drove down to the monastery so that she could meet with Brother Bernard, and Tom with Brother Jeremiah. Tom had noticed Jeremiah when he'd worshipped at SSJE. He was hard to miss. In his early seventies, well over six feet tall, broad-shouldered and bald with a beard that reached his barrel chest, he might have stepped off the pages of an illuminated manuscript. As they introduced themselves, Tom learned that the monk was a former Air Force fighter pilot who had almost died when his jet crashed in Korea. That he was a recovering alcoholic whose drinking almost drove him to suicide. That before coming to SSJE, he'd had a street ministry in New York City, where one of the drug addicts he was working with "went off on crack" and knifed him in the chest. "There's no reason I can think of why I'm still alive," he told Tom as they sat across from each other in a small room with a narrow window overlooking the Charles River, "except God still has work for me to do."

Brother Jeremiah seemed bigger than life, threatening somehow. Tom wanted to say, "Okay, you've done a lot, but you never lost a child," as if he were back at the Family Center for Grief and Loss, playing "my story is more dramatic than yours."

The monk smiled at him. "I talk too much. Which is only one of my failings as a spiritual director. But I'm the one Brother Bernard suggested, so you're stuck with me." He sat back in his chair. "Tell me why you're here."

Swinging his swivel-rocker from side to side, Tom told the story of Annie's death and his subsequent grief and guilt. He talked about Father Curtis Mathews and St. Mark's, Jonathan Bennett and meditation. He spoke of the Prodigal Son Retreat and how it had sucked him back into his black hole of despair. "It's not just in meditation that I'm upset. Last week I dreamed I was trying—unsuccessfully—to make love to my wife, and I looked over and saw a baby crawling along the side of our bed." He twisted his hands together. "I couldn't move. All I could do was watch, as the baby fell to the floor with a loud thud. I realized the baby was Annie. I woke up, hearing a voice—probably mine—screaming, 'No, not again!'"

Brother Jeremiah played with some kind of knotted bracelet he'd taken off his wrist. Tom drank the last of his cold tea and wondered if the monk had even been listening. Finally, Brother Jeremiah straightened up in his chair. "Is what you're feeling exactly the same as after Annie died?"

Tom gazed out through the narrow window. Wind rippled the Charles River. He said, "There's less guilt, more fear—well, not fear, exactly, but anxiety...No, make that dread. How about existential dread?"

Brother Jeremiah chuckled. "Wow!" He opened a tin of Altoids, took one, and offered the tin to Tom.

Tom shook his head. Brother Jeremiah slipped his bracelet back on his wrist. He gazed at the wall behind Tom. "Okay, here's some homework," he said. "Have you heard of *Lectio Divina*?"

Tom folded his arms. "That's 'divine reading,' isn't it? Where you slowly read a passage of scripture and meditate on a word or phrase that stays with you?" He was both pleased with himself for knowing the right answer and disappointed because, after reading about it with the meditation group, he'd tried it and it hadn't opened any doors. The words that always stayed with him expressed frustration or confusion about God.

"That's close enough for government work," Brother Jeremiah said. "Well, there's another kind of meditation sort of like it. You actually put yourself into an episode in the Bible, either as a main character or as an onlooker. It can be pretty overwhelming, especially if you put yourself into the flogging or the Crucifixion." He grinned. "But from the sound of things, I don't think you need to flog yourself any more than you already have." He picked up his tin of Altoids. "Why don't you spend your meditation time becoming part of the Parable of the Prodigal Son?" He popped another Altoid into his mouth and stood up, signaling the end of their session. "You might start by being the father for a while."

So for twenty minutes each morning, Tom tried to imagine himself as the father watching for his child. He pictured the hillside, the smell of the grass, the sheep bleating in the distance. He put a rock ledge on the hill to lean against. He envisioned a dirt road winding through a grove of trees in the distance, and, beyond that, fog lying on the horizon.

But as he wrote in his journal:

> I can't envision sending out love to Annie, because I can't imagine her receiving it. That would mean picturing my child now, in the present moment, not as the little girl learning to read, or the budding artist with the bright red streak in her hair, or the helpless child in the hospital. Every time I try to visualize my daughter walking that road back to me, a canyon opens in my imaginary landscape, keeping the two of us apart.

On Easter Sunday afternoon, while Christine stayed at the monastery writing another seminary paper, Tom sat at a wrought-iron table in front of Au Bon Pain in Harvard Square. The air smelled of exhaust fumes and sausages. Sun lit both the mottled branches of the sycamores overhead and the cigarette butts under his feet. A cacophony of languages babbled about him, while in the distance the nasal voice of a street musician wailed over his guitar:

REQUIEM IN STONES

*"Ten years ago, on a cold dark night,
Someone was killed, 'neath the town hall light."*

Tom sipped his coffee and watched a tall black man pirouette on the sidewalk before presenting two camera-clad tourists a copy of *Spare Change*, the newspaper written by the homeless. His eyes itched from not enough sleep. He felt lightheaded, tired, and yet, in a strange way, awakened. Instead of observing Easter this morning at St. Mark's, he and Christine had driven down last night to stay at the monastery and get up at 4 a.m. to join a small band of guests, following the Brothers as they processed from the bonfire in their garden to the chapel, all of them carrying candles.

The service had begun with the Great Vigil, a two-hour service of Old Testament readings. The only light in the church, coming from the candles, cast shadows on stone walls. Tom listened to creation stories from Genesis, Exodus, Isaiah, Ezekiel, and Zephaniah, remembering how he'd sat comforted by these stories in the Chapter House at Salisbury Cathedral in England. He longed to return to the feeling he'd had that day, of being embraced and warmed by the sunlight and the stones. He'd been cold now for more than a month.

Then the lights had come on in, a searing illumination of the granite walls and the stained-glass windows and flowers around the altar, and of Jesus on the cross. The organ had boomed and a trumpet had blared as they had sung "Jesus Christ is Risen Today." Alleluias rose and crashed like tidal waves. Tears spilled from Tom's eyes. He escaped out the aisle, made his way to the back door, and stood outside on stone steps until the morning sun and a cold wind off the river dried his face. When he returned, Christine looked at him worriedly. He reached for her hand and clutched it.

They remained holding hands as Brother Patrick, SSJE's Brother Superior, stood up to preach. Tall and ascetic, the monk reminded Tom a little of Curtis Matthews. His text was on the women at the empty tomb in Mark's Gospel:

1997

So they went out and fled from the tomb, for terror and amazement had seized them, and they said nothing to anyone, for they were afraid.

"I can understand their amazement," said Brother Patrick. "But why the terror? Why were they afraid? We are not told. So I ask you: why would you be afraid, then or now?"

Yes, why? That's what I've been asking myself again and again for the last six weeks.

"Well, perhaps they were afraid that Jesus's body had been stolen and that they were in danger themselves." Brother Patrick had a staccato delivery. "That's one possibility. These were violent times. Maybe there were grave robbers about. Maybe Pilate had changed his mind and sent soldiers to take the body away to a common grave.

"But I would say that there's another reason for their fear. One that keeps us from entering into the joy of Easter and the fullness of God's love. And that's the fear that Jesus really is alive again." Brother Patrick adjusted his glasses and referred to his notes. "For if Jesus really is alive, that means that everything we think we know about the way the world works, everything we think we know about life and death, is wrong. And that's scary. Even if we don't like the idea of death, we think we understand how it works. And this understanding gives us a certain security."

A cold worm wriggled across the back of Tom's neck.

"I suspect like most of us, the women in Mark's Gospel had become secure, not only about what they believed about death, but even secure in their vision of a violent and hostile world. Secure in their own suffering..."

Tom recoiled. Was he like the women in Mark's Gospel, afraid to confront the meaning of Easter? After Annie's death, he had dismissed the Easter story as a childhood fairy tale. Since then, he'd fixed his attention on trying to understand God. Over the last few years, however, his reading, his meditation, his retreats, had all moved him to a crossroad. Straight ahead was this thing called

"Resurrection," not the intellectual exercise—did Jesus' molecules reassemble themselves or not—but something that had or hadn't happened to his daughter. He had to make a choice. Either Annie was resurrected or she wasn't. It was time for him to say, "Yes, I believe" or "No, I don't believe."

He was afraid to make that commitment.

Sitting now in Harvard Square, Tom realized that over the years his Lenten preparations had become smoke screens. Exercises to help him deal with Annie's death. Diversions to keep him from thinking about the fact that Easter was about living, not about dying. Had he become secure, he wondered, even happy in his vision of himself as Grieving Parent? He thought of his angry reaction to Christine's poem at the Prodigal Son Retreat because she'd taken *his* story. Was fear of losing this story, this identity, the reason he couldn't picture Annie's return to him in his meditations? Did he want her only as memories pasted on the pages of a scrapbook? Did he want to keep the stone rolled in front of her tomb?

He watched a young couple and a little boy probably ten years old, all of them dressed up in what were probably new Easter clothes, walking past Au Bon Pain. He remembered the pants and socks he and Ed used to get this time of year, his mother in one of her hats and white gloves and high heels, his father in his gray fedora, holiday suit, and freshly shined shoes. Again he considered the father in the Parable of the Prodigal Son. The old man doesn't know whether or not his son is still alive. His friends and his older son probably declare he'll never see the boy again. That his child now lives in a distant country or sails the seas or lies dead from famine, disease, or foul play. "Face it," they say, "you've lost that child. Don't waste your time and your love searching for him."

But the Prodigal Father, as Brother Bernard called him, goes out on the hill every day, sending out his love to wherever his child may be, and if Tom was serious about his Christian faith, he'd do the same thing. He needed to stop hoarding his love—dwelling on old memories of his daughter—and send it out to Annie, trusting that she'd receive it.

1997

As he finished his coffee, a man and two children walked by. The girl was probably about five and held a bright-green balloon on a string. Tom tried once more to imagine himself standing on a hill, keeping watch across the canyon that separated him from his child. He substituted an olive tree for the balloon, replaced the sound of automobiles and voices with those of birds and sheep.

"I don't know where you are, kid, or what you're doing," he whispered, "or what you look like. But please know that I love you…I love you."

Gradually, Harvard Square dissolved, leaving him suspended in a sort of mist. He sensed someone standing with him. Together, they looked over the abyss and down the serpentine road toward the horizon. An arm gently fell across his shoulder. Slender fingers patted him.

And he knew—knew as absolutely as he knew she'd died eight years earlier—that Annie was with him. The distant road, the canyon, the hillside faded, became Harvard Square once more, and still she stood by his side, her arm around him, both of them gazing up at the blue-and-gold domes rising over the trees. And he wept, both out of joy because she'd come back, and out of sorrow because he couldn't put his arms around her.

Chapter Seventeen

2000

Tom leaned against a ledge by the shore of St. Columba's Bay on the island of Iona off the west coast of Scotland. Vaporous sunlight shimmered around him and white clouds lay low over the water. Waves crashed on the rocks and rolled in over a pebbled beach like a necklace, which breaking, cast pearls upon the stones.

Annie's voice whispered, "Pretty neat day I painted you, huh, Dad?"

Yeah, it is. Thanks, Kid. Tears welled, spilled, and dried in the sea breeze. The last years had been a pendulum swing between happiness and sadness. His daughter was always with him and at the same time she was never there. Even if he heard her voice, felt her touch, he couldn't hold her, see her face become more interesting as it aged.

He heard laughter. Two teenaged girls waded in the water toward him. More young people in shorts and backpacks wandered along the shoreline. Earlier that morning, he and Christine had joined the weekly pilgrimage around Iona's various holy sites, led by staff of the Iona Community, the ecumenical Christian group that ran religious activities on the island. But instead of the meditative walk he'd imagined, they'd arrived during this week's Community Youth Conference, and Tom found himself on a gallop, young people racing up and down hills and jumping over rocks like mountain goats, while he and Christine plodded behind, catching up at the stops along the way, always arriving at the tail end of a prayer.

The two girls who'd been wading deeper and deeper into the surf suddenly dove into the water, one after the other. They surfaced, screaming, water dripping from their hair and clothes. Tom smiled. In them he saw his daughter's energy, her radiance. At the same time, emptiness burned. He lifted his eyes to a rocky promontory jutting out into the ocean, layered like a cake—yellow turning to black, frosted with pink heather—and tried to focus on Annie's spiritual presence instead of on her physical absence. Feel her vitality both in these young people and in the magical landscape surrounding him.

Brother Bernard at SSJE had suggested Iona to them as a place to visit, touting the island as a "thin place," where the connection between God and humanity, the eternal and the temporal, is most apparent. Which was what Tom was looking for these days. While he might have felt closer to Annie than he had since her death, he still felt distant from God, as he realized how often he used to sit in meditation focused on his daughter when he thought he was focusing on God. Since the Prodigal Son Retreat, he no longer experienced that comforting cloud of presence during meditation, no longer saw lights or visions. Only a constant struggle with thoughts, where he often resorted to *Lectio Divina*, repeating passages of scripture—*For God alone my soul in silence waits...As the deer longs for the water brooks, so longs my soul for you, O God...My soul waits for the Lord, more than watchmen for the morning*—to get him through his twenty minutes.

Even though Iona reminded him of parts of Maine, there was also something different here. The quality of light. The way sound carried. The stones. Tom had never seen so many stones in one place. Yellow, pink, violet, white, gray, and green, sometimes all marbled together in one rock. The previous night he had read that some rocks on Iona are almost three billion years old. Holding one of them was the closest he could come to imagining eternity.

He saw Christine walking the shore, filling the pockets of her cargo pants with stones. In June she'd received her Master of Theology at Bangor Seminary, and after eight years of her studying and his holding them to their budget, they'd given this trip to each other. He knew she was picking up stones to bring back as gifts. To Diane and Sam in Wyoming. To her parents, now living in a retirement community in Lexington. She would choose some particularly nice ones—perhaps the marble ones flecked with green—to take to Nathan, in his second year of graduate work in herpetology at CSU, and to his girlfriend Maria, a high school counselor, and her five-year-old daughter Yazmin.

Tom and Christine's visit last winter had been like this day—bittersweet. When Yazmin danced down the walk of Nathan's and Maria's apartment in Fort Collins to meet them, she reminded Tom so much of Annie at that age, in the way she moved, that she frightened him. Later, when she looked at him with a shy smile and said, "Would you like to see my snow fort?" he was pleased, but once they were outside and she asked, "Will you help me make it bigger?" he held back, saying, "Shouldn't we ask your mother and Nathan if you need to have your mittens?"

Then Nathan came out with her mittens and a shovel. "Come on, Yaz," he said, "Let's make the biggest snow fort in Fort Collins!" He looked at Tom, and seemed to hesitate before asking, "Do you want to join us?"

Not sure whether or not he meant it, Tom said, "No, I'll go in. Thanks anyway."

He didn't understand why he felt estranged from his stepson. He couldn't put a finger on anything Nathan ever said or did to create the tension he sensed still separating them. No, Nathan was invariably polite, he was obviously eager to have him like Maria and Yazmin, and last winter he'd mentioned several times that he and Maria now belonged to the Society of Friends and attended worship every Sunday evening. But any conversation between Tom and Nathan always petered into awkward silence—a vacuum that Tom always expected Nathan to fill with angry accusations of his stepfather's poor parenting skills.

Here on Iona, Tom whispered a prayer he'd learned at SSJE:

"May we be at peace
May we know the beauty of our own true natures
May our hearts be opened
May we be healed."

"Could we gather together?" called Jeannie, their guide on the pilgrimage. As she did at every stop, she pulled a spiral notebook from her backpack. "As part of our pilgrimage," she read, raising her voice above the sound of the waves and the laughter, "we take two pebbles from the beach. One we throw into the sea as a symbol of something in our lives we would like to leave behind, while the other we take back with us, as a sign of a new commitment in our heart."

The young people raced down over the rocks. Tom followed slowly, stopping at one of the ledges to pick up a jagged piece of rock—ash-colored, like Annie's memorial stone in Ashton—narrowed at either end, about a half-inch thick, with sharp edges. He considered the rough edges of his heart, those parts still unable to trust God. He dug his thumbnail into cracked and pitted crevices, and thought of the emptiness within him. At the water's edge, he put his index finger around the rough edges of the stone, dipped his shoulder, and skimmed the rock across the water. It skipped three times and sank. He imagined the stone drifting to the bottom of the bay, thought of the currents working on it, the other stones rubbing against it year after year, smoothing away the rough edges.

He watched the circles spread out from where the stone hit the water. So many times over the past thirteen years he'd felt as if he were wandering in circles, revisiting the same feelings, like a mule harnessed to a chain; but today, at least, he sensed his circle of grief widening, fanning out into something larger, the way the circles of water were spreading into St. Columba's Bay and beyond that, into Iona Sound, and beyond that, into the Atlantic Ocean.

He turned, bent over, and after searching a bit, picked up a green stone shaped like a heart. *My commitment to...?* He wasn't sure, but he dropped it into his pocket. Then he noticed another stone, marbled red-and-green-and white, and picked that up to send to his brother. After finding Ed's address, he'd sent him a birthday card in March. In April, Ed sent Tom a card for his birthday, with a note: "Good to here from you No bullshit. It really is." Tom hadn't written back, but this would be a good excuse.

As he dropped the stone in his pocket, he saw Christine, her face glowing in the sunlight, walking toward him. He reached for her hand and they clambered up the thirty yards or so of small stones rising at an almost forty-five degree angle between the water and a field. The stones shifted, slid, and sank under their feet. Often the couple stumbled and, at one point, they fell to their knees, laughing. Finally, they gave up trying to walk straight up the incline and began to weave their way back and forth.

Reaching the top of the final tier of stones, Tom turned and looked once more out over St. Columba's Bay. The surf crashed and the pebbles shifted in a chorus of clanks, thuds, clatters, pings, rattles, and taps, a Sanctus that pulled at him as he and Christine trekked through the boggy field of pink-and-blue-and-yellow wild flowers, up over some craggy hills, and down across a low-lying pasture called the Machair.

The pilgrimage ended at St. Oran's Chapel, next to the abbey. The worn, twelfth-century stone walls of the chapel rose white against the blue backdrop of Iona Sound and, behind that, the rugged green hills on the Island of Mull. Tombstones and daffodils surrounded the small building. By the time Christine and Tom arrived there, teenagers huddled by the arched entrance, listening to the sound of guitars playing from inside.

2000

Consulting her notebook once more, Jeannie told them the pilgrimage traditionally ends at St. Oran's and the cemetery, because Christians have always celebrated the fact that it was in a burial place that the Resurrection faith began. She told them that—as they continued their various pilgrimages through life—they should realize they did not journey alone, that they had many companions walking with them in prayer and in friendship. She prayed:

"God bless each of us as we travel on.
In our time of need
May we find a table spread in the wilderness
And companions on the road."

While everyone else scattered, Tom and Christine ducked into St. Oran's Chapel and collapsed onto a stone choir stall in front of a small white altar. A single light burned from a votive candle suspended from the ceiling. The stark white walls and damp air reminded Tom of a cellar.

He sat in the silence—somewhere between sleep and meditation—as the companions who'd walked with him since Annie's death flickered through the chapel: Christine, her hair once again black, and Nathan in his new tie-dye cradling Claudius the corn snake; Curtis Mathews—now remarried and serving as rector of a big parish in Connecticut; Jonathan Bennett—still in Alaska as far as he knew; Angela, Penny, Doug, and the others at the Family Center for Grief and Loss; Brother Jeremiah—who still made him feel inadequate and defensive for some reason, but for whom he was grateful; even Martha, from whom he hadn't heard in ten years, but whom he often envisioned walking a parallel path through grief, and for whom, like the others, he prayed.

When he and Christine stepped outside into the graveyard, Tom's legs were stiff and his back was sore. While she wandered toward a stone wall and gazed across the sound, he examined the gravestones. Stone slabs, lying like gray tablets in the green sod, marked most of the gravesites. Many commemorated islanders lost at sea, some even younger than Annie had been when she died. Some of the stones were ancient, almost completely covered in lichen, smooth, any words or carvings obliterated by wind and rain.

He thought again of Annie's memorial stone and of how glad he was to have had one made. He'd taken a picture of the stone and sent it to Martha in a card, apologizing for not understanding her need to have Annie's ashes buried in her family plot. But Martha had never replied.

He wandered through the Iona cemetery a bit more and then called to Christine, "Hey, I just remembered. This is the graveyard where Duncan and Macbeth are buried. This is 'Colmekill.' I wonder if this big unmarked mound here is theirs."

She turned, sunlight reflecting off tear-stained cheeks. Her mouth was a half-smile, reflecting joy, embarrassment, sorrow—he couldn't tell.

"What's wrong?" He walked to her and put his hand on her shoulder. He felt her straighten.

"What did you throw away?"

It took a moment for him to understand her question. "You mean back at Columba's Bay?"

"Yes." Before he could reply, she said, "I threw away my muzzle."

"Oh?" The steep cliffs of Mull rose into low clouds on the other side of the sound. "You want to tell me what you mean?"

His hand still rested on her arm. She put her hand over his. "I thought I believed in Easter, thought I believed in resurrection. But I'm still with Mary in that poem I wrote at SSJE. I'm still in the tomb with a dead body, and I think a big reason is the way I've muzzled myself ever since Annie went into the hospital."

I will always love this woman, but I'll never understand her. "I know you've always felt we should have told Nathan that Annie was dying."

She withdrew her hand and began making circles with it, as if trying to clear away cobwebs. "But I've never known why I never told him," she said. "I know you asked me not to say anything, but I knew saying nothing was wrong. It's just recently that I've understood that the reason I didn't tell him was because I felt guilty for breaking up your family—I thought I'd done enough to hurt you and your daughter—and I couldn't stand the thought of breaking us up, too."

"You didn't break up my family." Tom jammed his hands into his pockets and tried to stretch out his back. "Martha and I never were a family in the first place. And even if we had been, I'm as responsible as you are."

She spoke slowly and softly. "I know you think you are, but, remember, I'm the one who wrote first. Admit it, Tom. You never would have written to me. I waited almost three weeks before I sent my letter."

He shrugged his shoulders and looked away. His back had begun to ache. He wanted to go back to their guest house.

"And once I put that muzzle on, I couldn't take it off. I didn't say anything to the counselor at the Family Center for Grief and Loss who told me I didn't belong there. I didn't tell Zack that Nathan would have been better off staying with us in high school. I didn't say anything to you when you went into that room or when you went off on those retreats of Bennett's every Easter instead of staying home with your wife and son." Her voice trembled. "All of that silence was wrong, and I'm—we're—still paying for it."

How happy she'd looked earlier, her face bathed in sunlight on St. Columba's Bay! How he'd imagined the two of them as they struggled together up the pile of stones, a team, striving hand-in-hand, laughing at life's challenges! Had he seen only what he'd wanted to see? He clasped his hands together and rubbed one thumb against the other. He thought of Lady Macbeth. *What, will these hands ne'er be clean?*

"I know I screwed up in those first years," he said, "but I thought I'd learned to listen. I didn't know you felt you still couldn't talk to me."

She put both hands on his arms. "Your not knowing is my fault, not yours. You've had to deal with every parent's nightmare—

the worst loss a person can have." Her grip tightened. "And you're finding your way. I need to find mine."

She reached into her travel vest. "What was it we heard?" she asked. "Take a pebble back as a sign of a new commitment? This is my commitment to finding my voice."

She held up the stone. Black and white and red layers swirled through it, the colors looking as fluid as they had in the heat of their creation.

"Now I'm the one who doesn't dare say anything," he said. Emotions circled like sea birds. Anger at her for disturbing his vision of the day. Shame for being so self-absorbed and not knowing the burden she'd been carrying almost ever since he'd known her. Gratitude for her saying he was her example of what she needed to do. Respect for the determination he heard in her voice. "What can I do to help?"

"A lot," she said. Behind her the sun twinkled off the water. "I'm going to need your emotional support, and I'm going to need more of our money." She leaned back against the stone wall. "As I was sitting in St. Oran's Chapel, I realized that what I really want to do when we get home is start working with women who are in prison. That at some level, I identify with them."

He stopped himself from patting her arm and saying they'd talk about it when they got home. Her decision to go to seminary had been one thing. She'd always been interested in theology. But he'd never heard her talk about prisoners or even prisons before. She was too old to make a career change. They couldn't afford what he assumed would be more education costs. She complained about some of the delinquents in her classes. How would she be able to stand working with convicted criminals? Not to mention that the work might be dangerous.

"And I guess I'm not asking you if it's okay," Christine said. Her voice was slow and steady. "I'm telling you, and I'm praying you'll understand. I want to do some part- time volunteer work first, get my Clinical Pastoral Education done next summer, and, if all goes well, retire from teaching the following year and move to full-time work."

2000

He gazed at the rippling waters of the sound, fear widening the gulf he sensed opening between them. He'd always considered her return to seminary a fairly harmless diversion, something to take up her time after Nathan moved away. These plans would seriously change their lives. Could they keep up with the house payments? Get another two years out of their ten-year-old Honda?

He looked back into her eyes, which were that mysterious color he couldn't identify. Damn it, though, she was right. For the last eleven years, she'd allowed him—without comment or criticism—to do whatever was necessary in his battles with grief and guilt after Annie's death. Now she was telling him that she had her own war to fight. She had let him find his way. It was time to put aside his ego, his presumption that her happiness depended exclusively on him, and let her find hers.

When her hand stroked his cheek, the channel narrowed. "Can you understand?" she asked. "I hope so."

He recalled when he'd first seen her mysterious eyes in the lobby of that college dormitory. He had thought her the most exciting woman he'd ever met. That same impassioned woman stood in front of him once more.

"I don't understand," he said, "anymore than I understood why, sixteen years ago, you'd want to write to a confused and timid couch potato like me." He took her hand with both of his. "But if you hadn't sent that first letter, and if we'd never gotten together, I'm not sure I'd be alive today. Maybe I'm being melodramatic, but without you with me after Annie died…" He drew her to him. She fitted her body against his. "I've never wanted you to be locked up in any kind of prison," he said, "and I won't keep you from going to prison now, if that's what you want to do."

She smiled and her eyes glistened. "Thank you," she whispered. They embraced.

"We can find Macbeth's grave later," she said. "Let's go back to the guest house."

In the soft, afternoon sunlight through the curtains, they made love, falling into an ocean rhythm, becoming one wave rising, cresting, and crashing on the shore. After supper, they walked back to the abbey for the Iona Community's evening service. Past St. Martin's Cross, they entered the Gothic doorway. They walked down the nave and found the last two empty seats in the choir stalls. Between the stalls ran several tables. Overhead, beams of timber arched like an upturned boat. On their right, light streamed from a high soaring window onto a marble communion table. Facing them, two Gothic arches rose over the choir stalls. An organ played a vaguely familiar hymn.

Christine leaned over and whispered to Tom, "I feel as if I'm at a reunion of flower children." He nodded. They sat surrounded by plaid shirts and tie-dyes and purple skirts and moon earrings. Several toddlers wore fool's caps. In jeans and floppy hats, the teenagers at the Youth Conference spread out between the choir stalls at a table covered with various brightly colored collages, many featuring peace symbols.

Tom thought of how much of his daughter's abbreviated life she'd spent working to end war and hunger and to promote equality. He imagined her here as a counselor, helping these young people to create their collages or tie-dye new T-shirts.

The order of service was familiar. The Gospel reading came from Mark: the story in which three of the disciples follow Jesus to a high mountain, where he is transfigured, and Moses and Elijah appear and God speaks. After which, Jesus, Peter, James, and John return to an arguing crowd and a young man possessed by a demon. Jesus drives out the unclean spirit and quiets the crowd.

One of the youth ministers, who didn't look much more than eighteen himself, gave a "Reflection on the Gospel." Speaking directly to the young people, he talked of mountaintop experiences. How, often, we feel transfigured by weeks such as this one, everybody working together in love and harmony. "But then," he said, "we're thrust back into the real world and its demons." He smiled at the kids. "I'm not talking about those creatures you see in the horror movies. I want you to expand your understanding of demons. Think of any conflicted situation in which you find yourselves."

Tom remembered when he saw his grief as an "alien," a giant cricket pounding against his chest. He smiled sadly. These days, his demons had more to do with a sense of being "alien-ated," isolated by the knowledge that he would never—at least not in his lifetime—have recompense for the loss of his child. He glanced over at Christine. *Or for the loss of her child.* He hoped Nathan would someday again come to Maine to visit, but there would always be a breach between them they could never close.

His eyes found a gargoyle carved into a stone arch, a face either in agony or fear, its mouth open, about to scream. But hadn't he always isolated himself? Erected barriers, hidden behind personas? This afternoon, Christine had reminded him that, even before Annie's death, he'd struggled to engage with the world. Even his most active years in Webber had been a way to avoid confronting a failing marriage and the Mr. A.P. facade slowly strangling him. Christine was right. He never would have written to her unless she'd written to him first, and he might never have told Martha about Christine if Martha hadn't found one of Christine's letters. No wonder his divorce and remarriage seemed so easy. He hadn't done anything. And now he stood on the sidelines, watching his wife plan the next step in her life.

He understood now why he reacted so defensively to Brother Jeremiah. The monk's social activism reminded him of how little he interacted with people, except from the front of a classroom.

"But the common figure," said the minister, "on both the mountaintop and in the real world, is Jesus, and it is Jesus who can reconcile the two experiences through his love."

Tom understood the image of Jesus on the mountaintop, shimmering in white. This was the Grand Tetons glowing in the sunset. This was the enfolding candlelight in the hospital chapel. This was Annie's handwritten *I love you*, splashed by the sunlight over Casco Bay, and her presence in the sun-dappled sycamores of Harvard Square. This was Christine's face earlier today, shining by

St. Columba's Bay. These were his "holy" moments, the rare times where he felt the presence of the Divine. And because he imagined God at these times, he could imagine Jesus there as well.

But probably because he had always been isolated and self-absorbed, he'd had trouble finding God in the everyday world, let alone that world of blood and shit and green bile he still remembered. As a consequence, he supposed, he'd never fully paid attention to the stories of Jesus in that world. Certainly not as part of his own story. But here was Jesus entering the crowd—casting out those demons—not as a shining figure descending from heaven like Superman, but as a man who looked like everyone else and who eventually would suffer his own agonizing death, a death Tom had, up until now, seen as a pale imitation of his daughter's. But no, wasn't Jesus's crucifixion God's cry, "I am here!" even in the worst of times, as well as in the best?

Years ago, Curtis Mathews had told him that God was with Tom both in the chapel at EMMC and when he learned of Annie's cancer, with him in the Ronald McDonald House, with him when Annie died. But Tom had decided then that if he were just strong enough, he wouldn't need God at all. Well, he needed God, and maybe the way to God was through Jesus.

"Pick up your cross and follow me," Jesus said. Maybe it was time to pick up his residual anger and his shame and his solipsism and follow Jesus into the world in which he'd always felt defensive and diffident. A world of disease and death, violence and runaway technology, unscrupulous politicians and religious extremists who made him hesitant to call himself a Christian.

Tom's backache, which had vanished in the late-afternoon lovemaking, returned. He shifted in his seat to find a comfortable position. But what would it mean to follow Jesus? Go to seminary like Christine? Stand on the street corner, preaching to the traffic? Knock on doors, asking people if they'd been saved? Get on St. Mark's Vestry? Join the choir the way he had in Webber?

"What are you going to do, Dad?"

2000

The voice came from his twelve-year-old daughter as she stood in the basement of Fellowship Hall in Webber's First Parish Church. On the cinderblock wall behind her, there were pictures of mothers holding starving children with thin arms and distended stomachs. The table in front of her featured plates of crackers, carrots, celery sticks, cut-up apples, orange slices, squares of cheese, and a loaf of bread. Note cards announced the prices: one cent per cracker, two cents for a vegetable stick, three cents for fruit, four cents per cheese square, ten cents for a slice of bread.

Annie stood behind the table with several members of her Sunday school. "Okay, Dad, you're the average third-world person. You have thirteen cents a day to spend on food. What are you going to eat?"

What had he said?

"What are you going to do, Dad?" His daughter looked up at him, her gaze intense, waiting for his answer.

"What are you going to do, Dad?" Her voice filled the abbey.

What am I going to do with the rest of my life?

Annie nudged him in the ribs. "Come off it, Dad," she whispered in his ear. "You know what to do." He sensed her pointing to the teenagers sitting around the table before him with their rainbow-colored messages, and to a pasteboard sign: "We are Happy Only When We Learn to Serve." He'd watched his daughter grow up working to serve others. Now, his wife was going to serve those in prison. The young people here on Iona were working to bring peace to the world. His job was somehow to join them.

"Tonight," the minister said, "as a sacrament of Jesus's love, we're going to have our Agape Service."

As four young people left their seats and walked to the communion table, Tom turned to Christine and shrugged his shoulders. He'd never heard of such a service. She pointed at their program. It read:

> Here it is always an open table: the invitation to share Communion is offered to everyone. There are still those,

however, who feel excluded by a sacrament about which Christians can have such different understandings. Sometimes an Agape may be the more appropriate way of expressing our unity in Christ. The Agape, using oatcakes, water, or, according to the occasion, something else special, is sacramental in the sense that every shared meal, and every aspect of our life as God's children, on God's good earth, can be called sacramental.

As people passed a plate of oatcakes and a chalice of water to one another, a young man whose skin appeared golden in the candlelight stood up in the double arches and played a jazz standard—*"Round Midnight," maybe?*—on a saxophone.

Tom mulled over the sacraments—the outward signs of God's love—which had helped him fill some of his emptiness after Annie's death. Everything from the circular window in the hospital chapel, to the King's College Choir singing on the River Cam, to the green stone in his pocket, to the man now playing the saxophone, to the boy around ten years old in front of him, leaning against his mother, his unlined face glowing with joy.

Sacraments. Grace.

The surest sign of God's grace to him was the woman standing beside him. She was a pure gift: unexpected and unearned. He still wasn't sure he deserved her. He broke off a piece of oatcake and gave it to her. He whispered, "May this sacrament give you the voice you need."

Christine offered him some water. "And the strength you need," she said.

Amen. She was probably referring to the strength he'd have to have to support her in her new ministry. But he prayed for the strength to engage in his own new commitment, to find a way to be of some service to the world, to fill someone else's emptiness, to make someone happy.

When the saxophonist finished, a young woman in thick glasses rose and invited the rest of the congregation to join hands and follow the youth into the refectory for refreshments. She concluded the service:

> "May the road rise to meet you
> May the wind be always at your back;
> May the rain fall softly upon your fields;
> May God hold you in the hollow of his hand."

The organ sounded forth. Another familiar hymn, "I Want to Follow Jesus." *Yes.*

Tom took Christine's hand. He felt a smaller hand slide along his other palm. He thought of Annie's long, thin fingers. He turned to see the boy who'd sat with his mother in front of them. They smiled at each other and joined the line dancing its way around the aisles, past the marble altar and under the gargoyles, through the Gothic arches out of the cathedral and into the gathering August twilight.

Chapter Eighteen

2000–2001

Flying home from Scotland, Tom made a list of service activities he might look into. Amnesty International. Advisor to the church youth group. Starting a grief group at church or at Jordan Mills High. Could he work in prison like Christine was planning to do? Serve in a soup kitchen? But once back at the beginning of another school year, his pile of uncorrected papers mounted and his interest faded. He wasn't really interested in social issues. He'd already advised a church youth group. He lacked the self-confidence to start any kind of new program. As September became October, his guilt for not being of some kind of service to others grew.

"Do you have any idea," he said to Brother Jeremiah, "how much you intimidate me—all your social activism?"

"There are a lot of ways to help others," said the monk. "What would have helped you when you were in pain?"

"No! I am not going to work with grieving parents."

Brother Jeremiah threw his hands into a shield in front of his face. "Okay, okay. But what about people who are sick—not necessarily dying or having cancer—people who are elderly or alone?"

Tom recalled his anger at how Gary Coffin had ignored him and his family during Annie's final months. Caring for those unable to care for themselves had always struck him as one of the church's most important activities. And he liked Julia Fremont, the retired priest from Rhode Island who chaired the Pastoral Care Committee. "That's an idea," he said.

At his first meeting in November, Julia asked him to visit Henry Shaw, a long-time parishioner now in the hospital.

"Do I pray with him or what?" Tom asked.

"No, just go in, say hello, and make a little small talk. I think he used to be in the Navy," she said. "The important thing is to let him know St. Mark's is thinking of him."

"Sure, no problem."

But after church on Sunday, as he drove into the parking lot of Jordan Pines Hospital and looked at its brick edifice, his hands began to tremble. The hospital looked nothing like the Eastern Maine Medical Center, yet as he passed through the revolving door into the lobby, old fear grabbed his stomach and started twisting. The elevator walls pressed in on him. Walking down the second-floor corridor, he saw the nurses trying to smile in the face of impossible demands, smelled the shit and the disinfectant, heard the moaning voices. When he found Henry's room and saw the old man sleeping, there was Martha, sitting on the bed beside Annie, rubbing her back and staring up at the ceiling, her face white as marble, the pain evident in her eyes, even as she spoke firmly and softly, "Crying won't make it any better, sweetie. It's a mess, I know, a helluva mess, but you've just got to tough it out, like you have so far. We're all proud of you, kid."

Tom turned away from Henry Shaw's room and walked quickly away.

On Monday, he told himself he was being ridiculous. It had been more than eleven years since Annie's death. He'd stop by to see Henry on his way home from school. But when he reached the turnoff to the hospital, he kept driving. Too near suppertime.

The next afternoon he had the same thought, then swerved at

the last minute onto the road leading to Jordan Pines. In the parking lot, he sat in his car, the motor running, his heart racing, as he clasped his hands and rubbed his thumbs. The setting afternoon sun through bare branches cast the parking lot into patterns of light and shadow, reminding him of dreams of Annie walking away from him in that rocky tunnel through spots of light. Why didn't he just go home to Christine? Sip some Wild Turkey bourbon, his latest indulgence? Hadn't he spent enough time in hospitals?

His daughter laughed. "Come on, Dad. Turn off the damn ignition, open the car door, and move your ass!"

This time he walked up the stairs to the second floor. At the door of Henry's room, he peered in. A woman—probably in her early thirties—stood by the bed. She glanced up. "Hi," she said. "Can I help you?"

"I'm...I'm Tom Jacobs of St. Mark's Church, and I thought I'd stop by to see how Henry was doing." He started to turn away. "I can come back another time."

"No, please, come in," she said. "I'm Leigh, Henry's granddaughter." She smiled and offered him her hand. Tom thought she was about the same age Annie would be. She spoke slowly and loudly to the gaunt figure in the bed: "Grandpa, this is Tom from St. Mark's."

Oxygen tubes ran into Henry's nostrils. He coughed a thick, mucus-filled cough. Leigh held a kidney-shaped bowl to his mouth. "Spit it out!" she ordered. She wiped her grandfather's face, stood up, and whispered, "He's really failed the last day or so. I think he's lost the will to live. He's eighty-eight and, since Grandma died two years ago, he's lived alone. I think he's been lonely long enough."

Tom reached down and picked up Henry's hand. It felt like an empty deerskin glove. Seeing the thin line of mucus trickling from the side of the old man's mouth, Tom remembered the night Annie died. "Mr. Shaw, I'm very happy to meet you," he lied loudly.

Henry Shaw's eyes opened and for a moment he stared at Tom intently.

"Who did you say you are?" His voice was faint. Filled with fluid.

Tom's chest burned while the rest of him shivered. "Tom Jacobs." He tried to speak slowly. "I don't think we've ever met. You go to the eight o'clock service and I go to the ten o'clock one." The divide between the two services—one silent and traditional, the other musical and contemporary—was notorious, and the two congregations seldom interacted. Tom leaned forward, trying to make eye contact. "I'm one of those 'Ten O'clockers.'"

"Ain't no such animal," Henry said, faintly. He coughed and closed his eyes.

Now what? As Tom straightened, his lower back pinched. He saw reflected in the window some jerk with a dopey expression on his face. What was he doing here?

He and Leigh talked for a few minutes about the *Farmer's Almanac's* prediction of a snowy winter, the good care the hospital provided, and their respective jobs. (She was an elementary school teacher.) She thanked Tom for coming, and he left, feeling inept and embarrassed. Two days later, Henry Shaw died.

At the December meeting of the Lay Pastoral Visitors, Julia asked Tom how his visit to Henry had gone. Tom shrugged his shoulders. "I'm not sure he even knew I was there."

"Well, the family expressed their gratitude to the church for your visit, so I'm glad you were able to see him." She smiled. "I've got somebody else for you to try this month. I don't know much about her, except her name is Nellie Wyman, and she's in the Alzheimer's wing of the Honeywell Nursing Home." Julia consulted a note card. "Her son lives in Bangor and has had to put her in a place down here until something opens there."

"Great," said Tom. "The woman suffers from dementia, she has no connection to this church, and doesn't know a soul from around here. Maybe I'll give her my lecture on The Lost Generation."

Julia laughed. "Who knows, she might like it." She patted him on the arm. "You'll be fine."

Honeywell Nursing Home was a one-story building behind

the Jordan Mills Hospital and beside a community garden of weeds and withered vines now partially covered by the season's first dusting of snow. Several equally withered people sat in the hallway under Christmas lights and Santa Claus cutouts, their heads disappearing into their bathrobes like turtles. Tom walked down a corridor, past more old people either sleeping or staring off into space. A receptionist referred him through a closed set of doors to a nurse, who looked a little like Jen White back at the Eastern Maine Medical Center. "Nellie's in Room 25," she said. "I'll introduce you."

They walked down a hall with pallid walls, upon which were more cutouts of Santas and reindeer and saccharine angels. The nurse, whose name was Georgette, knocked on the door of Room 25 and opened it. "Hi, Nellie! You've got a visitor."

Nellie Wyman stood by the window, looking out at a stand of birch trees. A navy-blue jumper hung around her like a teepee. Her brown hair was tightly curled and flecked with gray. She turned and looked intently at Tom, her mouth slightly open.

"Nellie, this is Tom."

Nellie looked at Georgette, then at Tom, then back out the window, then back at Tom. "Who are you?"

Tom felt his stomach sinking. "I'm Tom, from St. Mark's, the Episcopal church here in town."

Nellie's eyes darkened. "Isn't St. John's the Episcopal church in town?"

It took Tom a moment to understand. "No, St. John's is in Bangor," he said, remembering a service he had attended there when he went with Christine up to Bangor Seminary. "St. Mark's is in Jordan Mills."

"I think I remember you," Nellie said. "Do you know my husband?"

"Her husband died five years ago," Georgette whispered. She spoke to Nellie: "Why don't you show Tom around?" She mouthed, "She likes to walk."

Tom and Nellie set off down the hall, Nellie shuffling beside him in plaid slippers. She was about as tall as his armpit. "It's nice of you to come," she said pleasantly. "I'm awfully lonely." She stopped and peered up at him. "Who are you?"

"I'm Tom."

But Nellie was looking at the door on the right. "Who lives here?" she asked.

"This is Dick Butler," said Tom, reading the tag on the door.

"Oh, yes, I remember him. He goes to our church in Bangor."

Tom searched the hall for Georgette. *Do you humor people like this or tell them they're full of shit?*

Nellie looked at a picture on the wall of a field of flowers.

"That's a pretty picture," said Tom.

"Yes, those flowers are behind our house. Our house is just over the hill."

"That's nice."

"Who lives here?"

"Let's see. This says that 'Ursula Chapman' lives here."

Nellie frowned. Her eyes grew vacant. "I don't remember her. I'm so lonely." She looked at Tom. "You're awfully nice. Who are you?"

That night, he wrote in his journal:

> I keep chewing on her question. Who am I? I'm trying hard these days not to create personas like Mr. A.P., the Last Romantic, Mr. Wimp, or Grieving Parent. I've been focusing my daily meditation on what so many of the books I've been reading call the "real self," but so far, all I can identify is *what* I am—husband, stepfather, teacher, Episcopalian, Maine native, American, middle-of-the-road Democrat. Do I even have a real self?

Two more visits with Nellie further frustrated and confused him. He asked Brother Jeremiah at their monthly meeting, "Why am I doing this? She doesn't know where she is, she can't remember her life, and she has no idea who I am." He sighed. "I'm beginning to wonder that myself."

"This isn't about you," snapped Brother Jeremiah through his beard, gone completely white in the last year. "This is about God's Church. Not the Episcopal Church or the Methodist Church or the Church of the Great Gildersleeve." He reached into a bag of mentholated cough drops. "It's one of the things we're celebrating this time of year. God incarnate, God in the world, God's Church, the mystical body of Christ, from which no one is excluded, not even those who've stopped being aware of their inclusion."

The monk leaned back in his chair and put his hands behind his head. "And as for who you are, my friend, you are God's beloved. That ought to be enough. Merry Christmas, Tom."

In January, after Nellie's son found a nursing home for his mother in Bangor, Julia said, "You haven't had very good luck, have you? Why don't you go see Paul Tibbetts. He loves visitors."

Tom remembered Paul as a broad-shouldered man with a loud laugh who'd been Nathan's mentor during the boy's preparation for confirmation. Paul once invited Nathan to go sailing with him and his wife, but they'd had to cancel because of bad weather. Before they could reschedule, Paul suffered a stroke. Tom hadn't seen him in eight years.

Even having known the man, Tom's heart was tap dancing as he stood before the double glass doors of the assisted-living wing of Honeywell. Would Paul be upset that Tom hadn't brought Nathan to visit after his stroke? Or that he hadn't attended the funeral for Paul's wife four years earlier? The familiar cold knot in his chest flamed into his throat. His gastritis had returned and Dr. Sampson advised him to limit his caffeine to one cup of coffee a day and his alcohol consumption to four drinks a week. The caffeine Tom could do, but not the alcohol. Except for the week right around the anniversary of Annie's death, he didn't think he drank that much, but he still liked a couple of drinks before dinner and some wine with his meals. "I can no more stop at one drink in the evening than I can eat one piece of popcorn," he told Brother Jeremiah at their last meeting.

"Well, if you want to cut down on the booze, there's nothing I can do for you," Brother Jeremiah said, playing with his wrist bracelet. "But if you want to quit the stuff altogether, I'll do everything I can to help."

Wondering if it would be easier just to quit drinking rather than try to cut back, Tom walked down a carpeted hall with red walls that reminded him of raw liver, empty except for a lone figure ahead of him in a wheelchair. He recognized Paul's big ears. His head slumped over his chest. Eyes closed. Under a stained jersey and sweat pants, his body was thin and bent. His left hand rested on a soiled pillow like a club, the fingers bent into a fist, with thick-callused knuckles.

Tom came closer. Stopped. Started to turn around. He'd spent his adult lifetime imparting information to a classroom of anywhere from fifteen to thirty-five students. All in all, he'd liked most of the kids. Even, he supposed, loved some of them. But visiting one on one—no podium to stand behind, no lesson plan, no text to refer to—frightened the hell out of him. He felt beaten. He wasn't cut out for this pastoral visiting. If he was part of the mystical body of Christ, he must be a hangnail.

He realized Paul was staring at him. The man's blue eyes lit up. His voice echoed through the hall, "I know you!"

Too grateful to be embarrassed, Tom shook Paul's hand. For a moment Paul's grip was firm, then it weakened. "What brings you here?"

"To see you."

"Great! Let's go in my room, up the hall here. Give me a push, will you? I get tired of fighting with this damn machine."

Tom wheeled Paul into his room, in which there appeared to have been a recent explosion. Clothes, wheelchair parts, newspapers, paperbacks, and black composition books cluttered the floor and the windowsill. "Have a seat," Paul said. "There's a chair under that pile of books. Just shove 'em off."

Tom piled the books on the floor: volumes 3 and 4 of Will Durant's *Story of Civilization, The Essential Santayana,* Evelyn Underhill's *The Mystic Way,* something called *Courage to Change*—he couldn't read the rest of it. "That's quite a collection of books," he said, taking off his jacket and laying it over a pile of towels on the dresser.

"Oh, I try to keep my mind active, even if the rest of me is a sack of shit," said Paul.

Tom laughed as he caught a glimpse of the vigorous and profane man who'd been Nathan's mentor, but who was now held captive, struggling to break out of an invisible shell. At some level, Tom identified with that struggle.

He looked again at the stack of books. "Is there any particular one of these you'd recommend?"

"Oh, I like Will Durant, but I like history. My tastes these days are pretty personal. To be honest, I get more wisdom out of the Al-Anon book than I do any of the others. It's my Bible."

Tom picked up *Courage to Change* and read the subtitle: *One Day at a Time in Al-Anon II.* "You know, I'm not sure what Al-Anon is. How is it different from AA?"

Paul rolled his wheelchair closer to Tom. "The short answer is that AA is for alcoholics while Al-Anon is for families of alcoholics." He arched his back. *Must be tiring, sitting in that thing all day.* "Of course, it's more complicated than that. I used to go to meetings of both, but since my stroke, I can only get out once a week at the most, so I've had to make a decision. I decided that the root of my problems with booze goes back to my old man's drinking."

A curtain opened, revealing a vista Tom had always sensed but never seen. "Maybe I ought to read it," he said. "Both my father and my grandfather were alcoholics. And so is my brother."

"It would be better if you came to a meeting or six," said Paul. "Without the meetings, the book's nothing but a bunch of clichés and meaningless slogans."

"I'll think about it," said Tom.

"Just let me know. I'd love to have another way to get to the meetings, in case my regular ride can't make it."

Thinking that he really didn't need one more thing in his life, Tom changed the subject by gesturing at the composition books. "Are you a writer as well as a reader?"

Paul shrugged his shoulders. "I write a bit, although it's hard for me to hold a pen for very long." He reached over to a jar of green pens. "I like these fiber-points. They're easy to hold."

Tom remembered Annie used to write in green. Her words on the page by the ocean: *I love you.* "What do you write?" he asked.

"Poetry mostly. Not very good poetry, I'm afraid."

"Do you want to read me one? You don't have to if you don't want to."

"Are you sure?"

"Absolutely."

Paul picked up the composition book next to him on a metal tray table and flipped through it. "Bear with me. I don't get an audience very often." Tom saw that the handwriting sprawled across the pages and outside the lines.

"Here's one I sort of like." Paul's voice was raspy:

"I once sailed Penobscot Bay
Mount Desert to Deer Isle.
Sea gulls hurrahed
and granite tors
applauded my seamanship.

"Now, I roll my chair
from bathroom to dining room.
Old farts encircle me,
and nurses cheer
when I dress myself.

"Still, at night, I sail again,
hear ancient voices
from rocky hills:

'Fare thee well, Pilgrim,
until, like the tide, you return.'"

The poem brought to Tom's mind memories of picnics and walks with Annie on Mount Desert Island. His dreams, which had provided much of his healing. His own journey. "Thank you," he said. "Your courage is an inspiration."

Paul shrugged one shoulder. "Enough about me. How are you, and—let's see—your wife's name is Christine, right?"

Tom nodded.

"And Nathan. How's he doing?"

"Okay, I guess." Tom felt his shoulders sag. "He's in Colorado, working on a PhD. in herpetology. We don't see that much of him."

"You must be proud."

In all his shame over the fact that Nathan never visited, Tom rarely thought about Nathan's work, studying the use of snake venom to fight cancer. "Yes," he said, "I am."

"Now do you and Christine have other children? I forget."

Deep breath. "I have a daughter. She died of cancer at eighteen."

Paul's voice softened. "That's right. I remember now. Nathan talked about her a lot. Shit. What a shame. I'm really sorry." He slapped the arm of his wheelchair. "Life really sucks sometimes."

"Thank you," Tom said. He removed his glasses and wiped his eyes with the back of his hand. "That's one of the most honest things anyone's said to me in eleven years." He reached out and touched Paul's shoulder. "Now tell me about your children."

"Well, I'm afraid they've got the family disease." Sadness seemed to pull down the corners of Paul's eyes and jowls. "I've got a daughter, Margaret, who's hooked on heroin, and a son, Rick, who's an alcoholic. He at least came by at Christmas. She didn't even drop me a fucki…excuse my language…send me a card."

"That must be really hard."

"They're the main reason I go to meetings these days. I need a weekly infusion—just like a blood transfusion—so that I don't suffer because of what my kids do or don't do. They're both adults.

I can't control their behaviors and I can't do for them what they have to do for themselves."

Tom wished his mother had learned that, instead of trying to choreograph his every move. But what about the way he'd tried to control Christine? The way he'd told her not to let Nathan know about the seriousness of Annie's illness? The way he'd tried to talk her out of prison ministry?

Was he even trying to control his ex-wife? A year or so earlier, he'd awakened one morning, seeing his marriage to Martha come apart through *her* eyes. His inconsistent behaviors, his silent lies, his use of God to justify adultery. He had decided he needed to ask her forgiveness, so he wrote to one of his former colleagues at Webber High and found that Martha had remarried and had a new last name. He went online, found her new address, and sent her a birthday card containing an apology. No response. He tried again a few months later, with the same lack of results.

He could understand why he had written his first note, but why the follow-up? Had he been trying to manipulate her, too? She had all kinds of reasons for not wanting to talk to him again. Maybe he was just opening old wounds. Maybe he could go to at least one of those meetings with Paul.

An hour later, Tom wheeled Paul to supper. At the door to the dining room, he reached down and shook the man's hand. "I hope you don't mind if I visit you again."

Paul smiled. "I'd like that a lot, Tom. The days get pretty lonesome around here." He started into the dining room and stopped. "And think about those meetings."

"I will."

Tom walked back down the hall to the exit, his mind spinning. Too bad about Paul's kids. At least Ed was sending cards now. And would it be his fault if he didn't? Ordinarily, he'd have said yes. The same way it had always been his fault Nathan never visited. Did he know that he was the reason Nathan didn't come? Was he seeing a pattern of shame, and a sense of responsibility and a need for control that went back almost sixty years?

As he opened the door to leave, the January air, smelling of ocean, felt cold and fresh in his lungs. As usual, he felt better simply for having seen what he'd never been able to see before. A new moon grinned in the western sky. Snow glistened under the lights in the parking lot. He glanced at his watch. He'd stayed longer than he'd planned. For a moment, he was disappointed. Christine probably had supper waiting, so he wouldn't have time for his nightly belt of Wild Turkey.

He looked up at the emerging stars. *Good.*

Chapter Nineteen

2001

"Why doesn't your sister-in-law go to a place like the Family Center for Grief and Loss?" Tom asked Jim Silas. It was the first day of another new school year, and after the usual speeches from administrators and union representatives, followed by faculty and department meetings, Jim had followed Tom into his room.

"She looked into it," he said, perching on the corner of Tom's desk, "but she couldn't get anyone else in her family to go with her and the Center wants families." He leaned forward. "Couldn't you meet with her at least once? Come on, man. I'll set everything up."

Tom rubbed his thumbs together. Over the past year, he'd become relatively comfortable visiting old people in nursing homes; he was learning to think with what Al-Anon called "detachment" upon the problems of aging. Talking to someone who'd lost a child was something else. He stared at the wall—at the poster Annie had printed for him twenty years earlier titled "Why Write?"—at the line, "To exorcise our private ghosts." He remembered her angrily tearing up an earlier poster after he pointed out that she'd written, "To exercise our private ghosts." But that's what he was doing now. Letting his fears—of confronting new challenges, of being dragged back into old sorrows—out of their cages and taking them for an afternoon stroll. He felt ashamed and weak, but he couldn't do it. "No, I'm sorry, Jim. I can't help her."

Two weeks later, he took his first-period class to the computer lab. Tom heard a buzzing sound. Harry, a junior firefighter, said, "Mr. Jacobs, I've just got a page that says it's important. May I use the computer to check the news?"

Harry seemed a good kid. As far as Tom knew, being a junior firefighter was his one claim to distinction. "Go for it," he said.

A minute later, Harry said, "A plane has just crashed into one of the towers of the World Trade Center!"

During his late-morning planning period, Tom joined students and faculty in the library, watching again and again United Flight 175 sail into the side of the South Tower. As clouds of smoke and gray debris piled like snow on the streets, all he could think of was a city being cremated. He recalled Annie's tortured *ash…es, ash…es,* and felt himself shrinking into his shell, falling into the Void opening beneath him, as if he were once again walking these halls after receiving the news of his daughter's diagnosis.

He decided not to stick to any of his lesson plans for the rest of his classes, but in his A.P. class, the kids wanted to talk about the day's events in the light of their assigned reading from Annie Dillard's *Pilgrim at Tinker Creek.*

"I mean, why should we be surprised when people use violence?" asked Kate. "Look at the way she talks about Nature—cats with bloody paws, frogs sucked dry of life by water bugs, insects eating their mates."

"Violence and death are the ways of the world," Jed said. "That's why we've got to find the bastards—sorry, Mr. Jacobs—who did this and kill them before they do any more damage."

Tom found himself agreeing with Jed. Which thrust him back into his own anger at God. Not because God was somehow responsible for the acts of terrorists, but because in this world that God had created, responding with violence seemed the only way to stop violence, whether with noxious bombs to stop malignant terrorist cells or noxious chemotherapy to stop malignant cancer cells.

That night he and Christine attended a prayer vigil at St. Mark's. The church was about half full, as Father Larry Davison led them in prayer and an airing of feelings.

"The reason we're here," said Father Larry, "is that I'm deeply conflicted in my response to what's happened, and I wonder if you are, too." Tom felt better. His frustration had been building all afternoon and it was good to know he wasn't alone.

Father Larry stepped out from behind the pulpit and began pacing the dais. "As a Christian," he said. "I'm committed to finding nonviolent solutions to problems. I want to believe that violent retaliation is to become like those who committed these atrocities—murderers. But I admit to you that I'm angry and I want to strike back." Lights glinted off his shaved head as he stepped from the dais to the floor of the church. "Perhaps we can help each other out, as we turn our hopes, our fears, our anger, over to God, trusting in the Spirit to work through us. Who needs to talk?"

"We need to put aside politics and support our president," said Thad Damon, Jordan Mills' state representative.

"We can't go it alone," said Caleb Cox, a lawyer, "we need to ask the help of other countries…and, of course, God."

"Thank God for those brave firemen and policemen," said Marian Magnuson.

Betty Pelletier, a tall, well-tailored woman whose china-doll cheeks suggested Botox treatments, stood. "I want to take this opportunity to thank God," she said, "that my son is safe. His office was in the South Tower, and God gave him the sense to recognize the seriousness of the crash. And God protected my son four times! He showed Chuck the way down the stairs. He moved him out of the way of falling debris twice. He provided Chuck with a private boat to offer him a ride across the river to Hoboken." Her voice choked. "I'm so grateful."

Tom reached for Christine's hand and held it tightly. There were what, over 7,000 victims of these attacks? He was sure Betty's son was a great guy, but why did God save him and let 7,000 others die? Each of these victims had a mother and father. Even taking into account parents who'd died, it wouldn't be exaggerating to say there were at least 10,000 parents grieving tonight. He thought of their numbing pain, depression, anger, and guilt, their questions about God's justice and mercy.

The next day at school he told Jim Silas, "Okay, I'll talk to Rachel. But tell her I don't have any words of wisdom. Losing your kid sucks. Period."

She was waiting for him outside the Coffee Cat, Jordan Mills's new coffee shop. "Are you Tom? I thought you weren't coming." She barely acknowledged his outstretched hand. A stocky woman with fly-away hair, her black eyes flashed as her words resounded above the cacophony of voices greeting them as they walked through the door: "The first thing you need to know is that if I didn't have two other children, I'd have killed myself when Ryan died."

Seeing her face, the set of her jaw, those eyes, he believed her.

They bought coffees and cookies and sat down at a laminated wood table. "So when did your daughter die?" she asked.

So much for small talk. "Twelve years ago."

"I don't know how you've survived."

Tom shrugged. For a moment he felt guilty for living.

"Was she a good kid? I'll bet she was, you being a teacher and everything. Jim says you go to church. Ryan was a good kid, even though he got into some trouble when he was younger. And that's the thing. He'd just begun to put his life together. He'd done drugs, lost jobs, been married and divorced." Her voice rose in a crescendo of pain. "He was clean, he had a good job at the mill, he'd found Cindy, and then…" Her face contorted. Her arms flailed the air before she wrapped them around herself. Her voice fell. "It's not fair, goddamn it. It is not fair."

She sobbed into her napkin, while Tom stared down at his coffee. *What can I say? She's right.*

2001

"I thought I was beginning to get over it, but last week would have been Ryan's twenty-fourth birthday." She wiped her eyes, pinched off a corner of her cookie and dropped it on her plate as she looked at Tom. "I couldn't even get out of bed, let alone come to work," she said quietly. "I just lay in bed all day and cried."

Her voice dropped to a dead monotone. "I kept reliving that afternoon. Five months ago now. I was driving home from work—we live in Dathum, outside of Lewiston—when I saw flames and smoke coming out of the apartment house just down the street from us, where Ryan and his fiancée live...lived. I knew Ryan worked the night shift at the mill and that they were both in there. I remember stopping the car. Running toward the burning building. But nothing after that."

Tom imagined sirens splitting the air, the open door to her car, the heat of the flames shooting into the sky, the smell of wood and burning shingles and Christ knows what else. *Anyone who says, "God won't give you more than you can handle," ought to be drawn and quartered.*

Rachel's glassy eyes gazed over his shoulder. "Later, my husband told me that it took two firemen to keep me from running into the flames. I guess I screamed the whole time."

They talked about their families. Rachel worried most about her youngest daughter, whose grades had plummeted, and who'd started hanging with a wild crowd. Her older daughter seemed okay, except for being unable to forgive her brother for leaving them. Her husband, Jim's brother, spent all of his spare time sleeping and watching TV.

"I feel so goddamned alone." She reached for another napkin.

"It's hard," Tom said. "My wife wound up seeing a psychotherapist."

"I can't afford one of those," Rachel snapped.

"Well, I got a lot of help from the rector of my church. He was going through some hard times, too, and—"

Rachel's black eyes flashed. "Don't talk to me about religion!" Her body rocked back and forth to some internal rhythm. "Do you know that our Catholic priest showed up drunk at my house the day after Ryan died?" She pointed her finger at Tom like a gun. "And a week later, he showed up again and he was still drunk!"

Her voice ascended over the coffee shop, an aria of grief: "But it's not just the Catholics. Christ, some Protestant minister showed up that week, too, asking if I'd been saved. I just looked at him and said, 'Get the fuck off my doorstep!'"

Her hands dropped, along with her voice. She appeared exhausted. "What's wrong with these people?"

Tom's chest burned and his heart was palpitating. He'd forgotten to order decaf. He rubbed his thumbs together. He wanted to help her, give her some wise words about the grieving process, make her see him as someone who'd learned to control his emotions, someone worth coming here to talk to. But he knew he couldn't, and he felt himself sliding into despair.

Since he'd started attending weekly Al-Anon meetings with Paul, he'd heard a lot of sad stories. Stories of parents dealing with children in prison, strung out on drugs, trying for the second, third, or tenth time to stay sober. Children who'd become clean only to turn into "somebody I don't know anymore," as one woman put it the other night, "someone I don't really like very much." He listened to ugly childhood memories, where "I never knew whether my mother was going to sit down with me and show me how to knit or slap my face and tell me I was a piece of shit." Or where "I was the golden boy, the perfect student, the star of the football team—all so I could hear my old man say, 'I love you,' which of course, the bastard never did." Stories of marriages in which "my husband fell out of bed again, but I was proud of myself, because I left him there this time instead of trying to lift his two hundred and fifty pounds of drunken vomit back into bed."

But none of those stories moved him like Rachel's, and he was frustrated at not being able to help her.

He said a silent prayer to his Higher Power, God, Jesus—who or whatever he believed in these days—finding himself adapting T.S. Eliot: *teach me to care about this poor suffering woman, and at the same time not to care about her, so that she may find her way.*

An hour later, Tom and Rachel walked together out of the coffee shop into a wind-driven autumn day. They stood silently on the sidewalk. "Thank you," Rachel said, "you've been a big help."

How?

She looked at the sidewalk, then up at the sky, then back at the muddy concrete. "Could we meet again?"

Why? He hadn't done anything except foment a maelstrom of guilt and memories of Martha's broken voice on the telephone, his daughter's last faint, congested breaths, Nathan's eyes turning black as he held his clay monster—"He represents, like the anger."

Still, he said, "Sure, just give me a call."

She was crying again, tears etching her face. He bent to give her a hug, but as he did, she turned so that she was side-to. His awkward attempt at consolation reminded him of his efforts in the hospital to hug Annie as she lay tied down with tubes and catheters. But out of that memory, his daughter's presence rose within him. Grew larger and larger, until Annie was no longer inside of him, but on the sidewalk with him and Rachel and their anger, enfolding them all in her arms.

"Look, why don't we meet here next week?" he said.

Chapter Twenty

2005

Tom looked over at Christine. "How do you feel about some coffee?"

The florescent lights in the Jordan Mall accentuated age spots on his wife's angular face. Her hair, which now she usually pulled back into a bun, was a tapestry of black, gray, and white. Lines etched into her forehead and around her mouth conveyed wisdom but also sorrow, for which Tom, despite Christine's remonstrations—"Ever wonder how sad I'd look if I hadn't married you?"—felt responsible. He sometimes missed the free spirit who caught rattlesnakes and rode a horse through the Rocky Mountains.

He rose from his metal folding chair. But while he might occasionally wish for the woman he'd first met, the woman before him was stronger, more self-confident, more compassionate. And her eyes remained as mysterious as when he'd first looked into them. Under those incredibly long lashes, tonight they shone smoky gray.

Her smile was like sunrise over the ocean as she said, "Better make it decaf. I'm going to have enough trouble sleeping tonight as it is."

He nodded. Even though she'd led a Good Friday service this morning at the county jail and was sitting with him tonight

2005

behind this card table selling concert tickets, he knew that when they got home, she'd bake another batch of cookies. Nathan, Maria, and Yazmin were in Massachusetts while Nathan attended a herpetology conference at Harvard. Tomorrow, they planned to drive up to Maine for Easter, the first time Nathan had visited since high school, the first time he'd ever been in the house Tom and Christine had been fixing up for the last ten years.

Tom stretched his stiff back, felt the familiar dull ache. His latest CT scan read, "Severe narrowing of lower thoracic discs, vacuum disc phenomena, severe narrowing of L2-L3 disk, degenerative hypertrophic bone, mild compression, mild spinal stenosis, ossification, lower lumbar facet degenerative disease..." All in all, he was lucky, Dr. Samson told him, that he didn't have more pain.

Searching for the closest coffee shop, Tom peered over and around the shoppers who ebbed and flowed past him. Teens in oversized pants and undersized tank tops, men in baseball caps and leather jackets, young families, geriatrics—many of them veering off as if running into an electric fence when they saw the poster beside his card table: two hands coming together over the words "The Compassionate Friends—Supporting Family After a Child Dies." For years, Tom had chastised himself for not being more engaged with the world; his work in Al-Anon made him more aware than ever of the connection between his family's alcoholism and his isolation, but he also knew that even the most convivial parents find themselves isolated in grief. Most people don't even want to think about what it's like to have a child die. Don't want to "go there," as his brother might say.

It had been great to see Ed. A half hour after a surprise phone call the previous New Year's, Ed had driven into the driveway, still pierced and profane and angry ("AA and I are working on that"), but also clear-eyed and confident, celebrating five years of sobriety by visiting friends and family in Maine. He'd earned a degree in nursing and now worked primarily with AIDS patients in the San Francisco area. It was hard work, he said, dealing with the patients and their partners, but sometimes even harder having to struggle with societal bias, not only against AIDS, but against grieving.

"What really pisses me off," he told Tom as they stood on the frozen ground of the Riverview Cemetery outside Ashton, hunched against the wind coming off the Androscoggin, "are those people who want to see suffering as somehow good for you." A dusting of snow had fallen the previous night, and as his brother talked, Tom used his feet to brush the snow from the flat, granite stones honoring their parents and the matching memorial stone for Annie. "I don't know, they think it builds character or some fucking foolishness. Our whole goddamn society loves to hear stories of heroic struggles, determined resilience, cracking jokes on the deathbed." Ed's voice trembled in anger. "We don't want to hear how hard—how fucking frustrating and painful—it is for the patients and the people who love them."

You're preaching to the choir, big brother. In the sixteen years since Annie's death, Tom had gone through counseling, experienced spiritual epiphanies, shared the love of the world's most understanding woman, and still the pain was always there. Every Ash Wednesday, he could feel his body chemistry change. For the following six weeks of Lent, he was more apt to come down with a cold, yell at the motorist cutting in front of him, cry. Sixteen years, and he still didn't understand God or God's world, especially how the death of children fit into it. This world, his religion told him, was a better place because of the death of God's son, but he'd be damned if he could see how the death of his daughter improved anything.

He knew that, compared with millions of people, he was fortunate. He laughed. He loved. Hell, he lived. A few weeks before, he'd tried to contact Doug, the artist he'd grown to know at the Family Center for Grief and Loss, to see if he wanted to become part of the team Tom was putting together to start this chapter of Compassionate Friends. When he discovered Doug's phone was no longer in service, he called Doug's ex-wife, who said, "You hadn't heard? Doug's dead. He...committed suicide." Sally's voice broke. "The goddamn fool took his prize antique shotgun and blew his brains out. He never did anything halfway." Her voice disintegrated into sobs. "I blame myself. I should have kept in better touch with him."

Tom recalled Doug's booming voice, the way he filled the doorway at the Family Center for Grief and Loss when he entered the room, his eyes teary whenever he talked about his nine-year-old daughter.

And how, dear God, is the world a better place because of Doug's death and Sally's guilt?

As he joined the torrent of shoppers flowing through the mall, Tom saw Randy and Betty Jarosz pushing their son Timmy in his wheelchair. Timmy's "Ay-ay-ay" cascaded over the muzak as he waved his arms at window displays, while his parents, their mouths frozen into grim smiles, stared straight ahead. The Jaroszes went to St. Mark's. Tom had no idea what caused the poor kid's genetic catastrophe, but here was just one more reason that, while he could celebrate Easter intellectually, part of him—his heart, his gut, whatever—would always blame God for the suffering and death of innocent children.

Wrestling Jacobs. He couldn't remember when he'd first seen the connection between his struggles with God and his Old Testament namesake, but the Biblical Jacob had become his icon. Grappling with God was as much a part of whatever spiritual life he had as was attending church, meditating, or pastoral care.

He stopped in front of Starbucks, took a deep breath, and unclenched his fists. *Don't ask why, just ask for help.* Sixteen years, and those words he'd heard in the chapel still remained the only response possible to the death of a child. They explained, come to think of it, the reason he was spending the anniversary of his daughter's death sitting in the middle of a shopping mall. Why he planned to retire from teaching at the end of the year and set up a local chapter of Compassionate Friends. The time had come for him to pass on some of the help he'd been given to other grieving parents. While he appreciated what the Family Center for Grief and Loss did, its emphasis on families shut out people like

Christine and Rachel Silas who needed communal support.

Speaking of Rachel, when Tom returned with the coffees, he found her sitting at the card table, talking and laughing with Christine. After her afternoon at the supermarket downtown, selling tickets for this concert of local musicians to benefit Compassionate Friends, Rachel was showing pictures to Christine of her second daughter's wedding.

After Christine put away the latest picture of their granddaughter Yazmin, the three of them counted their money and found they hadn't done all that badly. They congratulated each other. Selling the concert tickets to raise money had been Rachel's idea, but Tom could also pat himself on the back for asking her to help him in the first place. Picking up the phone to call Rachel was the first time he could remember ever having taken the initiative on anything. He'd mumbled and stammered his way through a sales pitch before she'd laughed and said, "Oh, for Christ's sake, Tom, why don't you just come out and ask me?" He knew that without her the Jordan Mills Compassionate Friends would still be just a dream instead of a near-reality.

After saying good night to Rachel, Tom and Christine walked out into the parking lot, buttoning their coats. A full moon rose over a thin line of clouds. As they navigated some black ice, Christine reached for Tom's arm. When they got in the car, he turned on the radio. On "Oldies 101.5" the Everly Brothers sang,

"Things have really changed now that I've kissed ya, uh huh, My life's not the same, now that I've kissed ya, uh huh."

He leaned over and kissed Christine. "Uh huh."

She chuckled. "There have been a few changes since New Jersey, haven't there?"

He remembered the two of them groping like teenagers outside the dormitory. A lot of the time, they were still groping their way together. His left hand found her breast as he kissed her again. "Yeah, a few," he said. "Ready for a few more?"

2005

It was after midnight when Christine took the cookies out of the oven and Tom finished cleaning the bathrooms; still, they got up the next morning at 6:00 to clean the rest of the house. He unfolded the cot in the spare room that would be Yazmin's and took to the garage the box of Christmas wrappings and suitcases and several empty cardboard boxes they'd tossed in the room over the years. He put clean sheets on the bed, laid fresh towels on a clothes rack, and set Nathan's once-favorite book, *The Hotel Cat*, on the table beside the bed. He plugged in a nightlight, and dusted the Georgia O'Keefe painting that used to be over his and Christine's bed in the Newell duplex. Then he dusted Nathan's eighth-grade graduation photograph and Annie's spray of lavender-blue blossoms. After lunch, he brought the vacuum upstairs and did the floors again in this room and in the guest room across the hall.

He was keeping busy, the way he always did when apprehensive or upset. Four months since he and Christine had visited Nathan and his family, and the old gulf between Tom and his stepson remained as wide as ever. Now, they were coming to Maine. He felt that this weekend would be some kind of test: if he passed, the kids, as he thought of them, would return; if he failed, they would never set foot in the house again.

The problem was that Tom had no idea how to study for this exam. Somehow, somewhere, he'd lost his instruction manual on how to reach out to a stepson after sixteen years of failure.

He was suddenly very tired. He lay down on the bed in Yazmin's room, intending only to rest his eyes for a minute, but fell into a dream of walking along a rocky beach, similar to the one by St. Columba's Bay on Iona, except that the stones were bigger and the waves larger. The sea ebbed and flowed over and around his feet, as he walked over what he realized were gravestones. Tiers and tiers of gravestones, jagged and broken. A lichen-covered spire thrust out of the stones at an angle. He read the names on it carved in marble:

REQUIEM IN STONES

Thomas Andrew Jacobs
Christine James Jacobs
Nathan Zachary Shales
Maria Martin Shales
Yazmin Zoe Garner

Icy talons of panic clawed at him. He turned to run, but tripped just as a great wave crested and broke over him. Powerful currents pulled him out to sea. Tom struggled to turn toward shore, but the water fused with his body, as if knowing ahead of time every movement he would make, playing him as if he were some kind of instrument, plucking his muscles and tendons like musical chords, taking him further away from shore. He gasped for air, caught short breaths, but they weren't enough. The sky overhead tilted and swayed, and darkness inked his mind. *I'm going to drown*, he thought. Self preservation urged him to struggle harder, but instead, he stopped thrashing and surrendered. He began to sink. Looking down, he saw more gravestones on the bottom of the sea, marbled in greens and reds and blacks and browns and whites, rounded and polished.

And then he rose. Unseen hands lifted him to the water's surface and cradled his body, as warm currents bore him further and further out to sea. Fear disappeared. He would trust the current to carry him wherever he needed to go.

"They're here!"

Tom blinked. He heard the front door slam. Apprehension washed over him. Slowly, he rose from the bed and went downstairs on heavy legs. He had no idea what the weekend would bring and part of him wanted to turn around, go back to the spare room, close the door behind him, and return to his dream.

Come on, Jacobs, move it!

Christine was already in the driveway, hugging Nathan, Maria, and Yazmin. Tom came down over the front steps, searching for what to say, how to behave. Hugging Maria was easy; he liked her. She was a short woman, perhaps five feet two, with dark

2005

brown hair and eyes, a husky laugh, and a wide smile bookended with laugh lines. Next came Yazmin—*what is she, eight now?* Sometimes Tom thought of Annie when he saw her, but today she was nothing like his daughter—dark hair and eyes and skin, dressed in jeans and red cowboy boots. He had no idea what to say, so he tried to smile, hugging her awkwardly against his hip until she pulled away and went to her mother.

Then he looked at Nathan, who was taller than Tom now, thin, dressed in jeans and a plaid western shirt.

They shook hands. Tom thought of how easily Christine's father had always welcomed him into his home. *Why can't I do that?* After an awkward silence, he asked, "How was the traffic?"

"Fine," Nathan said, looking around the yard. "No problems."

They went into the house and took suitcases upstairs to the guest bedroom. Then they came and sat in the living room. Christine served her chocolate chip cookies. The adults drank coffee, Yazmin lemonade. They compared notes about the weather: "It's been warm in Maine—up to 50 all week." "Yeah, it's been in the 60s in Colorado." Nathan and Maria admired the house; Tom and Christine detailed the changes they'd made and the changes they wanted to make. The conversation lagged, until Nathan said he'd been sitting not only for the last two hours, but for two days in conferences. Would Tom and Christine mind if he, Maria, and Yazmin went for a walk?

"No, go ahead," Christine said. "Go down Emanuel Road, turn right on Bethel Street, right again on Shipley, and look for Penham Road, turn right and you're back to Emanuel. It's about a mile."

"Would you like to come?" asked Maria.

"No, I should see about dinner," said Christine.

"Tom?" The invitation sounded to him like an afterthought.

"No, I'll stay and help Christine."

After Nathan and his family left, Tom followed his wife into the kitchen.

"This is awkward," he said.

"That's okay," she said. "They're here. We're all nervous. We'll relax in a while."

He wasn't so sure. When Nathan, Maria, and Yazmin returned, Nathan was on his cell phone with his father. Tom knew Zack had recently undergone bypass surgery, but hearing Nathan's "You take care, Dad," reminded him that his stepson had never once phoned him. Nathan and Yazmin went upstairs to play Yahtzee, Maria went in the kitchen to help Christine, and Tom sat in the living room, thumbing through old copies of *The New Yorker*, wishing he still drank.

He relaxed a little at dinner. Everyone raved about Christine's lentil soup, salad, and homemade bread, followed by her Wellesley Fudge Cake and ice cream. Tom sat beside Maria, a therapist at Fort Collins High School, and talked with her about their respective school systems, agreeing that parents becoming more involved in their children's educations had both positive and negative implications. Maria's term "helicopter parents" to describe the hovering that was becoming more and more common these days appealed to Tom, and Maria wanted to hear about Compassionate Friends—"Nathan's told me how the Family Center for Grief and Loss helped him."

Nathan, however, sat through dinner in silence or talked to his stepdaughter, giving his mother only monosyllabic responses to her questions. Tom thought of the work Christine had put into getting ready for this weekend, and he felt both sorry for her and angry with her son. After dinner, he volunteered to clean up while the rest of them visited. Laughter drifted through the door from the living room. Apparently, Christine was telling Yazmin about Nathan at eight. Before Tom knew him. When he'd still been the bubbly, spontaneous kid with the bright eyes. Tom's sense of failure returned.

He went into the living room just as Nathan and Maria were getting ready to put Yazmin to bed. He gave the girl another awkward hug and then, while the rest of them went upstairs, walked outside. It was still above freezing, with a vague smell of earth.

2005

Overhead, the moon cast the world in patterns of yin and yang. He walked around the house, feeling different temperatures depending on the breeze.

"God, I wish you were here, kid," he said to the night. "You used to be able to talk to him. Show me what to do."

The wind flushed, and Tom thought about that infinitesimal pause one notices in meditation between the in and out breaths. Today was Holy Saturday, which he always thought of as being another such pause: between the agonizing exhale of Good Friday and the inscrutable inhale of Easter. When the breeze picked up again, it seemed to be coming from a different direction. He hoped it was an omen.

He returned to the house to find that Maria and Yazmin had gone to bed, and that Nathan and Christine were in the study. Nathan sat in the stuffed, granite-colored chair that Tom had once bumped up the stairs of the old duplex, jiggling both legs nervously. When Christine asked her son if he would like more wine or coffee or chocolate chip cookies, he replied, "Sure, all of the above."

"It's so good to have you here," Christine said, for probably the tenth time today. She set the cookies on the coffee table and poured Nathan and herself some wine. "Decaf, Tom?"

Tom nodded, even though what he wanted was to go to bed. But he should be polite for fifteen minutes or so. He swung the chair in front of the computer around, and sat down.

She poured Tom some coffee and offered a cookie to Nathan. He shook his head. "In a minute. First, I need to tell you that I'm here primarily because of Maria." Tom's stepson looked at Annie's watercolor over the bookcase. His knee pistoned nervously. "She's been telling me that I need to talk to you guys about some things." Tom's stomach dropped. "Some things I've kept bottled up for—I don't know—probably fifteen years."

Christine straightened in her chair by the window and folded her hands, her eyes fixed on her son. Although only twenty-eight, his face was weathered by the outdoors. In another year he would be Dr. Nathan Shales. *Amazing.* "Well, I guess the main thing I have to tell you," Nathan said, "is that I'm still mad at you, Mom, for tearing me away from my friends in Wyoming, and abandoning me once you brought me to Maine. Before Maria, I'd screwed up a lot of relationships because I never felt I could trust any woman."

"I take a lot of the blame for that," Tom said. "After Annie died—"

"No, I'm talking about before that. Mom always acted—or at least I thought you acted—as if I was in your way. You kept leaving me with all those babysitters while you and Tom went out by yourselves."

Christine and Tom stared across the room at each other. "Nathan, I don't think we went out without taking you with us more than three times in the four years you lived with us," she said. "Did we, Tom?"

"I don't even remember three times." Tom stretched his back. "I remember going to dinner at your department head's and I think we went to dinner and a movie one Valentine's Day…I can't remember another time. Maybe a faculty party or something. We didn't have enough money in those days to go out very often."

Nathan stared at the floor, scratching his head. "All I can remember is hearing the front door slam when you guys left and this terrible loneliness." His eyes went to his mother. "I thought you'd deserted me."

Christine frowned. "Well, Tom and I did leave you with your grandparents once—when Annie first went into the hospital. They came up to stay with you."

Tom's stomach churned. "That's right, and that was a time we probably should have taken you with us."

Nathan's eyes went back to the watercolor. "I always thought that picture was so cool." His voice dropped. "Maybe that's what I remember. Annie was the one who made me feel loved," he said. "And because I had no idea she was dying, I thought she'd deserted me, too." He looked again at his mother. "Then later, Mom, when you started clinging, I thought, 'Tough luck, lady, you're too late.'"

2005

Christine's face fell. Her mouth trembled. She started to speak but then bowed her head and began to cry.

Nathan dropped his eyes to the floor. Tom wondered if Nathan wasn't examining his memories. God knows *he'd* done it enough times: reviewing recollections, testing them, then running through them again. (*Are they really true?*)

"I don't know, Mom," Nathan said. "Maybe you two didn't leave me as much as I remember, but I do know that I felt alone a lot of the time I lived with you." His eyes jumped back to the painting. "Or maybe it is Annie's death that I've been so angry about for the last fifteen years, and not just you."

Tom clasped his hands and rubbed his thumbs together as a wave of old guilt broke over him. "In either case, you need to be angry with me. Being the new kid in a Maine school is tough, and I know I didn't do enough to help you." He shrugged his shoulders. "And then after Annie died…"

"Oh, there's always been part of me that's mad as hell at you for taking me away from my friends, and not telling me more about how sick Annie was," Nathan said. "But I never blamed you for her death. And now that I have my own child, I'm beginning to realize how much pain you must have been in. I have no idea what I'd do if Yazmin died."

Tom stared at Nathan's jiggling legs. Heard Christine quietly weeping. She rose from her chair and went into the bathroom, returning with a box of Kleenex. She dabbed at her eyes. "Nathan, you have every right to be mad at me. I might not have physically deserted you, but I'm sure I wasn't as emotionally present as I should have been." Her voice turned bitter. "I just assumed that I was such a great mother that I could spend my time focusing on Tom and Annie and still be there for you."

"Mom, I never said you weren't a good—"

"Please, let me finish." Christine began to cry again. "I was wrong and I'm sorry." She poured herself another glass of wine. "And then when Annie died—I knew we should have said more to you. But Tom was in such pain, and I felt caught in the middle."

279

She sipped her wine. Looked at the ceiling. "I've never been able to face confrontation, especially with those I love." She reached for another Kleenex. "When I was a kid, I used to leave the table whenever my parents had any kind of argument."

"I know what you mean about confrontation," Nathan said, holding out his empty glass for his mother to refill. "Maria is having to teach me how to argue." He watched the wine as Christine poured. "It was a tough time for all of us." He drank half of it in one swallow. "I'm just beginning to see how tough."

He swung his body toward Tom and leaned forward. "But Tom, why didn't you try to talk with me later? Every time you'd come to Wyoming or Colorado, I kept hoping you'd show some interest in me, in what I was doing." He ran his hands over his buzz-cut. "At least I thought you might say something when I was running cross-country. You who always talked about how much you liked to sweat. Or when Maria and I started going to Friends' Meetings, I thought we might talk about silence or meditation. But you never said anything. It's like there's this barrier between us."

Tom's throat tightened. He flinched, his face flushed, his stomach churned coffee up into his throat. How often he'd felt the same barrier, had at some level known he was the one who'd erected it. Still, there had always been another part of him waiting to hear Nathan say, "No, there's no problem, no wall between us." Now here he was, face to face with the malignant effects of his diffidence.

"I thought you didn't want me around," Tom said. "I knew I'd blown it when I didn't talk to you more after Annie died. And when you moved back to Wyoming, I guess I figured you were lost to me." He lifted his eyes to meet his stepson's, which were also swollen with tears. "I was ashamed of myself and I just stopped trying."

"But all you did was add to my sense that you didn't want me around. That you weren't interested in me."

Tom felt sick. "Nathan, I'm sorry."

Nathan said, "I moved back to Wyoming because I missed my friends, and I thought Dad needed me." His eyes swept to his mother and back to Tom. "He was pretty depressed back then, and you two had each other." He picked up a chocolate chip cookie. "Moving away had nothing to do with you," he said to Tom. "Actually, I thought you were a pretty decent stepfather. You never judged me, never wanted me to be someone else. I try to remember that when I'm dealing with Yazmin." He broke the cookie in half, and gave the other half to Tom. "The problem is, I always thought part of you was somewhere else, especially after I moved away." His voice broke. "I thought you wished I'd died instead of Annie."

They were all crying. *We should have done this sixteen years ago.* "No, I was the one who wished he'd died," Tom said. "I got so wrapped up in my shame and my guilt, it was hard even to notice anyone else." He ate Nathan's offering. "And when I did think about other people, I just knew they hated me, and so I wrapped myself that much tighter. Which kept me from reaching out to others." He tried to smile. "Like you, for example."

"And I felt ashamed and guilty for turning you against me," said Nathan. He ate his half of the cookie. "I'm starting to see what Maria means about people getting caught up in their own dramas."

"I've always thought of it as my story." Tom looked to Christine. "Our story."

"Yeah, well, Maria would say that a story is intended for someone else. That's what she tries to get kids to do in her group sessions. She says the problem is that people in pain slip into drama. That's more about being on stage and wallowing in your emotions."

"Sort of like my story is sadder than your story," said Tom. He needed to remember this conversation next year in Compassionate Friends.

"Exactly. That's what gets people in trouble. They isolate themselves."

"Oh yeah. Tell me about it."

Silence enveloped the three of them. Tom rubbed his thumbs

with his forefingers, Christine gazed at her lap and Nathan stared at Annie's stones.

Finally, he said, "Look, it's late. I've had a hard weekend and I'll bet you folks have, too."

"Thank you for being so honest," Christine said. "I hope we can talk more tomorrow."

"Come on, Mom!" Nathan laughed. "Not tomorrow, please!" He drummed his fingers on the arm of the chair. His voice dropped. "I need to work through some things first." His smile returned. "I will say I feel better having talked to you, and I'm pretty sure it won't be another fifteen years before we visit again."

"Maybe when your mother and I visit you next time," said Tom, "you could take us to a Friends' Meeting."

They stood together, and Christine held out her arms to her son and her husband.

Nathan laughed. "Group hug?"

"Why not?" said Tom, opening his arms.

Earlier, he'd been exhausted; now he couldn't sleep. He gazed up into the night, listened to Christine's breathing, and ruminated on the difference between his story and his drama. He thought of the masks he'd hidden behind over the years. They really were dramatis personae: Mr. A.P. in his matching ties and pocket handkerchiefs, the bearded Last Romantic, Mr. Wimp with his bottle of Scotch, Sisyphus, Grieving Parent perusing old photograph albums. Then he saw Wrestling Jacobs, flexing his muscles for another battle with God. An icon or another mask to hide behind? Maybe it was time to say goodbye to him as well. Tom recalled the afternoon dream—the peace he felt as he floated out to sea. Was it time to stop wrestling and surrender to the mystery that is God? He had no idea why innocent children had to die, but neither could he explain his and Christine's enduring love, his ongoing sense of Annie's presence in his life, and the quiet joy he felt when he thought of Nathan, Maria, and Yazmin sleeping in the adjacent rooms.

2005

He rose from bed on Easter Sunday about 5:00 a.m. without waking Christine, and went downstairs to get the package of yellow marshmallow Peeps he'd bought the day before for Yazmin. He might not know how to talk to her, but maybe the candy would be a way to make up for his lack of words.

Walking into the living room to begin hiding the candy, he was startled to see someone else already there. At first, he saw Annie in her tie-dyed shirt standing in the dappled morning light, but he realized it was Yazmin in a flowered nightgown, reading the Easter cards on the coffee table.

Oh shit. Now he wouldn't be able to surprise her. He turned to go, but she saw him. She knocked a card on the floor. "I wasn't stealing." Her voice quivered. "I was just looking. I couldn't sleep."

Before Tom had time to think about what he was doing, he was on one knee, holding her in his arms. "I know you weren't stealing, sweetie. You can look at all the cards you want. That's what they're there for." He smiled. "I couldn't sleep, either. Tell you what. Would you like to help me?"

So they hid Peeps behind lamps, in bookcases, and, at Yazmin's suggestion, in the plant pots on the windowsill. They went into the kitchen and Tom fried her an egg. While they were sitting at the kitchen table, Nathan and Maria came downstairs. "Mommy, Nathan!" She cried, "Guess what Grampa and I have been doing?"

Grampa. She'd never called him that before.

Lilies, tulips, daffodils, peonies, ferns, and hostas enveloped St. Mark's sanctuary. Tom stood, singing with Christine, Nathan, Maria, Yazmin, and the rest of the congregation, as the organ sounded and a timpani reverberated and two trumpets soared:

"Jesus Christ is Risen Today, Alleluia!
Our triumphant holy day, Alleluia!"

Memories streamed through the stained-glass windows: Annie in her oversized sweater singing this hymn at Saint Jude's seventeen years earlier, her eyes lighting up when she smiled at Nathan; holding his mother's hand as they walked to church behind his father and Ed; Scotty Hugh's face; Sunday dinner with his parents and grandparents.

> *"Who did once upon the cross, Alleleuia!*
> *Suffer to redeem our loss. Alleleuia!"*

Recalling his parents, he thought yet again of their legacy to him of shame and guilt. He'd forgiven them; they'd done the best they could, given their own dysfunctional backgrounds. But while he could work to avoid dramatizing his story, just as he would always grieve his daughter's loss, he would always carry the weight of his shame, either for what he'd done or what he hadn't done. Shame had always been the driving force in his life, stemming from the lessons his parents taught him—"What will the neighbors think?" Shame had led to his creation of various personas. Shame had caused the end of one marriage and threatened another. Shame had exacerbated his grief over Annie's death. Shame had almost killed his relationship with his stepson.

> *"Who endured the cross and grave, Alleluia!*
> *Sinner to redeem and save. Alleleuia!"*

It wasn't the physical pain of the Crucifixion, he realized, that made him wince at Jesus's suffering. It was the ridicule—the shame—that went with it. Being stripped naked, spat upon, mocked by soldiers, jeered at by crowds.

Tom bowed before the cross as it passed him, held high by white-robed Thad Allison and flanked by the acolytes, Bobby Parsons and Jessica Morrison, in red cassocks and white surplices. Still, at the end of each line, the congregation sang, "Alleluia—Hallelujah: Praise Yahweh; Praise Ye the Lord." Why? Why praise

God? Because God raised Jesus from the dead? Great, but what about the rest of us? What about Betty Pelletier, in the pew behind them, who was so quick to praise God for saving her son on 9-11, but who lost her husband a year later when he died from a blood clot during what was supposed to be a routine knee replacement? What about Roger in the meditation group, who'd lost one wife to breast cancer, and whose second wife had just been diagnosed with the same thing? Why should they sing *Alleluia?* What about his daughter-in-law, Maria, whose first husband had been killed in a helicopter crash during the Kosovo War when their daughter was a year old? Why should she sing? Or Nathan, thinking himself abandoned by his stepfather and mother for eighteen years?

But the fact was, the voices of these broken people were filling the church with music. Under her white shawl, Maria's face glowed with happiness as she sang. At every "Alleluia," she looked adoringly at Nathan, who grinned back at her. Christine's eyes (royal purple this morning) sparkled with joy as she circled her left arm around her son, and her right arm around him.

> *"But the pains which he endured, Alleluia!*
> *Our salvation have procured, Alleluia!"*

As the choir followed in black and white and Father Larry in his white stole ascended to the dais and took his place beside the great paschal candle, Tom wondered: in the same way that some of the notes in the hymn referring to Jesus's suffering are part of the "Alleluia," what if—instead of sorrow and joy, doubt and faith, despair and hope, being separate on some spiritual see-saw teetering up and down—sorrow isn't a piece of joy, doubt an element of faith, grief an ingredient of hope, shame a component of compassion? The hospital chapel had enveloped his pain and confusion. Annie's small circular *I love you* had overlaid his guilt. His daughter had held both him and Rachel Silas as they stood with their sorrows in a cold September wind. It wasn't that the pain had gone away; it was that it had become part of something or someone larger.

Is this how You work? Have I been struggling all these years, not against an opponent trying to wrestle me to the ground, but a lover seeking to embrace me?

Annie's voice rose inside of him; not the memory of her voice, but her voice, no longer a child's, but a graceful soprano.

"Now above the sky he's King, Alleluia!
Where the angels ever sing, Alleluia!"

It rose with the voices of Christine and Nathan and Maria and Yazmin and Marion Magnussen and Betty Pelletier and Roger and the others in the meditation group and the Lay Pastoral Visitors and rest of the St. Mark's congregation. Rose with the voices of Curtis Mathews and Jonathan Bennett and the Brothers of SSJE and Paul Tibbetts and his brother, Ed. Rose with the voices of his parents and grandparents. Rose as they lifted their collective All-le-lu-ias! through the doors and windows of the church, lifting Tom over the streets of Jordan Mills, over the fields and the rocky coastline, and into enfolding arms.

Acknowledgments
2016

First, I need to emphasize that although certain events in my life inspired some of the events in this novel, all of the characters in *Requiem in Stones* are just that: characters in a novel, with their own thoughts, words, and deeds. Literary creations really do, as other writers have said, take on minds of their own. There are times I'm glad I'm not Tom Jacobs and times I wish I were.

Now for the thank you's. The list is long and I hope I haven't left anyone out.

Thank you to my writing mentors—Diane Benedict, Richard Hoffman, Lee Hope, Barbara Hurd, Erin McGraw, Suzanne Strempek Shea, Michael Steinberg—for encouraging and challenging me. ("What do you mean here?" "You need to go deeper." "What would happen if…?")

Thank you to those in my writing groups for your guidance ("Why does this character change his name half-way through the chapter?") and support along the way: especially Sarah Arnold, Nancy Brown, Susan Casey, Jane DeMillo, Gro Flatabo, Pat Hager, Steve Lauder, Jean Peck, Penelope Schwarz, Maureen Stanton, Barbara Walsh, and Rebecca Welsh.

Thank you to my spiritual mentors—Jonathan Appleyard, Cynthia Bourgeault, The Center for Grieving Children, Ken Ferguson, Dan Warren, Br. James Koester, Br. John Mathis, and the Society of Saint John the Evangelist—for being there and for listening.

Thank you to Jane Karker and the staff of Maine Authors Publishing for helping me figure out what to do with the book after writing it.

To my family: Micah, Jeremy, Jaye, Roger, and especially Mary Lee—lover, supporter, writing and spiritual mentor—

who has picked me up and put me back together more times than she knows. Thank you for your love, your encouragement, and your understanding.

And finally to my daughter Laurie, who continues to guide me along the journey.

After retiring from teaching literature and composition at several high schools in Maine and from a position as a writing consultant at Bates College, Richard Wile published essays and reviews in numerous magazines and journals, including *The Christian Century, America, Fourth Genre,* and *Solstice: A Magazine of Diverse Voices.* He is a past winner of the Maine Writers and Publishers Open Writing Competition, and a finalist for the Maine Literary Awards in nonfiction. *Requiem in Stones* is his first novel.

He currently facilitates spiritual writing programs throughout the state as well as a weekly writing group for the homeless and materially poor in Brunswick, Maine.

Long active at St. Paul's Episcopal Church as a Lay Eucharistic Minister and Lay Reader, he is a Member of the Fellowship of The Society of Saint John the Evangelist, an Episcopal monastery in Cambridge, Massachusetts, and serves on the Board of the Northeast Guild for Spiritual Formation, an ecumenical community called to encourage and empower all who seek the presence and guidance of the Holy in their lives.